# His Virgin Bride

## MELANIE MILBURNE
## MAGGIE COX
## MARGARET MAYO

Published in Great Britain 2015
by Mills & Boon, an imprint of Harlequin (UK) Limited,
Eton House, 18-24 Paradise Road, Richmond, Surrey, TW9 1SR

HIS VIRGIN BRIDE © 2015 Harlequin Books S.A.

*The Fiorenza Forced Marriage, Bought: For His Convenience or Pleasure?* and *A Night With Consequences* were first published in Great Britain by Harlequin (UK) Limited.

*The Fiorenza Forced Marriage* © 2008 Melanie Milburne
*Bought: For His Convenience or Pleasure?* © 2009 Maggie Cox
*A Night With Consequences* © 2011 Margaret Mayo

ISBN: 978-0-263-25228-6
eBook ISBN: 978-1-474-00407-7

05-0915

Harlequin (UK) Limited's policy is to use papers that are natural, renewable and recyclable products and made from wood grown in sustainable forests. The logging and manufacturing processes conform to the legal environmental regulations of the country of origin.

Printed and bound in Spain
by CPI, Barcelona

# THE FIORENZA
# FORCED MARRIAGE

## BY
## MELANIE MILBURNE

**Melanie Milburne** says: 'I am married to a surgeon, Steve, and have two gorgeous sons, Paul and Phil. I live in Hobart, Tasmania, where I enjoy an active life as a long-distance runner and a nationally ranked top ten Master's swimmer. I also have a Master's Degree in Education, but my children totally turned me off the idea of teaching! When not running or swimming I write, and when I'm not doing all of the above I'm reading. And if someone could invent a way for me to read during a four-kilometre swim I'd be even happier!'

To one of my most loyal fans, Anu Sankaran, who has encouraged me from book one. Thank you so much for your lovely e-mails and fabulous personal reviews! This one is just for you. x

# CHAPTER ONE

EMMA looked at the Italian lawyer in heart-stopping shock. 'There must be some sort of m-mistake,' she said, her voice wobbling with disbelief. 'How could I possibly be included in Signore Fiorenza's will? I was just his carer.'

'It is no mistake,' Francesca Rossi said, pointedly tapping the thick document in front of her. 'I have it here in black and white. Valentino Fiorenza changed his will a matter of weeks before he died.'

Emma sat in a stunned silence. She had lived with and nursed the multimillionaire for eighteen months and not once had she thought something like this would happen. 'But I don't understand…' she said after a moment. 'Why on earth would he leave me half of his estate?'

'That's exactly what his son has been asking,' Francesca Rossi said with a speaking glance. 'I believe he is on his way over from London as we speak. As his father's only remaining heir one can only assume he was expecting The Villa Fiorenza and the bulk of his father's assets to pass directly to him.'

Emma chewed at her bottom lip for a moment. 'You said the terms of the will are rather strange….'

'They are quite unusual,' Francesca agreed. 'In order to

inherit your share you must be legally married to Rafaele Fiorenza within a month and stay married to him for a year.'

Emma felt her stomach drop like a gymnast mistiming a tricky manoeuvre on the bar. 'M-married in a month?' she croaked. *'For a year?'*

'Yes, otherwise the estate in its entirety will automatically pass to a previous mistress of Valentino's, a woman by the name of Sondra Henning. Did he ever mention her to you?'

Emma wrinkled her brow. 'No, I don't think so…but then he was a very private man. He didn't talk much about anything, especially towards the end.'

The lawyer leafed through the document before looking back up at Emma. 'Signore Fiorenza stipulated that upon marriage to his son you are to receive a lump sum of fifty thousand euros, and then for every year you remain married to Rafaele you will receive an allowance,' she said. 'A rather generous one, in fact.'

Emma's stomach did another fall from the bar. 'H-how generous?'

The lawyer named a sum that sent Emma's brows shooting upwards. 'I guess it does seem rather a lot to walk away from…' she said, thinking of her sister's recent phone call. Fifty thousand euros at the current exchange rate would not completely solve Simone's financial situation, but it would certainly go a long way to help her get back on her feet.

'It is a lot to walk away from,' Francesca said. 'Even without factoring in the allowance, the villa, as you know from staying there, is considered one of the most beautiful show-pieces around Lake Como. You would be a fool to forfeit such an asset, even a half share of it.'

'What is Rafaele Fiorenza like…I mean as a person?' Emma asked. 'I've seen photos of him in the press from time to time, but his father barely mentioned him. And as far as I know he wasn't at the funeral. I got the feeling there was bad blood between them.'

'I have not met him personally,' Francesca said. 'Apparently he left home when he was a young adult to study abroad. He is a high-flying stock trader now. But, yes, as you said he is often featured in gossip magazines throughout Europe and further abroad. Word has it he is a bit of a playboy and a very wealthy one at that.'

'Yes, I did get that impression,' Emma said, and then with another little crease of her brow added, 'but what if he doesn't agree to the terms of his father's will? If he's so wealthy why would he agree to be married to a perfect stranger?'

'The entire estate involves a great deal of money, even for a rich man,' Francesca said. 'Besides, the villa was where he spent most of his early childhood until he went to boarding school abroad. I cannot see him walking away from such a gold mine without at least inspecting the candidate his father chose to be his bride.'

Emma felt every fine hair on her body lift up like the fur of a startled cat. 'I haven't said I would agree to marry anyone,' she said, 'especially a man who didn't even have the decency to visit or communicate with his dying father.'

'Given he has had little or no contact with his father for the last decade or so you might have a hard time explaining your relationship,' Francesca said. 'I know you were employed as Valentino's carer but the press haven't always seen it that way and neither, I suspect, will Rafaele Fiorenza.'

Emma straightened agitatedly in her chair. When she had first taken on the position as Valentino Fiorenza's carer she had not been prepared for how the press would misinterpret her relationship with him. Every time she had accompanied him out in public it seemed the paparazzi were there to document it, often times misconstruing the situation to make her appear a gold-digger, content to hook up with a man three times her age. She still cringed as she thought of the last photo that had appeared in the press. Weakened by the progression of his bone cancer Valentino had been too proud to use a walking stick and had relied increasingly on Emma's support. The photographer had captured a moment where Emma's arms had gone around her employer's waist to keep him from falling, making it appear she was intimately involved with him. Even her sister Simone had rung her from Australia and asked if what everyone was saying was true.

'He can think what he likes, but there was absolutely nothing improper about my relationship with his father,' Emma said. 'Valentino was an invalid, for pity's sake. He employed me to take care of his day-to-day needs. I grew fond of him certainly, but that happens with just about every home care client I take on. Looking after someone as they count down their last days is incredibly poignant. I know it's not wise to become emotionally involved, but from the very first day Valentino Fiorenza struck me as a very lonely soul. He had wealth but not health and happiness.'

'Well, let us hope Rafaele Fiorenza understands the situation,' Francesca said. 'In the meantime I take it you are staying on at the villa?'

'Yes,' Emma said. 'I wasn't sure what else to do. Some of the staff have taken leave and I didn't want the place left unattended until I heard from the son. I've been looking for alternative accommodation but with not much luck so far. I let my previous lease go as Signore Fiorenza insisted I move in with him from day one.'

'You do realise of course that Rafaele Fiorenza stands to lose rather a lot if you do not agree to the terms,' Francesca said in a serious tone. 'Even though he might not need the money it would still be wise to take some time to think it over before you come to a final decision for his sake as well as your own.'

Emma shifted uncomfortably in her chair. 'I realise it is a difficult situation for him…but I'm not sure I can agree to such a thing. It doesn't seem…right…'

'There are a lot of people who would see it differently,' the lawyer said. 'They would not baulk at a short term marriage of convenience in exchange for a fortune.'

Emma nibbled at her bottom lip for a moment. 'You mentioned the marriage has to last a year. Is there any way of negotiating on that time frame?'

'No, I am afraid not, but, as I said earlier, for every year you remain married to Rafaele you will be paid an allowance.' Francesca rolled back her office chair and offered her hand across the desk. 'I hope it goes well for you whatever you decide, Miss March,' she said. 'Signore Fiorenza Senior was clearly very fond of you. He would not have been an easy person to nurse, I would imagine. The Fiorenza family has had its share of tragedy. The boys' mother died when they were very young children and if that was not bad enough the younger of the two boys, Giovanni, died in a tragic accident when he was about eight. Over the years Signore Fiorenza became increasingly bitter and reclusive, not to mention terribly stubborn.'

'Yes, he was certainly stubborn,' Emma said. 'But I couldn't help feeling it was all a bit of a front. He liked to rant and rave a lot but he was as soft as butter towards the end. I really liked him. I will miss him.'

'You never know, Miss March, the son may turn out to be perfect husband material,' the lawyer said with a wry smile. 'It would not be the first time a marriage of convenience in this country turned into something else entirely.'

Emma backed out of the lawyer's office with a strained

smile and made her way to the bank of lifts. But all the way
down to the ground floor she felt a fluttery sensation disturbing the lining of her stomach, like a thousand tiny moths all
frantically looking for a way out…

Every time Emma stepped through the elaborate wrought-iron
gates of the Villa Fiorenza she stood for a moment or two in
awe. The massive gardens set on four tiers were nothing short
of breathtaking, the lush green of yew hedges and elm and
beech trees and cypress pines a perfect backdrop for the
crimson and pinks and reds of azaleas and roses and other
fragrant spring blooms. The villa itself was equally breathtaking; set above the stunning crystal-blue beauty of Lake Como,
it was four storeys high and built in the neo-classical style
lending it an allure of old-world grandeur that never failed to
take Emma's breath away.

Most of the rooms of the villa were no longer in use, the
antique furniture draped in shroud-like sheets and the shutters
pulled tight across the sightless windows, giving the grand old
place a slightly haunted look. And without the presence of
daily staff bustling about the villa and gardens the sense of
loneliness and isolation was even more acute.

After she had spent more than a year looking after him in
his palazzo in Milan, Valentino Fiorenza had announced to
Emma six weeks ago he wanted to come back to the villa to
die. And now to Emma it seemed as if every breath of breeze
that disturbed the leaves on the trees were lamenting his
passing. She had loved spending time pushing him around the
gardens in his wheelchair, for, although towards the end he
had found speech difficult, she had sensed his enjoyment of
the peaceful surroundings.

The warmth of the spring weather brought out the heady
scent of wisteria and jasmine as Emma walked under the arbour

on the second tier of the gardens. She had just stopped to dead-head some of the milk-white climbing roses when a sleek black sports car growled throatily as it turned into the driveway at the back of the villa, like a panther returning to its lair.

She brushed a loose strand of hair out of her eyes and watched as a tall figure unfolded himself from the car. Even from this distance she could see the likeness to his father immediately: the loose-limbed, rangy build, the brooding frown, the chiselled jaw and the arrogant set to his mouth all spoke of a man used to insisting on and getting his own way. But, unlike his father, Rafaele Fiorenza was well over six feet tall and his fit body wasn't bent over double and ravaged by disease and his glossy black curly hair was thick and plenti-ful on his head and held no trace of grey. It was casually styled, the wide, deep grooves in amongst the strands suggest-ing he had used his fingers as its most recent combing tool.

Even though Emma had seen his photograph in the press a couple of times she realised now it hadn't done him justice. He was quite simply the most arrestingly handsome man she had ever seen.

He was dressed in casual trousers and an open-necked light blue shirt, the cuffs rolled back over his strong tanned forearms, an expensive-looking silver watch around his left wrist and a pair of designer sunglasses, which shielded the ex-pression in his eyes.

He slammed the car door and strode down the steps leading to the second tier, his long, purposeful strides bringing him within a matter of seconds to where she was unconsciously crumbling rose petals in her hand. 'Miss March, I presume?' he said in a clipped, distinctly unfriendly tone.

Emma hated talking to people wearing sunglasses, particu-larly the one-way lens type he was wearing. She always felt at a disadvantage not being able to read what was going on behind that impenetrable screen. She lifted her chin and let the petals float to the ground at her feet. 'Yes, that is correct,' she said. 'I take it you are Rafaele Fiorenza.'

He removed the sunglasses, his black-brown gaze sweeping over her contemptuously. 'And I take it you were my father's latest floozy.'

Emma automatically stiffened. 'I take it you have been misinformed, Signore Fiorenza,' she returned with arctic chill. 'I was employed as your father's carer.'

He gave her a cynical smile but it didn't involve his dark bottomless brown eyes. 'So you took care of all of his physical needs, did you, Miss March?' he said. 'I must confess my mind is having a bit of a field day with that information.'

'Then I would say your mind needs to drag itself out of the gutter, Signore Fiorenza,' she returned with a deliberately haughty look.

His smile went from cynical to devilish. 'So how do you feel about becoming my bride, Miss March?'

Emma tightened her mouth. 'I have no intention of doing any such thing.'

He stood looking down at her for a pulsing silence, his eyes unwavering as they held hers. Emma tried her best not to squirm under his piercing scrutiny but in the end she was the first to drop her gaze.

'I suppose you put him up to it, did you?' he asked. 'In a weak moment of his you talked him into signing away a fortune.'

'That's a despicable thing to say,' she said, looking back at him in affront. 'I had no idea what he had planned. The first I heard of it was when his legal firm contacted me about the terms of the will.'

'Do not take me for a fool,' he said. 'You were living with my father for a year and a half. That is the longest relationship he has had since my mother died. Everyone knows you were sleeping with him. It has been in the papers numerous times.'

Emma felt her cheeks burning but forced herself to hold his gaze. 'I did not have that sort of relationship with your father. The press made it up just to sell extra copies. They do that with anyone rich or famous.'

His dark eyes glittered with disdain. 'Come on, now, Miss March,' he said. 'You surely do not expect me to believe my father wrote you into his will at the last moment just because you smiled sweetly at him on his deathbed, do you?'

Emma sent him a flinty glare. 'I have never slept with your father. It's totally preposterous of you to even suggest it.'

His expression communicated his disbelief. 'My father was a well-known womaniser,' he said. 'You lived with him for well over a year before he publicly announced he was ill. It would be all too easy to assume you wormed your way into his bed to secure yourself a fortune.'

'I did no such thing!' she protested hotly. 'I only agreed to live with your father so long before his health deteriorated because he didn't want a profusion of carers coming in and out of his life. He was also concerned if people knew he was terminally ill when he was first diagnosed, his investment clients would leave him in droves. His illness progressed slowly at first, but a couple of months ago he realised the end was near. I did my best to support him through the final stages.'

'I just bet you did,' he said with a little curl of his lip. 'Although I must say you are not his usual type. He usually went for busty, brassy blondes. Pint-sized brunettes must have been a taste he had recently acquired.'

Emma felt the scorch of his dark gaze run over her again and inwardly seethed. 'I resent your reprehensible insinuations,' she said. 'I can see now why your father refused to even have your name mentioned in his presence. You have absolutely appalling manners.'

He had the audacity to laugh at her. 'What a prim little schoolmarm you are,' he taunted. 'Miss March suits you perfectly. I bet my father loved you putting him to bed.'

Emma was almost beyond speech and to her immense irritation she could feel her face flaming. 'You…you have no right to speak to me like—'

'I have every right, Miss March.' He cut her off rudely. 'My father would not marry you, would he? He swore he would never marry again after my mother died. But you obviously thought of a way to get your hands on the Fiorenza fortune by suggesting you marry me instead.'

Emma clenched her teeth as she battled to contain her temper. 'You are the very last man I would consent to marry,' she threw at him heatedly.

His eyes were like twin lasers as they held hers. 'You want more money, is that it, Miss March? I am sure I can afford you. Just tell me how much you want and I will write you a cheque here and now.'

Emma bristled at his effrontery. 'You think you can wave your wallet around and pay me?'

He gave her a scornful smile. 'That is the language of women such as you. You saw a big fat cherry just ripe for the picking in my father, did you not? You must have buttered him up rather well to get him to rewrite his will. I wonder what tricks you had up your sleeve, or should I say skirt?'

Emma had never felt closer to slapping a person. She curled her hands into fists, fighting for control, anger bubbling up inside her at his despicable taunts. 'How dare you?' she bit out.

He rocked back on his heels in an imperious manner. 'You are quite the little firebrand behind that demure façade, eh, Miss March? No wonder my father took such a shine to you.

Who knows? We might make quite a match of it after all. I like my women hot and flustered. I think you might do very well as my bride.'

Emma gave him a look that could strip paint. 'You are the most obnoxious man I have ever met,' she bit out. 'Do you really think I would agree to become involved with someone like you?'

He gave her another cynical smile. 'I am not sure I should tell you what I think right now, Miss March,' he drawled. 'You might follow through on your current desire to slap my face.'

Emma hated that she had been so transparent. It made her feel he had an advantage over her being able to read her body language so well. What else could he see? she wondered. Could he tell she was deeply disturbed by his arrant masculinity? That his sensually shaped mouth made her lips tingle at the thought of what it would feel like to have him kiss her?

Her reaction to him was somewhat of a bewildering shock to her. She was normally such a sensible, level-headed person. She had never considered herself a sensualist, but then she had so little experience when it came to men.

Rafaele Fiorenza, on the other hand, looked as if he had loads of experience when it came to women. His tall frame, classically handsome features and magnetic dark brown eyes with their impossibly long dark lashes were a potent combination any woman would find hard to resist. Emma could imagine he would be a demanding and exciting lover. She could almost feel the sexual energy emanating from him; it created a crackling tension in the air, making her feel even more on edge and hopelessly out of her depth. The thought of being legally married to him for any length of time was disturbing in the extreme. The lawyer had spoken of a marriage of convenience, but what if Rafaele wanted it to be a real marriage?

In order to pull her thoughts back into line she said the

first thing that came to her head. 'You didn't go to your father's funeral.'

'I am not one for hypocrisy,' he said, shifting his gaze from hers to sweep it over the property. 'My father would not have wanted me there, in any case. He hated me.'

Emma frowned at his embittered tone. 'I'm sure that's not true. Very few parents truly hate their children.'

His eyes came back to hers, his inherent cynicism glittering like black diamonds. 'I can only assume he thought by forcing me to marry his little nursemaid it might have some sort of reforming effect on me,' he said. 'What do you think, Miss March? Do your skills extend to taming decadent playboys?'

Emma could feel her colour rise all over again and quickly changed the subject. 'How long has it been since you were here last?' she asked.

He drew in a breath and sent his gaze back over the stately mansion. 'It has been fifteen years,' he said.

'You have lived abroad all that time?' she asked.

He turned back to look down at her. 'Yes. I've been primarily based in London but I have a couple of properties in France and Spain. But now my father is dead I intend to move back here.'

Hearing him speaking in that deep mellifluous voice of his did strange things to Emma's insides. He spoke English like a native and even had a trace of a London accent, which gave him a sophisticated air that was lethally attractive. She could imagine him travelling the globe, with a mistress in every city clamouring for his attention. He was everything a playboy should be: suave, sophisticated and utterly sexy. Even his aftershave smelt erotic—it had a citrus base and some other exotic spice that made her think of hot sultry musk-scented nights.

'Um…I have a spare set of keys for you,' she said as she led the way to the front door. 'And there's a remote control for the alarm system. I'll write down the code and password—they might have changed since you were here last.'

'I noticed you trimming the roses,' Rafaele said. 'What happened to the gardeners? Do not tell me my frugal father refused to pay them?'

Emma gave him another haughty look. 'Your father was very generous towards the staff,' she said. 'They were all provided for in his will, as I am sure you know. They are just having a couple of weeks' break. I was keeping an eye on things until you arrived.'

'What a multi-talented little nurse you are,' he said. 'I wonder what else you can turn a hand to.'

Emma fumbled through the collection of keys, conscious of his dark satirical gaze resting on her. Her heart nearly jumped out of her chest when his hand came over hers and removed the keys.

'Allow me,' he said with a glinting smile.

She stepped to one side, trying to get her breathing to even out while her fingers continued to buzz with sensation from the brief contact with his.

He opened the heavy door and waved her through with a mock bow. 'After you, Miss March.'

Emma brushed past him, her nostrils flaring again as she caught the alluring grace notes of his aftershave as they drifted towards her. She watched as he came in, his coolly indifferent gaze moving over the black and white marbled foyer with its priceless statues and paintings.

'It's a very beautiful villa,' she said to fill the echoing silence. 'You must have enjoyed holidaying here with all this space.'

He gave her an unreadable look. 'A residence can be too big and too grand, Miss March.'

Emma felt a shiver run over her bare arms that had nothing

to do with the temperature. Something about his demeanour had subtly changed. His eyes had hardened once more and the line to his mouth was grim as he looked up at the various portraits hanging on the walls.

'You are very like your father as a younger man,' she said, glancing at the portrait of Valentino Fiorenza hanging in pride of place.

Rafaele turned his head to look at her. 'I am not sure my father would have liked to be informed of that.'

'Why?' Emma asked, frowning slightly as she looked up at him.

'Did he not tell you?' he said with an embittered look. 'I was the son who had deeply disappointed him, the black sheep who brought shame and disgrace on the Fiorenza name.'

Emma moistened her lips. 'No…he didn't tell me that…' she said.

He moved down the foyer and stood for a moment in front of a portrait of a young woman with black hair and startling eyes that were black as ink. Emma knew it was his mother, for she had asked Lucia, the housekeeper. Gabriela Fiorenza had died of an infection at the age of twenty-seven when Rafaele was six and his younger brother four.

'She was very beautiful,' Emma said into the almost painful silence.

'Yes,' Rafaele said turning to look at her again, his expression now inscrutable. 'She was.'

Emma shifted her weight from foot to foot. 'Um…would you like me to make you a coffee or tea before I go?' she asked. 'The housekeeper is on leave, but I know my way around the kitchen.'

'You are quite the little organiser, aren't you, Emma March?' he asked with another one of his sardonic smiles. 'It seems even the staff are taking orders off you, taking leave at your say-so.'

She pulled her mouth tight. 'The staff are entitled to some time off. Besides, someone had to take charge in the absence of Signore Fiorenza's only son, who, one would have thought, could have at least made an effort to see him just once before he died.'

His expression became stony. 'I can see what you have been up to, Miss March. You thought you could secure yourself a fortune by bad-mouthing me to my father at every opportunity. It did not work, though, did it? You cannot have any of it without marrying me.'

Emma was finding it hard to control her normally even temper. 'I told you I had no idea what your father was up to,' she said. 'I was as shocked as you. I'm still shocked.'

He gave a little snort of disbelief. 'I can just imagine you having little heart-to-hearts with the old man, telling him how shameful it was his son refused to have any contact with him. I wonder did he tell you why, hmm? Did he allow any skeletons out of the tightly locked Fiorenza closet?'

Emma swallowed thickly. 'He…he never told me anything about you. I got the feeling he didn't like discussing the past.'

'Yes, well, that makes sense,' he said with an embittered expression. 'My father's philosophy was to ignore things he did not like facing in the hope they would eventually disappear.'

'Why *did* you leave?'

'Miss March,' he said, his look now condescending, 'I am not prepared to discuss such personal details with the hired help, even if you were elevated to the position of my father's mistress.'

'I was not your father's mistress,' Emma said crossly.

'I find that very hard to believe,' he said with another raking glance. 'You see, prior to arriving I did a little check on you, Emma Annabelle March.'

Emma's eyes widened. 'W-what?'

'I have a contact in the private-eye business,' he said, his hawk-like gaze locked on hers. 'This is not the first time a client of yours has left you something, is it?'

She moistened her lips with a nervous dart of her tongue. 'No, it's not, but I never asked for anything, not from anyone. I have had one or two clients who have left me small gifts but only because they wanted to show their appreciation. Nursing someone in the last weeks or months of their life can sometimes blur the boundaries for the patient. They begin to look upon you as a trusted friend and confidante.'

'All the same, such gifts must be quite a windfall to a girl from the wrong side of the tracks,' he went on smoothly.

'Not all people are born with a silver spoon in their mouth, Signore Fiorenza,' she said with a cold, hard stare. 'I have had to work hard to achieve what I've achieved.'

His dark, impenetrable gaze was still drilling into hers. 'According to my source you left your last client's house in a storm of controversy. Do you want to tell me about that or shall I tell you what I found out?'

Emma compressed her lips momentarily. 'I was accused of stealing a family heirloom and a large sum of money,' she said. 'I have reason to believe I was framed by a relative. The police investigating eventually agreed and the charges were dropped. In spite of my name being cleared the press were like jackals for weeks later, no doubt fuelled by the rumour-mongering of Mrs Bennett's family.'

'Is that why you moved to Italy from Australia?' he asked, his expression giving no clue as to whether he believed her explanation or not.

'Yes,' Emma said. 'I had wanted to work abroad in any case, but the Melbourne papers just wouldn't let it go. It made it hard for me to find a new placement locally. I had no choice but to start again elsewhere.'

'How did you get into this line of work?' he asked.

'I trained as a nurse but I found working in hospitals frustrating,' she said, trying to make him see that she was genuine, not the gold-digger he assumed she was. 'There was never enough time to spend with patients doing the things nurses used to do. Back rubs, sitting with them over a cup of tea, that sort of thing rarely happens these days. I started working for a private home-based care agency and really loved it. The hours can be long, of course, and it can be disruptive to one's social life when a client needs you to live in, but the positives far outweigh the negatives.'

'I am very sure they do,' he said with another mocking tilt of his lips. 'Inheriting half a luxury Italian villa and a generous allowance are hardly to be considered some of the downsides of the job.'

'Look,' Emma said on an expelled breath of irritation, 'I realise this is a difficult time for you, Signore Fiorenza. You have just lost your father and in spite of your feelings towards him that is a big thing in anyone's life, particularly a man's. I am prepared to make allowances for your inappropriate suggestions given you had no recent contact with him, but let me assure you I have nothing to hide. Your father was a difficult man, but I grew very fond of him. He was lonely and desperately unhappy. I like to think I gave him a small measure of comfort in those last months of his life.'

He stood looking down at her for a long moment before speaking. 'Let us go into the library. I would like to discuss with you how we are to handle this situation my father has placed us in.'

Emma felt her insides quiver at the look of determination in his eyes. 'There's nothing to discuss,' she said with a hitch of her chin. 'I'm going upstairs right now to pack.'

His eyes burned into hers. 'So you do not want what my father intended for you to have?'

She flicked her tongue across her suddenly bone-dry lips. 'It was very generous of him but I'm not interested in marrying for money.'

'Do you really think I am going to allow you to sabotage my inheritance?' he asked with a steely look.

Emma swallowed tightly. 'You surely don't expect me to agree to…to…marrying you…'

'I am not going to give you a choice, Miss March,' he said with implacable force. 'We will marry within a week. I have already seen to the licence. I did that as soon as I was informed of the terms of the will.'

Emma glared at him even though her heart was hammering with alarm. 'You can't force me to marry you,' she said, hoping it was somehow true.

His dark eyes glinted. 'You think not?'

*I hope not,* she thought as her stomach did a flip-flop of panic.

'Miss March,' he went on before she could get her voice to work. 'You will comply with the terms of the will or I will personally see to it you never work as a nurse in this country again.'

Emma sent him a defiant glare. 'I am not going to be threatened by you,' she said. 'Anyway, even if you did manage to sully my reputation in Italy I can always find work in another country. There is a shortage of nurses and carers worldwide.'

His lips thinned into a smile that was as menacing as it was mocking. 'Ah, yes, but then working as a nurse or carer you will not receive anything like the wage I am prepared to pay you to be my wife.'

Emma felt her defiant stance start to wobble. 'A…a wage?'

'Yes, Miss March,' he said with an imperious look. 'I will pay you handsomely for the privilege of bearing my name for a year.'

'How much?' she asked, and almost fell over when he told her an amount that no nurse, even if she worked for two lifetimes, would ever earn.

'Of course it will not be a real marriage,' he said. 'I already have a mistress.'

Emma wasn't sure why his statement should have made her feel so annoyed. She disliked him intensely, but somehow the thought of him continuing his affair with someone else while formally married to her was infuriating. 'I hope the same liberty will be open for me,' she said with a jut of her chin.

'No, Miss March, I am afraid not,' he said. 'I am a high-profile person and do not wish to be made a laughing stock amongst my colleagues and friends by the sexual proclivities of my wife.'

Emma glared at him in outrage. 'That's completely unfair! If you're going to publicly cavort with your mistress, then I insist on the same liberty to conduct my own affairs.'

His mouth tightened into a flat line. 'I will be discreet at all times, but I cannot be certain you will do the same. The way you conducted your affair with my father is a case in point. You lapped up the press attention whenever you could, hanging off him like a limpet when all the time all you wanted was his money.'

Emma clenched her teeth. 'I did *not* have an affair with your father. You can ask the household staff. They will vouch for me.'

His lip curled in scorn. 'You very conveniently sent them all off on leave, did you not?' he said. 'But even if they were here I am sure you would have convinced them to portray you as an innocent.'

She gave him a blistering glare. 'You're totally wrong about me, Signore Fiorenza, but I am not going to waste my time trying to convince you. You're obviously too cynical to be able to see who is genuine and who is not. Do you know something? I actually feel sorry for you. You are going to end up like your father, dying with just the hired help to grieve your passing.'

He ignored her comment to say, 'I expect you to act the role of a loving wife when we are within earshot or sight of other people, and that includes the household staff.'

Emma could feel her panic rising. 'But I haven't said I would marry you. I need some time to think about this.'

He looked at her for a long moment, his dark eyes quietly scanning her features. 'All right,' he said. 'I will give you until tomorrow, but that is all. The sooner this marriage starts, the sooner it ends.'

'I couldn't have put it better myself,' Emma muttered under her breath as he walked off down the long wide corridor until he finally disappeared from sight.

# CHAPTER TWO

EMMA didn't see Rafaele again until later in the day. She was picking up the fallen petals from a vase of fragrant roses in the library when he sauntered in. He had changed into blue denim jeans and a close-fitting white T-shirt, which highlighted his flat stomach and gym-toned chest and shoulders. His hair was still damp from his recent shower and his jaw cleanly shaven. He looked tired however; she could see the dark bruise-like shadows beneath his eyes and the faint lines of strain bracketing his mouth.

For the first time Emma started to think about his angle on things. This magnificent villa was his heritage; it had been in the Fiorenza family for generations. No wonder he was angry at how his father had orchestrated things. Forcing him to marry a perfect stranger in order to claim what should have been rightly his would be enough to enrage anyone.

But why had Valentino chosen *her* to be his son's bride? Emma had talked to him on one or two occasions about her difficult childhood, and how she wanted one day soon to settle down with a man she loved and have a little family of her own, to have the security she had missed out on as a child. That was when he had—she had thought jokingly—suggested she marry his wealthy, successful son and fill the villa with

Fiorenza babies. It was one of the few times he had mentioned Rafaele's name. She had tried on several occasions to get him to talk about his son but he had remained tight-lipped, and, sensing the subject was painful to him, Emma had decided it was better left well alone.

'I have made a start on some dinner,' she said. 'I wasn't sure what your plans were so I made enough for two.'

He gave her a sardonic smile. 'Are you rehearsing the role of devoted wife for our temporary marriage?'

'You can interpret it any way you like, but the truth is I was merely trying to be helpful,' she said, a little stung by his attitude when she had made an effort to understand his point of view.

He held her gaze for several heartbeats. 'I noticed when I was upstairs your things are in the room connected to my father's,' he said. 'If you were not sleeping with him as you claim, why did you use that particular room when there are numerous other suites you could have occupied?'

'I was planning to move out of there as soon as you informed me of your sleeping arrangements,' she said tersely. 'I wasn't sure if you would feel comfortable sleeping in the bed in which your father died.'

A shadow flickered briefly in his eyes, like the shutter of a camera opening and closing. 'Were you with him when he passed away?' he asked.

'Yes, I was,' she answered. 'He asked me to stay with him. He told me he didn't want to die alone.'

He turned and, walking over to the bank of windows, looked down at the view of the sparkling waters of the lake, his long, straight back reminding Emma of a drawbridge being pulled up on a fortress. She had seen a lot of grief in her time; it seemed as if each member of a family had a different way of expressing it. But something about Rafaele Fiorenza made her think, in spite of his obvious anger and hatred towards his father, somewhere deep inside him was a little boy who had loved him once.

'Signore Fiorenza?' she said after a long silence.

He turned and faced her, his expression giving no clue of what was going on behind the screen of his coal-black gaze. 'Rafaele will be fine,' he said with a stiff on-off smile. 'I do not think we need to stand on ceremony given the circumstances.'

'Um…I'll just go and move my things into one of the other rooms, then…' Emma said, moving towards the door.

'The Pink Suite is probably the most comfortable,' he said. 'It was my mother's favourite. She decorated it herself. It was one of the last things she did before she died. I remember helping her with the wallpaper.'

Emma turned back to look at him. His expression had softened, as if the memory of his mother had peeled off the hard layer of cynicism he usually wore. 'The housekeeper told me your mother died when you and your brother were quite young,' she said. 'That must have been very difficult for you.'

He gave her a humourless smile. 'Life goes on, eh, Emma? Death and disorder and disease happen to us all at one time or another. The trick is to pack as much enjoyment in your life before one or all of them get their claws into you.'

'Life is certainly harder on some people than others,' she responded quietly.

He came across to where she was standing and, before she could do anything to stop him, lifted her chin with the blunt end of one long, tanned finger. 'Those grey-blue eyes of yours are full of compassion,' he said. 'But then I wonder if it is for real?'

Emma could barely breathe. The pad of his thumb was now moving back and forth against the curve of her cheek, his dark mysterious gaze mesmerising as it held hers within the force field of his. She could smell the cleanness of his freshly showered skin and the citrus spice of his aftershave, a heady combination that was intoxicating. She could see the sculptured perfection of his mouth and thought again of how it would feel to have those very experienced lips imprinted on hers. She ran her tongue out over her mouth, her heart kicking like a tiny pony behind her chest wall and her stomach doing little jerky somersaults as his thighs brushed against hers.

'Is this how you worked your magic on him, sweet, shy, caring little Emma?' he asked. 'Making him so mad with lust he promised you the world?'

Emma shook herself out of her stasis and stepped back with a glowering glare. 'I-I would prefer it you would keep your hands to yourself,' she said, annoyed that her voice shook.

He smiled in that taunting way of his. 'I will keep my hands to myself if you stop looking at me like that,' he said. 'It gives me all sorts of wicked ideas.'

She frowned at him furiously. 'I'm not looking at you with anything but disgust at your insufferable behaviour. You are one of the most obnoxious men I have ever had the misfortune to meet.'

He was still smiling at her in that mocking way of his. 'Has anyone ever told you how cute you look when you are angry?'

She swung away from him, her face flaming. 'I'm going to see to dinner,' she said and, stalking out, clicked the door shut behind her.

Rafaele waited until she was well out of earshot before he let out his breath in a long, tired stream. He sent his hand through his hair and turned and looked down at his father's antique leather-topped desk. His gaze went to where a gilt-edged photograph frame was sitting next to a paperclip dispenser, but he didn't pick it up. He didn't need to turn it around and look at his younger brother's face to summon the pain.

He still carried it deep inside him…

\* \* \*

After Emma had transferred her things to the Pink Suite she made her way back downstairs to the massive kitchen, where through one of the windows she saw Rafaele out on the lower tier of the garden. He was standing with his hands in his trouser pockets, looking out over the expanse of verdant lawn fringed by silver birch trees, their lacy leaves quivering in the faint breeze. The same light breeze was wrinkling the surface of the lap pool, and a peahen and her vociferous mate were nearby, but it looked as if Rafaele hadn't even noticed their presence.

He stood as still as a marble statue, his tall, silent figure bathed in a red and orange glow from the fingers of light thrown by the lowering sun. The Villa Fiorenza was perhaps the most tranquil setting Emma had ever seen and yet she couldn't help feeling Rafaele Fiorenza did not find it so.

She opened the French doors leading off the terrace, the sound of her footsteps on the sandstone steps bringing his head around. She saw the way his expression became instantly shuttered, as if he resented her intrusion.

'I was wondering if you would like to eat outside,' she said. 'It's a warm evening and after such a long plane journey I thought—'

'I will not be here for dinner after all,' he said in a curt tone. 'I am going out.'

Emma felt foolish for feeling disappointed and did her best to disguise it. 'That's fine. It was nothing special in any case.'

He took the set of keys hanging on a hook on the wall. 'Do not wait up,' he said. 'I might end up staying overnight in Milan.'

'Did your mistress travel with you from London?' she asked.

'No, but what she does not know will not hurt her.'

Emma knew her face was communicating her disapproval. 'So faithfulness in your relationships isn't one of your strong points, I take it?'

'I am not sure I am the settling-down type,' he said. 'I enjoy my freedom too much.'

'I thought most Italians put a high value on getting married and having a family,' she said.

'That may have been the case for previous generations, but I personally feel life is too short for the drudge of domesticity,' he said. 'I have got nothing against children, but I like the sort you can hand back after half an hour. I have no place in my life for anything else.'

'It sounds like a pretty shallow and pointless existence to me,' Emma said. 'Don't you ever get lonely?'

'No, I do not,' he said. 'I like my life the way it is. I do not want the complication of having to be responsible for someone else's emotional upkeep. The women I date know the rules and generally are quite willing to adhere to them.'

'I suppose if they don't you get rid of them, right?'

He gave her a supercilious smile. 'That is right.'

Emma pursed her mouth. 'I feel sorry for any poor woman who makes the mistake of falling in love with you.'

'Most of the woman I know fall in love with my wallet. What they feel for me has very little to do with who I am as a person. As you have probably already guessed, I am not the type to wear my heart upon my sleeve,' he said, and then with a rueful twist to his mouth added, 'Perhaps I am my father's son after all.'

'Your father liked to give the impression he was tough, but inside he was a very broken and lonely man,' Emma said. 'I could read between the lines enough to know he had some serious regrets about his life and relationships.'

'What a pity he did not communicate that to what remained of his family while he still could,' he said with an embittered set to his mouth.

'I think he would have done so if you had made the effort to come to see him,' Emma said. 'Towards the end I couldn't help feeling he was lingering against the odds on the off chance you would visit him.'

His lip curled up in a snarl. 'He could have made the first move. Why was it left to me to do so?'

'He was *dying*,' she bit out with emphasis. 'In my opinion that shifts the responsibility to those who are well. He couldn't travel; he could barely speak towards the end. What would it have cost you to call him? These days you can call someone from anywhere in the world. What would it have cost you to give a measly five minutes of your time to allow a dying man to rest in peace?'

He stabbed a finger at her, making her take an unsteady step backwards. 'You know nothing, do you hear me? *Nothing* of what it was like being my father's son. You came into my father's life horizontally. You know nothing of what passed before. You were his carer, for heaven's sake. You were paid to wipe the dribble from his chin and change the soiled sheets on his bed, not to psychoanalyse the train-wreck of his relationships.'

Emma took a shaky breath. 'I realise this is an emotionally charged time for you, but I think—'

'I do not give a toss for what you think.' He raised his voice at her this time, his dark eyes flashing with anger. 'As I see it you exploited a dying man to feather your own nest. I find it particularly repugnant to be subjected to your lectures on what constitutes appropriate behaviour from his son when you clearly have no idea of what the dynamic of our relationship was like.'

She bit her lip. 'I'm sorry…I didn't mean to… I'm sorry…'

He let out a ragged sigh as he scraped his hand through the thickness of his hair. 'Forget about it,' he said, his tone softening. 'I should not have shouted at you. I am sorry. Put it down to overwork and jet lag. God knows I did not sleep a wink on the plane.'

'It's fine…really…I understand…it's a difficult time…'

There was a small tight silence.

'I am glad you were there for him when he died,' Rafaele said in a gruff tone. 'In spite of everything I am glad someone was there…'

'He was a good man, Signore… I mean, Rafaele,' she said. 'I think deep down he was a good man who had simply lost his way.'

He gave her a somewhat rueful smile. 'I am starting to think you make a point of seeing the good in everyone, Emma March. Is that something you learnt in your training or somewhere else?'

'No one is completely bad, Rafaele. We all have our stories, the history of what makes us the people we are. I am sure your father had his. It is a shame he didn't share his with you so you could understand the demons he had to wrestle with.'

'My father was not the sort of man to share anything with his family,' he said. 'He deplored weakness in others so I cannot imagine him ever getting to the point of confessing any of his own.'

'Were you ever close to him?' Emma asked.

His expression became shuttered again. 'He was not comfortable with small children, or even older ones when it comes to that.'

'What about your younger brother?'

His eyes turned to fathomless black. 'Has anyone ever told you that you ask too many questions?'

'I'm sorry…I just thought it might help to talk about—'

'Well, it does not help, Miss March.' He cut her off brusquely. 'And in future I would appreciate it if you would refrain from putting your nose where it is not wanted. Digging up the past serves no purpose. My father is dead and I am sorry if it offends your sensibilities, but I for one could not be happier.'

Emma stood in silence as he strode out of the room, the

echo of his embittered words ringing in her ears long after his car had roared out of the villa grounds and faded into the distance.

Emma's sister Simone called again not long after Emma had gone to bed. She sat up against the pillows and listened as Simone tearfully informed her how she had tried to apply for a personal loan only to find out there was a black mark against her credit rating. On further investigation Simone had found out her ex-partner had fuelled his cocaine habit by applying for various loans, using her as guarantor. Emma had listened in horror as Simone had described a visit late at night from a loan shark Brendan had used. The man had threatened Simone and her daughter, making it more than clear that if the money was not repaid within a week there would be unpleasant repercussions.

'I don't know what to do, Emma,' Simone sobbed. 'I'm so scared. When I picked up Chelsea from school I was sure we were being followed.'

'Have you called the police?' Emma asked, her heart thumping in alarm.

'I can't do that,' Simone said. 'You know how they treated me the last time when they came looking for Brendan. They thought I was lying about not knowing where he was or that he was using drugs. They made me feel like a criminal too.'

Emma chewed at her lip. Simone had always had it tough. In the past she had been there so many times for Emma, protecting her from one or both of their parents' drug-fuelled rages until finally the authorities had stepped in and placed both girls in foster homes. And then at the age of nineteen Simone had finally found happiness with David Harrison, but he had been killed in a motorcycle accident just six weeks after Chelsea had been born.

'Listen, Simone, I have a plan.' Emma took a shaky breath

and continued, 'It turns out the man I was nursing left me quite a bit of money in his will. It might take a few days to get it to you, but if you can tell this man Brendan owes the money to that you will settle the debt, perhaps things will calm down until you get some legal advice.'

'But, Emma, it's such a lot of money,' Simone said in anguish. 'I'll never be able to repay you, even if I do manage to take Brendan to court over this. It's not as if he's ever going to have any money to pay the legal fees, let alone the debt, even if the police do manage to track him down and arrest him.'

'I don't want to be repaid, Simone. I just want you and Chelsea to be safe,' Emma insisted. 'If things go according to plan you'll have enough money to relocate to another suburb or even to another state and make a fresh start.'

'Oh, Emma, that would be a dream come true,' Simone choked. 'I hate this place. It reminds me of our childhood, living with Mum and Dad stoned out of their brains all the time. I can't believe I didn't see it in Brendan. He was always so charming and loving. How could I have got it so wrong?'

'It's not your fault, Simone,' Emma said. 'You know what drugs do to people. They turn them into someone else. You have to move on for Chelsea's sake. It's not safe for her to be in such an environment.'

'You're right,' Simone said. 'If Dave was still alive he'd be so ashamed of me for subjecting Chelsea to this.'

'Honey, don't be so hard on yourself,' Emma said. 'I know how tough things have been for you. No one should have to deal with the stuff you've had to deal with. Just be strong, this will all go away and you'll never have to worry again.'

'I don't know how to thank you,' Simone said. 'I really don't know what Chelsea and I would do without you.'

Emma felt a little guilty not telling her sister the truth about how she was going about getting the money, but she reasoned that Simone had enough to worry about for the time being. If she were to tell Simone she was about to marry a man she had only met that morning, her sister would think she had gone mad.

*But then maybe I have,* Emma thought as Rafaele's handsome features came to mind. She gave the pillow a thump and settled back down but it was ages before she could relax enough to sleep…

Emma's eyes sprang open as the front door slammed. She heard Rafaele move about the villa with no attempt to keep the noise down, as if he couldn't care less about disturbing her, no doubt because he considered her an interloper in his family home.

She heard the sound of a glass shattering in the lounge room downstairs and then a course expletive cut through the still night air. She waited a few minutes, listening as various cupboards and drawers were opened and slammed shut as he began hunting through the main bathroom.

'Where the hell is the first-aid kit?' Rafaele's voice roared from the foot of the sweeping staircase.

Emma threw back the covers and, reaching for her bathrobe, tied it securely around her waist and came out on the third-floor landing. 'What's wrong?' she asked, looking down at him. 'Have you cut yourself?'

He swayed slightly on his feet as he held up his right hand wrapped in a hand towel. 'Yes, I have, as a matter of fact. Want to kiss it better, pretty Emma?'

She frowned at him as she came down the stairs. 'Have you been drinking?' she asked in a reproachful tone.

He gave her a sinful smile. 'So what if I have?'

She stood three steps above him to meet him eye to eye. 'Did you drive home in this state?'

He swayed towards her, the strong fumes of brandy wafting

over her face. 'No, I caught a cab,' he said. 'Wasn't that sensible of me?'

'It's not sensible to drink to excess even if you're not planning to be behind the wheel of a car,' she said. 'Let me look at your hand.'

He held it out to her and she gently peeled back the towel to find a gash near the base of his thumb that was still oozing blood.

'Am I going to make it through the night?' he asked with one of his mocking smiles.

Emma pursed her mouth and led him by his uninjured hand to the nearest bathroom. 'Sit on the stool,' she directed sternly as she washed her hands. 'You're very lucky, as it doesn't need stitching. I'll put a Steri-Strip on it to pull the edges together.'

She located the first-aid kit and set about cleaning the wound and dressing it. But she found it almost impossible to control the slight tremor of her hands as she touched him. His shirt sleeves were rolled back, revealing strong wrists with a generous sprinkling of dark hair, a potent reminder of his virility.

She was acutely aware of his closeness, his long legs trapping her between the basin and him at one point. He was such an intensely masculine man. She could smell the musk of his skin, this close to him she could see every pinprick of stubble on his jaw, making her fingers ache to touch him there, to see if her soft skin would snag on his rougher one.

She took an unsteady breath and tried to ignore the flutter of her pulse as his dark eyes locked on hers.

'You have very soft hands,' he said. 'I wonder if that prim little mouth of yours is just as soft.'

'I guess you'll just have to keep on wondering,' Emma said, trying to move to one side.

He stood up, his left arm blocking her exit. 'How about I kiss you and find out, eh, Emma?'

Emma gave a nervous swallow, her belly doing a funny little somersault at the smouldering look in his darker-than-ink eyes. 'I don't think that would be a good idea…'

He gave her a slow, sexy smile. 'Why not?'

She unconsciously ran her tongue over her lips. 'You know why not.'

'Is there someone else?'

'No…I mean, yes, there is,' she lied, but she knew the colour storming into her cheeks was betraying her.

'You are not a very convincing liar, Emma,' he said. 'If you were involved with someone else you would not be sending me those hungry little looks all the time, now, would you?'

'I'm doing no such thing,' she said. 'I don't know what you're talking about.'

He released her hand and placed the heated warmth of his palm at the nape of her neck instead. Emma couldn't stop the little shiver that coursed like a tickling feather all the way down her spine, loosening every vertebra along the way. Her heart began pick up its pace, the thud of her pulse so heavy she was surprised he couldn't feel it leaping beneath her skin where his hand rested.

'You want to know, don't you?' he went on in that same toe-curling, sensuous drawl. 'You have done it with the father, now you want to know what it feels like to do it with the son.'

Emma's eyes flared in shock at his crude statement. 'That's not true!'

'Did he make you come?' he asked.

She tried to push at him, but if anything it brought him closer, the stirring of his body against hers sending sparks of heat coursing through her lower body. Her breasts were jammed against his chest, her stomach hollowing out at the diamond-hard glitter of his dark gaze as it drilled into hers. 'L-let me go…' she choked. 'Y-you're drunk.'

He countered her paltry escape manoeuvre by placing his injured hand in the small of her back, his left hand now buried in the curtain of her hair. 'Perhaps a little, but that will not affect my performance,' he said. 'I can make you come like you've never come before.'

In spite of her outrage Emma could feel her body betraying her. His sultry promise set her senses alight at the thought of having him deep inside her, bringing her the sort of pleasure she had so far only dreamed about. She knew it was unusual in this day and age for a woman of twenty-six to be without sexual experience, but she had never met anyone she had been attracted to enough to take that final step. Getting involved with a playboy was not something she had ever contemplated and certainly not one as ruthless and arrogant as Rafaele Fiorenza. He was undoubtedly the most attractive man she had ever encountered, but allowing herself to be seduced by him was something she was determined to avoid if at all possible. He was an inveterate heartbreaker and she would do very well to remember it.

'I don't recall reading anything in your father's will that stipulated I have to satisfy your disgusting animal urges,' she said with as much acerbity as she could. 'Now, if you don't let me go this instant I will have to resort to slapping your face.'

He grinned at her, which wasn't quite the effect she had intended. 'You are quite something when you are all fired up,' he said. 'I bet you go off like a firecracker in bed.'

She drew in a sharp little breath, her eyes flashing him a warning. 'I don't have to put up with this,' she said. 'If you don't stop this I will pack my bags first thing in the morning to make way for Ms Henning.'

A nerve twitched at the side of his mouth, his eyes hardening to narrow chips of black ice. 'Are you blackmailing me, Emma?' he asked.

Emma lifted her chin. 'You bet I am,' she said. 'And you'd better not forget it.'

He looked at her for a long pulsing moment, his palm still on the nape of her neck. Emma tried not to show how unnerved she was by his closeness, but her heart was skipping every second beat with each drawn-out second that passed.

'You would walk away from a fortune such as this just to spite me?' he asked, dropping his hand.

Emma's neck was still tingling from the touch of his fingers. 'If I have to, yes. I refuse to be treated like a tramp. I do have some measure of pride, you know.'

'I am sure you do,' he said. 'But I wonder if you are calling my bluff.'

She gave him an arch look. 'There is only one way to find out.'

He smiled again, his dark eyes twinkling. 'Are you daring me to kiss you, Emma March?'

Her eyes widened in alarm. 'Of course not!'

'I am tempted,' he said, looking down at her mouth. 'In fact, I have never been quite so tempted.'

Emma spun on her bare feet to leave, but before she could take a single step he captured one of the ties of her bathrobe and towed her into his solid warmth like a wobbly dingy being drawn towards the safe harbour of a jetty. 'Thank you for fixing my hand,' he said. 'I really appreciate it.'

Emma had to fight against the overwhelming temptation to look at his mouth. 'It's fine…I hope it doesn't get infected.'

'If it does at least I will have you on hand to mop my feverish brow, will I not?'

She tugged her bathrobe tie out of his hold and gave him a testy glare. 'I'm sure your current mistress will do a much better job than me.'

His eyes moved over her face in a leisurely fashion, his

quiet assessment of her features even more disturbing to her than his verbal taunts. 'As of earlier tonight I have dismissed her services,' he said. 'She was starting to bore me, in any case. I have no time for emotionally needy women. They are too much hard work.'

Emma wasn't sure what to say in response. She felt a pang of empathy for the woman he had discarded so cavalierly. She wondered if he had called her or texted her on his mobile, not even bothering to wait until he could speak to her face to face. Either way she couldn't help wondering if the woman had done the unthinkable and fallen in love with him. It was a sobering reminder of what she was in for if she dared to allow her own feelings to get out of control.

'It's very late,' she said. 'You should go to bed. You look exhausted.'

He cocked his head at her. 'How about you tuck me in? I am sure you are very good at it. After all, isn't that what my father paid you to do?'

'I would have looked after him without any payment,' she said, even though she knew it was going to annoy him. 'In my opinion he was worth two of you.'

A flicker of anger flashed in his dark gaze. 'Are you telling me you were in love with him?' he asked.

She held his glittering gaze with an effort. 'Everyone deserves love, Rafaele; even, dare I say, someone as odious as you.'

She gave him one last frosty look and stalked out with the sounds of his mocking laughter following her all the way upstairs.

# CHAPTER THREE

WHEN Emma came downstairs the following morning Rafaele was leaning against the kitchen counter with a cup of coffee in one hand. He put the cup down and pushed himself away from the counter and came to stand in front of her. 'I believe I owe you an apology,' he said. 'I have no real excuse for my behaviour last night. I was not even drunk, not that it would have been any excuse even if I had been. It was a difficult day for me…coming back here after a long absence. I guess I had underestimated just how much of a strain it would be.'

'It's OK,' she said and, after a little pause, asked, 'How is your hand?'

'It is fine,' he said, holding it out for her to see. 'I do not think there will even be a scar. You did a good job.'

A silence hummed for several seconds.

'Have you come to a decision?' Rafaele asked.

Her grey-blue eyes moved away from his. 'I have…yes…' She ran the tip of her tongue over her lips. 'I have decided I will marry you. It's the most sensible thing to do and…and it's what your father wanted.'

Rafaele smiled to himself. He had known from the first moment she would not be able to resist getting her hands on a fortune. She thought she had it all stitched up now, but he wasn't going to let things go her way. Nor was he going to make life easy for her. He would marry her certainly, for there was no other way to get his inheritance, but he wasn't going to stay married to her any longer than necessary. Once the year was up that would be it. Although looking at her now with her slim but curvy figure dressed in a white sundress, he was tempted to make the marriage a real one. She had an air of sensuality about her that was intoxicating. He had seen the looks she gave him when she thought he wasn't watching. She was as attracted to him as he was to her. He had felt the tension passing between them like high voltage electricity. He could even feel it now. 'I am sure we will be mutually satisfied by the arrangement,' he said with an enigmatic smile.

A flicker of something came and went in her gaze. 'I would like to establish some ground rules,' she said.

'Such as?'

'This is a hands-off arrangement, correct?'

'If that is what you want,' he said. 'But if you change your mind just let me know.'

She gave him a withering look. 'I will not be changing my mind,' she said. 'As far as I am concerned this is a temporary businesslike arrangement. I hope I won't have to keep reminding you of that.'

*Oh, but she's damned good at this*, Rafaele thought, *deliberately withholding her charms to make me feel the lure of the chase.* He would bring her to heel, however, and a whole lot sooner than she realised. His body hardened at the thought of driving into her softness, claiming her as his until she forgot all about her affair with his father. She would be screaming *his* name in the throes of pleasure. She would be raking her nails down *his* back as he took her to paradise. 'You will not have to remind me,' he assured her. 'I will take my cue from you.'

Her gaze narrowed slightly. 'What do you mean?'

He gave another inward smile at her artifice. 'I mean that if you make the first move I will respond to it as any full-blooded man would do in the same situation.'

She gave him a condescending look. 'So any woman with a pulse will do for you—is that it?'

'You do yourself a disservice, Emma,' he said with a lazy smile. 'You are a very attractive young woman. I would be more than happy to consummate our marriage if you should require my services.'

Her cheeks pooled with angry colour. 'I am sure I will be able to survive the duration of our marriage without resorting to such a measure of desperation,' she clipped back primly.

Rafaele felt his groin kicking with anticipation. He had never felt such wild desire before. No wonder his father had agreed to give her half of his estate. Rafaele felt like offering her double what he'd already offered just to have her on her back on the floor right here and now. He had to fight not to show how she was affecting him. He schooled his features into indifference and reached for his coffee again. 'I will have some legal papers for you to sign later today,' he said.

'What do I need to sign?' she asked with a guarded look.

'A pre-nuptial agreement, for one thing,' he said. 'I am not going to be stripped of half of my assets when we terminate our marriage.'

'How soon do I get the money you offered?' she asked.

He held her grey-blue gaze. 'How soon do you want it?'

She lowered her eyes. 'I have some debts to see to…they're rather urgent.'

'If you give me your bank account details I will see to it the moment we get back from the church.'

Her eyes flew back to his. '*The church?* You mean we're getting married in a church?'

'Do you have a problem with that?'

She sank her teeth into her lower lip for a moment. 'No… it's just I thought a register office would be more appropriate under the circumstances.'

'I do not think our marriage would be considered authentic if we did not have it consecrated by the church,' he said. 'I will also arrange for a dress and veil for you.'

'You don't have to do that.'

'It is no bother,' he said. 'My mother's wedding dress and veil have been well preserved and you are much the same size as she was.'

Her eyes were wide grey-blue pools. 'I can't wear your mother's dress!'

'Why not? People will think it a loving gesture on your part,' he said. 'Besides, this is probably going to be the only time I marry anyone so I might as well do it properly.'

Emma chewed at her bottom lip in agitation. This was going to be much harder than she had expected. Somehow she had thought a quick civil service would make her feel less married. That was vitally important to her. She didn't want to *feel* married to him.

'I will get my mother's rings out of the safe for you,' he said. 'But of course they must be returned to me once our marriage ends.'

'Yes, of course…' she said. 'I wouldn't dream of keeping them.'

'The wedding will take place tomorrow.'

Emma's heart gave a sickening lurch. 'T-tomorrow?'

'Yes,' he said. 'The legalities will be seen to this afternoon. The ceremony will take place tomorrow at the Basilica of Saint Abbondio, the ancient cathedral in the town. Have you by any chance been there?'

'I haven't done a lot of sightseeing yet,' she said. 'I was too busy looking after your father.'

He paused for a moment, his eyes still holding hers before he continued. 'We will have a small reception at a function centre afterwards, but there will of course be no honeymoon.'

'I wasn't expecting one, I can assure you,' she said. 'Besides, I need to contact the agency in regards to finding a local placement.'

'You will not be returning to the agency while you are married to me,' he said.

Emma blinked once or twice. 'What did you say?'

His dark eyes challenged hers. 'I said you will not be returning to work. I have already contacted the agency and terminated your contract.'

Emma gaped at him. 'You did *what*?'

'You are now employed by me to act as my wife. I do not want people speculating on whether this marriage is the real deal or not. What if a client needed you to live in for weeks on end? No one would expect any wife of mine to be employed and certainly not as a carer.'

'Well, no husband of mine would ever expect me to give up the job I love to pander to his needs,' Emma tossed back.

'I am not asking you to pander to my needs, but if you feel the need to do so I will not stop you.'

She gave him a blistering glare. 'What am I supposed to do all day? Laze about the pool and paint my nails? I'll go stark staring mad.'

'Think of it as a holiday, Emma,' he said. 'You can explore a hobby or two. Most of the women I know would give anything for a year to indulge themselves at a rich man's expense.'

'You really need to widen your circle of women friends,' Emma said in a crisp tone. 'Most of the women I know value their self-respect and independence too much to be indulged like a spoilt child.'

'I am sure you will adapt very quickly,' he said. 'After all, you have had plenty of practice while living with my father as your sugar daddy. Money is your motive and always has been, has it not? Why else would you be marrying me if it was not for the money?'

Emma ground her teeth. 'I don't want the money for myself,' she said. 'Otherwise I wouldn't dream of agreeing to any of this. Do you think I want to be married to someone as loathsome as you?'

A muscle leapt in his jaw. 'Careful, Emma,' he warned. 'I will not tolerate insults from you once we are married.'

Her chin came up at a defiant angle. 'If you insult me I will insult you straight back.'

His eyes glinted. 'I will enjoy taming you, Emma March,' he said. 'You are a little wildcat under that demure façade, are you not? I can see the passion in your eyes; they flash with it like twin flames of grey and blue.'

Emma felt her stomach go hollow at the sensual threat behind his statement. Her heart was suddenly racing, her skin prickling all over and her face hot with colour. If it weren't for Simone and Chelsea, she would tell him right here and now where he could put his money and his villa. But then how many times had her sister stood in the line of fire for her? Simone had taken many a slap intended for Emma; she had even had her arm broken once when she had blocked their father from lashing out at her in a fit of rage. It was not going to be easy, but surely Emma owed her sister this chance. Rafaele might not be Emma's choice of husband material, but at least it was only a temporary arrangement.

She gave him a flinty look and moved past him to pour a cup of coffee. It annoyed her to see her hand shaking as she did so, but she comforted herself that her back was turned towards him so he couldn't see.

'The lawyer will be here at three p.m.,' Rafaele said. 'In the meantime I have some work to see to in my study. If there is anything else you need for tomorrow let me know and I will see to it that you have it.'

She cradled her coffee-cup in both of her hands as she looked at him. 'Thank you but, no, there's nothing I need.'

'What about your friends?' he asked. 'Is there anyone you would like to attend the ceremony?'

'No,' she said. 'Most of my friends are in Australia. I have a couple of new acquaintances I made while I was living in Milan but no one here.'

'What about your family?' he asked. 'Obviously it is too short a notice to get them here for the wedding, but have you told them?'

She shook her head. 'There's only my sister and my niece, but I didn't want to worry them.'

He frowned at her. 'What do you mean?'

She gave him a level stare. 'My sister has always been very protective of me,' she said. 'If I told her I was marrying a virtual stranger she would have a blue fit.'

Rafaele rubbed at his jaw for a moment. 'What if she finds out some other way? An announcement or photo in the press, for instance?'

She sank her teeth into her bottom lip as she put her coffee-cup back on the counter. 'I hadn't thought about that...'

'I have been doing some thinking,' he said. 'To give our marriage some sort of credibility we shall have to tell anyone who asks we met when you first began to look after my father and up until now we have conducted a long-distance relationship.'

'Do you think that will work?' she asked.

'It will have to work. I do not want the world to know I have been manipulated into a loveless marriage by my father's machinations from the grave.'

'I'm not going to lie to my sister,' she said with a spark of defiance in her eyes.

'As far as I see it you have already done so by omission,' he pointed out. 'Concealing the truth is the same as lying in my book.'

She gave him an arch look. 'And yet you are prepared to lie to the world about your relationship with me.'

'I am prepared to compromise quite a few of my standards in order to secure what is rightly mine, including sleeping with the enemy if she so desires.'

Her eyes flashed at him again. 'This particular enemy has no such desire.'

He smiled and stepped closer, close enough to take her chin between his index finger and thumb. 'Are you prepared to lay some money down on that, Emma?' he asked in a silky tone.

He felt her tremble under his touch and his groin leapt in response. Her mouth was like a soft, plump cushion of pink flesh just begging to be kissed. The more he thought about it, the more he wanted to do it. He lowered his head, slowly, watching as her eyes widened before her lashes began to come down, her lips parting slightly, her sweet breath mingling with his, giving him all the invitation he needed.

Emma came to her senses just in time. She slipped out of his light hold, her heart hammering, her breath catching and her senses on fire. 'What the hell do you think you're doing?' she said, rubbing at her chin as if he had burnt her.

'I was doing what you were all but begging me to do,' he answered smoothly.

She glared at him. 'I was doing nothing of the sort. You touched me. I didn't touch you.'

'You will have to touch me tomorrow. In fact you will have to kiss me in front of the congregation, so perhaps we should rehearse it a couple of times now.'

Emma couldn't quite control the flutter of nerves in her belly. 'I-I don't think that will be necessary,' she faltered. 'Surely we can just…you know…wing it at the time…'

He gave a wry smile. 'Wing it?'

'Ad lib,' she said. 'You know…go on instinct…'

His eyes darkened to black pools of ink. 'I thought that was exactly what I was just doing,' he said, 'and so were you if you were honest with yourself.'

'Maybe I was thinking of your father,' she said, even though she knew it would infuriate him. Better that than admit to him how much she had wanted him to kiss her. That was just asking too much of her pride, battered as it was.

His features went tight with anger. 'You gold-digging little whore,' he bit out savagely. 'I swear to God you will not be thinking of my father when I finally take you to my bed.'

His confidence fuelled Emma's defiance. She gave her head a little toss and gave him a taunting look. 'That is not part of the deal, Rafaele, remember? If you want the goods on display, then you will have to pay extra for them.'

A nerve pulsed like a jackhammer at the side of his mouth. 'Goddamn you,' he ground out. 'I am not paying another penny for a cheap little tramp like you. When you come to me you will do so because you want it so badly you cannot help yourself.'

Emma stood her ground as he brushed past her in a swish of anger-filled air that lifted the strands of hair about her face. She closed her eyes once the door clicked shut behind him, her chest deflating on an expelled breath, her throat tight with the effort of holding back a stray and totally unexpected sob.

* * *

Emma heard the lawyer arrive just on three in the afternoon and made her way downstairs to the library. She wished she had thought to ask Rafaele what he intended to tell his legal advisor about their relationship. As she came into the room she looked at him for guidance but his expression was impenetrable.

Brief introductions were made and she sat down and began reading through the wordy documents, deliberately taking her time before she signed the places marked with a sign-here sticker. Emma had no problem with signing a pre-nuptial agreement—several of her friends back home in Australia had done so when they had begun living with their partners or got married. She totally understood Rafaele's position, he couldn't risk a division of his assets upon their inevitable divorce, but somehow she wished things were different between them. She wasn't used to people taking an instant dislike to her. Even her parents, for all their faults, had not really hated her; they had just loved their drugs more.

She signed the last place and gave the lawyer a smile. 'Thank you for going to the trouble of printing a copy for me in English.'

'*Prego.*'

Once the lawyer had left Rafaele turned to Emma. 'I have left my mother's dress and veil in the dressing room upstairs. If it is not suitable will you let me know immediately so I can come up with an alternative?'

Emma arched her brows at him. 'You must have some very fancy connections in that little black book of yours if you can come up with wedding finery at short notice.'

'There are certain advantages in being extremely wealthy,' he returned with a stretch of his lips that was almost, but not quite, a smile.

'Yes, well, you're lucky, I suppose, that you've got that going for you in compensation for your other numerous short-comings,' she said with a pert tilt of her chin.

'If you are looking for an apology for this afternoon's discussion I am not going to give it to you,' he said.

'I wasn't expecting you to be civil,' she threw back. 'I know that about you at the very least.'

His black-brown gaze clashed with hers. 'You will know a whole lot more about me before this marriage is over, let me assure you.'

She gave a bored sigh and folded her arms across her chest. 'I can hardly wait.'

Rafaele felt his control slipping. She was goading him deliberately, making him feel things he didn't want to feel. He had never met a more infuriating woman, or a more desirable one. He wanted her so badly his body burned with it. The blood was already thick and heavy in his groin, the pulse of lust so strong he could feel it pounding in his ears. But acting on it was out of the question, or at least until they were officially married. She stood between him and his last link with his father. If he made a wrong move now she might pull the plug just to spite him. How could he trust her? For all he knew she might have cooked this scheme up with that cold-hearted bitch Sondra Henning. They could share the spoils of their victory, leaving him with nothing.

He was *not* going to let that happen.

He rearranged his features and forced his tense shoulders to relax. 'This is not getting us anywhere,' he said. 'We are arguing like children in a playground. Tomorrow is going to be difficult enough for both of us.'

'I couldn't agree more,' she said. 'That is why I am going to have an early night. If you want dinner you will have to make it yourself.'

Rafaele frowned at her churlish expression. 'I do not expect you to prepare my meals, Emma. That is what I have a housekeeper for. I have employed a temporary one to fill in until my father's lady returns from leave. She will start next week. I could not get anyone any sooner.'

'Have you told her our marriage is not a real one?'

'I did not see the necessity to do so,' he said.

'Isn't she going to think it rather unusual we will not be sharing a bedroom?'

'Many couples do not share a bedroom for a variety of reasons,' he said. 'I will tell her I am a very light sleeper if you like.'

'Fine,' she said and turned to leave.

'Emma?'

He heard her draw in a breath of petulance as she turned back to face him. 'Yes?'

He searched her features for a beat or two. 'I hope I do not need to remind you that I expect you to refrain from bringing any of your lovers back here to the villa.'

She arched her brows at him. 'Do I get the same guarantee from you?'

'Any affairs I conduct will be discreet.'

Her eyes flashed with sparks of grey-blue hatred. 'If you embarrass me publicly, then I swear to God I will do the same to you.'

Rafaele held her feisty glare. 'Do so at your peril, Emma. You might think you have got the upper hand now your goal of marrying a rich man is just hours away, but do not forget who you are dealing with. My father might have been a weak-willed pushover, but you will not find me so easy to manipulate. You put one foot out of line and you will live to regret it. I will make sure of it.'

She gave him an insolent look. 'Do you have any idea how much I loathe and detest you?'

His mouth tilted in a mocking smile. 'If it is even half of

what I feel for you, then I would say we are in for a very entertaining year of marriage.'

'I am not staying married to you any longer than necessary,' she said with another defiant glare. 'Once I have what I want I am leaving.'

'Believe me, Emma Money-Hungry March,' he drawled dryly, 'I will be the first on hand to help you pack your bags.'

She looked as if she was going to fling another retort his way, but suddenly seemed to change her mind. Instead she pressed her lips tightly together and brushed past him, her gait stiff with haughtiness. It was only later, much later, that he recalled seeing a glisten of moisture in her eyes before she had lowered them out of the reach of his.

# CHAPTER FOUR

WHEN Emma came downstairs the following morning wearing the wedding dress and veil Rafaele's mother had worn on her wedding day he felt a shock wave of reaction go through him. She had styled her chestnut hair into a smooth princess-like chignon at the back of her head, her flawless face lightly made up with foundation and eye-shadow and just a hint of blusher on her cheeks. Her lips were a glossy pink and the fragrance she wore floated down towards him with every cautious step she took as the dress's train followed her down the stairs.

He felt his throat go dry and had to swallow a couple of times to clear it enough to speak. 'You look very beautiful, Emma,' he said. 'I have never seen a more stunning bride.'

'I feel like a dreadful fraud,' she said with a little downturn of her mouth.

He took her by the elbow and led her out to where his car and driver were waiting. 'This is going to be the easy part. The priest tells us what to say and we say it. You have probably been to or seen enough weddings on television to know how to act. Just smile constantly and look adoringly at me.'

She gave him a surly look without responding.

He settled her into the limousine and took the seat beside

her, holding her hand in his. 'Stop frowning, Emma,' he said. 'Think about the money that is going to be in your bank account at the end of today. Surely that should bring a smile to any woman's face.'

She turned her head away to look out of the window. 'I can't wait for this to be over,' she said.

Rafaele felt the slight tremble of her fingers where they were resting against his. He gave her hand a little squeeze. 'Do not worry, Emma, it soon will be.'

The ceremony was very traditional even if the bride and groom had arrived in the same car, Emma thought as she mechanically repeated her vows. Then the moment came when the priest instructed the groom to kiss his bride. Emma could feel the anticipation of the congregation as Rafaele gently lifted the veil off her face. Her breathing came to a jerky halt in her chest as his eyes locked on hers. Her heart began to thud as he brought his head down, his warm, mint-fresh breath caressing the surface of her lips before he pressed his against them in a kiss that went from feather-light to red-hot passion within a heartbeat. Sensation exploded inside her as his tongue slipped through the softly parted shield of her lips to mate with hers in a blatant act of possession that sent electric shivers up and down her spine. Her breasts tightened and tingled simultaneously, her legs trembling so much she could barely stand upright and would have melted in a pool at Rafaele's feet if his hand hadn't been pressed to the small of her back, holding her against his rock-hard body. She felt the stirring of his groin against her, making her even more acutely aware of the formal ties that now bound them.

When he finally lifted his mouth off hers, Emma gave a tremulous smile for the benefit of the congregation, or at least that was what she told herself at the time. Rafaele smiled back, a warm, generous smile that made his eyes go very dark and the lines about his mouth relax, making him look all the more irresistibly handsome.

After the register was signed Emma stood sipping a glass of champagne an hour or so later, smiling until her face ached as she was introduced to the various colleagues and friends Rafaele had invited at short notice. Numerous people raved about her dress, remarking how it had made the wedding all the more special to think she had worn it in honour of Rafaele's much-loved mother.

One woman in particular, someone who had known Gabriela Fiorenza personally, came and spoke to Emma while Rafaele was engaged in a conversation elsewhere. 'I am so very glad Rafaele has found someone like you,' she said in heavily accented English. 'He always said he would never fall in love and marry, but that is because he did not want to end up like his father. Valentino did not handle Gabriela's death very well. He had been in love with her practically since childhood. And then losing poor Giovanni…' The woman crossed herself. 'God rest his soul.'

Emma wanted to ask what had happened to Rafaele's younger brother, but realised it might appear strange if she did so. As his bride she would be expected to know everything there was to know about Rafaele and his family, but, she realised with an unnerving quiver deep inside her belly as she met his gaze across the room, she knew very little…

Once the official photographs were taken and the wedding cake cut, Rafaele led her out to the car where the driver transported them back to the villa.

He turned to her once they were inside. 'I will leave you to get changed. It has been a long day. I will see to the electronic transfer of the funds I promised you, also I have some stocks and shares to look up on my computer, which may take some time, so if you will excuse me, I will say good-night.'

'Rafaele?'

His expression locked her out. 'The money is yours, Emma,' he said. 'That is what you wanted, was it not?'

She rolled her lips together, her eyes falling away from his. 'Yes…' she said. 'Yes, it is…'

'I will see you in the morning.'

Emma lifted her gaze, but he was already striding away down the hall towards the study as if he couldn't wait to get away from her.

Emma barely caught sight of Rafaele during the next couple of days. He came in late at night and left before she was up in the morning, which should have made her feel relieved but somehow didn't.

She did, however, get some measure of comfort from transferring Simone the funds to clear away the debt. She even decided to come clean and tell her sister about her marriage to Rafaele in case it was reported in the press back in Melbourne. Simone was shocked and expressed her concern about Emma marrying a man she barely knew, but Emma tried to reassure her by pointing out Valentino Fiorenza would never have insisted on such a scheme if he had not trusted his son to do the right thing by her.

'You're not going to do something stupid like fall in love with this man, are you, Emma?' Simone asked.

'Of course not!' Emma laughed off the suggestion but later, after she had ended the call, she wondered if she had tempted fate by being quite so adamant. She could still feel the imprint of his lips on hers and her belly gave a little twitch-like movement every time she thought of his tongue moving against hers.

The last thing she wanted to do was to develop feelings for Rafaele, but as she moved about the property she couldn't help thinking what it must have been like for him and his younger brother growing up without a mother. Every time she walked through the villa or gardens she imagined two little bewildered boys wandering around the huge mansion and grounds without the comfort and nurture of their mother. In many ways it reminded her of her own childhood, but at least she had had Simone to turn to. But then that also brought it home to her how lonely Rafaele's childhood must have been after the death of his younger brother Giovanni. Rafaele had only been ten years old at the time. The large rooms, though beautiful, were formal and rather ostentatious, the many priceless paintings and objets d'art clearly not conducive to the presence of a young child.

As she had guessed, Rafaele had chosen not to occupy his father's suite and instead had placed his things in one of the suites on the third level. For days Emma had felt uncomfortable even walking past his private domain, although she felt inexplicably drawn to the room every time she walked past to her own suite further along the hall. Finally she could stand it no longer, and, once she was confident she was alone in the villa, she opened the door and went in.

The huge bed was neatly made and several books were sitting on the bedside table, all but one of them in English. She could smell the trace of citrus in his aftershave lingering in the air and her nostrils automatically flared to take more of it in.

The sunlight slanted in at the windows, the dust motes rising like tiny wraiths in the air. Before she was even aware of what she was doing Emma moved across the room to sit on the bed, the creak of protesting springs sounding like a warning in the silence. She ran her hand over the pillow, smoothing out the indentation where his head had lain the night before.

She wondered if this had been his room while growing up at The Villa Fiorenza, but if it had been it held no trace of his previous occupation. His brother's room on the nursery floor, on the other hand, was like a shrine. When she had gone in there for the first time a few days ago she had been more than a little taken aback to find the wardrobe still contained his clothes; his shoes were still lying at the bottom with his socks stuffed inside as if at any moment he were coming back to claim them. His toys and junior soccer trophies lined every available surface and, even more disturbingly, the urn with his ashes held pride of place on the mantel above the fireplace. Emma had found it a little creepy being in there. She felt as if the house wasn't quite ready to let Giovanni Fiorenza leave even though, according to the inscription on the urn, he had died twenty-three years ago.

She looked at the photograph hanging on the wall; Giovanni had been as dark as his brother with the same deep brown eyes, but there was a relaxed and friendly openness about his features that wasn't present in his brooding older brother's. The photograph portrayed Rafaele as a rather serious young boy who looked as if he were carrying the weight of the world upon his thin shoulders.

Even though Emma had been in every room in the villa by now she had seen not a single photograph of Rafaele in the years since his brother had died.

She couldn't help wondering why.

Emma was in the salon falling asleep over a book the following evening when Rafaele came into the room. She put the book to side and got to her feet, suddenly feeling uncomfortable in case he somehow sensed where she had been mooching around earlier.

'That looks like a riveting read,' he remarked dryly.

She gave him a sheepish look. 'I guess I must be a little tired. I should have been in bed an hour ago.'

His brow creased slightly. 'I hope you are not overdoing things,' he said. 'I noticed you have taken all the covers off the furniture in the spare rooms. Surely that can wait until the new housekeeper starts in a day or so?'

'I thought the place needed airing,' Emma said. 'Some of those rooms look like they have been shut for years.'

He studied her for a moment. 'What are you up to, Emma? Making an inventory of all the valuables for when we finally divorce?'

'I am merely trying to make this place habitable,' she said, frowning at him crossly. 'It's a huge villa and too much work for one housekeeper. I don't know how Lucia had managed for as long as she has. No wonder she wanted a break.'

He held her fiery look for a tense moment. 'Were you waiting up for me, Emma?' he asked.

'No, of course I wasn't,' she said, annoyed with herself for the creep of colour she could feel staining her cheeks. He was so worldly and in control while she always felt so flustered and out of her depth in his presence.

'Actually, I am glad you are still up,' he said. 'Do you fancy a nightcap?'

'Um…OK…'

'What would you like to drink?' he asked, turning to the well-stocked drinks cabinet.

'A small sweet sherry…if you have it,' she said.

He poured himself a cognac after he'd handed her the sherry and came and sat beside her on the sofa, touching his glass briefly against hers. '*Salute.*'

'*Salute,*' Emma said and took a tiny sip.

'I thought only grey-haired Sunday-school teachers drank that stuff,' he said with a crooked smile.

Emma felt a little stung at what she perceived was a criticism. 'I suppose I must seem terribly unsophisticated to someone like you.'

'On the contrary, I find you rather intriguing.'

'I thought you said I was a money-hungry slut who was intent on making herself a fortune, or words to that effect,' she returned with a tart edge to her tone.

'I may have been a little hasty in my judgement,' he acceded. 'Although I guess only time will tell.'

'You can't quite accept there are still people in the world who genuinely care about others, can you?' she asked.

'You were being *paid* to care, Emma,' he pointed out. 'My father obviously did not know the difference. He fooled himself into thinking you were worthy of half of his estate. How does it feel now you have achieved your goal?'

'I told you before I did absolutely nothing to encourage your father's decision,' she insisted.

'He only changed his will once you had come into his life,' he said. 'How did you do it, Emma? How many times did you have to crawl into his bed to sweeten him up a bit?'

'That's a disgusting thing to say,' she said.

His top lip curled. 'My father always had a thing for women young enough to be his daughter,' he said. 'He liked to show them off like a trophy. It used to sicken me to see them fawning all over him. None of them had any time for my brother and I. They were after my father's money just like you.'

Emma got to her feet. 'I don't have to listen to this.'

His flashing dark eyes raked her mercilessly. 'So how did you manage it, Emma? Could he still get it up towards the end or did you have to give him a bit of encouragement with that pretty little mouth of yours?' he asked.

Emma lifted her hand to his face, but he blocked it with

one of his, the grip of his strong fingers almost brutal around her slender wrist.

'I don't think so, *poco moglie di miniera,*' he said. 'Not unless you want to face the consequences.'

She ground her teeth as she pulled at his hold. 'It's no wonder your father stripped this house of every single photograph of you,' she said with uncharacteristic spite. 'He must have hated being reminded of the sort of person you turned out to be. I have never met a more hateful despicable man.'

His fingers tightened even further. 'Perhaps I should give you an even better reason to hate me,' he said and tugged her towards him, her breasts pressed tight to his chest. 'After all, that is what you really want me to do, is it not? You have wanted it from the start. My father cannot have been much use to a young nubile woman like you. How long has it been since you had a real man in your bed?'

Emma threw him a heated glare. 'I wouldn't dream of demeaning myself by spending even a second in yours.'

His mouth tilted mockingly. 'Now that is very interesting you should say so, for you spent a whole lot longer than that on it this afternoon, did you not, Emma?' he asked.

Her eyes widened, her voice sticking at the back of her throat. 'I-I don't know what you're talking about.'

He picked up a lock of her hair and slowly wound it round one of his fingers. 'Little liar,' he said. 'Guess what I found lying on my pillow? A couple of chestnut-brown hairs that look to me as if they came from that clever little calculating head of yours.'

Emma knew she had no real way to defend herself, but it didn't stop her trying. 'I went in there to check if you needed any washing done,' she said. 'There was nothing else to it.'

He slowly unwound her hair, his eyes holding hers like a mesmerised rabbit. 'I know what you are doing, Emma,' he said. 'You are turning up the heat, bit by bit, just like you did with my father.'

'I am doing no such thing!'

'Can you feel what you are doing to me?' he asked, pressing her closer to where his lower body was thickening. 'Feel it, Emma.'

Emma felt it and it secretly terrified her. She had never felt the overwhelming power of physical attraction quite like this before, it smouldered like red-hot coals deep inside her, making her a slave to the senses he had awakened. She wanted to feel his commanding lips on hers again; she had been dreaming of it for days. She wanted to feel the hot brand of his mouth suckling on her breasts, her stomach, her thighs and the secret heart of her that throbbed and pulsed with longing for him even now.

'Damn you, Emma,' he growled, putting her away from him roughly. 'I want you but I hate myself for it. I swore I would never touch a woman my father had slaked his lust on first.'

'I didn't have that sort of relationship with your father,' Emma said in frustration. 'Why won't you believe me?'

'Do you expect me to believe he handed over half of his estate just because you smoothed the sheets on his deathbed?' he asked. 'I am not that much of a fool.'

'There's nothing I can say to convince you otherwise, is there?' she said. 'You want to believe your father set out to deliberately thwart you, but I don't believe he did.'

His mouth twisted with scorn. 'Oh, come on now, Emma. You're surely not going to tell me he had a last-minute change of mind and told you how much he really loved me, are you?'

'Why did you hate him so much?' Emma asked.

His expression became stony and the seconds ticked by before he answered. 'I didn't like him for many reasons,' he said. 'For the first few years of my life he was everything a father should be, but after my mother died he changed. It was like living at a perpetual funeral. He would snap at my younger brother and I for the most inconsequential things. In his opinion we were meant to grieve indefinitely, but Giovanni was too young to remember much about our mother. He was just a little child who was forced to walk around on tiptoe. I could not always protect him from one of my father's outbursts.'

Emma swallowed. 'Did he…did he physically abuse your brother or you?' she asked in a hollow whisper.

His lips tightened to a thin white line. 'Oh, he was far too clever to leave marks and bruises that could raise suspicion if noticed by others,' he said. 'He liked to use other, more subtle means of control. His modus operandi was more along the lines of emotional abuse, such as the systematic erosion of self-esteem and stripping away of confidence.'

'I'm so sorry,' she said, biting her lip momentarily. 'It must have been very painful for you growing up like that.'

'It is ironic that I have achieved the sort of success I have,' he said. 'Perhaps I would not have gone so far without the harsh lessons my father subjected me to, but in spite of that I can never find it in myself to forgive him.'

'He's dead, Rafaele,' Emma said. 'What point is there in hating him now? What will it achieve? You'll only end up bitter and twisted, not to mention desperately unhappy.'

'Is that what you told him in his last days?' he asked with a mocking set to his mouth. 'Forgive and forget? Perhaps there is a little of the grey-haired Sunday-school teacher in you after all.'

'From the very first day I went to his palazzo in Milan to look after him I felt he was struggling with some issues to do with his family,' Emma said. 'Over the months I gently encouraged him to make his peace with whoever he needed to. I tell all my terminally ill clients that. I think it's very important they leave this world with some sense of closure.'

'What was his reaction?' Rafaele asked.

She gave a soft sigh, a small frown creasing her smooth brow. 'He didn't say much, but I got the impression he was thinking about it a great deal. I think he found it very painful, you know…confronting the past, but then a lot of people feel that way. I felt sorry for him. I found him crying one day not long before he died. He was inconsolable but he wouldn't tell me what had upset him.'

'Were you there the day he contacted his lawyer?'

'No, but I think it must have happened one afternoon when I had taken a couple of hours off,' she answered. 'He never mentioned anything to me about a visitor coming and neither did Lucia, the housekeeper, who often kept an eye on him for me while I was doing errands.'

Rafaele wondered whether or not to believe her. She was certainly very convincing with her soft grey-blue eyes misting slightly as if she had genuinely been fond of his father. But how could he be sure? She had made all but a token protest about marrying him in order to gain her share of the estate, and even more damning was the scandal over her previous client back in Australia. He had looked up the newspaper articles on the Internet and read the various interviews with the family members, who had each painted Emma March as an opportunist who had inveigled her way into their senile mother's affections before stealing from her. That the charges were later dropped hadn't satisfied the family, who still staunchly believed Emma to have used the old woman's dementia to throw doubt on the case.

As he saw it, Emma was either a genuinely caring person who had become the unfortunate victim of a hate campaign by jealous relatives, or she was indeed a conniving con-artist with greed as her motive.

It sickened him to think of her playing up to his father

to manipulate him into changing his will in her favour at the last hour. The thought of her firm young body being pawed over by a ruthless old man like his father churned his stomach. But then he already knew how far a woman would go for money. The mistress his father had kept after Giovanni had died, Sondra Henning, was a case in point. Thirty-odd years his father's junior she had made no effort to hide her intentions. She had been a spiteful bitch when his father wasn't looking. She had subjected Rafaele to the lash of her tongue and the slap of her hand. He couldn't bear the thought of that home-wrecker taking anything else away from him.

Emma March might be a ruthless little gold-digger, but she had a sensual aura about her that was potently seductive. She wasn't classically beautiful by any means, but there was something about her girl-next-door vitality that drew him in like a magnet. Every time he touched her he felt the electrifying voltage of her body charging into his. Her slim but femininely curvy body made him ache to feel her writhing beneath him in the throes of passion. He wanted to feel his hard, thickened body driving into the yielding softness of hers until they both exploded. He wanted to feel her primly pursed mouth sucking on him until he burst with pleasure. He wanted to taste her, to explore her tender contours and bring her to the pinnacle of fulfilment he knew she craved. He had seen it in her eyes almost from the first moment they had met. That hungry, yearning look was unmistakable.

'It has all worked out rather brilliantly for you, has it not, Emma?' he asked. 'All your hard work has paid off. Either way you win.'

She looked at him hesitantly. 'I'm not sure what you mean…'

He smiled a cynical smile. 'You have a roof over your head for the duration of our marriage and a guaranteed income at the end of it, a windfall most people would not dream of seeing in a lifetime.'

'I keep telling you I was never interested in your father's money,' she said. 'As far as I can make out he apparently wanted you to spend some time at The Villa Fiorenza and the only way he thought he could bring it about was to tie you here with me.'

Rafaele snapped his brows together. 'This villa has been in the Fiorenza family for several generations. I spent some of the happiest years of my life in this place before my mother and brother died. I will be damned if I will let one of my father's whores take even a single pebble from the driveway without my permission.'

'I'm not planning on making things unpleasant or difficult for you,' she said. 'You can live your life and I'll live mine. We don't even have to communicate with each other if we don't want to.'

'Your very presence here makes things difficult,' Rafaele muttered as he set his glass down with a loud thwack. 'But perhaps that is what you and my father planned.'

She frowned at him. 'I'm not sure what you're suggesting, but I can assure you I am finding this as difficult if not more so than you. The sooner we end this farce, the better, as far as I am concerned.' With one last searing glance, she stalked out, leaving him with just his empty glass for company.

# CHAPTER FIVE

AFTER their exchange Emma did her best to avoid Rafaele, although at one point she watched him from her upstairs window as he swam lap after lap in the pool, his strong, leanly muscled body carving through the water with effortless ease. She felt a little guilty drinking in the sight of him, but she couldn't seem to drag her eyes away. His body was so wonderfully built; lean but powerful, muscular without being over-bulky. His olive skin was a deep even brown as if he had recently spent some time somewhere tropical. His black hair was like wet silk as he vaulted out of the water, the water droplets on his body glistening in the afternoon sun. As he reached for his towel he looked up and locked gazes with her, the lazy smile he sent her seeming to suggest he had known all along she was up there staring down at him.

Emma turned from the window with her heart doing little back flips in her chest, her face hot and her pulse racing out of control. She was deeply ashamed of her reaction to him. She felt like a gauche schoolgirl instead of a grown woman. He had only to look at her and she felt her colour begin to rise both inside and out. That dark smouldering gaze of his set her senses alight every time it rested on her and it seemed there was nothing she could do to stop it. It galled her to think he of all people had such an effect on her. He was an unprincipled playboy, a man who used women as playthings, discarding them when they no longer appealed to him. She knew if she was fool enough to succumb to his potent charm he would break her heart and think nothing of it. After all it would be the perfect revenge to get back at her for what he was convinced she had done to profit from his father's will.

The new housekeeper came to work at the villa each morning, along with the team of gardeners, which left Emma with even less to do to occupy her time. She caught up on some reading and went for long walks about the town, visiting some of the places she had read about in her travel guide. The tourist season was in full swing by now and she mingled with the crowds, stopping for coffee at one of the many cafes until the heat of the day brought her back to the villa.

After a few days, once the staff had left for the day Emma made the most of the warm weather by dipping in and out of the pool. The water was cool against her heated skin and she closed her eyes and floated on her back, enjoying the sounds of the garden, the birds twittering in the shrubs and trees, the gentle lap of water and the soothing tinkle of the wind chimes hanging in the arbour.

'Mind if I join you?' Rafaele's deep voice sounded from the deck of the pool.

Emma jerked upright, water shooting up her nose as she tried to find her feet. 'You scared me!' she said, blinking the water out of her eyes. 'I thought you'd gone out.'

'I did, but I have been back about an hour,' he said. 'I thought I might find you out here. How is the water?'

'It's…lovely,' she said, trying not to stare at his leanly

muscled body. He was dressed in black bathers, the close-fitting Lycra outlining his masculine form so lovingly she felt her breath hitch in her throat.

He dived in and swam several lengths, the effortless motion of his arms and legs making Emma's earlier efforts seem rather pathetic by comparison.

'Want a race to the other end?' he asked as he came up close by.

'I'm not quite in your league,' she said with a self-conscious grimace.

'Come on, Emma, be a devil,' he said. 'I will give you a head start.'

Emma took a deep breath and threw herself into it, her arms going like windmills and her feet and ankles flapping with all their might. She thought she was in with a chance until she felt one of his hands grasp her by one of her ankles and pull her backwards through the water. She came up spluttering, and as she twisted round to face him her hands somehow landed on his chest, her legs tangling with his under the water. 'You cheated!' she spluttered.

He smiled at her. 'One thing you should know about me, Emma, is I do not always play by the rules.'

She gave him a reproachful look. 'In my book you're not a winner unless you've won fair and square.'

His hands settled on her hips, his lower body brushing against hers as he kept them both afloat. 'Ah, yes, but then I make it a point of always winning,' he said, looking down at her mouth.

Emma could hardly breathe. His mouth was so close she could see the pepper of stubble on his jaw, his warm breath like a caress as he came even closer. 'D-don't…' she said in a hoarse whisper.

He lifted one brow. 'You do not want me to kiss you?'

She looked into his dark, smouldering gaze. 'I think it's best if you don't…'

'Why is that?' he asked, still holding her against him.

'Um…I think it's not wise to complicate things…'

One of his hands moved from the curve of her hip to settle at the back of her neck beneath the wet curtain of her hair. 'How will it complicate things if I kiss you?' he asked.

Emma took a tight little swallow. She knew exactly what one kiss would do. As it was she had been trying to stamp out the memory of the wedding kiss without success. 'I don't want to…to develop feelings for you, Rafaele,' she said.

His eyes searched hers for a long moment. 'You think that is likely to happen?'

'I'm not a casual hook-up type of person,' she said. 'After this…arrangement is over I want to get married and have a family. I'm twenty-six years old. I don't want to leave it too late to settle down. I want stability and commitment. You're not the person to give me those things.'

A hard light came into his eyes. 'Nor was my father, but that did not stop you from talking him into giving you a fortune.'

Emma pulled out of his hold. 'You're starting to sound like a broken record, Rafaele. I'm not even going to waste my breath denying it again.'

'Have dinner with me tonight.'

She frowned at him. 'What?'

'Let's go out for a meal,' he said. 'Let's do it the old-fashioned way. Guy meets girl, that sort of thing. Let's forget about my father and take it one step at a time.'

'Rafaele…this is crazy,' she said.

'What is so crazy about two people going out to dinner and strengthening their acquaintance?' he asked. 'After all, we have got to live together for months on end—wouldn't it be better if at the end of it we were friends instead of enemies?'

'I can't imagine us ever being friends.'

'Only because we got off to a bad start,' he said. 'I am not always such a brute you know. I can be quite charming when I put my mind to it.'

*Yes, well, that's what I'm worried about*, Emma thought. She was having enough trouble keeping her head as it was. God only knew what would happen to her heart if he laid on the Fiorenza charm at full strength. She had seen a glimpse of it already, that lazy smile and those dark, smouldering eyes had set her heart racing a few times too many. 'All right,' she said. 'I'll have dinner with you, but only because it's the housekeeper's afternoon off.'

He grinned at her, a boyish grin that sent her stomach into another dip-and-dive routine. 'You really know how to annihilate a man's ego, don't you?' he said.

Emma felt an answering smile tug at the corners of her mouth. 'I'm sure yours should be listed as one of the great wonders of the world,' she said. 'In fact I bet it can be seen from outer space.'

'I can see I am going to have to work extra hard to improve your opinion of me,' he said. 'But who knows what a bit of wining and dining will do? I am going to have a bit more of a swim before I get out and have a shower. Is eight-thirty OK with you?'

'Sure,' Emma said, moving to the side of the pool, her stomach already fluttering with excitement. 'I'll be ready.'

When Emma came downstairs close to eight-thirty Rafaele was waiting for her in the salon. He had been reading through one of the weekend papers and rose to his feet as she came in, his gaze running over her appreciatively. 'You look stunning, Emma,' he said, 'absolutely stunning.'

'Thank you,' Emma said shyly.

'I thought we could eat at a restaurant at Villa Olmo,' he said as he led the way out to his car. 'Have you had a chance to visit it yet?'

'No, but I've walked past it a couple of times,' she said. 'It's very grand, isn't it?'

'It's the most famous residence of Como,' he informed her. 'The villa owes its name to an elm tree that in ancient times grew inside the park. The architect was Simone Cantoni and now the town of Como owns it and uses it for various exhibits. The restaurant is situated to the right of the villa.'

'I've made a bit of a start on my sightseeing,' Emma said. 'I've been to Duomo, the cathedral, and to the Volta temple and on the Funicular so far.'

He glanced at her. 'Did you walk up to the lighthouse?'

'Yes, it was an amazing view from up there,' she said. 'I didn't want to leave.'

'The funicular has been running from the end of the eighteen hundreds,' he said. 'From the top you can make out the castrum, the rectangle that made up the old establishment of the Roman town. You can even see the first basin of the lake and the villas and plains that lead to Milan.'

Emma looked at him. 'Did you miss all this while you were living abroad?'

He took a moment to answer. 'Yes, I did miss it,' he said. 'There was many a time I wanted to come back, but it was impossible.'

'Do you really think your father would have turned you away from the door?' she asked.

His hands tightened on the wheel, the only sign Emma could see of his tension. 'When I left fifteen years ago he made it quite clear I would not be welcome to return. I did not bother testing him to see if he meant it or not.'

Emma made an exasperated sound. 'But don't you see

how you were being as stubborn as him? I am sure he would have welcomed you with open arms if you had come back.'

He gave her a flinty look. 'Still trying to defend him, Emma?' he asked.

She compressed her lips for a moment. 'I'm not doing any such thing; I just think two wrongs never make a right.'

His expression was mocking as he came around to open her door. 'He did a good job on you, didn't he?' he said. 'But then he bought your allegiance.'

Emma stepped out of the car, flinging him a glare over one shoulder. 'Could we talk about something else for a change?' she asked. 'I thought you said this evening's outing was going to be about building our acquaintance, not talking ad infinitum about your late father.'

He shut the car door and took her elbow in the cup of his palm. 'You are right,' he said, and led her towards the restaurant entrance. 'I am not being a very good date so far, am I?'

Emma cast him a glance. 'No, but believe it or not I've had much worse.'

'Is that some sort of compliment?' he asked with the hint of a wry smile.

Emma didn't get the chance to answer as the *maître d'* came to lead them to a table in the little courtyard outside. A short time later they were seated with drinks and a plate of warmed olives and fresh crusty bread set in front of them.

Rafaele picked up his glass and slowly twirled the contents. 'So tell me, Emma,' he said. 'Marriage and kids is high on your to-do list, is that right?'

'If the right person comes along, then yes.'

'Are you one of those young women who have a checklist on what they are looking for in a man?' he asked.

'I don't see a problem with sorting out what you don't want from what you do,' Emma said.

'So what's on your list?'

'The usual things,' she said. 'Faithfulness, a sense of humour and a willingness to be emotionally available.'

'You did not mention money.'

'That's because it's not as important as love.'

He gave her a cynical smile. 'It is always important, Emma,' he said. 'At least it is for all the women I know.'

'I don't agree,' she said. 'Your father is a perfect example of how money doesn't buy love. He had more money than he knew what to do with and yet he didn't have the love and respect of his son.'

'That's because he did not want it,' he said. 'Now, I thought we were not going to talk about him—or have you changed your mind?'

'I'm just trying to understand you, Rafaele.'

'I do not need your understanding, Emma,' he said. 'What is it about women that they always want to pick apart a man's brains? Now, be a good girl and choose something to eat. I am starving after my swim.'

Emma let out a sigh and busied herself with the menu, all the while conscious of the way her body was responding to his close proximity. She knew his desire for her was purely a physical thing on his part; he was between mistresses so why wouldn't he want a quick fling with her to satisfy the primal urge to copulate? Her cheeks grew hot as her brain filled with images of him in the throes of making love, his strong, tanned naked body glistening with sweat as he pumped his essence into the secret heart of her until she…

'Have you had too much sun today, Emma?' Rafaele asked. 'Your cheeks are bright red.'

Emma fanned her face with the menu. 'Um…it's still a bit hot, don't you think?'

'Would you prefer to move indoors where there is air-conditioning?' he asked.

Her eyes fell away from his. 'No…I'm fine out here,' she said and picked up her drink. 'I like being outdoors.'

'I suppose you must spend a great deal of time indoors in the role of a nurse.'

'Yes…if the patient is housebound.'

A small silence passed.

'How ill was my father towards the end?'

Emma brought her eyes back to his. 'He was very ill,' she said softly. 'He had to have high doses of morphine to control the pain so he spent the last couple of weeks drifting in and out of consciousness.'

'So you sat by his side and did everything you could to make him comfortable.'

Emma hunted his expression but found nothing to suggest he was needling her. Instead she thought she saw a flicker of regret pass through his ink-black eyes as they held hers. 'Yes…that is exactly what I did…' She waited a second or two before adding, 'Rafaele…sometimes people change when they know they are about to die. I think your father would have contacted you, but he ran out of strength. I wish now I had done it for him.'

There was a rueful set to his mouth as he spoke. 'I probably would not have listened if you had.' He drew in a breath and added, 'We were too alike if the truth be known. I never quite forgave him for not protecting my mother and he never quite forgave me for not protecting Giovanni.'

'What happened to your brother?' Emma asked.

He picked up his glass and stared down into the contents for a moment. When his eyes came back to hers they had a brittle edge to them that warned her she had come a little too close. 'I did not bring you out this evening to talk about the past and what can never be changed,' he said. 'You have told me all I needed to know and as far as I am concerned I have done the same for you. The rest of my family are dead and buried. I am the only one who remains. Let that be the end of it.'

Emma frowned at him. 'Why do you keep pushing everyone away?' she asked. 'Don't you care how other people feel about you?'

'I am not responsible for other people's feelings,' he said. 'I am only responsible for my own.'

'It sounds to me like you don't have any feelings,' she said. 'Or if you did you switched them off years ago.'

'I have feelings but I choose not to let them get out of control. I do not see the point in being anyone's slave. Once you care too much for someone they can exploit you. That is why I do allow myself to become too attached. It is easier all round. No one gets hurt, or at least not intentionally.'

'So you won't allow yourself to love anyone, not even the women who share your body and your bed,' Emma said in disgust. 'Don't you realise how much you're short-changing yourself?'

He gave her one of his annoyingly indifferent shrugs. 'That is the way it is.'

'Well, I hope that one day you meet someone who turns your neatly controlled world upside down,' she said. 'I hope you fall in love and hard, and then get unceremoniously dumped just so you know what it feels like.'

He gave her an unaffected smile. 'Are you putting a curse on me, Emma?' he asked.

Emma rolled her eyes at him. 'You're impossible. I don't know why I even bother talking to you.'

He smiled lopsidedly as he signalled for the waiter. 'You talk to me because deep down you like me,' he said. 'I am the bad boy you are desperate to reform.'

She gave him a withering look. 'I know when I'm beaten and you are definitely in the too-hard basket,' she said. 'I'm starting to think you're way beyond redemption.'

'Yes, well, that is what my father thought,' he said. 'Didn't he tell you what a wastrel I was?'

Emma frowned at his embittered tone. 'No, he didn't say anything of the sort. I told you, he barely mentioned you the whole time I was living with him. Besides, I didn't want to upset him by prying.'

He smirked. 'It would not do to upset the goose who was about to hand you the golden egg.'

She glared at him heatedly. 'That's just so typical of you,' she said. 'You have a tendency to measure everyone else by your own appalling standards. Just because you regularly use people to get what you want doesn't mean other people will necessarily act that way.'

He held her gaze for several beats. 'I have found most people work things to their advantage,' he said. 'It is hard-wired into human nature.'

'I feel sorry for you,' Emma said. 'You are so cynical you can't possibly enjoy life.'

He gave her an indolent smile. 'On the contrary, Emma I enjoy life very much,' he said. 'I have a good income, good food, good wine and good sex—what more could a man want?'

Emma could feel her face burning, but soldiered on regardless. 'I hope you're not going to conduct any of your sordid little affairs right in front of my nose,' she said. 'It would be totally nauseating to see a host of vacuous women simpering after you like you're some kind of sex god.'

'You surely do not expect me to be celibate for the duration of our marriage, do you?' he asked with a twinkle in his dark gaze.

Emma moistened her dry lips. 'I…no…well…I…'

'I have not been celibate in a very long time,' he said, still watching her with that smouldering gaze.

She shifted restively in her seat. 'Yes, well, the rest will probably do you the world of good, I would have thought.'

'What about you?' he asked.

She looked at him warily. 'W-what about me?'

'What is your longest stint being celibate?'

She dropped her gaze from the penetrating probe of his. 'Um…a fair while…' she answered vaguely.

The waiter came at that moment to take their order, giving Emma a much-needed chance to regroup. She buried her head in the menu, hoping Rafaele couldn't see how ruffled she was at his choice of conversation. She felt so unsophisticated around him, like a child playing at grown-ups. She didn't have the aplomb to laugh off such a personal topic, nor did she have the experience.

Although she knew enough about her body and its responses to know what physical pleasure felt like, somehow she suspected the pleasure Rafaele Fiorenza would dish out would leave her solitary explorations sadly lacking. She had sensed the sensual potency of him that afternoon in the pool. His hardened body brushing against hers had ignited spot fires beneath her skin; she could feel them smouldering even now. Her wayward body was pulsing at the proximity of his long strong legs so close to hers. She had hers tucked as far back beneath her chair as they would go and yet she could still feel the magnetic pull of his body. She couldn't get her mind away from the thought of having his legs entangled with hers the way they had been in the pool, his hair-roughened thighs rubbing against her smoother ones, the heat and power of his erection so tantalisingly close she had felt the throb of his blood pounding against her belly.

The waiter's request for her order brought Emma out of her

reverie and, after choosing the first thing she saw on the menu, she sat back and took a reviving sip of the white wine Rafaele had ordered for her.

He was still watching her in that indolent way of his, as if he was quietly assessing her character. It made her feel a little exposed, as if he could see through the layers of her skull to what she had been thinking about him just moments ago.

'Why are you blushing?' he asked. 'I thought at first it was sunburn but that colour keeps coming and going in your cheeks.'

Emma sat bolt upright. 'I'm not blushing,' she said, even though she knew it wasn't true. She could feel the twin fires burning on her face and wished, not for the first time, she wasn't so out of her depth.

He gave her a knowing smile. 'I think it is rather cute,' he said. 'I do not think I have made a woman blush in years.'

'I'm sure it wasn't from lack of trying,' she quipped wryly.

His smile widened. 'No, that is indeed probably true.'

Emma picked up her glass and took another tentative sip, conscious of his gaze resting on her. Her pulse fluttered in response to his contemplative scrutiny, each of the fine hairs on the back of her neck prickling as if he had touched her there the way he had done earlier in the pool.

'What do you intend to do with your share of the villa at the end of our marriage?' he asked.

She set her glass back down and met his eyes. 'I'm not sure...I haven't thought that far ahead...'

'Would you consider selling it to me?'

She nibbled at her bottom lip for a moment. 'That seems a bit unfair, making you pay for something that really should have been yours in the first place,' she said.

His expression was unreadable. 'You are at perfect liberty to do what you like,' he said. 'We are now joint owners. But if you wish to sell at the end of the time I would like to make the first and final offer.'

'It's a beautiful property,' Emma said. 'It would make a fabulous family home. I wish I could afford to buy you out at the end of the time, but I can't. I would never be able to afford the maintenance costs, for one thing.'

'My half is not going to be for sale,' he said with an implacable edge to his tone.

Emma's forehead wrinkled in a frown. 'It seems rather a large place for a bachelor.'

'Perhaps, but I want to retain ownership regardless.'

'So will you live here permanently?' she asked.

'For some of the year perhaps,' he said. 'I am thinking of appointing a manager to keep the place running while I am away.'

'That sounds like a good idea,' Emma said. 'It would be a shame for it to be empty for long periods.'

He went silent for several moments, his gaze focussed on the contents of his wineglass. 'I have missed the place,' he said almost wistfully. 'I am not quite ready to let it go. There are some ghosts to lay to rest first.'

Emma was starting to see there was more to Rafaele Fiorenza than she had originally thought. It was no wonder he liked to hold the balance of control in all of his relationships. After his experiences as a child he would abhor being vulnerable in any context. He would never allow himself to love anyone in case they turned against him or deserted him.

He reminded her of a wounded wolf who would only attend to his pain in private. She felt her animosity towards him soften, the anger she had felt from the first moment of meeting him melting away to be replaced by compassion and an acute, almost painful desire to understand.

What had put those lines of strain about his mouth or those dark shadows that came and went in the black-brown depths of his gaze? What made his smile teasing and playful one minute and bitter and cynical the next? What would it take to crack open the hard nut of his heart she wondered. What dark secrets were locked away in there?

# CHAPTER SIX

AFTER the waiter had brought their meals to the table, Emma concentrated on the delicious seafood risotto set before her, in an attempt to get her emotions in check. What sort of romantic fool would she be to fancy herself in love with Rafaele? She barely knew him and, besides, anyone could see he wasn't a for ever type of guy. She could sense the restlessness in him, the way he worked so hard and played harder, to escape whatever demons drove him.

Emma put her fork down and reached for her wineglass to find his dark, contemplative gaze resting on her. Her heart suddenly felt as if a silk ribbon were being pulled right through the middle of it, making her breath catch in her throat.

'You mentioned the other day you have a sister,' he said. 'What happened to your parents?'

Emma put her glass back down with a little clatter against her dinner plate. 'I would have thought your private investigator contact would have told you when you had him dig up the dirt on my background.'

Rafaele let out a rusty breath. 'I am sorry, Emma, but if you had been in my position you would have done the same.'

She held his gaze for a beat or two, but dropped it to say, 'I haven't seen either of my parents since I was twelve years old when my sister and I were taken into foster care. Our parents were both heroin addicts. The prolonged drug use fried their brains. They died within months of each other, my father from a stab wound from a drug deal gone wrong, my mother from an overdose.'

Rafaele frowned as her quietly spoken words sank in. No wonder she had been so upset about him looking into her background. It also explained why she was so keen to have financial security to make up for what she had missed out on as a child. His own childhood had been painful enough, but to have such incompetent and potentially dangerous parents would have been soul-destroying. He could see now why she had hooked up with his father, to find an older father-figure who would indulge her every whim. Rafaele wouldn't go as far as excusing her for prostituting herself in such a way, but at least he understood her motive for doing so.

'I am sorry you had such a rough time of it,' he said. 'I have always thought it is a pity one cannot choose one's own parents. It would certainly make life easier for many children growing up.'

Her eyes came back to his. 'I guess so…but it's a parent's responsibility to be the adult in the relationship once children come along. Children don't ask to be born. They deserve to be loved no matter what.'

'That is one of the reasons I do not want to have children,' he said. 'It is too risky. How can I guarantee I will even like the child, let alone love it?'

Emma felt an inexplicable pang deep inside at his words. 'I'm sure you would love your own flesh and blood,' she said. 'One of the few benefits of coming from a difficult background is recognising the pitfalls to avoid when you become a parent yourself. You wouldn't make the same mistakes your father made, I'm sure of it.'

His smile was a little crooked. 'No, but I would probably make new ones,' he said. 'Then in thirty-odd years I would have a son or daughter who hated my guts. No way am I going to put my head in that particular noose. I am staying out of the parent trap.'

'But what if it were to happen?' Emma asked, still frowning slightly. 'What if one of your mistresses got pregnant by accident?'

The line of his mouth tightened a fraction. 'Firstly I would find it a little hard to believe it was an accident,' he said. 'I always take precautions and so do my sexual partners. In fact I insist on it.'

'Precautions can fail,' she pointed out. 'My sister Simone fell pregnant while on the pill. She was only nineteen at the time. If that happened to one of your partners would you expect her to have a termination?'

'I realise that is a decision best left to the woman concerned,' he said. 'An unwanted pregnancy is devastating to many women. I would not insist on her going through with it unless she was convinced it was the only option for her.'

'Wouldn't you want to be involved in its upbringing?' Emma asked.

He drew in a breath and reached for his glass once more. 'I am not sure a child should be in regular contact with a reluctant father. Children are not stupid. They work out pretty quickly who is genuine and who is not.'

Emma frowned at him. 'But don't all children deserve to have contact with both of their parents if at all possible?' she asked.

'In an ideal world, yes,' he said. 'But it is hard for men these days. It seems to me we are damned if we do and damned if we do not. We are called selfish for not wanting to procreate, and then if we do agree to father a child we are the worst in the world for not contributing enough in terms of housework or child care, even though we might be working every hour God sends to keep food on the table.'

'I hadn't really thought about it from that angle,' she confessed. 'But I still want to have a family. I just have to find a man who wants the same thing.'

'You have got plenty of time yet,' Rafaele said. 'Why not have a bit of fun while you still can?'

She gave him a guarded glance. 'I hope you're not suggesting what I think you're suggesting.'

He reached across the table and picked up her left hand, the pad of his thumb stroking over the backs of her fingers. 'What about it, Emma?' he asked. 'Want to have some fun with me before we call it quits?'

'I'm not sure it would be all that much fun for me,' she said with a haughty little glare.

He brought her hand to his mouth, the slight rasp of his skin against her fingers making her stomach fold over. 'I would make sure it was fun for you, *poco moglie di miniera*,' he said, and translated in a low sexy drawl, 'little wife of mine.'

She tried to pull out of his hold, but his fingers around hers subtly tightened. 'You're only doing this because you see me as a novelty. It's because I won't fall at your feet just like every other poor deluded woman out there, isn't it?'

The movement of his lips as he gave her a wry smile grazed her bent knuckles, sending another ripple of awareness through her body from her breasts to her thighs. 'I admit you are becoming a bit of a challenge to me,' he said. 'I have not had to work so hard at getting a woman to agree to have an affair with me before.'

Emma gave him another glare as she pulled her hand out of his, this time with success. 'I thought you said you weren't interested in sleeping with someone your father had slaked his lust on first? Those were your exact words, weren't they?'

His eyes held hers fast. 'Did you sleep with him, Emma?'

She returned his level stare. 'No, I did not.'

Rafaele sat back in his chair and surveyed her heightened colour, wondering if she was lying to him or not. He wanted to believe her, but knowing his father as he did he couldn't imagine him handing over half of his estate without some sort of inducement from her. His father had always been so mean with money; it didn't seem possible he would have given something away for free.

Admittedly Emma was nothing like any of his father's previous mistresses, but that didn't mean he hadn't fallen for her understated beauty and beguiling aura of innocence. Rafaele could see beyond the prim and proper façade she adopted to the passionate woman simmering beneath. She was a feisty little thing with her flashing grey-blue eyes and pouting mouth, her sensual allure so powerful he could barely keep his hands off her every time she was in the same room as him.

He wondered if she was holding him at bay deliberately. Had she done that with his father, leading him on and on until he finally agreed to give her what she wanted? If so, what was it she wanted from him? She already had half of the estate secure in her hands. Nothing he could do or say could take it away from her. But did she want more, and, if so, what?

'If you say you did not sleep with him, then I suppose I shall have to accept that,' he said after a pause.

'I have no reason to lie to you about something like that,' she said. 'What could I hope to gain by doing so?'

'I am not sure,' he said, rubbing at his jaw. 'I am still trying to figure that part out. Eighteen months ago you had not even met my father, now you own half of his estate. I am trying to join the dots but so far with little success.'

Emma reached for her glass. 'Maybe he wanted you to

learn to trust people,' she said. 'Perhaps he sensed I wouldn't do the wrong thing by you.'

'Interesting theory, Emma,' he said with an unreadable smile. 'But I wonder if he really knew you. You caught him at a vulnerable time. He was dying and his judgement may well have been impaired. For all I know you could have talked him into this madcap scheme.'

Emma compressed her lips. 'Of course *you* would think that, wouldn't you?' she said. 'You don't want me to be anything but a scam artist, do you? What if you're wrong about me, Rafaele? What then?'

He studied her for a lengthy moment. 'If that is the case I guess I will have to get down on bended knee and beg your forgiveness,' he said. 'But it is hardly something you would be able to prove either way, is it?'

Emma could think of a very good way of proving it, but didn't like to inform him of it. It wasn't that she was ashamed of her inexperience; it was more a case of not wanting him to ridicule her. Somehow that seemed particularly important. Besides, she could just imagine what he would say. She could even imagine his teasing smile.

'I don't have to prove anything to you,' she said instead. 'You can believe me or not, it makes no difference to the truth.'

'So you don't do recreational, just-for-the-hang-of-it sex?'

'No.'

'Pity,' he said. 'I think we could be dynamite together. Fire meets ice, that sort of thing.'

'I think any woman with half a brain would give you a wide berth,' she said. 'You won't commit, you're incapable of falling in love and you don't want kids. For the thinking woman you're a very bad deal, Rafaele.'

He gave her a bone-melting smile. 'But I make up for it in other ways. Even thinking women like hot sex, do they not?'

Emma hated that she blushed so readily. 'I can't speak for other women, but personally I would rather share my body with a man who treats me as an equal, not as a sex object.'

'I do not see you as a sex object, Emma. I just think we could be really good together.'

'Oh, yes, but for how long?'

He gave a could-mean-anything shrug. 'I am not one for setting time limits,' he said. 'Physical attraction has its own timetable.'

'Yes, but in your case it lasts about as long as the life cycle of a flea,' she said. 'Or maybe even a gnat.'

He gave a low chuckle of laughter. 'You are *so* damned cute. I bet you do not even know how long a gnat's life cycle is.'

Emma tried to purse her lips, but somehow it ended in a lopsided smile. 'You're incorrigible. You really are.'

He picked up her hand again and brushed his lips over the back of her knuckles, his dark-as-midnight gaze holding hers. 'But you like me anyway, right, *mio piccolo*?'

Emma didn't answer but the words seemed to ring in the silence all the same: *I like you. I like you too much.*

# CHAPTER SEVEN

THE drive back to The Villa Fiorenza took only a few minutes, but Emma suddenly found she didn't want the evening to be over. Rafaele had relaxed over dessert and coffee, chatting to her about his work as a share trader, telling her some amusing anecdotes about some of the people he'd met and the places he'd visited. She knew she was being a fool for letting her guard down around him, but for some reason the cold breath of common sense couldn't seem to penetrate the warm mantle of complacency that had settled around her in his company.

As he led the way to the front door of the grand old house Emma could smell the pungent clove-like scent of night stocks from the massive herbaceous border running along one side of the property. The purple and white pendulous blooms of sweetly scented wisteria hung in a fragrant arras from the trellis on one of the walls, and the melodious twinkle of the wind chimes hanging in the summer house carried over the garden on the slight breeze, setting an atmosphere that was as intoxicating as a mind-altering drug.

'Why don't we take a nightcap out to the arbour?' Rafaele said once they were inside. 'It is too nice a night to be indoors.'

'That sounds lovely,' Emma said, wondering if he had somehow read her mind. She had been thinking how nice it would be to sit out in the garden, breathing in the fragrant air and looking up at the peepholes of stars and planets in the dark blue blanket of the sky.

A few minutes later she followed him out to the summer house, minus her heels, the soft, slightly damp carpet of the springy lawn tickling the soles of her bare feet.

Rafaele handed her a cognac and patted the swing seat beside him. 'You look like a nymph or a sprite,' he said with a smile.

Emma returned his smile with a warm one of her own. 'I love nights like this,' she said, curling her toes as she sat on the seat next to him. 'I love the sounds and smells of a garden late at night. It's like another world out here.'

He placed his foot against the frame of the arched doorway to set the swing in motion. The gentle rocking motion brought their bodies closer together on the seat. Emma could feel the strong length of his thigh within a breath of her own, her shoulder brushing against his upper arm. Her skin tingled as he laid his left arm over the back of the seat, his fingers within touching distance of the nape of her neck. It would be so easy to turn and face him, to reach up and stroke her fingers over the lean planes and angles of his face, to explore the contours of his sensual mouth.

'You have not touched your cognac,' he said, looking at the glass she was cradling in her hands.

'I haven't got much of a head for alcohol,' Emma confessed. 'The wine we had at dinner has already addled my brain.' *And my common sense*, she thought wryly as she placed her untouched glass on the nearest ledge.

The long silence was measured by the sound of crickets chirruping in the background, the soft plop of a frog landing in the lily pond sounding like a distant gunshot.

Rafaele turned to look at her. 'Did you ever bring my father out here?' he asked.

Emma couldn't read his expression, his face was in shadow, but she sensed tension in the question. 'Yes...a couple of times,' she answered. 'He found it peaceful and the fresh air was good for him after being confined indoors for so long.'

Another silence slipped past.

In spite of the darkness Emma could feel the slow burn of his gaze as it held hers. 'What are you thinking about, Emma?' he asked.

She self-consciously tucked a loose strand of hair behind her ear. 'I was thinking how we're probably going to be eaten alive by mosquitoes,' she said with a rueful tilt of her mouth.

The white slash of his smile cut across his shadowed face. 'Or what about gnats?'

She screwed up her mouth at him. 'Do gnats bite?'

'I am not sure,' he said as he set his glass to one side before turning back to face her.

Emma sat very still as he lifted his hand to her face, his index finger tracing over the curve of her top lip. She couldn't breathe; she couldn't even speak, so mesmerising was his feather-light touch. She watched as in slow motion his head came down, his mouth so close she could feel the warmth of his breath skating over her lips. She sucked in a sharp little breath as his lips pressed against hers, once, twice, and then the third time with increasing pressure.

His mouth was like a brand, searing her lips with the imprint of his, stirring her senses into a frenzy of heady excitement. The first slow and yet determined stroke of his tongue against the seam of her lips sent her pulse skyrocketing, the rasp of his masculine jaw with its stubbly growth against the tender skin of her face making her feel utterly feminine in a way she had never felt before.

He explored every corner of her mouth in a leisurely fashion, the drugging movements of his mouth on hers making her forget all about her reasons for not getting involved with him. Desire began to pulse hot and strong in her veins with each thrust of his tongue against hers, the erotic promise in his kiss unmistakable.

His teeth nibbled at the fullness of her bottom lip in tiny, tantalising tug-and-release bites that made her legs turn to water. Her feminine core melted, she could feel the dew of desire anointing her intimately, her breasts swollen and aching for the attention of his hands and lips and tongue.

He pulled her to her feet, her legs hardly able to keep her upright as his mouth lifted off hers to blaze a fiery trail of kisses along the sensitive skin of her neck, each hot blast of his breath inciting her need of him to fever pitch. She was melting in his arms, discovering a passionate facet to her personality she would never have believed had existed until now. Where was her self-control? Where was her level-headedness and cool composure? They seemed to have been swept up in the conflagration of her senses under the sensual mastery of his touch.

His lower body ground against hers, leaving her in no doubt of his arousal. It was thick and hard against her, making her body tremble all over with a clawing need for fulfilment.

His mouth came back to hers with renewed fervour, the pressure of his kiss increasing as his erection burned with insistent force against her traitorous flesh. She could feel the hollow ache of her body, the tight walls of her womanhood preparing for the onslaught of his thickened presence. She felt as if she would die if he didn't bring to completion what he had started. Her body was crying out for release from this sensual torment. There was no part of her that wasn't sizzling from the heat of his touch. He was like a fire in her blood; somehow he had circumvented her firewall of common sense and turned her into a desperate wanton, a slave to the passion he had awakened.

Rafaele lifted his mouth off hers to look down at her with eyes dark with desire. 'Let's take this inside—or shall we get it over with right here on the floor?'

Emma flinched as her conscience gave her an unwelcome but timely nudge. No wonder he thought she was his for the asking. She had practically melted in his arms. Shame flooded her cheeks and to disguise it she stepped out of his hold, her expression full of cold disdain. 'You might not have liked him much, but at least your father had much more class than you,' she said with a cutting edge to her tone. 'He would never have dreamed of insulting me the way you have done.'

His eyes became diamond hard. 'What is wrong, Emma? Are you expecting a little more finesse? I thought you would be used to doing it rough since you have been servicing my father. He would not have been too fussy about where he had you. Or maybe he got sentimental in his old age and whispered sweet nothings in your ear.'

'That's a disgusting thing to say!' Emma said, her face fire-engine red.

'What about it, Emma?' he said. 'How about we get down and dirty while we are married? You are up for it, I can tell.'

She gave him a paint-stripping glare. 'I wouldn't dream of tainting myself with the likes of you.'

His smile was deliberately taunting. 'I can afford you, Emma. If it is more money you want I have plenty of it. I have ten times the wealth of my father.'

'I want nothing from you,' she bit out. 'I would rather die.'

'You are such a transparent liar,' he said. 'If the way you kissed me is anything to go by I can almost guarantee it will not be long before we end up sharing much more than this villa.'

'I did *not* kiss you,' Emma said through tight lips. 'You kissed me. You took me completely by surprise.'

His eyes began to glint. 'Ditto. You totally rocked me. I

had no idea how passionate you are behind that school-marmish façade you are so fond of displaying to the world. But it is all an act, isn't it, Emma? That is how you got my father's attention, wasn't it? You reeled him in like a minnow on a line.'

Emma felt like slapping him, but in truth she was frustrated at herself for falling under his sensual spell so incautiously. How could she have been so stupid? He had wined and dined her, setting the scene for seduction, and she had fallen for it so readily. It made her feel so foolish but also very hurt.

Deeply hurt.

He had no feelings for her. He despised her. How could she have been lulled into thinking anything else? Tears suddenly blurred her vision and desperate to keep them hidden, she pushed past him with a hastily muttered goodnight.

'Emma?' He caught up to her in a couple of strides and tipped her face to one of the fingers of light coming from the villa. He frowned as he dabbed at a rolling tear with the blunt pad of his finger. 'Tears?' he asked, sounding surprised.

Emma shoved his hand away and glared at him. 'You must think I'm so naïve,' she bit out. 'You think you can just crook your finger and have me dive head first into your bed, don't you?'

'It was just a kiss, Emma,' he said in a dry tone.

'It was *not* just a kiss!' she railed at him.

'What was it then?'

'It was a blatant attempt to seduce me, that's what it was,' she said with a livid grey-blue glare.

'If I was serious about seducing you, Emma, you would be flat on your back by now and letting the neighbours know in no uncertain terms how much you were enjoying it,' he said with a smug little smile.

Emma opened and closed her mouth at his audacity. 'I can't believe you just said that!'

'I said it because it is true,' he said. 'I am not going to play games with you, *cara*. I am prepared to bed you any time you like. But that is all I am offering, so you had better be clear on that. No strings, just good old-fashioned bed-wrecking sex. Take it or leave it.'

She threw him a caustic look. 'I'll leave it, thank you.'

'Fine, but if you change your mind just let me know,' he said. 'I think we could be dynamite together.'

'I won't be changing my mind,' Emma said, with perhaps not as much conviction as she would have liked. His evocative comments had unravelled her resolve to an alarming degree. Her body was on fire just thinking about the pleasure he was promising. She was in no doubt of his ability to be as good as his word. She could see the smouldering look in his dark eyes. She could still feel the imprint of his lips on hers. Her mouth was tingling even now, the tiny nerves beneath her skin leaping and jumping from the passionate pressure of his. What was it about this man that made her feel so out of control? Was it because she had decided he was off limits? Was some perverse part of her determined to have him in spite of her convictions?

He had made it more than clear what he wanted. He was attracted to her certainly, but only as a means to an end. Once he got what he wanted she would be discarded, just as he had discarded his numerous other mistresses.

It hurt Emma to realise how much she wanted it to be different. How had that happened in such a short space of time? She had hated him the first time she had met him and yet it was difficult to dredge up such intense feelings now. There was something about him that drew her in like a moth to a deadly flame. He intrigued her, he excited her and he made her feel things she had never felt before. She truly wondered if she would ever be the same now she had tasted his potent passion on her lips. Would every kiss she received from this point on be measured by the heat and fire of his? Would any future lover of hers fall short of his blistering benchmark? Would she always feel short-changed and frustrated as a result?

'I'm going inside,' she said, turning away again.

His hand stalled her. 'Wait.'

Emma felt the steel bracelet of his fingers and suppressed a tiny shiver. She looked up at his face, her breath catching at the back of her throat at the intensity of his dark gaze as it meshed with hers. 'I-I can't do this, Rafaele…' she said. 'It's not right.'

His thumb found her pulse, the drumbeat of her heart beating against his skin. 'But you want to, don't you, Emma?' he asked softly.

Emma compressed her lips to stop them from trembling, her heart pumping so hard she could feel it against her sternum. It would be so easy to throw caution to one side and step into his arms. It would be so easy to press her still-swollen lips to the sculptured curve of his.

*It would be all too easy to fall in love with him…*

'Go on, admit it,' he said. 'You want me just as much as I want you.'

She drew in a prickly breath. 'I want a lot of things I can't have, Rafaele,' she said. 'Wanting something doesn't make it right.'

The hard look came back into his eyes. 'Is it because of my father?' he asked. 'Do you still have feelings for him even though he is dead?'

Emma frowned at him. 'Why must you persist with this?' she asked. 'Just let it go, for God's sake.'

'Damn it, Emma,' he growled. 'I hate the thought of you with him. It sickens me to my stomach. I cannot get it out of my mind. I keep seeing him pawing at you like some animal.'

She gave him an ironic look. 'Isn't that what you've been doing to me?'

His brows snapped together and his hand fell away from her wrist. 'Is that what you think?' he asked.

Emma wished she hadn't said it. The anger was coming off him in waves. The air crackled with it, the tension building to an intolerable level. 'No…no, of course not,' she said. 'I'm sorry…I shouldn't have said that.'

'No, you should not,' he said through tight lips. 'You were with me all the way, Emma. You were hot for it.'

She felt her face fire with colour at his blunt crudity and her own traitorous transparency. 'You know, I was really starting to like you earlier this evening, but now I think I will stick to my first impression of you,' she said with a blistering glare.

He gave her a mocking smile, but anger was still glittering in his eyes. 'And what might that be?'

She pulled in a tight little breath. 'You're an unscrupulous, selfish bastard who uses people without conscience.'

'And do you know what my impression of you is, Emma?' he threw back.

'That's hardly necessary considering you've used every available opportunity to tell me,' she said with bitterness sharpening her tone. 'A tart, a whore, a slut, the list goes on and on.'

'You are a clever little cat with an eye on the main chance,' he said as if she hadn't spoken. 'You want it all, don't you, Emma? That's what you are counting on, isn't it? That I will walk away before the year is up and by doing so hand you the lot.'

'I don't want you to walk away from what is rightly yours,' she said. 'I'm trying my best to do the right thing by you. I admit there are certain advantages for me, but I'm not interested in taking your inheritance from you.'

'But you want the money.'

'Yes, but not for the reasons you think,' she said.

Rafaele looked into her grey-blue eyes and wondered if she was being straight with him. He wasn't used to trusting people, but he found he wanted to trust her. She was getting under his skin in a way he had never believed possible.

He hadn't thought a kiss could reveal so much. He had kissed a lot of women in his time, but no one had affected him quite as Emma did. The shy hesitancy of her responses had been totally enthralling. He could still taste her sweetness in his mouth. He could still feel the soft press of her slim body against his; it had left a branding outline on his flesh.

His desire for her was even now pulsing through his blood. He could feel it charging through his veins, making him hard at the thought of sinking into her velvet warmth. He had never wanted a woman more than this one. She awakened every primal desire in his body. Her sensual allure was totally bewitching, which was no doubt why his father had fallen under her spell.

But he wasn't a fool like his father. He would have her on his terms and his terms only, even if it took him every bit of the next twelve months to achieve it.

'What do you want the money for?' he asked.

'It's for my sister, Simone.'

He frowned. 'Your sister?'

She nodded. 'She lost her husband when my niece was a baby. She has never dated anyone else until recently, but it turned out to be a total disaster. He left her with massive debts. He fraudulently used her name for a loan with a dodgy creditor who was making some nasty threats about repaying it.' She gave a jagged little sigh and continued, 'I sent the money I got when I married you to her.'

Rafaele kept his eyes on her. 'It all seems rather convenient, does it not?' he said. 'It seems to me that my father's death came at rather a good time for you and your sister.'

Her grey-blue eyes flared with shock or was it anger? He couldn't quite make up his mind. 'Are you suggesting I did something to hurry up your father's death?' she asked.

'You stood to gain by it, though, did you not?'

Her face paled. 'I told you, I had no idea what was in your father's will. This is your home, Rafaele. I think deep down your father wanted you to have it.'

'He went a strange way about it,' Rafaele growled.

'Yes, but sometimes the things we have to work the hardest for are the things we end up valuing the most,' she said. 'Perhaps your father was trying to tell you something.'

'My father was always trying to tell me something,' he said bitterly. 'Like how I was the one who should have died that day, not Giovanni.'

Emma stared at him with wide, shocked eyes. 'Surely he didn't say that?'

He gave her a grim look. 'He did not need to. It is true. I should have been the one to die.'

She put a hand to her chest. 'Oh, Rafaele…'

'I was the older brother, I was supposed to protect him, but instead I killed him.'

Emma felt her stomach give a sudden lurch. The atmosphere between them had changed. She hesitantly pressed him for more details. 'W-what happened?'

His eyes looked soulless and bleak. 'I was teaching Giovanni to play cricket… It was his turn to bat. I didn't think I had thrown the ball too hard, I was always so careful, but somehow it hit him on the temple and he fell like a stone.'

Emma gasped. 'No one could blame you for that. *No one*,' she insisted hoarsely.

'Perhaps some would say I was just a child myself and could not be held responsible,' he said. 'But I did not see it that way and neither did my father. I spent the next eight years apologising for my existence. Every time my father looked at me I saw the hatred and disappointment on his face.'

Emma felt her heart tighten at what he had gone through.

She could see the pain etched on his face, the deep grooves at the side of his mouth and the almost permanent lines on his forehead making her realise he was not the shallow, selfish man she had first thought. He was a deep and complex man, a man who had been cruelly hurt by the vicissitudes of life, a man who had locked away his heart to avoid further pain. A man almost crushed with a guilt that should never have been laid upon his shoulders.

A man she was one step closer to falling in love with…

'Thank you for telling me about it,' she said softly. 'I can only imagine how painful it must be to do so. It explains a lot…about everything…'

'This place is full of my guilt, Emma,' he said, waving his hand towards the giant shadow of the house to the left of him. 'Even the floorboards creak with it. My father left Giovanni's room the way it was to drive home the point.'

Emma bit her lip. 'Maybe you're reading too much into that,' she said. 'A lot of parents find it very hard to let go after the death of a child. Getting rid of their things is like saying they didn't exist. It's a way of holding on to them for as long as possible.'

'For twenty-three bloody years?' he asked.

She let out a little sigh. 'I guess everyone has their own time frame.'

'Stop defending him, Emma,' he ground out. 'He wanted me to suffer.'

'You were ten years old, Rafaele. Just a little boy. You were not to blame. It was an accident. Can't you see that?'

'Do you know what it is like, Emma?' he asked, his dark gaze almost black with pain. 'Do you know what it's like to be holding your dead brother's body in your arms, begging God or whoever is out there to breathe life back into his lungs until your throat is red raw from screaming?'

Emma felt a sob catch at the back of her throat. 'I-I'm so sorry…'

He raked a hand through his hair. 'I would have given anything to save him. We had already been through so much with the loss of our mother. He looked to me for everything, but in the end I killed him.'

Emma couldn't speak. The anguish on his face was too heart-wrenching. She wanted to reach out and hold him to her, to offer what comfort she could, to help him move on from the pain of the past.

'After we came home from Giovanni's funeral my father didn't speak to me for months afterwards. He could barely be in the same room as me. I was packed off to boarding school and on the rare occasions when my father was here at the villa when I was on holiday he kept himself busy with his latest mistress, usually a young woman not much older than me. After I finished school I left the country. I had no reason to think he was anything but relieved when I finally packed my bags and left.'

Emma put a hand on his arm. 'Rafaele…you need to forgive yourself,' she said. 'You can't carry that guilt for ever. Your father was wrong to put that on you, but perhaps he was feeling guilty himself. Why wasn't he out there playing cricket with his young sons? Have you ever thought of that?'

'I have thought about it a lot,' he said. 'But even if he did feel marginally responsible he never let on. I do not even know where he was the day Giovanni died. He would never say. All I know is it seemed an eternity before he got back…'

Emma brushed her tears away with the back of her hand. 'I'm so sorry…so very sorry…'

He drew in a deep uneven breath as he looked at the house. 'I am going to make a start on clearing out Giovanni's room in the next day or so. It should have been done years ago.'

'Would you like me to help you?' she asked.

He turned back to look at her again. 'No, thank you all the same. This is one job I probably need to do alone.'

A little silence crept from the shadows of the garden towards them.

Rafaele got to his feet. 'I am going to take a walk around the gardens,' he said. 'Do not wait up. I will see you in the morning.'

She stepped up on tiptoe and pressed a soft-as-air kiss to his cheek. 'Goodnight, Rafaele,' she whispered.

Rafaele stood and watched as she made her way back to the house, the soft, ghost-like tread of her bare feet making no sound on the dew-kissed, spongy grass.

# CHAPTER EIGHT

WHEN Emma came downstairs the next morning Rafaele was out on the sun-drenched terrace with a pot of freshly brewed coffee beside him, the morning paper spread out before him on the wrought-iron garden setting. He was dressed similarly to her, in a close fitting white T-shirt and shorts to counteract the early heat of the day. He had recently showered, his hair was still damp and she could smell the sharp citrus tang of his aftershave as she came closer.

He turned his head as he heard her approach, his expression giving no hint of the anguish she had seen there the night before. 'There is enough for two if you would like some,' he said, indicating the coffee-pot with a careless waft of his hand.

'Thanks,' she said. 'I never feel truly awake until I've had my first caffeine hit.'

'I will go and get a cup for you,' he said, rising to his feet. 'Would you like a croissant? I jogged down to the bakery first thing this morning.'

Emma gave him a rueful smile. 'You're making me feel guilty, talking about early-morning jogs,' she said. 'I'm not normally so lazy, but I didn't sleep well last night.'

His expression was mask-like, although Emma thought

she saw something flicker in his eyes as they held hers. 'I hope it wasn't something I said.'

She let out a tiny sigh. 'It was everything you said. I feel like I've totally misjudged you. You're not the person I thought you were. I'm sorry. I hope you can find it in yourself to forgive me.' She looked up at him appealingly and added softly, 'I'd like us…I'd like us to be friends.'

The silence stretched for a moment or two.

'Is that pity I hear in your voice, Emma?' he asked in a flint-like tone.

She frowned at him. 'No…no, of course not,' she said. 'I'm just glad I now know what happened to your brother and how it affected you and your father's relationship. Life has been very hard on you. I didn't realise how hard until last night.'

His eyes glittered darkly as they seared hers. 'So it explains why I am a complete and utter bastard, does it, Emma?'

She compressed her lips. 'That's a choice you make,' she said. 'You don't have to be that way. Lots of people have tragic backgrounds and yet manage to move on without letting it ruin their life and all their relationships.'

'I have not let it ruin my life,' he said. 'And as for my relationships, that is my business and my business alone.'

'I think you have let it ruin your life,' Emma countered. 'You lock yourself away from feeling. I suspect you've done it for years. You're doing it now. As soon as anyone gets close you put up a wall of resistance. You let your guard down with me last night and now you're regretting it. That's why you're being so cutting and unfriendly towards me now.'

He gave a mocking laugh. 'So little Emma now wants to be friends with me, does she?'

She tightened her mouth without answering.

He stepped closer and, capturing her chin between his finger and thumb, tipped her gaze to meet his. 'How far are you prepared to take this offer of friendship?' he asked. 'All the way upstairs to my bed?'

Emma felt her stomach go hollow as he brought his hard male body even closer. Her tongue darted out to moisten her lips, her heart beginning to ram against her ribcage as she felt his arrant maleness springing to turgid life against her. He placed a hand in the small of her back, pressing her even closer so she felt the pounding of his blood against her softness.

And then his head came down…

The kiss was explosive. Their tongues wrestled and tangled, darted and dived and submitted and conquered simultaneously. Emma became breathless with growing excitement, her body on fire as his mouth commandeered hers with bruising passion. Her lips throbbed with the pressure, she even thought she could taste blood at one point, but wasn't sure if it was hers or his, as she had nipped at his bottom lip with just as much fervour as he had hers.

His mouth was still locked on hers as he shoved aside the thin straps of her top and bra, his hands cupping the slight weight of her breasts, her pert nipples driving into the moist heat of his palm. The tingling pleasure wasn't nearly enough. Emma wanted more of his touch and leaned into him, whimpering her need into the hot cavern of his mouth.

Her breathing came to a screeching halt as he lifted his mouth off hers to suckle on each breast in turn. She arched her back as the rasp of his tongue laved her tender flesh, her fingers grasping him by the shoulders to anchor herself as sensation after sensation coursed through her.

He brought his mouth back to hers, his tongue a thrusting force she welcomed with the shy dart of her own. She heard him make a sound at the back of his throat and her skin lifted in goose-bumps of feverish excitement at how she was affecting him. She could feel the heat and weight of his arousal pressing against her and reached boldly between their locked bodies to explore it with her fingers. He groaned again as she brushed her fingertips over the summer-weight linen of his shorts, the proud bulge of his body making her feel heady with feminine power. She wanted to touch him intimately, she wanted to feel the satin of his flesh in her hands, to shape him, to feel the surge of his blood, to tantalise him the way he was tantalising her.

'God, I want you,' he said against her mouth. 'I am going crazy with you touching me like that.'

His feverish confession incited Emma to slide down the zipper on his shorts, her searching fingers moving aside the final barrier of his underwear. Her breath caught as she felt his body leap against her hand, the smoothness and strength of him rising out of the springy masculine hair making her belly crawl with desire. She looked down at him, her eyes going wide at the size of him as he quivered against her tentative feather-light touch.

'Harder, Emma,' he said on a gasping breath. 'Touch me harder and faster.'

She did as he said, her own body quaking with the need to feel him fill her and explode with the banked-up energy she could feel throbbing against the pads of her fingertips.

He placed his hand over hers, stilling the movement. 'Stop,' he said, giving a little shudder. 'I am going to come right here and now if you do not stop.'

'Would that be a problem?' Emma asked on an impulse too strong to withstand. The desire to pleasure him was suddenly irresistible. She wanted to see how much he wanted her, to witness the way his body responded to her caressing touch.

His eyes were so dark she couldn't see his pupils. 'I am in the habit of abiding by the principle ladies come first,' he said.

Emma quickly made a token effort to locate her reasons

for not sleeping with him, but not one of them was at the fore-front of her brain. All she could think of was the thousands of reasons she wanted to be in his arms: the passion, the excitement, the pleasure and the thrill of experiencing the rapture of his possession.

But if her mind was her traitor, so too was her body. It was already pressing against him insistently as his mouth came down to hers, her arms going around his neck, not even a sound of resistance escaping from her throat as he lifted her bodily in his arms and carried her into the house.

He didn't take her as far as his bedroom. The largest sitting room was the closest, and, letting her slowly slide down the length of his aroused body to stand on the carpeted floor in front of him, he looked down at her with that scorching gaze of his.

'Take your clothes off,' he commanded.

That should have been Emma's cue to stop this madness, but somehow her hands went to the bottom of her top and pulled it over her head, dropping it to the floor at her feet. She hesitated for the briefest moment before taking off her shorts, leaving her standing before him in her pink lace bra and knickers.

'And the rest,' he said, his dark eyes feasting on her hungrily.

Emma felt her belly give two hard kicks of desire. 'You first,' she said with a little hitch of her chin.

His lips twitched slightly, but then he wrenched his T-shirt over his head before stepping out of his shorts and underwear, his legs apart, his arms folded across his broad chest.

Emma swallowed as she looked at him. He looked magnificent, lean and tanned and toned and devastatingly virile. His erection was bobbing slightly, as if eager to get on with business. She couldn't take her eyes off it. Had *she* done that to him?

'Come here,' he said with a glittering look.

She took one shaky step towards him. 'Rafaele…I—'

He placed the end of his fingertip against her lips. 'You talk too much,' he said. 'Right now I want you to feel.'

Emma was awash with feeling; her entire body was tingling and leaping with excitement at what was ahead. She felt as if she had waited her whole life for this moment. He was her nemesis—the one man who had tempted her out of her sensual stasis.

It was a shock to her how much she wanted him. It pulsed through her with such force it almost frightened her. She had been so very determined not to succumb to his potent sexual allure and yet here she was quivering to feel him thrust inside her.

She put her hands behind her back to unhook her bra, her breathing ragged as he watched her reveal her nakedness. His eyes darkened and his throat moved up and down as she tugged her lacy knickers down. She saw his eyes flare as he took in her feminine form, a pulse leaping in his jaw as he fought for control.

'You are beautiful,' he said huskily.

Emma felt her heart swell at the compliment. She had never considered herself anything other than average, and yet somehow now in front of him she felt as if she were the most exquisite creature on earth. Her natural shyness fell away, her desire to pleasure him knowing no bounds as she stepped up against him, her softness against his hardness. 'So are you,' she said in a breathless whisper as her hands skated over his chest before going lower.

He sucked in a breath as her fingers trailed through the dark hair that arrowed downwards, his erection thick and hard against the enclosure of her hand. Such power and yet such vulnerability, Emma thought as she stroked him.

'Enough,' he groaned and pushed her hand away. 'I want to taste you.'

Emma shivered as he pushed her down to the floor, the almost primitive urgency thrilling her. He parted her thighs, his warm breath like a caress as he kissed his way up from her knees to the secret heart of her. She drew in a rasping breath as his fingers tenderly parted her feminine folds, the first stroke of his tongue making her back arch off the floor. A flood of sensations swamped her, tingling electric-like feelings that left her mindless as her body's impulses took over. She felt the first flicker of a spasm and shrank back from it in nervous apprehension.

Rafaele's hands on her thighs softened into a soothing caress. 'Relax for me, Emma,' he said. 'Go with it, *cara*.'

'I-I can't…' she said breathlessly.

'Yes, you can,' he said gently. 'I am probably rushing you. I will slow down.'

*It's not that*, Emma wanted to say, but somehow couldn't quite bring herself to do so. How could she tell him she was a virgin? After what he had assumed had occurred between her and his father would he even believe her?

As if he sensed her uneasiness with such raw intimacy he moved up her body, kissing her deeply as his weight pinned her beneath him. She sighed with pleasure as his erection nudged against her moist folds, the sensation of him being so close but not close enough almost unbearable. She began to squirm under him, her body instinctively searching for his.

Suddenly he was there, in one slick, tearing thrust he was inside her, the gasping cry of discomfort she tried to suppress not quite as inaudible as she had hoped it would be.

He reared back, his weight resting on his arms as he looked down at her. 'I am rushing you, aren't I?' he said. 'I thought you were ready for me. You felt ready for me. I am sorry— did I hurt you?'

She shook her head, her bottom lip caught between her teeth.

His eyes narrowed slightly. 'What's going on?' he asked.

Emma felt tears prick at the backs of her eyes. 'I should have told you…I'm sorry…'

His gaze narrowed even further. 'Told me what?'

She took a gulping swallow. 'I've never done this before… you know…had sex…'

Rafaele stared at her in stupefaction. *'What?'*

She bit her lip again, her eyes sprouting tears. 'I know I should have told you but I didn't think you'd believe me…'

He felt a knife twist in his chest. 'You mean you're…you're a…a *virgin*?'

She winced as if he had just insulted her. 'Do you have to say it like that?' she asked. 'It's not something I should be ashamed of.'

He stared at her for a moment, his mind whirling. What had he done? Oh, dear God, what had he done? He thought of all the times he had thrown his filthy accusations at her, never for a moment thinking she had been anything other than the conniving slut he'd believed her to be.

*His father hadn't slept with her.*

It was almost too much for him to take in. Why had his father left things the way he had? What had he hoped to achieve by involving Emma in such a convoluted way? If she hadn't been his mistress, then why give her half of his estate? What possible reason could he have had for doing such a thing?

His father hadn't known Emma before she came to look after him. She had been a total stranger to him and yet he had tied things up to her advantage, giving her the trump card, leaving his only remaining heir at her mercy. Had his father known how he would react? Had he planned this? Why had he used an innocent girl to get back at his estranged son?

Rafaele carefully lifted himself off her, his insides twisting with guilt as he saw a smear of her blood on his body. His throat felt raw and tight and he inwardly grimaced as she hastily tried to cover herself, her face aflame, her grey-blue eyes looking wounded.

He handed her the shorts and top she had taken off earlier before stepping into his own. 'I am sorry, Emma,' he said heavily. 'I had no idea. I wish you had told me.'

She scrambled back into her shorts and top, her bra and knickers scrunched up in her hand, her eyes shying away from his. 'It's not your fault,' she said. 'I shouldn't have let things go that far…I don't know what came over me…I'm deeply ashamed…'

Rafaele touched her on the arm, his gut clenching again as she flinched away as if she found his touch abhorrent. His hand fell back to his side. 'Do not be ashamed,' he said. 'It was my fault, in any case. I have done nothing but pressure you into having an affair with me. I have no excuse, other than I truly believed you to have seduced my father in order to get your hands on his estate. I can see now I have done you a great disservice. I would not blame you if you walked out right here and now. It is exactly what I deserve.'

She lifted her gaze to his. 'I'm not going to walk out on you,' she said. 'This is your home, Rafaele.'

He scraped a hand through his hair, not at all surprised to see it was still shaking slightly when he brought it back to his side. 'Did my father know you were a virgin?' he asked.

She blushed to the roots of her hair. 'No, of course not! Why would I tell him something like that?'

He gave her a wry look. 'Why indeed?'

Her mouth flattened crossly. 'I had no idea when I came downstairs this morning that we would…you know…'

'Come on, Emma,' he said with a touch of impatience fuelled by his lingering guilt. 'You came down here this morning with every intention of handing me pity on a plate with you served as a garnish.'

'That's not true!' she said. 'I wanted to clear the air between us, that's all.'

He hooked one brow up sceptically. 'That was some flag of friendship you were waving,' he said. 'Do you kiss all of your friends like that?'

She gave him a brittle glare. 'You started it. You kissed me first.'

'Ah, yes, but then you stuck your hand down my shorts,' he said with a twisted, humourless smile. 'That is going a little further than friendship, I would have thought.'

Her cheeks were fiery red, her eyes flashing with sparks of irritation. 'Do you have to rub it in?' she asked. 'I told you I'm thoroughly ashamed of myself. I can't believe I acted like that. I lost control completely, but I can assure you it won't happen again.'

'Pity,' he said. 'I was just starting to enjoy myself.'

Emma drew in a prickly breath. 'Don't make me feel any worse than I already do,' she said. 'I realise it must have been…uncomfortable for you…to be left like…like that…'

'You mean unsatisfied?' he asked.

Her throat went up and down. 'Yes…I suppose that's what I do mean…'

'Put it out of your mind,' he reassured her. 'I am not going to die because I didn't get my rocks off. I can handle a bit of frustration now and again.'

'Yes, well, I'm sure it doesn't happen very often,' Emma said with a little pang of errant jealousy.

'No, not if I can help it,' he said. 'But then boys will be boys, eh, Emma?'

Emma wondered if he was mocking her again. The differences between them had never been more apparent. He was a cynical, experienced playboy who took pleasure how and where he wanted, while she was a romantic fool in search of a home-and-hearth-happy-ever-after. 'Are you laughing at me?' she asked.

He stroked a finger down the length of her cheek. 'Why would I do that, Emma?' he asked, looking at her with those darker-than-night, unreadable eyes.

Emma felt her spine start to unhinge. 'You probably think I'm an old-fashioned prig,' she said. 'Someone who hasn't lived life at all.'

'I do not think that at all,' he said with a little frown beetling his brows.

'I know I'm far too old to be without experience, but I haven't found anyone I liked enough to take that step,' she said. 'I wanted to be in love with the person first. I didn't want it to be just a physical thing.'

His frown deepened. 'So why did you let me make love to you just then?' he asked.

Emma felt her colour rise again as his probing gaze held hers. 'I-I'm not sure…'

The line of his mouth tightened. 'So it *was* just a pity lay,' he said crudely. 'I guessed as much.'

'That's not true,' she said, biting her lip again.

He moved away from her, his expression locking her out once more. 'It will not happen again,' he said, unwittingly driving a stake through her heart. 'It *must not* happen again.'

Her throat closed over until she could barely speak. 'If that's what you want…'

His eyes clashed with hers, pain glittering in their ink-black depths. 'Do you know what I want, Emma? *Do you?*'

She shook her head, fresh tears suddenly blurring her vision.

'I want my life back,' he bit out as he raked a hand through his already tussled hair. 'I want to start over. I want to pick up that cricket ball and throw it into the pond instead of towards my brother's raised bat.' He took in a breath and added hollowly, 'And I want to rewind the clock to the day before my mother died so I could have told her how much I loved her while I still had the chance.'

Emma choked back a sob as he continued in the same bitter, heart-wrenching tone, 'I do not even know if I ever told her that I loved her. Everyone throws those three little words around so casually these days, but I do not remember if I did or not. I was only six years old at the time. If I did I have never said those words since, not to anyone.'

'You can't shut off your feelings for ever,' she said. 'I am sure you are more than capable of loving someone. I am sure of it.'

He drew in a ragged breath. 'I am sorry for what happened here this morning, truly sorry,' he said. 'I must have some sort of curse on me; all I seem to do is wreck people's lives.'

'You haven't wrecked my life,' Emma said softly.

'I hurt you.' He gave her an agonised look. 'I made you bleed, for God's sake.'

'I'm fine...really I am,' she said.

'Maybe you should see a doctor to make sure...'

'That would be embarrassing and totally unnecessary,' Emma insisted. 'Really, Rafaele, please don't cut yourself up about it. It was bound to happen some time or other, if not with you then someone else.'

He came back to where she was standing and, reaching out with one of his hands, gently brushed her hair back off her forehead with a touch so tender Emma felt as if someone had placed an industrial-sized clamp on her heart. He didn't say anything; he just stood there with his eyes holding hers, his thumb moving in a rhythmic fashion against the softness of her cheek.

'I'm glad it was you, Rafaele...' she told him in a whisper-soft voice.

His hand dropped away from her face. 'Why?'

She drew in a little hitching breath. 'Because you made me feel things I have never felt before.'

Pain flickered briefly in his eyes. 'Do not make this any harder than it already is for me, Emma,' he said. 'You are young and far too inexperienced for someone like me.'

'Why do you say that?' she asked.

'I say it because it is true,' he said. 'This attraction I feel for you will burn itself out in no time at all. It always has with everyone else I have been involved with. It is the thrill of the chase. It is a primal urge that all men feel, some more than others.'

'If I wasn't so inexperienced would you be pushing me away right now?' she asked.

'If I thought you were developing feelings for me, then, yes, I would push you away, for your own good.'

Emma felt another piece of her heart crack. 'Isn't it up to me to decide what is good or not good for me?' she asked.

His dark eyes flashed at her angrily. 'Stop this, Emma. Stop it right now. It is not going to go any further than this. It should not have gone this far, damn it to hell.'

Tears began to course down her face and she scrubbed at them with a jerky movement of her hand. 'Do you hate me so much?' she asked.

He swore under his breath and reached for her, pulling her into his chest, bringing his chin down to rest on the top of her head. 'No, no, no, *mio piccolo*,' he said huskily. 'Maybe before...but not now...not now...'

Emma nestled closer, her cheek pressed against the deep thudding of his heart. 'Then...then can we be friends?'

His hand continued stroking the back of her head as if he

wasn't quite ready to release her. But after a moment or two he eased her away from his chest to look down at her uptilted face. 'You are a sweet person, Emma,' he said. 'Anyone would be proud to have a friend as caring and giving as you.'

Emma rose up on tiptoe and pressed a brush-like kiss to his lips. 'Thank you for saying that. I think it's the nicest thing you've ever said to me.'

He grimaced ruefully. 'Yes, well, I have not exactly been handing out the compliments to you, now, have I?'

She smiled up at him. 'So we got off to a bad start? That doesn't mean we can't forgive and forget.'

Something came and went in his dark eyes. 'I can handle the forgiving part, Emma,' he said. 'It is the forgetting that is the most difficult. I do not know if I will ever be able to do it.'

'You are too hard on yourself,' she said. 'If things had been the other way around, would you have wanted your brother to punish himself the way you have punished yourself?'

He looked down at her for a long moment. 'No, you are right. I would not expect him to do so. It was an accident, a tragic accident that might not have happened a second or even half a second later.'

'I think your father came to that conclusion too,' she said. 'He must have thought about how he had handled things and at the last minute realised how wrong he had been.'

'But why involve you?' he asked as he released her from his light hold. 'What did he hope to achieve by that?'

Emma wrinkled her brow. 'I don't know… We might never find out why. Sometimes that's just the way it is. There is no clear-cut explanation for why people do the things they do. But I feel very strongly he would not have left his estate to both of us if he didn't think we could be of help to each other in some way.'

He gave her another rueful look. 'I have not exactly been

much help to you so far, have I? I have torn strips off you at every opportunity, and then to add insult to injury I have robbed you of an experience that should have been precious and memorable, and turned it into a disgusting display of out-of-control male lust, hurting you in the process.' He shouldered open the door and added bitterly, 'I will never forgive myself for that and neither will I forget it.'

Emma winced as the door clicked shut behind him. *I will never forget it either*, she thought, and, once she was certain he was out of earshot, burst into tears.

# CHAPTER NINE

WHEN Emma came downstairs that evening for dinner, Carla the new temporary housekeeper informed her in fractured English that Signore Fiorenza would not be joining her as he had been called away on business and would be away for the rest of the week. Emma did her best not to show her disappointment, but inside she felt crushed that Rafaele hadn't bothered to tell her about his trip face to face. What the housekeeper made of the relayed message, Emma didn't like to think. She had already seen Carla's raised brow when she had come out of the Pink Suite that morning. The housekeeper had clearly thought it rather strange the brand-new bride of Rafaele Fiorenza did not choose to share his bed at night.

'Thank you, Carla,' Emma said and, pushing aside her pride, asked: 'Did he happen to mention where he was going?'

'London,' the housekeeper said. 'I think he has a...how you say it in English...a mansion there?'

'Yes, that is correct,' Emma said. 'A mansion.' *And a mistress*, she added in silent anguish.

'I will serve you dinner now.' Carla gave a little bow of her head.

'It's all right, Carla,' Emma said. 'I can fend for myself this evening. You've had a long day as it is. Please take the rest of the night off.'

The housekeeper wavered uncertainly. 'Are you sure, Signora Fiorenza?'

Emma stretched her lips into a tight smile. 'Yes, I'm very sure. I'm not very hungry, in any case. I think I'll have an early night.'

'As you wish,' Carla said, and with a polite nod backed away.

Emma blew out a long sigh once the housekeeper had left. Rafaele couldn't have chosen a better way to communicate how much he regretted their passionate interlude that morning. He obviously wanted to put as much distance as he could between them so he wouldn't be tempted into finishing what he had started. She cringed as she recalled his statement that his attraction for her was just a transitory thing that would soon burn itself out. Could he so easily dismiss what they had shared?

Emma couldn't. She could still feel an intimate ache inside where her untried muscles had been called into sudden play. Thinking about his thick, hard body filling hers made her body fizz with sensation, as if sherbet instead of blood were flowing through her veins. Recalling the feel of his naked flesh under her fingertips, the tantalising taste of his kiss and the cup of his warm hands on her breasts made her need for him so intense, a giant hole opened in the pit of her stomach. He had awakened her to needs she had barely known existed. Those needs were now suspended, unsatisfied and all the stronger because they had been roused to fever pitch.

Emma swung away from her thoughts and made her way back up the stairs, coming to a halt outside Rafaele's brother's room, and with just a moment's hesitation she opened the door and stepped inside.

The bed had been pushed up against the wall and several boxes were now in the middle of the floor, some with toys and books, and others with clothes and shoes as Rafaele had begun the painful process of packing away his younger brother's things.

Emma bent down and picked up a rather tattered-looking teddy bear sitting on the top of the box of toys, the brown velvet pads of his paws almost worn away where little fingers had stroked, perhaps looking for night-time comfort. She felt tears welling at the backs of her eyes for the little boy who had been in the right place at the wrong time, and for Rafaele who had had to live each day since with a sinkhole of guilt and despair in his soul.

She tucked the teddy bear close to her chest, deciding that this little guy wasn't going to the charity shop or the attic or wherever else Rafaele intended the rest of Giovanni's things to go.

On her way to bed a couple of hours later, Emma had more or less given up on Rafaele calling her, but the telephone next to her bed suddenly began to ring so she picked it up and answered it somewhat tentatively. *'Buongiorno?'*

'Emma.'

Emma felt her spine shiver at the sound of her name on Rafaele's lips. 'Oh…it's you…' she said, injecting each word with some of her hurt at being abandoned so readily.

'Are you OK?' he asked.

'Yes.'

'You do not sound it.'

'Then you are imagining things,' she said. 'I'm fine.'

'Emma…' she heard him pull in a breath '…I had to leave in a hurry. Something came up, something urgent. I had to catch the first available flight to London to sort it out.'

'You could have told me yourself instead of getting the housekeeper to do so,' Emma said. 'I felt such a fool. We're supposed to be acting like a married couple, remember?'

'I am sorry you were embarrassed but—'

Emma cut across him in frustration. 'Married couples are supposed to talk to each other. It's called communication.'

There was a tense little pause.

'Emma, I would have told you personally but you were lying down in your room. I did not wish to disturb you.'

'How do you know I was lying down?' she asked.

'I knocked on your door and when you didn't answer I opened it,' he said. 'You were sound asleep.'

Emma felt a faint shiver pass over her at the thought of him observing her without her knowing. 'You should have woken me up.'

'You looked exhausted, that is why I didn't,' he said. 'I was in a rush, in any case.'

'You could have phoned me once you were on your way in the car or even at the airport,' she said, not quite ready to relinquish her sense of pique. 'Why didn't you?'

He let out an impatient sound. 'Must we have this conversation?' he asked. 'I didn't realise you expected me to clock in and clock out.'

'I'm sure that's what you expect me to do,' she threw back resentfully. 'I bet if I left some vague message with the housekeeper or one of the groundsmen that I was going away for the best part of a week you would have something to say about it.'

'I would indeed,' he said, 'but that is because you are my wife and I will not have my reputation damaged by inappropriate behaviour on your part.'

Emma felt her anger towards him escalate. 'I'm hardly the one in this marriage to act inappropriately, now, am I?'

'What is that supposed to mean?' He bit each word out like small hard pebbles hitting against a glass surface.

'I'm n-not the one with a lover in every city throughout

Europe,' she said, struggling to keep her voice steady as her emotions started to bubble over. 'That's you.'

'Emma, you are overwrought,' he said in a gentler tone. 'It is understandable given what happened this morning. That is one of the reasons I came away when I did. I think we both need some space to regroup.'

Emma bit down on her lip to stop herself from crying.

'Emma?' he said. '*Cara*, listen to me…please.'

She gave a tell-tale little sniff. 'S-sorry…it's just I don't know what you want from me…'

Rafaele closed his eyes and with his free hand used his finger and thumb to pinch the bridge of his nose until he winced at the pressure.

What *did* he want from her? Something he had no right to ask of her. She was after security and safety and he was not the one to give it to her. He didn't trust himself. He had never been good at relationships. He got restless and bored within weeks of sleeping with a new partner. It happened every single time. It would not be fair to have an affair with her, only to walk away when the curtain came down on the year required to fulfil the terms of his father's will.

He had misjudged her so badly he couldn't bear to add insult to injury by offering her a convenient affair. She deserved so much better. She deserved to have someone who could love her and protect her, to nurture her and meet all her needs. It would pull her down to have someone like him in her life. He couldn't give her the children she wanted. *How could he?* What sort of father would he be? He didn't feel comfortable around children. The nightmares never went away. He would wake up in his bed, soaked in sweat, his heart thumping, and his mind filled with images of his brother lying lifeless on the ground.

'Emma…' He took a deep breath and continued, 'It was

not my intention to confuse you. But everything is different now. It has to be.'

'But what about what I want?' she asked.

Rafaele's fingers tensed around his phone. 'I cannot give you what you want.'

'How do you *know* that?'

He blew out another tight breath. 'I just know it. I am not the settling down type. You told me you wanted a proper love-match marriage and children eventually. That is just not going to happen with me.'

'Because you're still punishing yourself,' she said. 'You're robbing yourself of one of the richest experiences in life.'

'My father clearly did not find it so,' he reminded her bitterly.

'Your father was as stubborn and proud as you,' she said. 'But have you ever thought what it was like for him losing your mother so young? He was probably devastated, left with two little boys to rear. One of the guests at the wedding told me he had loved your mother since childhood. Can't you imagine how lost he must have felt when she died so unexpectedly?'

Rafaele frowned and changed his phone to his other hand, flexing his fingers to ease the tension, but it crawled up from his hand to stiffen his neck instead. 'He did not talk about my mother,' he said. 'Not once in all the years after her death. He was the same with Giovanni. The day of my brother's funeral was the last time I heard Giovanni's name mentioned by him.'

'And yet he kept Giovanni's room as he had left it for all these years,' she said softly. 'And your mother's wedding dress was as perfect as the day she had worn it and the room she had decorated all by herself untouched. Can't you see how deeply he must have still been grieving? Perhaps he was just unable to express it the way you expected him to.'

Rafaele felt a growing ache in the region of his heart, like a very large hand reaching inside his chest and slowly squeezing. He couldn't speak for a moment as his throat was so tight. How would he ever know now what his father had thought and felt? Emma was right about him being as stubborn as his father. Over the past decade he could easily have made an effort to make contact, but he had been too pigheaded to do so. He had told himself he didn't want to see that look of loathing on his father's face ever again. The months and years had rolled by and now it was too late.

'Rafaele?'

He gave himself a mental shake as Emma's soft voice pierced his painful thoughts. 'This is not a good time for me, Emma,' he said. 'I have hours of work ahead of me. I will call you in a day or two.'

There was a stiff little silence.

'Are you seeing her?'

He frowned. 'Seeing who?'

'Your mistress.'

Rafaele waited for a two-beat pause. 'I no longer have a mistress. I told you I ended that relationship before we got married.'

'But we're not really married, are we, Rafaele?' she said. 'You don't want it to be real because you would rather have the freedom to see other women whenever you want.'

'I am not seeing anyone at present,' he said. 'Now, please stop this nonsense before I lose all patience with you.'

She couldn't stop. She was so frustrated she had to keep going. 'If you're going to have a lover on the side I think I should be allowed to do the same.'

Jealousy rose like a red-hot lava flow inside Rafaele at her defiant statement. He had never felt anything quite like the force of it before. The thought of her young and tender, untutored body being taken by someone else made him sick to his stomach. What if they were too rough with her as—God forgive him—he had been? She needed to be gently and patiently initiated into the rhythm of lovemaking, not rushed or pressured.

Rafaele suddenly realised *he* wanted to be the one to show her the pleasure her body could give and receive. His body was still humming with the sensations her touch had evoked that morning. He could still taste her sweetness in his mouth, he could still feel the softness of her lips and he could still feel the satin and silk of her naked breasts against his hands.

'No,' he stated implacably. 'I will not allow you to take a lover.'

'I'm not asking for your permission, Rafaele,' she said in an arch tone.

Rafaele ground his teeth as he pulled his anger back into line. 'The only lover you will be taking during our marriage will be me, do you understand, Emma? No one else. Just me.'

'But you said—'

'I know what I said but I have changed my mind,' he interrupted her curtly. 'When I return to Como our marriage will be a real one in every sense of the word. Get the housekeeper to help you move your things into my room. I want you in my bed when I get home.'

Emma felt a frisson run up her spine at his toe-curling command. Her body came alive, every place he had touched or caressed that morning started to quake with longing, the nerves beneath her skin leaping and bouncing in anticipation. Her breasts felt tight and full and her inner muscles gave a couple of tiny contraction-like pulses as if already preparing for the invasion of his aroused length. Desire flowed thickly through her veins, making her almost giddy with it. Her heart picked up its pace, her skin peppering with fine beads of perspiration as she tried to control the in-and-out of her choppy breathing.

'Did you hear me, Emma?' he asked in that same commanding tone.

'Y-yes…I heard you…'

*'Non aver paura, mio piccolo,'* he said in a deep but gentle voice. 'Do not be frightened, my little one. I will not hurt you the next time.'

Emma's belly did a little freefall of excitement. 'When are you coming home?' she asked.

'I would come on the next flight if I could, *cara*, but I am afraid that is impossible,' he said. 'I really do have urgent business to see to. There is a rather large share portfolio I am interested in. I am meeting with the chief executive of the company in a few hours. If all goes well I will be home on Saturday evening. Can you wait for me until then?'

Emma suddenly felt wretchedly ashamed at how she had practically begged him to come home to her. She had come across as a wanton, desperate for sex, blackmailing him with the threat of another lover to bed her. What full-blooded man wouldn't take her up on her offer? It wasn't about feelings on his part, or at least not emotional ones. It was about sex. A purely physical need that could be met with any number of women, but she in her naivety had put her hand up the highest.

Emma mentally cringed at her clumsy attempt at seduction. She was such a novice. Had she forgotten why he had married her in the first place? He wanted The Villa Fiorenza, not her. She was the annoying caveat his father had attached to his will. All she had to do to confirm it was to ask him how long he wanted their marriage to continue.

*Go on*, the sensible part of her brain urged, *ask him. Ask him if he wants to stay married beyond the year set down in the will.*

Emma couldn't do it. She didn't want to know. Why torture herself with a timeline? What good would it do to spend each day ticking off the calendar, another piece of her heart breaking beyond repair as the inevitable end approached?

'Emma?'

His deep velvet-toned voice jerked her back into the moment. 'Um…you don't have to hurry back if you're busy.' She faltered. 'I understand you have a business to run and…and people to see.'

'I would much prefer to see you than an overweight CEO, but that is just the way it is for now, *mio piccolo*.'

Emma wished that niggling voice in her head would go away. She desperately wanted to believe him, but her doubts kept sneaking up and tapping her on the shoulder long after she had put the phone down after saying goodbye.

The next few days passed so slowly Emma felt as if lead weights had been strapped to the hands of the clock. Each minute seemed to limp past, making her feel uncharacteristically restless and edgy.

Emma had not yet moved her things into Rafaele's suite. It seemed such a huge step to take, to occupy his bed while he wasn't there as if they had a normal relationship. Nothing about their marriage was normal. She had a ring on her finger and a certificate that declared them legally married, but Rafaele still had a chip on his shoulder about his father and until that was resolved she didn't think he would ever move on enough to allow her a space in his heart. Her love for him had gradually crept up on her. She hadn't realised how intense her feelings were until she had finally been brave enough to pull back the screen of denial.

Of course she was in love with him.

She hadn't stood a chance under the blowtorch of his bad-boy charm. She had melted like butter, her body recognising from the first moment when they had locked gazes he was the one for her. He was the one man who had sent her senses spinning, turned her world upside down, her bones to liquid and her heart to mush. One look had started it, one smile had encouraged it and one kiss had confirmed it. What would making love to completion with him do to her already out of control emotions?

The housekeeper came in with the papers on the Saturday morning, her expression giving nothing away for free, but Emma sensed a pitying attitude in the way Carla retreated without once meeting her eyes.

Emma soon found the reason why on the gossip pages of one of the British scandal sheets. There was a photograph of Rafaele leaning in close to a gorgeous blonde woman wearing an evening dress slit to the navel, her full-lipped mouth pouting to receive his kiss. Emma closed her eyes and tried to get the image out of her brain, but when she opened them again it was still there, taunting her, reminding her of how stupid she had been to think she had even stood a chance.

The woman's name was Miranda Bellingstoke, a rich heiress to a fortune in stocks and shares, just the type of socialite wife Rafaele Fiorenza would have chosen if his father hadn't interfered. A woman who knew how to carry herself, a woman with a pedigree longer than her perfect, cellulite-free legs, a woman who didn't have a single drug-addicted skeleton in her closet, a woman who knew how to meet his needs and who had no doubt been meeting them the whole time he was in London. The article hinted as much. It speculated how Ms Bellingstoke's involvement with the high-flying Italian stock trader seemed to be on again in spite of his recent marriage to an Australian woman.

Nausea lifted Emma's stomach contents to her throat and she swallowed against it, fighting against the imminent collapse of her spirit. At least the journalist hadn't mentioned

Emma by name, but still the shame of being identified as the poor, ignorant wife, the last to know of her husband's affair, clung to her like filthy mud.

It was more than obvious the 'urgent' business he had to see to was five feet ten and weighed less than Emma did at five feet five. How could she compete against that? Rafaele was used to sophisticated women of the world. He had probably been laughing about her inexperience to his worldly mistress, no doubt relating to her how Emma had prostrated herself, pleading to be shown what it meant to be a woman in passionate command of a man who had so much experience he deserved a doctorate.

Emma felt herself shrinking in shame. How could she have been so dumb? It was obvious now how this was going to pan out. He would travel back and forth to London 'on business' leaving her back at the villa to twiddle her thumbs waiting with bated breath for his return. What better revenge for how she had supposedly insinuated her way into his father's affections? He would get exactly what he wanted with a little bonus thrown in.

*Her.*

But it wasn't going to go all his way, not if she could help it.

She would be more than ready for him when he returned; she would have her resolve hardened, her chin at a combative angle, her heart under lock and key.

Emma heard the low growl of his car a few hours later and straightened her spine as she waited for him to come in. She heard the firm tread of his footsteps on the marbled floors and his voice echoing throughout the large foyer as he called her. '*Cara*, I am home. Where are you, *la mio bella moglie*?'

She walked stiffly out of the salon, her chin held high, her eyes glittering with wrath. 'Here I am,' she said.

His gaze ran over her, a quizzical light in their dark depths. 'Emma, has something happened? You look…tense.'

'How was your business in London?' she asked. 'Satisfying?'

A frown brought his brows together. 'I achieved what I set out to achieve, if that is what you are asking, but somehow I get the feeling it is not. What is going on? Why are you looking at me like that?'

Emma gave him a hard little glare. 'You lied to me. You said your affair with your mistress was over but it's not, is it? I saw you with Miranda Bellingstoke in the paper.'

A flicker of irritation passed over his features. 'I did not lie to you, Emma. I am no longer involved with Miranda.'

Emma clenched her hands into fists. 'But you saw her while you were there, didn't you? There's no point denying it as I saw the photo of you with her in the London paper.'

He sucked in a breath and dragged a hand through his hair. 'All right,' he said with a hint of weariness. 'I did see her, but not intentionally. The CEO I was dealing with suggested we have a drink once we had sorted out the business end of things. Miranda happened to be at the same bar.'

Emma rolled her eyes. 'How very convenient.'

His jaw went tight. 'I did not plan to see her, Emma. She came over to where we were standing at the bar and, if the truth be known, made rather a nuisance of herself.'

'Would you like to see the press's version of Miranda making a nuisance of herself?' Emma asked with a little curl of her lip.

He set his mouth. 'I do not see the need to defend myself to you, Emma,' he said. 'After all, you have experienced the bias of the press first hand, have you not? I would have thought you would be the first person to give me the benefit of the doubt.'

Emma could see his point, but still those little finger-prod doubts kept nudging her. She felt so confused. He was a playboy. He was used to his freedom. He had only married her because he'd had no choice. Would she ever feel secure enough to trust him?

He stepped closer and gently lifted her chin so she had to meet his gaze. 'Have you changed your mind about making our marriage a real one?' he asked.

Emma looked into his bottomless black-brown eyes and melted. How could she say no to him when she loved him so much? Even if she could only have him for the rest of the year wouldn't that be better than not at all? 'No…' Her voice came out whisper-soft. 'No, I haven't changed my mind.'

He began to stroke her cheek with the pad of his thumb. 'I should have warned you how intrusive the press can be. I do my best to ignore them, but occasionally they go too far.'

She lowered her eyes a fraction. 'I guess I really don't have any right to be jealous…it's not as if we're in love…or anything…'

He looked at her for a second or two. 'No, perhaps not, but no one likes to feel they are being double-crossed.'

Her eyes came back to his. 'So…so while we are…together there won't be anyone else in your life?'

Again he took a moment to answer. 'I suppose we should make some sort of agreement that if one of us develops an interest elsewhere, we should inform the other of it so as to avoid unnecessary embarrassment. How does that sound?'

*It sounds as if you are never going to fall in love with me and are making sure you have a quick exit route*, Emma thought in silent despair. 'Fine,' she said with a tight smile. 'Best to be up front and honest about these things.'

Rafaele tucked a strand of her hair behind her ear. 'I am going to have a shower and a shave and come back down to the salon and pour us both a drink. Have you eaten?'

'Ages ago, but what about you?'

'I had a snack on the plane but I could do with something light,' he said, tugging at his tie. 'Has Carla left anything for us?'

'I will go and get it ready for you.'

He bent down and pressed a brief kiss to her forehead. 'I have been thinking of nothing else but holding you in my arms and making love to you.'

Emma let out a shuddering breath of anticipation as she looked into his dark eyes. 'I've been thinking about it too…'

He smiled and brushed his mouth against hers in a hot-as-fire-but-soft-as-a-feather kiss that set her heart racing. 'Hold that thought,' he said with a smouldering look. 'I will not be long.'

# CHAPTER TEN

WHEN Rafaele came downstairs after his shower Emma had poured a ruby-red glass of wine for him and set a plate of salad and a freshly made omelette on the coffee-table.

'Is Carla still here?' he asked as he sat down and picked up the knife and fork.

'No, I made it myself,' Emma said. 'I thought it would be nicer than reheated pasta.'

'That was kind of you,' he said. 'Are you going to have something? What about a glass of wine? Can I pour you one?'

She shook her head. 'No, I had an orange juice a while ago.'

He resumed eating; pausing now and again to chat to her about the weather in London and other inconsequential things, but Emma only listened with one ear. She drank in the sight of him, the way his mouth tilted at the corners when he smiled and the way his eyes softened when they met hers. He looked tired, but not tense this time. She hoped it was because he was glad to be back at the villa with her.

Rafaele pushed his empty plate aside. 'Come here,' he commanded softly.

Emma got up on unsteady legs and sat beside him on the leather sofa, shivering with delight when his arm came around her shoulders and brought her closer. She looked into his eyes, her heart skipping a beat at the passion she could see burning there.

He brought his mouth down to hers in a slow, sensual kiss that made all the fine hairs on Emma's body stand to attention. His tongue slipped through the soft barrier of her lips and she began to suck on its tip, delighting in the way he groaned with pleasure as he deepened the kiss.

His hands shaped her through her clothes, his mouth still locked on hers, his body pressing hers down on the sofa until she felt the hard length of him probing her intimately.

Rafaele lifted his head and looked down at her passion-swollen lips. 'This is not the place to do this,' he said. 'I want you to be comfortable and relaxed.'

Emma was swept away on a tide of such longing she was hardly aware of Rafaele lifting her and carrying her upstairs to his bedroom. She clung to him, her mouth crushed beneath the pressure of his, her heart rate racing out of control as he laid her on the mattress.

'Are you sure about this, Emma?' he asked as he came down beside her, his warm fingers splayed possessively on her hip. '*Really* sure?'

She looked at him with love shining in her eyes. 'I'm sure,' she said. 'It's what I want. I want you. I want you to make love to me.'

He kissed her mouth, a hard, brief kiss that burned with sensual promise. 'I cannot help feeling I should not be doing this,' he said as he lifted up her T-shirt to expose her breasts.

'But you want to, don't you?' Emma asked, squirming as his mouth began to suckle on her engorged flesh.

'Damn right I do,' he growled, and moved to her other breast. 'I think I have wanted to do this from the moment I met you.'

Emma gasped with pleasure as he moved his mouth down from her breasts to the tiny cave of her belly button, his tongue circling the indentation before moving lower. She automatically tensed but he spoke to her softly, his deep, sexy voice soothing her into relaxing as he subjected her to the most intimate of erotic caresses. Her body quivered, each sensitised nerve beginning to vibrate with pleasure under the exquisite torture of his mouth and tongue.

'Come for me, Emma,' he coaxed her gently.

Emma felt her body start to convulse, it was suddenly out of her control, the waves of rapture swamping her, leaving her breathless and euphoric and even more hopelessly in love.

She stroked her fingers through the thickness of his hair and let out a shaky sigh as the last tremors of pleasure rippled through her. 'I can't believe that just happened…' she said. 'I didn't know it would feel like that…'

Rafaele moved up her body, settling himself between her thighs, one of his legs splayed over one of hers. 'It will get better,' he said. 'It takes time to get used to a new lover. We have to learn each other's rhythm and pace.'

'Teach me how to pleasure you,' she said, tracing the outline of his mouth. 'Teach me everything.'

He brought her hand to his erection, letting her feel his rigid contours, hoping it would help her relax enough to accept him. 'I do not want to hurt you, Emma,' he said. 'It's important you relax as much as possible, don't tense up. I will let you set the pace, just tell me whenever you need me to stop.'

She bit her lip in that endearing way of hers. 'OK…'

He reached past her to take out a condom from the bedside drawer and, opening the tiny packet, handed it to her. 'You can put it on me, if you like.'

She peeled it back over him, the tip of her tongue between her teeth in concentration, her fingers soft and tentative as if worried she might hurt him. He found it a new experience being with someone so caring and sweet and so trusting. He was used to lovers going after what they wanted; the slightly aggressive and raunchy sexuality of modern women had never bothered him before now. Sex for him had been always been a totally physical thing. He had always been perfectly content with that, but now he wondered if he had missed out on something along the way.

He drew in a breath as her fingers began stroking him, the movements so deliciously tantalising he thought he might not last the distance. He pushed her back down, and, propping his weight on his arms, gently lowered his pelvis to hers. He touched her delicate folds, the sweet honey of her body slick against his fingers. 'Remember, Emma,' he said. 'Any time you want to stop, just tell me.'

'I don't want you to stop,' she said a little breathlessly.

He stroked her some more, inserting one then two fingers, letting her grip and then relax around him until he pushed deeper. 'You feel so wet and warm and tight,' he said, fighting for control.

'I want you inside me,' she said, shifting her body restively beneath him. 'I want you inside me now.'

He smiled over her mouth as he bent to kiss it. 'Don't be so impatient, *cara*,' he said. 'There is plenty of time. We have got all night.'

She kissed him back, her tongue tangling with his, her breathing coming in little gasps as he prepared to enter her. He took it very slowly, easing into her tight warmth until he felt she was ready for more of him. Bit by bit he advanced, his senses spinning as her small body enclosed him, the feel of her around his thickness making him want to selfishly plunge in and explode. It took every gram of patience and control to hold back, he could feel the pressure building inside him; he was almost shuddering with the effort of holding back, his skin breaking out in fine beads of perspiration as he coaxed her into accepting his full length.

She tensed momentarily at one point and he instantly eased back, and, propping himself up again, brushed the damp hair away from her forehead. 'How are you doing?' he asked.

'I'm fine…I think I'm fine now…'

He pushed in a bit further. 'You feel so good, Emma,' he said.

Emma pushed her hips up to take more of him, her mouth on his neck in hot little kisses that spoke of her own building need. He sucked in a harsh breath and began to gently thrust, the rocking motion sending her senses into a tailspin. Her skin was peppered with goose-bumps of pleasure as he increased the pace; she was with him all the way, her body so slick with moisture she could feel nothing but the smooth, hard glide of his body within the tight cocoon of hers. Her body began to fizz and tingle with each deepening thrust, her back arching, her legs stiffening in that prelude to paradise. She was so close but not quite there when he brought his fingers into play against her, the gentle but purposeful action intensifying the tight coils of pleasure until they suddenly unravelled, leaving her shuddering and quaking and sobbing her way through an explosive, earth-shattering orgasm.

Emma lay beneath him, her body still quivering as she felt him prepare for his own release. She felt it in the growing tension of his muscles on his back where her fingers were still digging into him, and she felt it in the way his pace began to step up, the pumping action of his body as it thrust into hers signalling he was getting closer and closer to that final blissful moment. He surged forwards, the quake of his body as he spilled himself sending her skin out in another layer of pimply goose-flesh, her body feeling every single shuddering pulse of his.

The silence was measured by the sound of their hectic breathing. Emma closed her eyes and breathed in the musky scent of their lovemaking, her senses still spinning at the heady pleasure she had felt in his arms. His body was heavy on hers, but she didn't want him to move. She loved the feel of him relaxed and spent on top of her, his face buried against her neck, the in and out of his breathing feathering along her sensitive skin.

'You were amazing, Emma,' he said, the movement of his lips against her skin making her shiver in reaction.

'So were you,' she responded shyly.

He leaned up on his elbows to look down at her, his brows close together over his eyes. 'Did I hurt you?' he asked.

Emma shook her head. 'Not much… A little at first but you were so gentle with me.' She smiled and lifted herself up to plant a soft kiss on his mouth. 'Thank you.'

He returned her kiss with a lingering one of his own. 'You are welcome,' he said, and carefully lifted himself off her, discarding the condom in the process.

He pulled her to her feet and held her against him for a moment, his hands resting on her hips, their bodies touching pelvis to pelvis. Emma felt the stirring of him against her and pressed herself closer, but he held her from him with a rueful smile. 'No, Emma,' he said. 'You will be too sore.'

Emma had to dampen down her disappointment. Her body was on fire all over again and she didn't want anything to spoil their new-found harmony, even if it was only physical. 'What if we have a shower together?' she asked, looping her arms around his neck.

His eyes flared with desire as he looked down at her. 'You ask too much,' he said in a mock growl. 'Do you think I will be able to control myself with you splashing around naked beside me?'

She gave him a coquettish smile. 'I could always put on a bathing costume if that would help?'

'Don't you dare,' he growled and, sweeping her up in his arms, carried her through to the *en suite*.

The fine needles of water were hot and caressing against Emma's skin, but nowhere near as caressing as Rafaele's dark brown gaze as it ran over every inch of her. Everywhere his gaze rested her body sprang to zinging life, her mouth, her breasts, the flat plane of her stomach and lower to where her feminine mound was already contracting with growing need.

'I knew this would be a mistake,' he murmured against her neck as he nibbled at her sensitive skin, his hands splayed on her bottom, holding her against his arousal. 'But I can't seem to help myself. You are driving me crazy. You have been doing it from day one.'

Emma tilted her head so she could feel his lips and tongue near the base of her ear. 'I like how you make me feel,' she said, clutching at his broad shoulders. 'I didn't know my body could feel the things you make it feel.'

'You make me feel some amazing things as well,' he said, and kissed her on the mouth, his tongue delving deep as his lower body rubbed against hers, the rough abrasion of his hair-roughened skin making her desire for him all the more uncontrollable.

Emma trailed her fingers from his neck, down his chest, circling his flat brown nipples before going lower to where his erection pulsed and throbbed with longing. She sank to her knees in the cubicle, the steamy water cascading over her shoulders and back as she brought her mouth towards him.

His fingers dug into her scalp to hold her at bay. 'You don't have to do that, Emma,' he said a little breathlessly. 'That is a big ask for a new lover, especially an inexperienced one.'

She looked up at him. 'But I want to pleasure you. I want to know how to make you feel the way I did when you did it to me.'

He brushed the wet hair back off her face. 'I don't want you to do anything you are not comfortable with,' he said. 'I can pull out before things go too far.'

Emma took an unsteady breath, her hands grasping his thighs as she brought her mouth to him, breathing over him first before she tasted him tentatively with the tip of her tongue. She felt him jerk back in response, his fingers digging even further into her hair as he tried to anchor himself against the sensual onslaught to come. It gave her all the confidence she so very badly needed. She licked at him like a hungry cat, her tongue discovering his rigid contours: the thickened shaft with its satin-like skin stretched to snapping point, the musky scent of his arousal filling her nostrils, the pulse of his blood thrumming against the sweep of her tongue.

'Oh, God,' he groaned, beginning to sag at the knees. 'I can't take much more of this.'

Emma kept at him, her mouth sliding over his engorged length, back and forth in a purely instinctive fashion until she felt him suddenly tense, his whole body locking in that pivotal moment when control finally slipped out of reach. She felt the convulsing shudders of his body; she received the spill of his life force, the warmth of him anointing her in one of the most intimate acts possible.

He pulled out of her mouth with a muttered expletive and hauled her almost roughly to her feet. 'You did not have to do that, Emma,' he said. 'I do not want you to feel you have to bend over backwards to please me all the time. We are supposed to be equals.'

'We can only be equals if you come to care for me as much as I care for you,' she said, sliding her hands over his rock-hard pectoral muscles, her eyes gazing into his. 'I love you.'

He frowned at her, his body going tense. 'Emma…' He gave a little sigh and continued, 'You are confusing love with sexual desire. In the first rush of attraction it is an easy mistake to make. Believe me, what you are feeling now will peter out over time.'

'I don't believe that,' Emma said. 'This is not just sexual attraction. *I love you.*'

'A lot of women develop strong feelings for their first lover,' he said. 'You have waited longer than most so it is natural you would form a stronger attachment than normal, but it does not mean it is the real deal.'

'How can I convince you it is?' she asked.

He let out another heavy sigh as he ran his hands from her shoulders down to her wrists. 'I do not want you to love me, Emma,' he said. 'I do not want to be responsible for your un-happiness. I am not good at relationships. I do not like hurting people, but at times it is inevitable. I am selfish and pig-headed and enjoy my freedom too much. Let's just enjoy this while it lasts.'

'How can you not want to be loved?' she asked as she fought back tears. 'What is the point in living if no one loves you?'

'Stop it, Emma,' he said brusquely as he reached past her to turn off the shower spray. 'I told you the rules. I would ap-preciate it if you would stick to them.'

Emma followed him out of the shower, her heart contract-ing at his keep-away-from-me manner. He had just made love to her with such exquisite tenderness. Didn't that mean he felt at least something for her?

No, she reminded herself painfully. It did not.

She wrapped herself in a towel and turned away from him in case he saw the distress she felt. How could she have been so foolish? She had blurted out her feelings so gauchely. No wonder he had pulled away. She cringed at her lack of sophis-tication. Hot, scalding shame rushed through her again at how she had begged him to make love to her like the sex-starved singleton she was.

'Emma,' Rafaele said as he touched her on the shoulder. 'Look at me.'

Emma stiffened under his touch. 'Leave it, Rafaele,' she said without facing him. 'Please don't make me feel any more of a fool than I already do.'

He tugged her around to face him, his hands going to her waist to hold her steady, and his eyes locking on hers. 'I want you, Emma,' he said. 'Make no mistake about that. I want you.'

*But not for ever*, Emma thought with a little sag of her shoulders as his mouth came down. She gave herself up to his kiss, her arms going around his waist, holding her to him tightly, wondering even as she felt his body quiver with longing against hers how long it would be before he tired of her and finally let her go.

Emma woke up alone the next morning, but when she turned her head she could see where Rafaele's had been resting on the pillow beside hers. She reached out and touched the indention, her nostrils flaring to take in the fragrance of their lovemaking lingering on the sheets. She moved her body experimentally, the tiny tug of her inner muscles reminding her of the mind-blowing passion they had shared during the night. He had been so tender and considerate she had felt tears come to her eyes. Her love for him felt as if it were taking up all the available space inside her chest. She felt it pulling on her every breath with a bittersweet poignancy.

The door of the bedroom pushed open and Rafaele came in bearing a tray with freshly brewed coffee, fruit and croissants. 'Rise and shine,' he said with a smile. 'Breakfast is here.'

Emma dragged herself upright and blinked the sleep out of her eyes. 'What is it about morning people who think everyone should be awake and fully functioning at dawn?' she asked with a mock scowl.

He grinned at her as he laid the tray across her knees. 'Do you need a wake-up kiss, Emma?' he asked, and, leaning forward, pressed his mouth to hers, the brush stroke of his tongue setting her senses alight.

He pulled back and looked at her for a moment. 'Mmm, I am thinking the coffee is too hot in any case,' he said, and lifted the tray off her knees and set it on the floor.

'What are you doing?' Emma asked as he began to haul his T-shirt over his head.

He gave her a burning look and reached for the zipper of his jeans. 'What do you think I am doing?' he asked.

'It looks like you're getting undressed,' she said, and suppressed a little shiver as he stepped out of his jeans. She could see the tenting of his underwear and her heart began to race as he came towards her.

He pulled the sheets off her in a ruthless fashion, his dark gaze feeding off her hungrily. 'You look more beautiful every time I see you,' he said.

'My hair's a mess,' Emma said breathlessly as he came down on top of her.

'It looks wonderful to me,' he said against her mouth. 'You look like you have spent the night making wild, passionate love.'

She squirmed with delight as his erection probed her intimately. 'That's because I did spend the night making wild, passionate love,' she said with a coy little smile.

He eased his weight off her. 'Are you sore?'

'A tiny bit,' she said. 'But it's a nice sore.'

His eyes went very dark as they held hers. 'Maybe I should leave this until later,' he said.

Emma grasped at his shoulders to stop him pulling back from her. 'No, don't you dare,' she said. 'You kissed me so now you'll have to finish what you started.'

His eyes glinted. 'So it's like that, is it?'

She stroked her fingers down to where his body pulsed. 'Yes, it is,' she said, pushing aside his underwear.

He sucked in a breath and pushed her back down to the mattress. 'You're a fast learner, *la mio bella moglie*,' he growled playfully.

'Yes, but then you're a great teacher.' Emma gasped as his mouth closed over her breast, her senses spinning as he circled her nipple with his tongue.

He moved to her other breast with the same exquisite caresses, his hand sliding down to explore her tender folds, making her toes curl in delight.

'I want you inside me,' she said, opening her thighs even further, her hands searching for him to guide him into her slick warmth.

She watched with bated breath as he applied a condom, his body so aroused she could see the veins rippling along the shaft.

He came back over her, his weight supported by his elbows as he looked down at her. 'I should have asked this earlier, but are you on the pill?'

Emma hesitated for a nanosecond. She had begun taking a low-dose pill a few months ago to help control her cycle, but she had not always been very vigilant in taking it. She would have to see a doctor to get a new prescription, in any case.

'Emma?'

'Yes,' she said, promising herself she would make an appointment with a doctor as soon as possible. 'I take it to keep my periods regular.'

He searched her features for an infinitesimal moment. 'I do not want any accidents,' he said. 'Condoms can some-times break.'

'There won't be any accidents,' she said. 'I'm safe.'

He held her gaze for another moment or two. 'Just to reassure you, I had tests done recently,' he said. 'You will not catch anything from me.'

Emma hated being reminded of his playboy lifestyle. She

felt as if she was just a number in a long line of women who had briefly occupied his bed. She knew as soon as he was finished with her someone else would step up and take her place. It was gut-wrenching to think he might only be using her in order to secure his inheritance, but her love for him demanded she spend what little time she had with him to show him how genuine her feelings were. What else could she do? She was locked here with him for the next few months. It would be unbearable if she had to watch on the sidelines while he conducted an affair with someone else.

'I'm glad to hear it,' she said a little stiffly.

'What's wrong?'

'Nothing's wrong.'

He captured her chin to stop her from turning her head away. 'Yes, there is,' he said. 'You are jealous.'

She gave him a glittering glare. 'Why should I be jealous?' she asked. 'You've been very open about the fact you've slept with hundreds of women.'

He gave her a wry look. 'Hardly hundreds.'

'How many, then?' she asked.

He frowned at her darkly. 'I am not going to give you a list of names and numbers, Emma. They have nothing to do with us.'

'Us?' She elevated her brows. 'That's hardly a word to describe you and me, is it? We're not a couple in the real sense of the word. We're only together because we were forced into it.'

'You do not think what happened yesterday makes us a couple?' he asked.

'It was sex, Rafaele. Even strangers have sex; it doesn't make them a couple.'

'We *are* a couple, Emma,' he said. 'I want you to be my lover for as long as we are happy together.'

Emma wished she had the strength of will to get out now before she got her heart broken, but her body was already responding to his thick, hard presence. She dug her fingers into his taut buttocks to bring him deeper, her breath coming in choppy gasps as he began an erotic rhythm. Her nerves began to hum with tension, her body feeling as if a hundred earthquakes were about to erupt inside her. The pressure built in every muscle of her body until she was teetering on the edge, finally pitching forwards into blissful oblivion.

She felt him come close behind her, his body tense and hard before it pumped its way into paradise, his arms tight around her, his face pressed into her neck as he cut back a harsh groan of ecstasy.

It was a few minutes before he moved or spoke. He lifted himself up on his elbows and pressed a soft kiss to her mouth. 'You are mine, Emma,' he said. 'Body and soul, you are mine.'

*But for how long?* Emma silently wondered as she kissed him back with all the tenderness she felt for him. She only hoped it would be long enough to melt the ice around his heart.

# CHAPTER ELEVEN

OVER the next few weeks Emma found herself relaxing more and more into the role of Rafaele's wife. Lucia the housekeeper returned after her much-needed break, not even blinking an eye at Emma's occupation of Rafaele's suite of rooms. If anything she seemed rather pleased and smiled every time she encountered Emma.

'It is good,' Lucia said in her heavily accented voice. 'Signore Fiorenza would be very pleased. It is what he wanted for his son.'

Emma frowned as she helped the housekeeper fold some towels. 'What do you mean, Lucia?' she asked. 'Are you saying Signore Fiorenza Senior talked to you about the terms of his will?'

The housekeeper looked a little sheepish. 'He talk a little bit one night a week or two before he passed away,' she said. 'He wanted Rafaele to be happy. He think he wasting his life with loose women. He told me he thought you would make Rafaele a good wife. You are kind and gentle and would love him, not for his money, but for him.'

Emma stared at her. 'Signore Fiorenza told you that?'

'Yes, many times,' Lucia said. 'You are perfect for Rafaele, Signorina. You love him, *sì*? It has all worked out.'

Emma chewed at her lip with her teeth. 'Signore Fiorenza

was taking a big gamble,' she said. 'What if I hated his son on sight and refused to marry him?'

Lucia gave her a knowing look. 'Even if you had hated him you would not have watched his inheritance slip away,' she said. 'Signore Fiorenza knew that you would do the right thing by his son. He trusted you. And now it has worked out exactly as he planned. The Villa Fiorenza will soon be filled with yours and Rafaele's *bambinos*.'

Emma didn't have the heart to tell the housekeeper how unlikely that was. Instead she smiled and finished folding the towels, her heart aching for what could never be.

Over dinner a few evenings later Rafaele announced he had to travel back to London on business and would be away for a few days. Emma waited with bated breath for him to ask her to accompany him, but the request was not forthcoming. She sat as he talked about other things, her heart sinking so low she began to feel ill.

'You're not eating, *cara*,' he said, indicating her untouched meal. 'Do you not like Lucia's cooking?'

Emma gave him a forced smile and picked up her fork. 'Of course I do... It's lovely...'

'If you would prefer Carla to return that can be arranged,' he said. 'I am inclined to agree with you that this place is too much for Lucia.'

'I'm not sure Lucia would like to think she has reached her use by date,' Emma said. 'She loves it here. In any case I don't mind helping her with the heavier tasks.'

He frowned at her. '*Cara*, there is no need for you to scrub the floors and do the dishes. I pay other people to do those things. You are my wife.'

Emma gave him a weak smile. They had been married nearly seven weeks and she still didn't know if she would wake up tomorrow to find he had found someone else. It was like living with the sword of Damocles hanging over her head. She had even stopped saying she loved him. What was the point? He never said anything in return.

He reached for her hand and stroked his long fingers over the back of hers. 'You look pale, *tesore mio*,' he said. 'Have I been keeping you up too late at night, hmm?'

Emma suppressed a tiny shiver as his dark eyes speared hers meaningfully. The passion that flared so easily between them felt like another presence in the room; she could feel it circling the table, coming closer and closer until her body was quaking in reaction. Her legs felt shaky, her palms moist and her inner core melted as she thought of him pinning her with his hardness as he had done so earth-shatteringly earlier that evening. The experience of having him take her from behind had sent shock waves of delight rippling through her; the rough, almost primal coupling had sent shivers racing up and down her spine. He was a demanding and energetic lover, but a sensitive and considerate one. Just looking at him made her body tremble all over with desire, the skin on the back of her neck prickling as she thought of him driving into her warmth, taking her to the highest pinnacle of pleasure time and time again. Over the last few weeks together she had grown in sexual confidence, she knew how to pleasure him and delighted in doing so at every opportunity.

She didn't like thinking of him pleasuring other women in the past; instead she took what comfort she could in the fact he had been with her every night, his desire for her knowing no bounds.

Rafaele lifted her hand to his mouth, holding her gaze as he pressed her bent fingers to his lips. 'I would take you with me to London except I will be tied up in meetings the whole time,' he said. 'But I promise to take you somewhere else for a short break next month. Where would you like to go? Paris? Monaco perhaps?'

'Anywhere would be lovely,' Emma said softly. 'I just want to be with you.'

His fingers tightened momentarily on her hand. 'You are very sweet, Emma,' he said with a slight rasp in his voice. 'You deserve someone much nicer than me.'

'I don't want anyone else but you,' she insisted.

He released her hand and picked up his wineglass, his expression locking her out. 'I leave first thing in the morning,' he said. 'I will be back on Sunday or maybe even Monday, I am not sure.'

'You have meetings on a weekend?' Emma asked, not quite able to remove the air of suspicion in her tone.

His eyes became hard as they held hers. 'I hope this is not leading where I think it is leading.'

'Tell me something, Rafaele,' she said with an embittered look. 'Do you wake up each morning and tick another day off the calendar?'

'It's not like that at all,' he said with a frown.

She glared at him. 'Isn't it?'

'No, of course not,' he said. 'I enjoy having you around, Emma. You are good company.'

'Why don't you say what you really think?' she asked. 'It's not about the company and scintillating conversation I offer you, is it?'

His mouth was pulled tight. 'Don't do this, Emma.'

'It's the on-tap sex, isn't it, Rafaele?' she continued bitterly. 'Anywhere, any time, any position. That's what you want from me, isn't it? That's all you'll ever want from me, isn't it?'

'You are becoming hysterical,' he said with ice-cold calm.

'You called me a whore from the very first day,' she bit out resentfully, 'but what I didn't realise then was how quickly you would turn me into one.'

His brows snapped together. 'You are nothing of the sort,' he said. 'I have apologised for what I thought back then.'

'But you still think it, don't you?' she asked. 'Deep down inside there's still a part of you that won't accept I was just your father's carer. You see me as the conniving slut who stole half your inheritance, and nothing is going to change that, is it?'

'I do not think anything of the sort,' he clipped back. 'Emma, for God's sake, I am in absolutely no doubt I was your first lover. What sort of man do you think I am to doubt you after that?'

'You don't love me. You make love to me, but you don't love me.'

'I do not want to continue this discussion,' he said stiffly. 'You are not being reasonable.'

'I'll show you how reasonable I can be,' she said with another fiery glare as she pushed back from the table. 'I'm not going to wait around holding my breath for you to pull the rug from under my feet. I'm going to pack my bags and leave right now.'

The nerve flickered at his mouth again as he got to his feet. 'If you do I will make you regret it,' he said through clenched teeth. 'The press will hound you, I can guarantee it. What the Bennett family said about you in Australia will be nothing to what I will reveal about your activities here. I have contacts. One word from me and your reputation will be unsalvageable in any country.'

Emma stopped mid-stride, her stomach dropping in alarm. 'You would do it, wouldn't you?' she said. 'You heartless, selfish bastard, you would do it and think nothing of it, wouldn't you?'

His eyes glittered with steely purpose. 'If you walk out on me you will regret it, I guarantee it. Don't make me do it, Emma. I don't want to hurt you.'

She looked at him in disdain. 'Don't lie to me,' she bit out. 'You would take great pleasure in hurting me. I know you would.'

He put his hands on her shoulders and brought her towards him. 'Emma, listen to me,' he said, his tone now gentle. 'I do not want things to get ugly between us. We have been thrown together by the machinations of my father. That is not your fault and neither is it mine. It is fortunate we enjoy each other's company so that we can see this through in order to get what we both want.'

'But I can't have what I want, can I?' she asked with tears stinging her eyes. 'You don't love me...you're never going to love me...'

He let out a heavy sigh. 'I care for you, Emma,' he said. 'I know it is not quite the same as the three magic words you crave, but it is more than I have felt for any other woman I have been involved with before.'

'It's not enough,' Emma said. 'I thought it would be but it's not. I want to be loved. I want to feel secure. I can't live with this shadow of uncertainty hanging over me. I never know from one day to the next if it's going to be my last with you. You hold all the power in our relationship, which means you have the least to lose if the relationship fails.'

'I cannot give you what you want,' he said. 'I don't want the same things in life.'

'Only because you're afraid of being let down like you were before,' she said. 'You lost your mother when you were young. That is enough to shatter anyone's sense of security. Then you lost your brother in the most tragic of circumstances, leaving you with a father who was unable to function as a mature adult. Everyone you have ever loved has deserted you one way or the other. Can't you see how that has impacted on how you view all of your relationships?'

He dropped his hands from her shoulders as if she had burned him. 'I do not need you to psychoanalyse me, Emma,' he said tersely. 'I am well aware of my shortcomings. Now stop this nonsense and sit back down and eat your dinner.'

Emma resumed her seat and began to pick at her food, but her stomach churned as she forced each mouthful down. She wondered if this was what people described as lovesickness. The gnawing ache was almost unbearable; it made her feel clammy and faint. Eventually she gave up and, pushing the plate away, got to her feet. 'Will you excuse me?' she asked. 'I think I'll go to bed. I'm not feeling well.'

Rafaele rose from the table with a frown. 'You should have told me earlier,' he said. 'No wonder you have been so tetchy. What can I get you?'

'Nothing,' she said, putting a hand to her damp forehead. 'It's just a little headache. I'll be fine once I've had a rest.'

He came around and placed his arm around her waist, guiding her upstairs with the gentle solicitousness Emma found so very confusing since he maintained he didn't love her. 'I will sleep in one of the other rooms tonight so as not to disturb you,' he said.

'You don't have to do that,' she protested.

He gave her a wry smile. 'I have to leave at an ungodly hour in any case,' he said. 'Now get into bed and I will bring you a glass of water and some paracetamol.'

Emma crawled into the big bed and closed her eyes against the swirling nausea as she waited for him to return...

Rafaele came back into the bedroom to find Emma fast asleep, her face still far too pale, the bruise-like shadows beneath her closed eyes making his gut suddenly clench. He sat on the edge of the bed and, pushing the silky hair off her face, gently stroked her smooth brow. She made a child-like murmur and nestled against his hand, the movement so trusting he felt another blade of guilt slice through him. He should never have allowed things to go this far. She was young and inexperienced, of course she fancied herself in love with him. It wouldn't last, he was sure of it. And then where would he be? He wasn't used to feeling so vulnerable in a relationship. Every time he made love to her it was a totally new experience, his pleasure reaching heights it never had before. Seeing her blossom with sensuality was captivating, she was such a generous lover, shy but adventurous, her passion a perfect match for his.

But how could he give her what she wanted? She had no idea of how things had been set up. If she were to find out about the codicil to his father's will she would no longer be talking about loving him. She would hate him and how could he blame her?

He bent down and pressed a soft kiss to Emma's temple and she blinked sleepily and looked up at him. 'Rafaele?'

He brushed his thumb over her slightly parted lips. *'Qual e´ il mio piccolo?'* he asked.

She placed her hand over his and held it to her cheek. 'I'm going to miss you,' she said.

*'Sto per perdere anche voi,'* he said, and then translated, 'I am going to miss you too.'

The villa was achingly empty once Rafaele left the following morning. Emma heard him leave first thing and felt immediately disconsolate. The days stretched ahead of her interminably. She couldn't imagine how she would survive when their marriage was brought to its inevitable end.

She pulled back the covers and got to her feet but was so quickly assailed by a giant wave of nausea she stumbled to the *en suite* and was promptly sick. She staggered out after the bout of sickness was over, but she still felt so wretched she had to lie down again.

A little thought began to gnaw at her like a tiny mouse nibbling at a crumb, and, although she tried to ignore it, it wouldn't go away.

It couldn't be possible.

It *couldn't* be.

They had used protection.

She was back on the pill.

Her hand crept to her belly, her thoughts still whirling out of control. She couldn't remember the last time she had been physically sick. It didn't seem possible she could have fallen pregnant in such a short space of time.

Panic clutched at her insides with claw-like fingers. How could she tell Rafaele? He had never promised her anything but an affair. She had been the one to profess love, not him.

Emma knew she had to have a test before she worked herself into a state of hysteria. There was no point in worrying about something that might not have even happened. She could easily have picked up a bug of some sort. After all, she had worked tirelessly looking after Valentino Fiorenza; it had drained her more than she had realised, leaving her run-down and vulnerable.

She got dressed and walked down to the town centre to the nearest pharmacy and in her rather fractured Italian managed to relay to the assistant what she wanted. She felt every eye on her as she took her purchase and left, wondering if she had been wise to buy the test locally, given everyone knew she was Rafaele Fiorenza's new wife.

The test was positive.

Emma stared at it for several heart-chugging seconds, her pulse so heavy she felt every beat of it in her fingertips as they clutched at the basin in the *en suite*.

The phone started to ring in the bedroom and she left the test on the counter to answer it. *'Buongiorno, Villa Fiorenza.'*

'*Buongiorno*, Emma,' Rafaele said with a smile in his voice. 'I see you are practising your Italian.'

She ran her tongue over the dust-like dryness of her lips. 'How is your business trip?'

'It is the usual run of boring meetings,' he said. 'How are things with you?'

'Um…things are fine…' she said, trying to inject some life in her tone.

'You sound distracted, Emma.'

'I-I'm not.'

He gave a soft chuckle of laughter. 'Are you missing me, *tesore mio*?'

'Are you missing me?' Emma asked in return.

'What do you think?' he asked.

She felt the velvet drape of his voice all over her skin and suppressed a little shiver. 'I think you have probably found some way to distract yourself,' she said. 'I can't imagine you pining away in your hotel room all on your own.'

There was a small silence.

Emma heard the thud thud of her heartbeats and felt another wave of nausea wash over her. She swallowed thickly and clasped the phone a little tighter to keep control.

'You have no need to be jealous, Emma,' he said. 'I have told you before, I am not interested in anyone but you.'

'For the moment,' she said in an embittered tone.

He gave an impatient sigh. 'I have not got time for this. I have another meeting in a few minutes.'

'In the bedroom or the boardroom?' she asked.

This time the ensuing silence had a menacing quality to it.

'If you want me to find someone else to make the accusations you toss at me true, then that can easily be arranged,' he said. 'Is that what you want?'

What Emma really wanted was for him to love her the way

she loved him, but she knew it was pointless telling him. 'No…no, of course that's not what I want…' she said in a broken whisper.

'I want you, Emma,' he said in a tender tone. 'I wish you were here with me now.'

'I wish I was there too,' she said, caving into his charm. 'I miss you.' *And I am carrying your baby*, she wished she could add if circumstances were different.

'I will be back as soon as I can,' he said. 'Take care of yourself while I am away.'

'I will…'

There was another little pause.

'Emma?'

'Yes?'

'Nothing,' he said after a moment. 'It can wait. I will talk to you when I get back.'

Emma hung up the phone once he'd ended the call and went back to the *en suite*, and, picking up the pregnancy test, looked at it again to make sure she hadn't been imagining it. The truth stared back at her, making her heart pump with dread all over again…

# CHAPTER TWELVE

EMMA was in the pool enjoying the peace of the evening when Rafaele returned. She hadn't heard his car on the gravel driveway and felt at a disadvantage when he came out to the deck and found her dripping wet as she hastily tried to wrap a towel around herself.

His hands stilled her clumsy movements and the towel slipped to deck at her feet. 'You don't have to be shy with me, Emma,' he said. 'I like seeing your body. It is beautiful.'

Emma felt suddenly exposed. Could he see how her breasts were slightly bigger? she wondered. Her cheeks grew hot under his lazy scrutiny and one of her hands crept to the flat plane of her belly, just to reassure herself there was no sign of the tiny life growing there.

He bent his head and kissed her soundly on the mouth. 'You know something, Emma?' he said, looking down at her with that sooty gaze of his. 'Right now all I want to do is kiss you and take you to bed. I have missed you more than I realised.'

Emma could feel herself weakening and nestled closer, her arms going about his neck to bring his mouth down to her. 'I missed you too...so much.'

His mouth connected with hers in a prolonged kiss of passion, his tongue thrusting against hers in a sexy motion that sent her senses spinning out of control. His hands cupped her breasts, moulding and shaping them possessively until she was boneless in his arms. She felt his erection pressing against her, its rock-hard presence a heady reminder of all the pleasure he had shown her before.

He lifted his mouth off hers to kiss her neck before going lower to where her breasts ached for his attention. He undid her bikini top and suckled on her tantalisingly, her nipples pushing against his tongue in their eagerness. She whimpered as he turned his attention to her other breast, his hot mouth like a brand on her quivering flesh.

He placed his hands on her hips, bringing her against him as his mouth returned to hers with renewed vigour.

Emma rubbed up against him feverishly, her body clamouring for his possession. Every nerve ending was screaming out for release, her body so ready for him she felt the humidity of her need between her thighs.

As if he sensed her growing urgency he helped her out of her bikini bottoms, his fingers searching for her slick warmth with devastating accuracy. She squirmed as he touched the tight pearl of need, the sensations rocketing through her.

Just when she thought she could stand it no more he suddenly turned her around. Emma's breath locked in her throat as she heard his zipper come down. She whimpered in excitement as he parted her legs for his entry, the anticipation of that first deep thrust almost sending her over the edge then and there.

He surged forward, a deep groan of pleasure bursting from his mouth as her tight muscles clenched around him. 'God, I have been dreaming of this the whole time I was away,' he said, grasping her by the waist to keep her in place.

Emma was beyond speech. Each rocking thrust was bringing her closer to the ecstasy she longed for, his guttural, almost primal sounds of pleasure like music to her ears. She felt him search for her again, those long, clever fingers intensifying the sensations until she was panting breathlessly as the first waves of release began to wash over her. She shuddered convulsively, the hard, repeated thrusts pitching her headlong into an orgasm so intense it was like fireworks going off in her head.

He kept pumping; his strong thighs braced either side of hers, his fingers digging into her waist as the pressure inexorably built. Emma shivered as she felt him get closer; she loved that moment when he finally lost control. It was the only time he ever allowed himself to be vulnerable; it made her feel as if she was the only woman in the world who could do that to him.

With one last groan he was there, the breath going out of him as his essence spilled into her tight warmth, his chest rising and falling against her back as he held her in the aftermath.

Emma breathed in the musky scent of him, the sensation of his fluid between her thighs intensely erotic.

His hands moved from her waist to cup her breasts, his body still joined to hers. 'I should have used a condom,' he said, 'but I couldn't wait. That is how much you affect me.'

Emma could feel herself tensing and forced herself to relax. 'I'm sure it will be OK…'

He began to nuzzle beneath her left ear. 'You smell so nice,' he said. 'Like orange blossom with just a hint of chlorine.'

She gave a little shiver as his tongue circled the shell of her ear. 'Maybe we should go upstairs,' she said somewhat breathlessly. 'I wouldn't want Lucia to see us like this.'

'She has gone home for the day,' Rafaele said as he pressed his mouth to the nape of her neck. 'She was leaving as I came in.'

Emma tilted her head sideways, her skin breaking out in

goose-bumps as his lips and tongue moved over her. She felt his body thickening again and her belly began to quiver in reaction.

'Can you feel what you are doing to me, Emma?' he asked against her neck.

She began to writhe as he moved against her. 'Yes…'

'I can never seem to get enough of you,' he said, rocking back and forth, slowly at first, his body growing harder with each movement.

Emma started to gasp as his speed picked up. Her legs were trembling as his hands went to her hips, her inner core so alive with nerve endings every surging movement of his body within hers made her quake in delight.

'Do you like it like this, Emma?' he asked as his thumbs rolled over her tight nipples.

'Yes,' she said, sucking in a breath as he thrust deeper. 'Oh, yes…'

'You like how I make you feel, don't you, *cara*?' he asked.

Emma whimpered again as he drove harder. 'You know I do…'

His hands went back to her hips, his fingers splayed possessively. 'Your body fits mine perfectly,' he said. 'I like the feel of you skin on skin. Yours reminds me of silk, so soft and smooth under my fingertips.'

Emma shuddered as his fingers found her feminine cleft, the coaxing motion against her sensitised flesh making her breathless with excitement. She couldn't hold back her response, it hit her in a series of pounding waves, tossing her about like a bit of flotsam, her body so spent she felt limbless.

She felt him shudder his way through his release, the sheer force of it reverberating through her body where it was pressed against his.

After a long quiet moment he moved back and gently turned her in his arms. 'Why don't you go upstairs and have a shower while I make a couple of calls?' he said. 'I will not be long.'

Emma felt her doubts returning and wondered who he intended calling at this time of night. 'I can wait with you while you make the calls,' she offered.

His expression became mask-like, but not before she saw that camera shutter flicker in his eyes. 'No, Emma,' he said, re-zipping his trousers. 'I have some private matters to discuss with a client. It would not be appropriate for me to conduct such a conversation within the hearing of someone else.'

'This is how it's always going to be, isn't it, Rafaele?' she asked bitterly. 'You're content to make love to me, but not to share any other aspect of your life.'

His mouth tightened. 'Watch it, Emma,' he said. 'You are starting to bore me with this jealous wife routine.'

'Why don't you send me away, then, Rafaele?' she said. 'Why not dismiss me from your life like all your other mistresses?'

He stood looking down at her with a nerve ticking at the corner of his mouth. 'I do not need this right now. I have only just walked in the door; I do not want to be drawn into a point-less argument with you.'

She gave him a churlish look. 'You won't give me anything but your body. It's not enough, Rafaele. I want more.'

He let out an impatient sound. 'I am going to the study,' he said. 'I will see you in the morning.'

'So you've finished with me for this evening, have you?' she sniped at him. 'You've slaked your lust and now I'm to go away like a good little whore until you need me to service you again.'

A hard look came into his eyes. 'I have not treated you as a whore and you damn well know it.'

She turned away in distress. 'Sometimes I wish I still hated you. It would be so much easier than this…'

Emma felt him come up behind her, his hands coming to rest on her shoulders. 'I do not want you to hate me, Emma,' he said gently. 'That is not what I want at all.'

She turned back to face him. 'But you don't want me to love you either, do you?'

The pads of his thumbs moved in a slow caress of her cheeks as he cupped her face in his hands. 'Love is something I am not so sure of,' he said. 'People say they love each other all the time and the next day they are at each other's throats. How can anyone know if what they feel is genuine?'

Emma looked into his dark eyes. 'I can't speak for other people, but I know what I mean when I say I love you.'

His eyes searched hers for a long moment before he released her. 'Go to bed, *cara*,' he said softly. 'I will be up shortly.'

Emma turned over in bed early the following morning to find Rafaele propped up on one elbow looking at her. She shoved her tussled hair out of her eyes and gave him a coy smile as she thought of the tumultuous passion they had shared the night before when he had finally come up to bed. She trailed her fingers from his sternum towards his groin as she had done only hours ago.

He captured her hand and held it against his chest. 'There is something we need to discuss,' he said in a tone deep with gravitas.

Emma felt her stomach lurch. She looked at him uncertainly, her heart thumping so hard she was sure he would feel the blood pounding in her fingertips where they were pressed against him. 'Y-yes?' she said in a scratchy whisper.

His dark, inscrutable eyes were steady on hers. 'Why didn't you tell me you are not on the pill?' he asked.

Emma stared at him in silence for several heart-chugging seconds, her mouth growing dry.

'Why, Emma?' he asked, his expression darkening with what looked suspiciously like anger. 'You have had numerous opportunities to tell me, but you have not done so.'

Emma swallowed unevenly. 'I...how do you know I'm not on it?'

This time the anger was unmistakable. She could see a jackhammer-like pulse beating at the corner of his white-tipped mouth. 'Because I looked, that is why,' he said.

She rolled her lips together for a moment. 'Looked where?' she asked.

'In your toiletries bag in the bathroom,' he answered. 'There was no sign of any contraceptives in that or your handbag and I would like to know why.'

Emma pulled out of his hold and got off the bed to glare down at him. 'I would like to know why you think you have the right to search through my belongings without my permission.'

His mouth tightened even further as he stood up and faced her squarely. 'You gave me the right when you agreed to be my lover,' he said. 'Now answer me, damn you. Why didn't you tell me?'

'It's none of your business, that's why,' Emma said, stung at the brutish manner of his inquisition. This wasn't going anything like she had planned, she thought in despair. She had wanted to prepare him, to wait until she felt secure enough to deliver her bombshell, but somehow he had pre-empted her.

His eyes narrowed into dark slits. 'You are trying to trap me, aren't you, Emma?'

Emma felt frighteningly close to tears. 'No, that's not true. We've always used condoms and I know this isn't for ever so I just thought—'

'You just thought what?' he barked at her savagely.

She flinched and shrank back against the wall. 'I-I thought it would be all right…'

'When was your last period?'

She turned away, nausea rising like a tide inside her.

He let out a vicious expletive and strode around the bed to grasp her by the upper arms, his fingers biting into her flesh almost cruelly. 'Think, damn it! When was it?'

Tears stung at the backs of her eyes. 'Stop,' she choked. 'You're hurting me.'

His grip loosened a fraction, but his expression was still livid. 'You have done this deliberately, haven't you? For all I know you could already be pregnant.'

Emma swallowed convulsively and averted her gaze from the searing blaze of his, her heart hammering, her skin beading with nervous perspiration.

The silence was suddenly so intense it rang like clanging bells inside her head.

Rafaele bit out a rough expletive and brought her face back in line with his gaze. 'You are, aren't you?' he said, and after a tight pause added hoarsely, '*Mio Dio*…you already are.'

She ran her tongue over her lips. 'I don't know how it happened,' she said. 'We used a condom every single time…you know we did, apart from yesterday by the pool.'

'And apart from the first time,' he reminded her coolly.

She looked at him in confusion. 'But you didn't…you know…come inside me that time.'

'There are literally thousands of sperm in pre-ejaculatory fluid,' he said. 'It only takes one to do the job.'

Emma bit her lip until she tasted blood. 'I'm sorry…'

He stepped away from her. 'I should have known you would try something like this,' he ground out. 'How long have you known?'

She swallowed again. 'I did a test a couple of days ago…'

His eyes glittered with fury. 'And you didn't think to tell me?'

'I-I was going to but…but I was frightened you would be angry.'

'Have I not the right to be angry?' he asked as he reached for his clothes.

Emma watched as he dressed, her heart feeling like a cold, hard stone in her chest. 'I'm not getting rid of it,' she suddenly blurted into the stiff silence. 'You can't make me.'

He left his shirt hanging undone as he came over to where she was still standing. 'Do you really think I would demand that of you?' he asked, frowning heavily.

She gave him a pointed look. 'Wouldn't you?'

He blew out a breath and sent his hand through his hair once more. 'I might be a bit of a bastard at times, but surely you don't think I am that big a one.'

'I don't know what to think…' she said. 'I didn't expect this to happen.'

'No?' he asked with a cynical curl of his lip. 'A temporary marriage was not enough for you was it, Emma? You wanted a child thrown in to make things really interesting.'

'How can you think that of me?' she asked in rising despair. 'From day one you set about to seduce me. You assumed I was a slut and made it your business to get me into bed to prove your point. The way I see it my being pregnant is your fault rather than mine.'

His jaw clenched so hard Emma heard his teeth grind together. 'So you wanted to make me pay and pay dearly for misjudging you,' he said through tight lips. 'What better way than to make sure I was tied to you permanently.'

'I wouldn't want my baby to be exposed to someone so incapable of loving it,' she threw back.

His mouth was a thin, flat line of anger. 'You seem to be forgetting something, Emma,' he said in a chilling tone. 'If you are in fact expecting a child it will be mine just as much as yours. I will have just as much say as you in its upbringing, perhaps, given my financial position and legal contacts, even more so.'

Emma felt a quake of alarm rumble through her. She knew he was more than capable of doing what he threatened. The courts were much more accommodating of fathers' rights these days. He wouldn't have much difficulty convincing the authorities he would be a more suitable custodian, especially since the press hadn't done her any favours in how they had reported the Bennett family's aspersions on her character. She would have a mammoth fight on her hands if she took him on in a legal battle, and she already knew who would be the loser…

'This is not the way my life is supposed to be,' she said, trying not to cry. 'The only man I've ever slept with is you and now…' her chin gave a little wobble and her eyes sprouted tears '…and now I wish to God I hadn't.'

He placed his hands on her shoulders before she could spin away. 'I am sorry, Emma,' he said in a gruff tone. 'I am being an unfeeling bastard as usual.'

Emma gave a little sniff and burrowed closer, her cheek pressed flat against the thudding of his heart, her arms going around his bare waist beneath his open shirt. She felt his breath disturb the top of her head and felt his chest rise and fall in a sigh. One of his hands began stroking the back of her head, the movement so tender she wondered all over again if somewhere deep inside, in spite of all his denials, he felt a smidgeon of affection for her.

'I am not doing a great job of this, am I?' he asked in self-deprecation. 'All I seem to do is make you cry.'

She lifted her face off his chest to look up at him. 'It's all right,' she said. 'I know this is difficult for you.'

Rafaele brushed her hair back off her forehead. It was going to be much more difficult for her, he reflected, frowning as he thought of the implications for her. She was thousands of kilometres away from her only family, her sister and her niece; married to a man she had met a little less than two months ago, a man who had treated her like trash and yet she claimed to love him.

Did he deserve such a woman?

Would the curse he had had on others' lives impact on hers? Hadn't it already?

'This changes everything,' he said, surprised his voice came out at all, let alone sounding so in command. The truth was he wasn't in command. He had tried to keep his life simple, no ties, no false promises, no guarantees…no love…

Rafaele realised with a lightning-like jolt that he wanted to be loved, but, more than that, he wanted it to last. He had spent so many years avoiding being disappointed, long, lonely years locking his heart away in case someone let him down while he wasn't on guard. Emma had somehow pierced that firewall and caused utter mayhem with his rigidly controlled emotions. She had turned his neatly ordered world upside down. He would never be the same again now she had come into his life. If she walked away now it would destroy him. His gut clenched at the thought of revealing his vulnerability to her. Would she use it to exploit him? How could he be sure?

'What do you mean this changes everything?' she asked, looking at him with a worried pleat of her brow.

'Our marriage will not be temporary,' he told her.

Emma's eyes went wide. 'N-not temporary?'

'We have a child on the way,' he said. 'We will continue our relationship in order to raise him or her the way neither of us was raised—with love and solid commitment from both its parents. It is important that our marriage from hence forth be as normal as possible.'

'This is hardly what anyone would call a normal marriage.' Emma felt the need to remind him.

He pulled her closer towards him. 'I do not know about that,' he said, resting one hand on the small of her back. 'It feels rather normal to me. You are wearing my ring, you have taken my name and you have my child in your womb.'

'But you don't love me.' She addressed the words to his chest, her heart contracting with pain.

He tipped up her face, his eyes holding hers. 'That is everything to you, isn't it? You want the words, but aren't the actions far more important?'

Emma felt her breath come to a halt in her chest. 'W-what are you saying?'

His mouth twisted ruefully as he brushed another tendril of hair off her face. 'To tell you the truth, I am not sure,' he said. 'All I know is I have never felt like this before with any other woman.'

Emma blinked back tears. She knew a pregnancy wasn't an ideal reason for staying in a loveless marriage; children put a strain on even the strongest relationships, but she knew Rafaele would not do anything to compromise his child's welfare, certainly not after what he had experienced in his own childhood. She had every confidence he would fall in love with his son or daughter on sight, hoping against hope that perhaps in time he might come to feel something deeper for her than sexual desire.

'I will try to be a good wife for you,' she said. 'I know this isn't what you wanted, but I will do my best to support you and our child.'

'Do you think it will be a boy or a girl?' he asked.

'I don't know and it's too early to tell, but would you like to know before the birth?'

'What would you prefer?'

'I think I'd like to be surprised,' she said. 'But if you want to know beforehand I won't stop you.'

He gathered her close. 'I have to go to Milan today to sort out some legal business.'

Emma looked at him hopefully. 'Can I come with you?'

He held her gaze for an infinitesimal moment. 'Not this time, *mio piccolo*. I have to leave now.'

'But I would like to come with you,' she said. 'I could do some shopping or something while you see to your business.'

'No, Emma.' This time his tone was implacable. 'I want you to take care of yourself. You are carrying my child, don't forget. I would not like anything to compromise his or her well-being. That is after all why we are staying together, is it not?'

Emma felt his words like a stinging slap across the face. 'Oh, yes,' she said with a querulous look. 'How could I forget?'

He reached for his bathrobe and tied the ends together. 'I am not going to be goaded into a fight. I realise this is a rocky time for you during early pregnancy. Your hormones and your emotions are all over the place.'

'My emotions are all over the place because I don't know where I stand with you,' she threw back tearfully.

He drew in an impatient breath. 'All right,' he said, raking his hand through his hair. 'I love you. Does that make you feel better?'

'You d-don't mean it,' Emma said and started to cry. 'Y-you're only saying it to placate me.'

He muttered a curse and came over to her, hauling her into his arms and holding her close. 'I mean it, Emma,' he said gruffly. 'I love you. I am not used to revealing my feelings. I have never allowed it to happen before. But I do love you.'

Emma desperately wanted to believe him, but how could

she be sure? He now had what he had wanted: the villa was in his hands. Even if they divorced he would still maintain possession of the bulk of his father's estate.

He dropped a kiss on the top of her head. 'Go back to bed, *cara*,' he said gently. 'I will bring you some tea and toast before I leave.'

Emma crawled back into bed, annoyed with herself for pushing him. She had been so desperate for a confession of love, but now she had it she felt let down and empty. Was it always going to be this way between them, her pushing and him pulling away?

# CHAPTER THIRTEEN

WHEN Emma woke a couple of hours later Rafaele had left, but she was touched to see a plate of toast and a cup of tea sitting on the bedside table next to her. Even though it was lukewarm she sipped at the tea and nibbled on the toast until her stomach began to settle.

After her shower she went down to the town centre to make an appointment at the medical clinic for a pregnancy check-up. The female doctor was heavily booked but the receptionist was able to squeeze Emma in for the following day.

Emma was coming out of the clinic with her appointment card in her hand when she saw a woman coming towards her rather purposefully.

'Signora Fiorenza,' the woman said, coming to stand in front of Emma, more or less blocking her escape. 'Do you have a moment?'

'Y-yes?' Emma said, hoping the woman wasn't a journalist. 'How can I help you?'

'We have not met, but I am sure you have heard of me,' the woman said. 'My name is Sondra Henning.'

Emma felt a flicker of alarm like an electric current run up her spine. She didn't like the ice-cold blue of the woman's eyes, nor did she care for the thin-lipped smile.

'Yes…I have heard of you,' she said and offered her hand. 'How do you do?'

Sondra's hand was like a cold fish against hers. 'It's all worked out rather nicely for Rafaele, hasn't it?' she said. 'He couldn't have asked for a more biddable wife.'

Emma frowned. 'I'm not sure what you mean…'

Sondra's smile didn't reach her eyes. 'You agreed to the terms of his father's will, in good faith, I imagine, but then perhaps he hasn't told you about the codicil to Valentino's will.'

Emma felt her stomach tilt sideways. 'W-what codicil?'

Sondra's cat-like gaze ran over Emma insolently. 'Valentino knew Rafaele was a playboy with no intention of ever settling down so at the last minute he added a codicil to his will. It stated that on the event of his marriage to you he would become the principal shareholder of Valentino's investment company. It is worth several million, a nice little inducement to matrimony, don't you think?'

Emma swallowed against a thick tide of rising nausea. 'I don't believe you,' she said. 'I was never informed of any codicil by the lawyer who handled the will.'

Sondra's lip curled. 'That is because Valentino insisted you were not to see it,' she said. 'He wanted nature to take its course, so to speak. He knew you would fall in love with Rafaele, most women do, but what he was not so sure of was whether Rafaele would fall in love with you.'

'He has fallen in love with me,' Emma said. 'He told me so this morning.'

Sondra gave her a pitying look. 'Oh, dear,' she drawled. 'You have got it bad, haven't you, my dear? Of course he would say he loved you. And perhaps he does in a way. After all, you have made him a very rich man.'

'He doesn't need any more wealth,' Emma said in a desperate attempt to defend Rafaele. 'I don't believe he would have acted so callously. I don't believe it.'

'You can always call the lawyer and find out for yourself,' Sondra said. 'Now that you have been married to Rafaele for a couple of months there would be no reason to keep it under wraps.'

'How do you know so much about all this?' Emma asked. 'You haven't been intimately involved with Valentino Fiorenza for years and as far as I recall you never once visited him while I was taking care of him.'

'Ah, but I did visit him and regularly,' Sondra said with a smugness Emma found offensive. 'And as to being involved with him…' She gave another conceited look. 'There are different levels of involvement. It was in my interests to keep Valentino as a trusted friend and confidante. After all, we had a history, one I wasn't keen on him disregarding when it came to the issue of his will.'

Emma felt the cold hand of contempt clutch at her insides at the avaricious tone of the other woman's voice. 'But I don't recall you ever coming to the palazzo in Milan, and Lucia has never once mentioned you coming to see him at the villa here.'

Sondra gave Emma a cold-hearted sneer. 'That old crone is too old to be looking after a place the size of The Villa Fiorenza,' she said. 'She doesn't see the dust on the chandeliers let alone who walks in and out of the back entrance. And as for the palazzo in Milan, that was all too easy. I phoned Valentino whenever you were out on an errand. I had an agreement with Rosa the housemaid there.'

Emma's insides tightened even further. 'An…an agreement?'

Sondra's smile was all the more sneering. 'Rosa always let

me know when you were going out so I could talk to Valentino in privacy on the telephone.'

Emma was still frowning so hard she felt an ache between her eyes. 'If you were so close to Valentino why didn't he ever mention to me you had phoned or visited him?'

'I asked him not to, that's why. I told him I was dating a very jealous man who wouldn't understand my continued affection for an ex-lover. Fortunately for me, Valentino agreed to our little secret. I think it fed his ego that I had never stopped caring about him. In any case, he knew what the paparazzi were like given what they had reported about his supposed involvement with you. As I was one of the few friends he had he didn't want to cause trouble for me.'

'Is that why you didn't come to his funeral?' Emma asked. 'Because of what your new lover might think?'

Sondra inspected her talon-like nails, her gaze averted, Emma suspected deliberately. 'I wanted to remember Valentino as he was the last time I saw him,' Sondra said, but her tone lacked sincerity.

'When *was* the last time you saw him?' Emma asked.

Sondra returned her cold gaze to Emma's. 'It was a couple of weeks before he died,' she said. 'I had to wait until you left the villa to get more medication or whatever errand you were running. Lucia was out talking to one of the gardeners so I let myself in. It was then Valentino told me what he had decided to do.'

Emma frowned again. 'You mean about the will?'

'No,' Sondra said with a glint in her cold eyes, 'about his relationship with Rafaele.'

Something about the woman's cat-with-the-canary smile bothered Emma. 'What do you mean?'

'Valentino told me he had just written a long letter to his son,' Sondra said. 'In it he had begged for Rafaele's forgiveness for how he had treated him over his mother's and then his brother's death. It seems you had worked some sort of miracle on Valentino's hardened soul, Emma. He said as much himself. He decided he wanted to put things right before he died. He knew he didn't have long to go.'

'I don't remember him asking me to post a letter to his son,' Emma said. 'And I'm sure if he had got Lucia to do it she would have told me about it.'

'That is because he didn't ask you or Lucia to post it,' Sondra said with a malicious glint in her eyes.

Emma felt her heart begin to slam against her sternum. 'Who...who did he ask to post it?' she said, her voice coming out slightly strangled.

'Oh, Emma.' Sondra gave a cackling laugh. 'Valentino was right. You *are* as innocent as a dove.'

Emma's skin began to prickle all over. 'You took the letter...' she said hollowly. 'You took the letter but...but you didn't post it...'

Sondra's expression turned bitter. 'Of course I didn't post it. Valentino Fiorenza broke my heart. He refused to marry me. He wanted a mistress, not a wife. No one was ever going to replace his beloved Gabriela. Do you know what that was like for me? I was competing with a dead woman and there was no way I could win.'

'So you waited all this time to get back at him in the most despicable way,' Emma said, her stomach churning with disgust. 'You pretended to still care about him in those last months of his life just so you could have your revenge.'

'Revenge, as they say, is a dish best served cold,' Sondra said with a disaffected smile. 'And you can't get any colder than a dead man in his grave, now, can you?'

Emma swallowed back a mouthful of bile. 'When did you find out about the codicil?'

'That was only recently,' Sondra said. 'I have a friend who works in the legal firm handling Valentino's affairs.'

'That's a breach of client confidence,' Emma pointed out. 'Your friend could be criminally charged.'

Sondra gave another careless shrug. 'That is of no concern to me.'

Emma set her mouth. 'What exactly is your concern?' she asked.

'I am offering you a chance to get back at Rafaele for using you,' she said. 'If you leave him before the year is up I will let you retain your half share of the villa. And if you choose to sell it I will pay you double what he offers for it. I have some money an uncle left me. We could both have our revenge on the Fiorenza men—what do you say?'

'I say no,' Emma said coldly. 'I will have no part in hurting Rafaele even more than he has already been hurt. What you did is unforgivable, not just to Rafaele, but to Valentino. He waited in vain for his son to contact him. It broke his heart, I am sure of it. He went to his grave believing his son hadn't forgiven him. That is no doubt why he never talked about it with me. He felt such a failure as a father. He was so bitterly disappointed. So terribly hurt. How could you do that? How can you live with yourself?'

Sondra opened her handbag and pulled out an envelope with a broken Fiorenza wax seal on the back. 'Give that to that arrogant bastard of a husband of yours,' she said. 'Better late than never, right?'

Emma clutched the envelope with a shaky hand, her heart feeling so heavy she could scarcely breathe, watching in silence as Sondra Henning strode off just as purposefully as she had approached, until she rounded a corner and disappeared.

* * *

Emma was waiting for Rafaele in the salon when he returned from Milan. He came in carrying a bunch of blood-red roses and handed them to her with a wry smile. 'For you, *mio piccolo*,' he said. 'For being so patient with me.'

Emma took the roses and put them to one side. 'Rafaele…I need to talk to you,' she said, 'about the codicil on your father's will.'

Had his expression become shuttered or was she imagining it? Emma wondered as she searched his face.

'How did you find out about that?' he asked after a small but tense pause.

'I ran into Sondra Henning this morning in town,' she told him. 'She came over and introduced herself. She said you had agreed to marry me, not just because of the villa, but because you stood to gain millions from your father's company. Is that true?'

Rafaele let out his breath in a long uneven stream. 'I knew once you found out about that wretched codicil you would think that,' he said. 'That is why I went to Milan this morning. I met with the lawyers and set up a trust in your name. You are now the principal shareholder of my father's company until such time as our child is able to take control.'

Emma's mouth dropped open. 'I don't believe it…'

He gave her a crooked smile. 'Why is it you do not believe a word I say, *mio piccolo*?' he asked. 'I finally summon up the courage to tell you I love you and you think I am fibbing. How on earth am I going to convince you it is true?'

She blinked back tears of happiness. 'You really mean it, don't you?' she asked. 'You really love me.'

He blocked the pathway of her tears with the pad of his thumb. 'I love you so much it hurts,' he said in a husky tone. 'I did not think I had the capacity to love so deeply. For years

I had shut myself off from feeling. But you, *cara*, with your big heart and caring ways, changed all that.'

'Oh, Rafaele…' Emma said. 'There's something else Sondra Henning told me…'

He went very still as if he sensed what was coming. Emma took a breath and in a gentle voice told him about the letter his father had written to him and how the wicked spitefulness of Sondra Henning had ruined any chance of Valentino making peace with his son. When she had finished, Emma handed him the letter with tears in her eyes.

'Have you read it?' Rafaele asked.

She shook her head. 'No, that letter was meant for you, no one else.'

He gave her a smile that was shaded by sadness. 'Would you excuse me for a moment or two?' he asked.

'Of course,' she said softly. 'Please…take your time.'

He went over by the bank of windows and opened the unsealed envelope, his eyes travelling down each page until he came to the end.

It seemed a long time before he looked back at Emma and when he did she could see the film of moisture in his eyes, making her own tears run all the more profusely.

Rafaele came back to stand in front of her. 'I do not know how to thank you, Emma, for what you have done,' he said.

She creased her brow at him. 'What have *I* done?'

He touched her face with his fingertips. 'You are an angel, do you know that? An angel sent down to this planet to make stubborn people like my father and I change our ways. If it had not been for you I would still hate my father. I would still be blaming him for all that was wrong in my life.'

Her eyes were glistening with tears. 'You don't hate him any more?'

He shook his head. 'Even if I had not seen this letter I had already decided to forgive him,' he said. 'You were so right when you said he was consumed by grief. He loved my mother so much he couldn't cope with the shock of her loss. There was no grief counselling in those days, he soldiered on in the only way he knew how, which was to bury himself in bitterness and denial.

'And then he was hit with the blow of Giovanni's accidental death. He blamed himself; he says so in the letter. He felt guilty that he hadn't been an involved father, leaving us for long periods on our own while he worked too hard and too long. His affair with Sondra Henning was his attempt to find a replacement mother for me after Giovanni's death, but of course it backfired. She wasn't interested in mothering some other woman's child. She wanted him to herself, but he would never agree to it. That proves more than anything how much he cared for me.'

'Oh, darling,' Emma said, tearing up again. 'You have been through so much.'

'He loved me, Emma,' Rafaele said, still trying to get his head around the fact. 'He loved me but just didn't know how to communicate it.'

Emma lifted her hand to his face and gently stroked the stubbly growth on his cheek. 'Now who does that remind you of?'

He smiled and pulled her close. 'Now, about that honeymoon we never had. Where would you like to go? I have cleared my diary so I am all yours for as long as you want.'

Emma looked up at him with love shining in her eyes. 'How long does a normal honeymoon last?' she asked with a playful smile.

He gave her a sexy grin in return. 'I do not really know,

but I can tell you one thing for sure,' he said, and paused as he planted a kiss on the end of her nose.

'What's that?' she asked, wrinkling her nose in delight.

He scooped her up in his arms and carried her towards the stairs, his dark eyes smouldering with passion. 'This one is going to last for ever.'

# BOUGHT: FOR HIS CONVENIENCE OR PLEASURE?

BY
MAGGIE COX

The day **Maggie Cox** saw the film version of *Wuthering Heights*, with a beautiful Merle Oberon and a very handsome Laurence Olivier, was the day she became hooked on romance. From that day onwards she spent a lot of time dreaming up her own romances, secretly hoping that one day she might become published and get paid for doing what she loved most! Now that her dream is being realised, she wakes up every morning and counts her blessings. She is married to a gorgeous man, and is the mother of two wonderful sons. Her two other great passions in life—besides her family and reading/writing—are music and films.

# CHAPTER ONE

'DO YOU remember what happened, Elizabeth?'

His voice sounded as if it came from a long distance away—like a voice in a dream. Drifting in and out of consciousness, Ellie didn't try particularly hard to stay focused. Somehow the sensation of cotton wool nothingness that had been cocooning her seemed far more appealing right at that moment than anything else. There was a great desire to sink back into its warmth and protection as quickly as possible, and avoid experiencing the all too unsettling wave of discomfort and fear that kept flowing through her like rivulets of ice every time she became conscious.

Something bad had happened. Why was this man forcing her to try and remember it? For a scant moment her eyes fixed on his hard, chiselled face, but she quickly closed them again because studying the unforgiving rigid lines of jaw, mouth and cheekbone that confronted her made her feel bad somehow...as if she'd done something wrong...something *really* wrong. *If only she could remember what it was.*

Yet maybe it was best that she didn't remember. Thankfully, the cottonwool fuzziness returned just in time. No more trying to recall things that might cause pain and distress. She was in hospital. That much she *did* know. That was quite enough knowledge of her predicament to be going on with...

He cut a sombre, rather intimidating figure in his black suit, and she wondered vaguely if he might be in mourning for someone. Why was he there almost every time she opened her eyes? What was he waiting for?

The tantalising threads of some kind of personal connection hovered frustratingly close, but right then the final link was beyond her. However, the sickening feeling persisted that *she* had been the cause or at least the catalyst for something dreadful. Deliberately veering her thoughts away from trying to imagine what, she focused on the plain, uninspiring room, with its nondescript oatmeal-coloured walls and the hospital scent that permeated everything around her. She sensed a heaviness in the lower part of her body. Glancing down, she realised for the first time that both her legs were in plaster. Making a little sound of distress, she turned her cheek into the pillow and again shut her eyes...

One day not long afterwards Ellie woke up to a face she *did* remember...and it belonged to her father.

'Don't worry, my girl.' He patted her hand as though she were a small, defenceless child. 'Your old man knows what to do. I'm going to take you away from all this just as soon as I can. Tommy Barnes knows a thing or two about how to blend into the background and disappear. I haven't spent the last twenty years doing what I do without learning a few tricks!'

'Make-up's ready for you now, Dr Lyons. Just follow Susie, will you? She'll take care of you.'

Ellie really couldn't attest to enjoying being a guest on these anodyne afternoon television programmes. Neither had she particularly taken to the label the London media had dubbed her with ever since she'd helped the drug-addicted son of a high profile politician who had been living on the streets. 'The pony-tailed psychologist'. It made her feel about fifteen, and Ellie abhorred the idea of ever being that young and inexperienced again. Some things in life *did* get better with age, she'd found. The path that had led her to where she was now had been strewn with quite a few large rocks, but even so she had managed to survive the journey and make a good life for herself.

And the most surprising thing of all was that her dad had helped—in his own muddled, haphazard, seat-of-the-pants way. He'd come up trumps for Ellie after her accident five years ago, and moving from London to Scotland had been one of the best moves of her life. It had definitely given her added impetus to complete her studies in psychology and qualify for the work she'd longed to do.

About a year ago an opportunity had come for her

to return to London and work in the East End at a
project that was particularly dear to her heart—the
plight of young people sleeping rough on the streets.
Knowing something about feeling abandoned and
alone, she knew a great urge to help as many of these
kids as she could. But for this week at least she was
located south of the river—staying at a charming little
bijou hotel in Chelsea, not far from the Kings Road,
funded by the cable TV company that had hired her to
do a week-long special on the troubled teenage offspring of some B-list celebrities.

*She could have done without this particular obliga-
tion.* The small counselling practice she had set up in
Hackney was growing, and what with her commitments
at the centre for the homeless she needed to be back
where she could do the most good—doing the 'real'
work she'd studied so hard for. But the money for this
particular stint was too good to turn down. The profile
she'd unwittingly earned was at least helping Ellie to
plough some money back into the centre, and she would
continue to do whatever she could to help increase the
meagre funding the project struggled to get by on.

Back at the hotel, after Ellie had done the show, she
was waylaid by the young receptionist, with her perfect
plum-coloured crop and smoothly ironed uniform, as
she stepped through the revolving door into the foyer.

'There's someone waiting to see you, Dr Lyons. I've
shown him into one of the meeting rooms along the
corridor, so that you can have a little privacy. Room
number one.'

Immediately wary, Ellie frowned. She couldn't be too careful in her line of work, she'd found. Because of its nature, people sometimes got angry, and occasionally even tried to seek her out to give her a piece of their mind. It was the last thing she felt like doing—placating some irate viewer, or a relative of someone she'd tried to help or advise.

'Who is he?' Ellie enquired. 'Did he leave a name?'

She tried to stifle a yawn as the young receptionist swept her with a curious, interested glance. Unspoken was her realisation that this was someone seriously impressive—and what had he to do with someone like Ellie?

'Mr Nikolai Golitsyn,' she announced, with some authority.

'Are you sure?'

Ellie's legs had turned into a river, sucking all her strength down, deep down, into its surging, heaving depths. Her head started to swim and for a moment her gaze went out of focus. *Nikolai Golitsyn…* It was a name that haunted her dreams and belonged to a man who had caused her more tumult than even her wayward father had done. Although she dreaded seeing him again, underneath that dread was a longing that had not lessened in its emotional intensity over the passage of time.

'I'm perfectly sure, Dr Lyons!' The receptionist took umbrage at the mere suggestion she might have got her facts wrong.

No longer tired, but acutely awake and alert as if she dangled off a cliff edge with bloody fingernails and a thousand feet drop below her onto treacherous sharp rocks, Ellie chewed down anxiously on her lip. *How had he found her after all this time?* Her father had covered their tracks so carefully—even suggesting she take up her mother's maiden name and shorten Elizabeth to 'Ellie'. But her reluctant recent high profile had presented the very real possibility that her previous employer *would* at last discover her whereabouts, and from time to time she had nervously contemplated that.

Touching the tips of her fingers to her neatly tied back wheat-blonde hair, Ellie wasn't surprised to feel them tremble. The sheer dread that surged through her blood made her feel dangerously weak for a second.

'Thank you,' she murmured to the girl behind the desk.

'You're welcome!'

All offence at Ellie's possible doubt in her competence banished—the girl's answering smile was as bright as a May full moon. *It was the smile of someone who'd been raised within the warmth and comfort of loving family, with friends around her to cushion life's blows. Someone who had yet to learn that life could be hard.*

Unable to prevent the wave of envy that washed over her, Ellie patted down some stray fair hairs she'd dislodged from her ponytail, then smoothed down the trousers of her smart black trouser-suit. Trying hard not to feel like a condemned prisoner, she headed down the thickly carpeted corridor to the designated meeting room.

'Hello.'

The everyday greeting that she automatically offered sounded incongruous even to Ellie's own hearing.

The man seated at the long, highly polished meeting table—drumming his fingers as though his patience had already been stretched to extreme limits—rose slowly to his feet. At the very first glance he exuded the kind of electricity and energy that made the air feel charged and potent. He was tall and—although lean—clearly packed the kind of toned, ruthlessly honed muscle beneath his clothes that could easily intimidate. In fact that was an understatement. Those broad, iron-hard shoulders nestling beneath the finest bespoke tailoring would surely give an attacking army pause?

The personal emotional threat he represented to Ellie was like a hovering menace that rattled her peace of mind and all that she had worked so hard for, and she sucked in a steadying breath. Seeing his military-cut fair hair and still-chiselled features, her initial assessment of his appearance was that the intervening years had been kind to Nikolai Golitsyn…but the bitterness edging his mouth and the cheekbones that slanted like cruel gashes in his face told a *different* story.

'Elizabeth.'

The ice-blue eyes narrowed searchingly, and Ellie sensed the piercing, laser-like quality of them, feeling a helpless shiver of disquiet and fear down her back.

'I prefer to be called Ellie these days.' She sounded defensive, and more than a little scared, and she couldn't help but despise herself for it. Where was her training when she needed it?

'I am sure you do.' The Russian's lip curled cynically. 'I am sure you would have preferred to remain anonymous for the rest of your life as far as I am concerned—but you should have known that was never going to be remotely possible. And you have helped my case considerably by putting yourself in the public eye. I confess my surprise that you did so, but perhaps you grew too confident that I would have given up my search for you a long time ago? If that it is true then you have only yourself to blame for your arrogance!'

The compelling face before her hardened like a glacier, and Ellie's stomach plunged like a stone. By now she had hoped to be enjoying a long hot bath in her suite, mulling over the day and the two new clients she had acquired for the programme. *Not* coming face to face for the first time in five years with the man who had caused her to flee the city she'd grown up in because he'd blamed her for causing his brother's death!

Her throat felt dry as scorched earth, and Ellie longed for a glass of cool water to ease the discomfort. 'I have nothing to either hide or run away from any more!' she declared. 'The only reason I left like I did was because my father was concerned about me. He wanted to take me to a place where I could properly recover from my injuries and recuperate!'

'I do not believe that was the only reason you disappeared as you did. Otherwise why the change of name—*Dr Lyons*?' Stating her name—her new name—with ironic disdain, Nikolai walked towards her.

Ellie froze, no longer wishing for a cool drink but instead for some benevolent divine force to intercede and suddenly make her invisible. But disappearing was only ever going to be a temporary reprieve. She'd always known that. Much better to stand and confront her demons no matter how intimidating they were!

Garnering all her courage, she schooled herself not to show fear—but it wasn't easy. Even five years ago— his hair fashionably longer, and the skin across his sculpted features more relaxed, less stretched and spare—Nikolai Golitsyn had made her wary. There'd been something about him…something provocative, enigmatic and powerful…that had made her muscles clench with tension whenever she'd found herself in his company. His brother Sasha had once goaded Ellie with his assertion that Nikolai had a ruthless streak that would shock her to her bones, should she ever have cause to anger him, and that forgiveness just wasn't part of his make-up. Once you got on the wrong side of him…look out!

But then Sasha *would* have said that. He had always been jealous of his more successful, enigmatic older brother. His own easy charm had won him many friends, but Nikolai's dependable solidity and hard-working ethic won him the respect and admiration that the younger man had craved. Ellie had learned that from day one in her role as nanny to Sasha and her sister Jackie's baby girl, in the imposing Park Lane house where she had agreed to live after Jackie had died in childbirth.

The brothers' rows had made the walls shake, she remembered. But despite what Sasha had asserted Nikolai had always seemed to be the first to want to heal any rifts.

'Why did you come to see me?' she asked now, willing her pounding heart to somehow calm down as Nikolai drew nearer.

'You can ask me that? After all that has happened?'

He spoke several languages besides his native Russian, and his English was near perfect. But right then his native accent was unmistakable—even pronounced. Beneath it seethed a vast sea of anger and resentment. All directed towards *her*.

'What happened to Sasha was the most t-terrible thing,' Ellie stuttered. 'I'm willing to talk to you—of course I am—but there's nothing new I can tell you about what happened, I'm afraid.'

'Is that so?'

'I know these years since you lost your brother must have been very hard for you, but my hope has always been that when we met again you would somehow have come to realise that the accident wasn't my fault, and that we could move away from any suggestion of blame or recrimination.'

'Is that what you hoped? Well, I have to advise you that such futile hope is both a travesty and a complete waste of time! Instead of talking to me after the inquest, which is what you should have done, or at least seeing for yourself that your niece was all right, you chose to run away with your disreputable father. Since then have clearly made a pleasant and successful life for yourself!

Of course you want that to continue! But now you must begin to realise that it might not. Why you agreed to drive Sasha that day in *my* car, when you had only just passed your test and I had told him to stay put until I returned, has dogged my every waking hour. Trust me when I tell you I will not rest until I finally learn the reason!'

Nikolai had barked that question at Ellie outside the court on the day of the inquest, and her father had put his arm round her and sworn at him in his daughter's defence.

'Leave her alone!' he had cried. 'Don't you think she's been through enough?'

Again Ellie longed for a drink to help lubricate her painfully dry throat.

'I still can't tell you the reason. You surely can't have forgotten that I hurt my head in the accident and lost all memory of what happened that day? In all this time I'm sorry to say it's never returned. It's like a lost piece of a jigsaw that I just can't find...no matter how hard I try. The doctors told me at the hospital that it could return all of a sudden or maybe not at all. I'm sorry if you find that hard to accept, but it's the truth!'

'How very convenient for you!'

Experiencing genuine heartfelt anguish at Nikolai's caustic response, Ellie linked her hands tightly together in front of her. Did he think it was easy for her, losing the memory of a whole day? No matter how terrible it had been? Some might say it was a blessing, but all she knew was that doubt, fear and guilt had lain heavy on her heart ever since—because she couldn't even

remember *why* she would have got into a car with Sasha
and driven when she had barely passed her test.

Although charming, Sasha had been reckless and un-
predictable, and losing Jackie had seemed to unbal-
ance him even more. He had made no attempt to bond
with his baby daughter at all and, if Nikolai hadn't
stepped in and given her a home the child would have
been starved of all the love and affection that was her
birthright, Ellie was sure. But it was Sasha's seriously
addictive behaviour that had disturbed Ellie the most,
she remembered.

'It's not convenient for me in any way! How could
you say such a thing? Don't you think what happened
left its scars on *me*? And I'm not just talking about
physical ones!'

'Yes. You would know all about the psychological
scars of such a trauma, would you not, Dr Lyons?
Especially the ones associated with extreme guilt!'

Ellie actually stepped away from the man confronting her, because his barely contained fury seriously
disturbed her. The smartly furnished conference room
suddenly felt like a tomb to her, and she grasped at her
rapidly melting composure. But the seams holding back
strong emotions from the aftermath of that distressing
time were slowly bursting apart.

'I don't deny that I have guilt—but that's because I
left Arina, not because I know I caused the accident!
How can I admit to such a dreadful thing when I don't
even remember what happened?' she cried.

'My brother was only twenty-eight years old,

Elizabeth… Too young to die so senselessly. Not to know why he died in such a way means that I cannot simply lay his spirit to rest and forget! What do I tell his daughter when she is grown? Have you ever thought about that?'

Feeling numb, Ellie couldn't find the words to answer him.

'The fact that he died is not the worst of it! What I cannot forgive is that when you decided to get into the car with him and take the wheel you also took Arina along for the ride! She was just a baby! What could you have been thinking?'

Ellie knew that Arina had survived the terrible accident that had killed her father and maimed her nanny and aunt without a scratch on her, strapped securely into her baby seat. The collision they'd had mercifully only crushed the front of the car, leaving the back miraculously intact. The Divine had *definitely* been looking out for the infant that dreadful day, and Ellie had often wept with gratitude. She could never have left if she had known the child was hurt. If she had been killed along with her father, Ellie would have wanted to die too! The thought that the little girl might have been harmed in any way still had the power to give her nightmares…

'How can I answer that? Haven't you been listening to anything I've said? I took my responsibilities extremely seriously as far as looking after my niece was concerned, and all I know is I would never have done anything to put her in jeopardy!'

'But you *did* put her in jeopardy—did you not, Elizabeth? She could easily have been killed along with her father!' Nikolai threw her the most contemptuous glance imaginable, and right then Ellie honestly *did* feel like dying.

But she quickly reminded herself she'd suffered enough regret and distress to last her ten lifetimes, and knew it would serve no purpose whatsoever to cease-lessly revisit those debilitating emotions. Life moved on. *She* had moved on—even if the man in front of her hadn't. It still appeared that he wanted to punish and blame her for what had happened to his brother.

Hugging her arms over her chest, Ellie moved her head slowly from side to side. 'I would never have allowed anything or anyone to harm the baby... I adored her! I—I... '

'What?'

'I loved her... I still love her.'

It was obvious that Nikolai was in no mood to listen to reason. But Ellie's compassion as well as her training told her that she needed to remember he was in pain too. He had lost his only brother, and had suffered the shock of learning that his beloved baby niece had been in the car too. She had to forgive him his anger and resent-ment, even if it wasn't in her power to reveal to him what had really happened that day. But *he* had to accept that five years had gone by. What did he want Ellie to do? Give up on her own future because she had lived and Sasha hadn't? Was that the punishment he wanted to exact? No doubt he was furious about the perceived success she had made of her life since the accident, and the irony of that was hardly lost on her. She didn't *feel* like a success.

'I understand your need to know what happened. I really do.' She shrugged sympathetically, and the most illogical hope suddenly surfaced inside her. Could she somehow make contact with the more human side of him? Was she crazy even to try?

Nikolai Golitsyn had always been an enigma to her: reserved, self-contained and sometimes chillingly aloof. When Ellie had first worked for him she had often wondered what it would take to breach those iceberg-like walls he seemed so frequently to retreat behind when in company. Occasionally she had been party to glimpses of intriguing warmth in his character—especially when he'd been around his small niece—and that had provoked Ellie's helpless interest in the man even more. The idea that there was some softness lurking somewhere inside that intimidating frame of his had been disturbingly appealing.

'Don't you think I'd like to know too? I feel like a sculpture that's accidentally had too much stone chipped away. It's left me feeling hollow and uneven inside. And I know…I know that I'll never be the same again.'

Nikolai slid his hand into his trouser pocket and sighed deeply—but without the smallest trace of sympathy. 'Whether your memory returns or not, you and I have some unfinished business—and there is no escaping that fact!' His jaw visibly hardened. 'You will soon learn that there are consequences for running away like you did, Elizabeth.'

Ellie blanched, 'Consequences?'

'I have to go now. But I have a table booked in the hotel restaurant in a couple of hours' time. I will expect you to join me there for dinner. Do not even think of refusing me!'

There was a knock at the door and, unable to disguise his impatience, Nikolai called out, 'Yes?'

A large man with close-cropped hair, immaculately suited and with the kind of physical frame that suggested moving mountains would be as easy as treading on an ant to him, put his head round the door. Remembering that from time to time Nikolai employed the use of such men as bodyguards, Ellie shivered. The man spoke briefly in Russian, and Nikolai answered equally as briefly. The man left.

'I am late for my next meeting,' Nikolai snapped, as if it were entirely Ellie's fault.

She touched a nervous but indignant hand to a button on her jacket and frowned. 'You sound like you're looking for some kind of revenge... Is that it?'

Even as she articulated the words her body started to tremble. Chillingly, her reaction only seemed to amuse Nikolai. He smiled, and she watched his broad shoulders lift in a careless shrug.

'Call it what you will, *Dr Lyons*... But however you like to refer to it... however you might psychoanalyse what appears to be a crude desire on my part to make you suffer...just know that you *will* pay!"

# CHAPTER TWO

*THE change in her was subtle, but nevertheless arresting.* After his encounter with Elizabeth, Nikolai had for the first time in years sat through a business meeting and not been able to give the matter in hand his full and utmost attention. His usually meticulous and organised mind had been completely hijacked by thoughts about Arina's aunt and former nanny.

Now, as he entered the lift of the same hotel she was staying in, to go up to his suite—he had made the reservation as soon as his sources had informed him that she would be staying there—he reflected on the meeting they had had, his mind and body in turmoil. For so long Elizabeth Barnes's whereabouts had consumed him, and he had begun to believe that disturbing memories of her would be all he'd ever have. Then he had chanced to catch a glimpse of her on television being interviewed—and discovered that she was Dr Ellie Lyons now.

Nikolai had barely been able to think straight, he had been so shocked and furious. But beneath his rage and tumult were feelings that were not so easily explained or quantified. He seemed to be gripped by something unnameable and compelling that existed just below the surface of his everyday thoughts about her.

A wave of memory submerged him. When he had seen her last she had been almost coltishly lean. Now, five years had developed those youthful angles into the most arresting curves. Her face, which had always verged on being breathtaking—with those luminously clear rain-washed eyes and that soft curving mouth—had become even more so. And the lustrous corn-coloured hair tied back in that businesslike ponytail was the perfect setting to showcase such beauty. *She was an absolute gift to the world of television.* Not only was she a practising psychologist at a time when the world seemed fascinated by other people's relationship problems and wanted to hear them discussed on a regular basis, but she looked like a flaxen-haired angel too!

Torn and angered by the troubling direction of his thoughts, Nikolai flexed his fingers and willed the lift to reach his floor. The last thing he wanted to do was admit that Elizabeth's beauty disturbed him! There was far too much at stake here for him to become side-tracked or distracted by her undoubted physical appeal…especially when the lady had categorically proved she absolutely could not be trusted.

Once inside the plush hotel suite, his body brimming with the kind of restless energy that could not be contained, Nikolai opted to go back downstairs to the gym.

Starting to disrobe on his way to the bedroom, he discarded his jacket and tie and then started on the buttons of his Savile Row shirt. Lifting some weights and running on the treadmill would help pass the time until dinner, when he and his reluctant companion would meet up once again.

He grimaced bitterly at the thought, at that moment feeling nothing but resentment and a desire to punish where she was concerned. Kicking off his handmade leather shoes, he arrived in the bedroom, but barely registered its fine furnishings and understated elegance. Having inherited an oil business from his father at just twenty-four, to him hotel rooms—however opulent and well appointed—were merely a necessary convenience, that was all. He much preferred to return home after meetings whenever possible, and as he owned several houses all over the world home could be any place he chose.

When he was in London, he and Arina resided at the house in Park Lane from where, on that fateful day five years ago, Elizabeth had driven his brother Sasha to some unknown destination…

For months after her aunt's disappearance Arina had sobbed herself to sleep most nights, unable to be soothed by either Nikolai or the first of what had turned out to be a stream of hopeful replacement nannies. None of them had forged the almost maternal bond Elizabeth had. How could they? Undoubtedly the blood-ties the infant shared with her aunt had helped her form a strong attachment to her, and Arina had clearly been disturbed by the fact she was no longer in her life.

What Nikolai could not forgive was that, knowing such a bond existed between them, Elizabeth had still callously deserted them without so much as a hint that she planned to leave so suddenly. Add to that the shocking discoveries that had been brought to light after the accident—a family heirloom found in the car after it had crashed, clearly stolen, plus his increasing belief that Elizabeth must have been having an affair with Sasha for her to commit such a reckless act as to drive the car for him—Nikolai had barely known how to subdue the rage that had consumed him.

When she had absconded after the inquest he had utilised a lot of time, money and expert help in trying to locate her whereabouts, and her disappearance had caused him no end of sleepless nights and stress-filled days. What had *really* happened on the day of the accident? He *burned* to know. Elizabeth's sudden flight had screamed her guilt to the rooftops, and it had definitely fuelled Nikolai's desire to somehow make her pay. Whatever else transpired, that terrible day had robbed him of his brother and Arina of her father—and she had definitely played her part in the tragedy that had taken place.

Now that she eluded him no longer she would quickly see that the perfect little life she had fashioned for herself for the past five years was definitely going to undergo some radical changes—one way or another…

\* \* \*

Ellie chose a simply designed black cocktail dress to wear to dinner. The irony of the colour was not lost on her. Ever since she'd set eyes on Nikolai Golitsyn again it was as though a violent darkening storm had threatened the pleasant meadow she'd been walking in, and truth to tell she was frightened. It hadn't sat well with her all these years that she'd agreed to fall in with her father's advice to simply disappear and then get herself a whole new identity, but at the time she'd been far too traumatised to argue. *Recent events had prompted even more painful reflection.*

Her father had been diagnosed with Parkinson's disease, and although his illness had undoubtedly forged a closer bond between them, and she perfectly understood why he had taken her away, Ellie wished she'd fought her ground and stayed to talk to Nikolai. Maybe if she'd stayed he would have eventually stopped blaming her for Sasha's death, realised that somehow his brother *must* have had a major part in events given his proclivity to be both reckless and intoxicated? In time he might even have come to accept that Ellie really *couldn't* recall what had happened that day and forgiven her at last.

If all that had transpired then she would still be looking after her niece now, and wouldn't be burdened by the most dreadful guilt that she *had* indeed abandoned her sister's child in her hour of need. But, even though she had a deep and abiding regret about leaving so suddenly, Ellie believed her father had acted with the best of intentions too. By being there in *her* hour of need she knew he had somehow hoped to make it up to her for all his years of emotional and physical neglect of her and Jackie when they were younger.

Fear of the consequences if her fate should be left to Nikolai had also inspired his actions. A man who had such enormous wealth and power at his fingertips could never be trusted, her father had warned. It would be like living with a time-bomb! If he chose to bring a private case against Ellie she would have little defence, considering that she had lost her memory. There was no telling how he and his fancy lawyers might twist things to their advantage! Yes…it was better that she had moved right away from him, until the sorrows and mistakes of the past were a little less raw and blunted by the passing of time…

Staring at her reflection now in the full-length mirror, Ellie touched a trembling hand to the balconette bodice of her dress, with its simple shoestring straps. *God! She looked as pale as sugar frosting!* What she wouldn't give for a little sun in some warmer climes, to bronze her skin and brighten her up! But that was going to be impossible, given her schedule at both the practice and the centre. Add to that this recent bout of television work, and she'd be lucky to grab a moment she could call her own…let alone have a holiday!

But her disappointment about not being able to look forward to a break paled into insignificance when Ellie thought about meeting up with Nikolai again. Her stomach lurched. It was unlikely she'd be able to swallow even a morsel of food all evening, confronted with his glowering accusing face across the table! He had looked even more frighteningly fit and intimidating then she'd remembered, and Ellie knew he had meant every word of that threat he'd left her with earlier... There would be were consequences for what he saw as her cold-hearted desertion...

'I took the liberty of getting us a table where we would have privacy.'

*I'll bet you did*! Ellie thought nervously as she sat in the padded velvet chair the smartly suited *maître d'* had pulled out for her. Tucked away in the most secluded corner of the hotel's elegant dining room, with its artistic silk panelling on the walls and its brass chandeliers fashioned in intricate Celtic knotwork hanging from the ceiling, they would have privacy in plenty.

In more ways than one their location couldn't be faulted. Their position overlooked a charming stone patio with a plethora of terracotta tubs filled with still abundant trailing pink and white blossoms, glinting in the pale light of late summer evening. It was breathtakingly pretty. The blooms surrounded a pretty fountain commanded by a modern sculpture.

Reluctantly withdrawing her admiring gaze from the appealing view, Ellie attempted to focus on the wine list the waiter had left them to peruse. Absently stroking the fine white linen napkin that had been draped on her lap, she fought hard against another intense desire to flee. And again she knew she would do no such thing.

Whatever the consequences Nikolai intended, she would stay and face them.

If nothing else, Ellie was desperate to see Arina again. She was, after all, the closest link she had to her much loved sister, and now that her father's health was cause for concern she longed for the chance to somehow make amends and be part of her niece's life again. Ellie also wanted Nikolai to know that she wasn't about to follow the same escapist route she'd taken five years ago.

'Are you happy for me to select the wine?' he asked, civil-voiced and Ellie glanced back at him in surprise, not trusting the polite veneer.

'Go ahead,' she replied. 'I'm certainly no expert!'

'Maybe not with wine,' Nikolai commented smoothly. 'But clearly you have become an expert in psychology.'

'I may have got the necessary qualifications, but it takes a lifetime to be really expert at anything. And even then I'll still be learning! I mostly think of myself as an enabler…somebody who can help a person in trouble take the next step towards healing and hopefully give them some useful tools to help themselves.'

'Your humility is commendable…although your current high profile in the media is somewhat at odds with that, wouldn't you say?'

Having expected his derision at some point, Ellie wasn't disappointed now. Her whole body tensed. 'I'm not interested in having *any* sort of media profile, for your information! It only happened that I appeared on television because a local reporter where I worked got wind of a case I'd worked on and the client's father was well known.'

Nikolai named the politician concerned, with his trademark ice-cool equanimity, and Ellie grimaced. She might have known he would have all the information he needed at his fingertips.

'I have that reporter to thank for helping me locate *you,* so I cannot regret his interest!' he continued, with a faint ironic lift at the edges of his disturbingly sensuous mouth. 'A bottle of Château Lafite Rothschild will fit the bill perfectly to celebrate our timely little reunion, I think. The wine was named after a French politician, so perhaps it is fitting, yes?'

Knowing very little about wine, but silently concerned that it sounded frighteningly expensive, whatever it was, Ellie stayed mute.

'You need not look so overwhelmed!' her companion remarked in mock amusement. 'Naturally I will insist on footing the bill, so do not fret. The cost makes no difference to me. I have already expended too much time, money and concern over your whereabouts over the years as it is! I am only relieved that in the end my searching was not in vain! Tell me…why Scotland? Who did you know there? My informants certainly did not discover any extended family in that location, or anywhere else in the UK!'

His comments made Ellie revisit afresh the gravity of the horrific event that had changed her life for ever, and the devastation she had undoubtedly left behind her. As well as that came the disturbing realisation that

Nikolai had not resumed his life in the way she'd hoped he would, forgetting all about her. For long moments she struggled to give voice to her racing thoughts.

'I don't know why. It's just a place like any other...a place where nobody knew us...where we could make a fresh start. My father was worried about me. That was why he took me away,' she finally explained.

'What was he worried about? That I would hold you in some way responsible for what happened to my brother despite the verdict reached by the courts?'

The cold slash of Nikolai's chilling voice immobilised Ellie in her seat. Nervously she met the burning blue of his fiercely focused gaze, and it was like glancing into a frosted lake in deep midwinter.

'Well, he was right!' he spat out, laying down the wine list just as the soft-footed waiter returned to take their order.

Ordering the wine in a calmly controlled tone that was miraculously devoid of the rage he had just expressed, he told the man to give them a few extra minutes so that they could deliberate over the menu.

In the ensuing stomach-churning silence Ellie stared hard at the printed words in front of her in the leather-bound book, but they might have been written in Sanskrit for all the sense they made to her distracted gaze.

'Have you decided?' her stern-faced companion asked after less than a minute, the question sounding more like an impatient demand.

'A Caesar salad will be fine,' Ellie answered, hardly caring what she ate.

At a nod from Nikolai, another waiter peeled away from a nearby table and took their order. When they were alone again, Ellie set the menu aside and reached for the jug of water that was on the table, offering it to Nikolai first. He responded with a curt nod.

The barely contained animosity he emitted locked every muscle in her body with fear. Any threats this man made would not be empty ones, she knew. He had both the means and the will to make her suffer. *As if she had not suffered enough—and in ways he probably couldn't even begin to imagine…*

'How is—how is Arina?' Finally plucking up the courage to enquire about the one thing she was desperate to know most of all, Ellie knew her voice was barely above a whisper.

Nikolai's frozen glance did not thaw for even a second. 'Do you not think you relinquished the right to know that five years ago?'

'I never stopped caring about her…no matter what you might think!'

'But you obviously did not care enough, or you would not have deserted her like you did!'

'I didn't mean to just leave her like that. You make it sound like it was a pre-meditated decision, and it wasn't! I was hurt and traumatised from the accident, and for the first time in my life I let my father take charge and look after me. Was that so terrible? If you had seemed less closed-off and unapproachable, I would have talked to you about it… But—'

'What?'

'I knew you were hurting badly yourself…emotionally, I mean. You'd lost your brother…why wouldn't you be? I know what a loss like that is like. The last thing I expected was that you would want me to stay on and take care of Arina. How could we possibly co-exist under the same roof when it was clear that you hated me after what happened? Besides, I thought your wife might want to play more of a part in Arina's upbringing when I left.'

'Veronika and I are no longer married. We divorced not long after you disappeared.'

All the muscles in Nikolai's face seemed to freeze for a moment, and Ellie felt genuine shock ripple through her at his news.

'However I might have appeared,' he continued gravely, 'you should have put Arina's welfare first…not your own! You simply ran away—like the coward I now know you to be!'

The comment was like a sharp-bladed dagger plunged into Ellie's chest, and the pain that ensued took her breath away.

'I'm not a coward!' She slammed her hand down hard on the table and the glassware and crockery rattled. It felt as if every pair of eyes in the room was on her, but she was sick with misery and hurt at the unfairness of Nikolai's cruel remark.

She understood his need to vent—he must have been storing up resentment over the years, desperately needing someone to blame. But Ellie had suffered too.

'Is there no understanding or forgiveness in your

heart at all?' she appealed. 'It's been five years, Nikolai!
Do you honestly think it will help you come to terms
with your grief any better by holding onto blame?'

It was the first time she had used his name, and she
saw the flicker of surprise in his eyes.

'The answer to the first part of your question is no.
There *is* no forgiveness in my heart where you are concerned, Elizabeth! I trusted you and you paid me back
with nothing but deceit! You abandoned us...not caring
what happened and clearly thinking only of your own
position!'

Her stomach clamped in a vice of pain, Ellie glanced
forlornly round at the other diners in the chic hotel restaurant, imagining she saw only pleasure and happiness
reflected on their faces—states of mind that were a
million miles away from what *she* was currently experiencing.

Inhaling deeply, she turned back to Nikolai. 'How
did I deceive you? I only left because I was hurt and in
shock. Since when has that become a crime? And you're
wrong if you think I didn't care about what you and
Arina were going through. *Especially Arina*! There's
not a day that's gone by when I haven't wondered how
she is! I'm so, so sorry if I added to her suffering and
yours by going away. What more can I say?'

'You ask how you deceived me?' Nikolai drawled,
the low-pitched timbre of his arresting voice sending
an explosion of hot little shivers down Ellie's spine.
'Well...I will tell you. It is my belief that at the time of
the accident you were having an affair with my brother.'

'What?'

'Not only were you having an affair, but you were also planning to elope with him—taking the baby with you! It is my belief that is why you were in the car together that day!'

'That's ludicrous!'

'Is it, Ellie?'

His unexpected use of the shortened version of her name made Ellie stare at him for a suspended moment. Then the adrenaline flooding her body after his unbelievable words kicked in, and she felt quite ill at the implications that crowded in on her.

'How do you know?' Nikolai suggested with deadly softness, his gaze making a dazed prisoner of hers. 'When you say you cannot remember anything? You two always seemed pretty close, and what other reason would you have had for agreeing to drive him that day? If he had wanted to go somewhere alone he would have rung for a cab…not taken you with him!'

A small helpless groan left Ellie's throat, and she shook her head in frustration and misery at the yawning space in her mind where her memory should be. 'Look…I know I can't remember what happened that day, why I should have been in the car with him and Arina, but I'd swear on my life that your conclusion is a million miles away from the truth!'

The returning dark, condemning gaze on her companion's face said he didn't believe her, and Ellie's spirits sank even lower. No wonder he was furious with her if he thought that she'd been having an intimate relationship with his brother and planning to run away with him, taking the baby with them!

'And you're wrong about us being close. I offered Sasha comfort and support after my sister died, that's all! And after you suggested that I move into the Park Lane house and look after Arina full-time you *know* how infrequent his visits were. Sometimes he could be gone for weeks on end!'

'There is something else.'

Ellie hardly dared breathe.

'A valuable jewel was found in the wreckage of the car after the accident—a diamond necklace belonging to my mother that I kept in a locked casket in my bedroom. You must have heard Sasha arguing with me about money before I left to go to the office. Obviously it was stolen to help fund your new life together! Did the two of you plan the theft together, or was that something you decided on all by yourself?'

Laying her palms down on the fine linen tablecloth, Ellie desperately needed something to anchor her. All of a sudden her world felt like a wild storm-tossed sea, and she was drowning in it. Breathing out a harsh breath, she made herself look Nikolai straight in the eyes.

'Haven't you been listening to me at all? Sasha and I weren't having an affair, and I know nothing about any necklace being stolen! I know you won't believe me, because I can't prove it, but I *do* know my own nature—and I would cut off my hand before I took anything that wasn't mine from anybody!'

Nikolai shrugged. 'Unfortunately, Ellie, all the evidence seems to suggest that you *are* indeed guilty. It is not just the necklace. Other things went missing from the house around that time too. And the fact that you disappeared so suddenly after the inquest would make anyone suspicious! Your father must have known what you had planned, and he took you away so that you would escape punishment! Who knows? Perhaps he even helped you steal the necklace and those other things?'

'No! Is that why you searched for me?' Her voice was hoarse now, and Ellie's hand moved nervously against her throat. 'Because you wanted to prosecute me for theft as well as blame me for the accident?'

'If not you, Ellie…then your father! He has spent time in prison before for theft, has he not?'

The Russian sighed, as though it was all a mere formality, and Ellie's blood ran colder than any ice-packed river as she looked into that handsome, unforgiving face.

'What would you do in my position?' he asked. 'I have been both deceived and betrayed. Do you not think I deserve to be compensated in some way?'

'You can't involve my father! He's done nothing…I know he hasn't! And he's not a well man! Going to prison again would likely kill him!'

'How dramatic you are! I see there is indeed fire beneath that deceptively cool air you exude.'

'Don't mock me! If you're so set on accusing me of crimes I know nothing about let alone have participated in, and if you want compensation—then perhaps there is a way I can somehow pay you back? We should talk…work something out. I'll do anything as long as it doesn't involve my father! Please, Nikolai… Whatever you decide, leave him out of it!'

# CHAPTER THREE

STUDYING the flawless buttermilk complexion of the lovely face before him, and steeling himself against her heartfelt plea, Nikolai sensed a renewed sting of fury and something perhaps equally disturbing but more personal sweep through him at the thought of Elizabeth with his brother.

Before he knew it, a blood-heating memory surfaced inside him, of an unforgettable encounter with her the day before the accident. It had been evening, the baby had long since been put to bed, and Nikolai had been looking over some important documents concerning a meeting he was due to attend the next afternoon. There was a lot of small print and equally as much red tape to wrestle with. Usually he didn't flinch for a second over such tasks, however tedious, but at that moment a world of onerous responsibility had weighed him down like an iron cloak across his shoulders, and he had longed to throw it off.

He had been groomed to take over his father's multi-million-pound oil empire when he should have been enjoying his youth—just as Sasha had been allowed to enjoy his. He had spent every minute of his day dealing with the complexities and demands of running a hugely successful business. All of a sudden the realisation had come to Nikolai that he was fatigued and disenchanted, and that the only thing he really longed for right then was his freedom… And not just from his sense of duty and responsibility. Veronika and he had barely been speaking to each other, and on the rare occasions when they were actually home at the same time lived in a state of near excruciating stalemate—neither of them having the time or energy to bring the increasingly brittle marriage to its deserved and grateful end. Nikolai had long suspected she might be seeing someone else.

Unexpectedly, Elizabeth had knocked on the door, shaking him out of his agonising introspection, and he had been grateful. She had brought him a cup of tea made just the way he liked it—black with sugar and lemon. When she had first arrived at the house to work he had been instantly drawn to her warmth and shyness, and her eagerness to learn new things. When she had exposed an interest, he had personally schooled her in the intricate art of making his favourite beverage in the highly decorated brass Samovar that had originated in Moscow and had belonged to Nikolai's great-great-grandmother.

Her thoughtful gesture in bringing him the tea, and the radiance of her presence, had acted like a soothing balm to Nikolai's soul, and he recalled smiling up at her with much more warmth than usual, his worries temporarily forgotten. He remembered Elizabeth placing the mug carefully on the side of the desk, and how fascinated he'd suddenly become with the graceful contours of her small, pretty hand as she'd uncurled it from the porcelain. A powerful desire had consumed him to discover if the flawless texture fulfilled the idea of satin and silk, as its appearance so alluringly suggested.

Compelled by some irresistible force he hadn't been able to fight, Nikolai had reached out and cupped his palm over her knuckles, momentarily holding her captive. A bolt of electricity had harpooned through him like lightning, and Elizabeth had been equally affected. Her sweet breath had whispered over him like hushed gossamer silk, and Nikolai had gazed into her eyes and seen the same helplessly wild longing that he had known must blaze in his own hot glance.

'By all the saints!' Before he'd known it he'd been rising to his feet and cupping the back of her head, to free the pale ivory comb that confined her hair. It had fallen onto her shoulders like warm summer rain, drifting softly onto a sunlit meadow, and trickled through Nikolai's fingers like smooth, silken skeins of pure spun gold. He had caught his breath in sheer delight, the parameters of his world narrowing down to just the vision of her lovely face. His senses on fire, he had touched his lips to hers, finally drinking at the exquisite well that promised to satisfy his thirst and heal his wounds like no other…

Wrenching his mind free of the distracting and

stirring memory, Nikolai forced himself to return to the present. The fact was—if his suspicions were correct—the lovely face and bewitching but treacherous lips before him had also been caressed by his brother, and it made him wonder if he had imagined the mutually hungry response and naked need in her eyes that day five years ago? Or was it simply that Ellie, as she called herself now, was a girl who took pleasure in teasing men with her beauty and sexuality just because she could?

Even though he had no evidence to support the idea, it was utterly distasteful to Nikolai's strong sense of male pride that she might employ such disingenuous behaviour—even once—and it completely doused the heat that had automatically flared inside him. But he knew that it would undoubtedly surface again. He had always been attracted to his brother's beautiful sister-in-law, and could no longer deny it. But he had been married when she had dropped out of college to come and take care of Arina after her sister's death.

Sasha had been in no fit state to take care of the baby himself, so had agreed to let Nikolai take charge of things. And, although there had been a definite maturity about the way Ellie had conducted herself, and also the way in which she'd taken care of her small charge, there had been a touching innocence about her too, and because of her comparative youth Nikolai had fought hard against his growing attraction for her.

'So—' he broke some bread between his fingers '—we will eat our meal and I will take some time afterwards to consider what kind of compensation I would like from you, Ellie.'

She pulled her gaze away from him, but not before Nikolai saw the tide of hot colour that rushed into her cheeks. Was it caused by anger, embarrassment, or something else? *Like that illicit kiss they had shared the evening before the accident*? His interest deepened.

'In the meantime…I'd like to see Arina,' she said, injecting a determined note into her soft voice.

Immediately Nikolai's fierce sense of protectiveness towards the little girl who had become his pride and joy surfaced, and he already knew his answer. 'That is not something I am going to agree to straight away—and I am sure you can guess at the reasons why. Arina is my daughter now. Yes…after Sasha died and Veronika and I split up I officially adopted her. After such an upsetting start in life she is happy and well-adjusted, and I am not about to jeopardise her happiness in any way—no matter how much you say you desire to see her again!'

'What do you think I'm going to do, Nikolai? Try and force her to accept me and like me?' Ellie's eyes were round with hurt. 'I didn't tell you before, but now that I've got used to the idea I'm *glad* that you found me! Yes—glad! I've wanted to see Arina for so long— even if it's only for a few minutes. She is my sister's only child, and I meant what I said when I told you I loved her and have never stopped loving her!'

'You will have to let me think about it. First of all I will need to see for myself the kind of person you have become in the years we have been apart, and whether you are indeed someone I would want involved in my daughter's life.'

'You make me sound like the very worst criminal!'

'Where Arina's well-being is concerned, I take no chances.'

'That's all I want, Nikolai.' Suddenly she looked close to tears. 'A chance! A chance to prove to you I'm neither a liar *or* a thief!'

'Trust has to be earned and built up… Especially when it has been shattered as badly as it has been in my case!'

The waiter brought the wine Nikolai had selected, and while the man expertly poured it into the waiting slim-stemmed glasses after his nod of approval he concentrated his gaze once more on the increasingly distressed expression on his beautiful companion's face. In a weak moment, Nikolai took pity on her.

'Arina has been at school full-time for about a year now—since she was five. She seems much enamoured with it.'

'Jackie always loved school…At least she coped with it much better than I ever did! How do you—how do you manage taking Arina and collecting her every day with your work commitments now that—now that your wife is no longer with you? Does she still have a nanny?'

'Between my housekeeper and my au pair we manage very well. Elsa—the au pair—is in charge of the school run, and Miriam—my housekeeper—also helps out when she is needed. Arina is fond of them both.'

'You have never—you've never thought about re-marrying?'

Ellie's question took Nikolai by surprise for a moment. After the soul-destroying relationship he had shared with Veronika he'd told himself he would avoid making a similar horrendous mistake again like the plague! Apart from occasionally thinking that Arina would benefit from having a mother in her life, he would not be human if he did not admit to feeling lonely from time to time too...lonely for a tender, loving woman who would not only warm his bed but would be a true partner in every sense of the word.

Women to warm his bed Nikolai could easily find...but someone tender and genuinely caring of his welfare...*that was another story entirely.*

'Not lately,' he replied, finally answering the question. 'But then I have preferred to devote my time and energy to taking care of Arina rather than invest it in a relationship. Besides, I have my work as well, and that also takes up a lot of my time.' He leaned forward a little across the table. 'What about you? Why are you still alone, Ellie?'

She bit down on her lip. 'How do you know I'm alone?'

'Because since I saw you on that television pro-gramme a month ago my sources have revealed that besides your father there is no one in your life... No one and nothing else to care about but your work!'

'You've had people checking up on me?'

'Under the circumstances I did what had to be done.'

Her returning glance was reproachful. Nikolai

shrugged it off. It hardly mattered what she thought of his methods when she had treated him and Arina with little or no concern at all!

Taking a careful sip of his wine, he inclined his head approvingly. 'A good choice,' he remarked, allowing a corner of his mouth the briefest lift upwards. 'Even if I do say so myself!'

The man had a charismatic allure that would always guarantee him plenty of female attention, Ellie mused somewhat resentfully. She was drawn like a magnet to the arrogant, almost autocratic set of features before her. Imaginative fantasies about what the hard, fit body beneath the expensive tailoring he wore would be like in bed would inevitably always be aroused too. And women would feel that same helpless pull towards him even if he was a pauper!

Ellie shivered as the familiar unbidden, disturbing fantasy stole into her mind...fuelled by her dizzying recollection of that kiss they had shared five years ago.

Having only been kissed once before by a boy at college—and pretty clumsily at that—nothing in the world could have prepared Ellie for the barely civilised and frightening passion of Nikolai's sizzling kiss. Even before his lips had made contact with hers, when he had simply covered her hand with his, an electrical bolt had shot through her insides and flooded her with the kind of heat more generally associated with the tropics. And when he had penetrated her mouth with his hot, silky tongue, Ellie had barely known how she remained standing.

She would have given him anything he'd asked for right then…anything…if only the telephone had not rung and shockingly broke them apart. Then guilt that he was married—and fear that taking things further would mean nothing to him—had sent her dashing from the room and back upstairs to her bedroom. To spend nearly the whole night lying awake, longing and wondering what it would be like to go to bed with the one man she had finally admitted she cared for and desired more than any other she had ever met…

But she had long ago given up on her impossible fantasy of being with Nikolai—and Ellie now sadly resigned herself to his hate and scorn instead.

'You study me very carefully beneath those eyes of green fire, Ellie.' His voice turned soft and beguiling all of a sudden. 'What do you see, I wonder? A wealthy, arrogant man who believes he can do anything he likes because money can open doors that remain firmly shut to those that do not have it?' He chuckled, amused at his own joke. 'Then you would be right. I cannot deny it!'

Ellie made no reply. She couldn't. Her throat was stinging to the point of pain, and she feared if she said anything emotion would overwhelm her. Bad enough to be accused of being somehow complicit in the car accident that had killed his brother, and of being his lover to boot, without knowing that this man—the one man she had secretly always admired and wanted— despised her and wouldn't even let her see her niece, her own flesh and blood, until she had somehow proved to him she was worthy of such a privilege! There was certainly no call for humour in thc situation as far as she could see...unless of course it was of the blackest kind!

Plucking the starched white linen napkin from her lap, Ellie dropped it onto the table and rose determinedly to her feet. 'I'm sorry...but I suddenly don't feel very hungry any more.'

'Where do you think you are going? Sit down immediately!'

'I'm not a child! Don't you dare—'

'I said *sit down*!'

She froze at the undertone of menace in that deeply rich voice.

'Unless you want to risk making a scene—and very likely ruin your so far unblemished professional reputation for good—I would think very hard before you turn your back and walk away from me, Dr Lyons!'

Uncomfortably aware that they were already the unwelcome cynosure of several pairs of interested eyes, Ellie sank slowly back down into her seat. Right on cue the waiter appeared with their food.

'Perhaps when you start to eat you will find that you have an appetite after all? You are looking distinctly pale all of a sudden.'

'Can you wonder why?'

'No doubt it has been quite a shock to see me again, when you had obviously hoped to remain undetected by my radar for good.'

Withdrawing the angry retort that burned on her lips, Ellie forked some food into her mouth. Certain that she

would be numb to any sensation of pleasure at all in
what she ate, she was surprised to find that the crisp and
bright Romaine lettuce, the anchovies and crunchy
croutons, were really quite delicious. Her tastebuds responded with silent, hungry appreciation.

'This is good!' she remarked.

'Even the most average fare can taste like the best
meal you have ever eaten when you are hungry.'

'I suppose in your world this food might be considered average, but I still say it's very good!'

'You were once a part of my world—remember?'

His lowered tone got her attention. Ellie laid down
her fork beside her plate. In the twelve months that she
had lived in the Park Lane house looking after the baby,
Nikolai had taken her to dine in some of the most exclusive restaurants in the world. Often they had been in
places where he had fabulous homes—Long Island in
New York, for instance, and Rome, Moscow and Monte
Carlo, as well as here in London. Veronika had rarely
accompanied them because her job as chief designer for
a smart European fashion house had already entailed
plenty of travelling.

*Only in her heart of hearts had Ellie confessed to
being glad about that.* She had also noticed that Nikolai
did not act as if he missed his wife…not at any time.
Now she recalled that the opportunity to visit those
fabulous locations and stay in the realms of such un-
mitigated luxury had been like a fantastic dream for a
girl raised mainly in the fostercare system and sometimes in children's homes. But the way Nikolai now

asserted she was once part of his world—as though he were suggesting she had meant something far more meaningful than someone who'd taken care of his niece—rubbed an already tender nerve raw.

'I was still just an employee of yours, even though we had a personal connection in Arina!' she exclaimed, the emotion she feared giving way to gripping her even more strongly.

'I treated you well, did I not?' His stunning azure gaze narrowed.

'Yes, you did. But—'

'What?'

She had been going to blurt out something about his brother but, forcing herself to calm down, quickly thought better of it. There was still Arina to consider, and the poor child had surely suffered enough, being deprived of both natural parents, without Ellie bringing the taint of more painful shadows into her young life.

Shrugging unhappily, she tried to concentrate on her food, but her hunger had fled. Her serious-faced companion didn't seem to notice that she'd stopped eating.

'So…you still like children?' he said, dipping some bread into the fragrant carrot and coriander soup he had ordered.

'Of course!' His remark prompted an image of the adorable baby that had been her niece, and Ellie's heart swelled with longing. 'Won't you tell me a little about how Arina is now? What she looks like and her personality? I've tried so many times to imagine her, but…'

'She is mischievous, and full of life, but she has

moments when she is just in a private little world all of
her own. She has inherited my brother's dark colouring rather than your sister's fairer looks. Her hair is as
black as treacle, and she has big blue eyes the colour
of the sky—and already she has the boys in her class
lining up for her attention!'

'A real heartbreaker, then?'

'Yes…a heartbreaker.'

Nikolai's smile broke across his face like the rising
of the dawn following a grim black night, and hearing
the love and pride in his voice, Ellie was helplessly
moved. One thing that did stand out in her memory was
his unwavering devotion to the little girl. He had loved
her from the outset. How many other men in his demanding position would have taken on the serious
lifelong responsibility of another man's child—even if
that man *had* been his brother? Whatever his
faults…nobody could criticise him for that.

Before she'd gone to work for Sasha and Nikolai,
Ellie had experienced two previous jobs as a nanny—
one for a doctor's family and the other for a couple who
had both been solicitors. Her natural affection for
children and her own desperate desire to somehow
redress the balance of her own love-starved childhood
had meant working as a nanny was the perfect job. But
then Jackie had persuaded her to go to college and work
towards getting a qualification in psychology—something Ellie's sister knew she had also yearned for.

When Nikolai had met her in the hospital just after
Jackie's shocking death, and they had all discussed the

baby's future and who was going to raise her, Ellie had had no hesitation in giving up her degree course to go and live in his house and take care of their niece. Sasha had all but gone completely to pieces, and Nikolai had instructed him to go away for a few weeks and try and get his head together.

At that first ever meeting with him Ellie had been quite overwhelmed by the handsome Russian. By the time she'd left that day—even though she'd been numb with grief and sadness over her sister—she hadn't been able to get his piercing blue eyes out of her mind. He'd suffered too, she'd seen. In spite of his staggering wealth and privileged position. Some great sadness had been walled up behind that unforgettable gaze, and Ellie had deduced again that outward appearances could be deceiving. She'd become adept at reading people and faces, and that was one of the reasons she had veered towards studying psychology—that and a heartfelt wish to somehow ease the mental and emotional suffering of others wherever she could…and try and understand herself too.

'She was just the loveliest baby to take care of!' she exclaimed now. 'I honestly can't wait to see her again.' Her suddenly self-conscious gaze met and held Nikolai's, and the smile that was like the dawn breaking vanished from his austere lips, as though he immediately regretted or even *resented* sharing it with her.

'What about having children of your own?' he asked gruffly. 'Have you ever thought about that?'

Ellie frowned. 'Yes…as a matter of fact I have. But

for that to happen I'd have to be in a stable and loving relationship—I wouldn't bring a child into the world otherwise! Anyway…I don't think that's going to be on the cards for a long time yet. Right now I think I am needed much more elsewhere.'

'By your clients, you mean?'

'Yes.' Raising her glass of wine to her lips, she took a small conservative sip and placed it back down on the table. 'What about you?' she enquired of the man sitting opposite, her heart thudding nervously at her temerity in asking such a question. 'Would you like children?'

'As a matter of fact I would. Arina has brought more joy into my life than I ever thought possible and a brother or sister or both to join her would be very much desired. But…like you…that is not on the horizon for me right now. Now, let us continue with our meal, shall we?'

# CHAPTER FOUR

UNABLE to stem his impatience as he waited for Ellie to emerge from the television studios, Nikolai could hardly believe he had let her out of his sight after they had had dinner together last night. He still did not trust her, but apart from forcibly detaining her or kidnapping her, frankly what else could he have done?

At the back of his mind he supposed he still feared that she'd flee again, but this time Nikolai had instructed Ivan his bodyguard to keep a watch on her movements. So far she was exactly where she said she'd be, but something else had been gnawing away at him after their meeting. Thinking back to the events that had led up to the car accident, he had reluctantly started to acknowledge that he had played *his* part in what had occurred that terrible day too. It was not an easy admission to make. A man who prided himself on making good decisions, that day Nikolai had made what was probably the very *worst* decision of his life. Sasha had been drinking heavily, and that was one of the reasons they had rowed so bitterly. His brother had also been demanding more money to fund his out of control and soulless lifestyle, as well as displaying his usual unbelievable indifference to his daughter's welfare.

In the year since he had lost Jackie, Sasha had failed to improve his life in any way…it had been as if he was hell-bent on destroying himself too. All things considered, Nikolai had certainly had plenty of reasons to be mad at him that day. But what he could not begin to fathom was how or why he had never suspected before that there might be something going on between him and Ellie—because that was the conclusion he had reached, and it would not go away. Why else would she have driven him that day, and risked getting into the most dreadful trouble when it had been Nikolai's car she was driving and he had warned his brother to stay put until he returned from his meeting?

If he had suspected that they were closer than he had thought then Nikolai never would have left the two of them alone together that afternoon. It had been vital that he get to his office for a crucial meeting, but he should have insisted that Ellie simply bring Arina and go with him. Not left her behind with the man she'd agreed to run away with, taking the baby with them! The meeting had been set up for Nikolai to formally present and then sign an employment contract that would guarantee the jobs of over one and a half thousand migrant workers in the city. He had not wanted to delay, as people's livelihoods depended on it, so Nikolai had reluctantly left Ellie and his niece alone with an already unstable

Sasha, and hastened to his office to meet with his board and do what had to be done—telling himself that by the time he returned to Park Lane his brother might have calmed down sufficiently for Nikolai to be able to talk some sense into him.

Little had he known that by the time he got back Sasha would be dead and Ellie would be lying unconscious in an ambulance, on her way to hospital, with a kind policewoman comforting a sobbing and terrified but thank God *unhurt* Arina until they could reach Nikolai and tell him what had happened.

A tight band of tension squeezed his temples in a vice, and he briefly shut his eyes. When he opened them again he saw Ellie hurrying from the uninspiring redbrick building that housed the television studios towards him—her footsteps slowing the nearer she got to the car. She was wearing a red blazer, a white blouse and a knee-length black skirt with black hosiery. *Nikolai found himself fascinated by her slim and shapely legs.* For the first time since meeting up with her again he noticed that she walked with a slight limp. It was not something that everyone would immediately observe, but it was a limp just the same.

A wave of unexpected emotion crashed in on him. His hours of waiting by her hospital bedside for her to regain consciousness after the accident returned. Hours that had turned into days before—back in the land of the living—she had seemed to have forgotten who he was, and had just stared at him from time to time with a sad far-away look in her eyes—a melancholic gaze that even in his grief and rage over Sasha's death had somehow pierced his soul…

'Hi,' she greeted him a little breathlessly, as the electronic window beside Nikolai slid down. 'Sorry if I'm a bit later than I said. The director wanted a word with me.'

'Get in,' he replied, struggling to maintain his equilibrium, and unbalanced further by the strangely powerful effect of her summery perfume and her beautiful face.

'Where are we going?' The perfectly smooth skin on Ellie's brow tightened a little, as if she was fighting the urge to escape him after all.

'I am taking you to dinner. Where else did you think we were going?'

She flushed a little. 'I was hoping you might have relented and would let me see Arina,' she admitted softly.

'Not yet. We have still got some talking to do. How was your day at the studios?'

'All right.' She lifted her shoulders in a shrug.

Again, her scent arrowed acutely into Nikolai in an explosion of erotic sensuality, and it had the effect of tightening the iron muscles in his abdomen like a vice in his bid to stay immune.

'But the studio lights shining on me all day were too hot, and I felt like I was melting! It can make it pretty hard to think straight when I'm supposed to be giving people advice! It's definitely not an environment I would regularly like to work in.'

'I think a lot of young women would envy you the opportunity of being filmed and having the rest of the country watching you!'

'Because they crave their fifteen minutes of fame, you mean? I wish I could tell them how empty that is! It means nothing. When the admiration and applause dies away you still have yourself to face!'

Silently, Nikolai agreed, and he felt a distinct surge of approval that she echoed his own feelings on the whole concept of fame and celebrity. As well as knowing the emptiness of it, he was also a person who relished his privacy, and whenever that was intruded upon by the press or the media in general he resented it mightily.

'So? What kind of food would you like to eat tonight? The choice is yours. We can go anywhere.'

'Must we go to another restaurant? I'm feeling rather tired tonight, and I would much rather eat at home. I can put together some pasta and a sauce, if that would suffice and you'd care to join me?'

Nikolai's eyebrows shot up in surprise. An invitation back to where Ellie lived had not featured in his thoughts at all. He'd believed that she was far too wary of him to put herself in such a potentially vulnerable position. Yet it was an opportunity that he would not hesitate to take advantage of. Since their conversation last night an idea had taken root in his mind and would not leave him. Considering it now, Nikolai thought that it would probably be better put to her in the confines of her own home rather than in a public place where anyone might eavesdrop.

'Pasta would be just fine,' he agreed. 'Tell me your address and I will instruct my chauffeur.'

When the car pulled up in the street outside where Ellie lived in London's East End, Nikolai, having observed the general area as they drove—the graffiti-scrawled hoardings, the rubbish littering the streets, the damaged cars and the air of neglect—told his chauffeur to leave. When the time came he would get a cab home, he declared.

He put his hand beneath Ellie's elbow as she opened her front door. It was not easy to shrug off the automatic urge to protect her from harm, even though she had caused him no end of turmoil and distress. Already knowing he hated the idea of her living in such a run-down and dangerous area, Nikolai wondered why she had chosen to make her home there.

Ellie refused to feel embarrassed about where she lived, or the fact that her tiny flat was not full of the things most people in the crazy consumer-ridden world they lived in knocked themselves out working to buy. Most of her furniture was second hand, but it didn't bother her one jot. The fact was her little home was clean and tidy and it was *hers*. When she finished work each day, after meeting the demands of clients and the people at the homeless shelter, it was a most welcome haven, and she never stopped being grateful for it.

'There's a hook behind the door if you want to hang your coat up,' she told Nikolai as breezily as she could manage, still shocked at herself for inviting him.

Briefly going into the living room, she threw her blazer onto the overstuffed striped sofa with its cheerfully displayed cushions, then made her way back out into the long galley kitchen to start cooking. Kicking off her shoes with a heartfelt sigh, she was more than glad to feel the cool wooden floorboards beneath her hot and tired feet. But suddenly every muscle in her body stiffened at the sight of the charismatic man who came and stood in the doorway. For a stunning moment he regarded Ellie with something that she momentarily fooled herself might be warmth. *Why had she invited him here, into the one place that she truly felt safe?* His presence compromised that feeling of safety more than anything else in her world right now.

Reaching for the tall glass jar of dried spaghetti in an overhead cupboard, she felt her throat lock in sudden anguish. She so wanted him to see that she was good…decent…not someone he should revile. She was a person who could be trusted…a caring aunt whose greatest wish in the world was to be able to see her deceased sister's child again… Maybe while he was here, Ellie could at last convince him of that?

Upstairs in a bedroom drawer, she had a small pile of birthday and Christmas cards, notes and letters she had written to Arina over the years. But she had never plucked up the courage to send them in case Nikolai merely destroyed them.

'Do you want a drink while I'm cooking?' she asked. 'If you open the fridge there's a bottle of white wine in there.'

Nikolai fetched the wine without replying, and as he did so Ellie placed two small glasses on the worktop. 'It's a screw top,' she told him over her shoulder as he studied the label on the bottle, 'so you don't need an opener.' She flinched. She couldn't help it. She was pretty certain that Nikolai had *never* drunk wine from a bottle without a cork—let alone one that wasn't vintage or expensive.

'Can I do anything to help?' His gaze moved interestedly round the kitchen, skimming the calendar with its scenic view of Lake Derwent in the Lake District, the large antique clock with Roman numerals that Ellie had bought from a local flea market, and the fridge magnets with warm-hearted sayings that she was in complete agreement with. His focus swiftly returned to his companion.

*Could he help?* Such an idea was so incongruous that Ellie couldn't help but display her amusement.

Nikolai's dark blond brows came together in a genuinely perplexed frown. 'What is so funny?'

'I suppose I just don't see you as someone domesticated…that's all.' Her smile was gently teasing. 'Wealthy businessman and all that.' But Nikolai stared back at her without commenting, merely looking at her as if he might never stop. To cover her embarrassment Ellie grabbed the bottle of wine and poured some into both glasses. She lifted hers straight away. 'Cheers!'

'I can cook and clean just as well as the next man,' he remarked wryly at last, the devastating blue eyes alight with unexpected humour. 'I can even make beds if the situation calls for it!'

Of all the domestic tasks he could have listed to illustrate his point, why had he picked *that* one? Ellie wondered, panicked, feeling her face flame. 'Then you'll make some lucky woman very happy one day, I'm sure!'

'You would settle for that, Ellie?'

Suddenly Nikolai was behind her, his warm breath lifting the fine tiny hairs at the nape of her neck and shockingly making her nipples prickle inside her bra and grow tight. Her whole body went rigid as a statue.

'You would settle for a man who would help you in the house…cook, clean and…make beds? I think I can offer you a little more than that!'

Confused by the announcement, as well as shocked by his nearness, Ellie spun round. 'What are you talking about?'

'Why not prepare the food and we will talk after dinner?'

'I want to talk now! What did you mean, Nikolai?'

His features inscrutable, he reached past her for his glass of wine. '*After* dinner,' he insisted.

Again Ellie found herself in a position where she could barely eat a thing. Her mind could hardly fathom his odd remark, and her anxiety round him increased.

After making a good job of eating the spaghetti with tomato and basil sauce she had made, Nikolai suggested they move into the living room, where they could be more comfortable, Ellie reluctantly led the way, speculating worriedly about what would take place next, and able to do little about the wild hammering of her heart. Remaining silent as she switched on the lamps and closed the curtains against the encroaching night, Nikolai elected to remain standing when Ellie sat down on the edge of the comfortable couch.

'Remember we talked yesterday about how you might compensate me for what happened?' he began.

All she could do was stare apprehensively.

'Well, I have come up with a way. You want to see Arina and be in her life again…yes?'

Ellie jerked her head in the affirmative, but still said nothing. She was waiting. Waiting to see just what form this *compensation* Nikolai talked about would take before considering the fall-out. *She was pretty sure there would be fall-out.*

'Well…there is a way in which you can see her each and every day, Ellie,' he continued gravely, all humour long gone from his spectacular blue eyes. 'You can agree to become my wife and return to Park Lane to live with us.'

There were some occasions in life when someone spoke words that elicited such monumental shock that you were struck speechless. For Ellie, *this* was one of those moments. The hands that had been previously folded calmly in her lap moved restlessly down to her sides, and she smoothed them nervously across the silky cotton mix of her skirt in a bid to steady them.

'This is the way you want me to compensate you?' she heard herself ask, her voice sounding strangely like someone else's. 'By becoming your *wife*?'

'Yes.' Sounding abrupt, Nikolai moved across the room to the bay window, lifted an edge of the plain cream curtain and briefly peered outside. Not too far away someone brashly honked a car horn, and the sound splintered through the silence of the room like breaking glass.

Turning back to Ellie, his features were full of foreboding, even in the soft glow of lamplight. *He was suggesting that she become his wife and yet he looked like he was going to the guillotine*, she thought unhappily, her stomach churning sickeningly.

'It will, of course, only be a marriage of convenience. I think you must already guess that?'

'Let me try and get this straight.' Rising to her feet, Ellie garnered all the dignity and courage she could muster to face him. 'Are you saying that the only way I get to see Arina again and be in her life is if I agree to this—this "marriage of convenience" with you?'

'That is correct. I have been thinking for some time now that Arina needs a mother, and as I have no one in my life at the moment to fulfil that role, and indeed am in no hurry to enter again into the state of matrimony for any other reason than that of convenience, after already having one failed marriage behind me, it would seem the ideal thing for me to do is to make you my wife, Elizabeth.'

By the mere fact he had referred to her by her original name—the name by which he had known her and then come to *despise* her—Ellie knew Nikolai was deadly serious about what he was proposing. Her heart seemed to crash into her ribcage in alarm and distress.

'But you don't even like me!' she declared, emerald eyes sparkling with helpless tears.

'It hardly matters.' The broad shoulders lifted carelessly. 'Seeing as this will not be a marriage that has come about by the normal route of most such liaisons. It is purely a business arrangement. The point is that you were always good with Arina…and you can be again. Of that I have no doubt. Only this time you will sign a binding contract that you will keep to this agreement of ours and not renege on it. If you try, then I will make sure you will rue the day that you were born, Elizabeth Barnes!'

'Ellie,' she answered defiantly, lifting her chin and inwardly recoiling at such a threat. 'I'm Ellie Lyons now, and I answer to no one but myself!'

Nikolai's mouth twitched in amusement. 'But soon you will be Mrs Golitsyn, and then you will answer to *me*!" he declared, taking no little satisfaction at the thought.

'And if I refuse to marry you?'

'Then you will never see or get the chance to speak to Arina again.'

'You can't do that! She's my sister's only child!'

'Watch me.' Nikolai's mouth was grim. 'Refuse this marriage, Ellie, and risk the consequences of me bringing a private case against you for the death of my brother and the attempted theft of the necklace and other items that disappeared—or marry me and achieve the closeness with Arina that you say you have long craved. The choice is yours.'

'What am I supposed to—?'

'I will give you twenty-four hours to make up your mind. If you agree, then we will discuss the terms of the marriage in more depth. If not…' His glance flicked over Ellie as if she would be beneath his contempt if she chose the latter route.

'And if I do agree…when can I see Arina?' Ellie already knew she had no other option but to accept Nikolai's unconventional proposal, even though it flooded her with many real fears and concerns.

Right at that moment she would not allow her mind to explore too closely what it would mean for her personally. Later, when she was alone, she would think about that. All she knew was that she had already missed out on five years of her niece's life, and she had no intention of missing out on the rest of it because of the bitterness of the man that had now become her father. She *owed* it to Jackie to do this.

Suddenly she admitted frankly to herself what had really prompted her return to London last year. It hadn't just been the opportunity to work there…Arina had always been on her mind, and in her heart, and more than anything else Ellie had been hoping against hope to see her again…

# CHAPTER FIVE

IN THE cab on the way home last night, after he had left Ellie, Nikolai had reached another major decision. *He had decided to let her see Arina.* He was fairly certain that once she had set eyes on her sister's child again it would be practically impossible for her to refuse the marriage of convenience he had suggested. But Nikolai had a hidden agenda. Suddenly…*shockingly*…since spending time with her again he'd found himself impatient to make Ellie his wife.

Of all the women he could desire, want, need…*she* was the one who crowded thoughts of any others out. It hardly made sense to him, believing as he did that she had betrayed him with his brother and risked both his life and Arina's by driving the car that day, but Nikolai could not deny to himself what he felt.

When she came out of the television studios that afternoon he was waiting for her, with the declaration that he was taking her home to see her niece. Her bewitching emerald eyes swam with tears, but she quickly wiped them away and got into the car, simply murmuring 'thank you' and after that falling silent.

Electing not to say very much himself on the short journey to the house in Park Lane, Nikolai dwelt on the upcoming meeting between his daughter and her aunt, her former nanny, instead. They would clearly all need time to adjust to the new situation he was proposing, but he prayed that Arina would quickly learn to accept Ellie as her new mother once they were married, and as a result grow more confident with a more permanent female influence in her life.

His daughter's happiness meant everything to him. And even if it meant that for him there would never be the prospect of truly falling in love with a woman again—he was willing to make that sacrifice to guarantee his daughter's well-being.

Turning his focus to the plan he was devising for Ellie's long-term presence in their lives, he told himself it was only right that she should sacrifice some of the freedom she had stolen to pursue her chosen career when the child she had deserted had needlessly suffered because of her. *And it wouldn't be for ever…*just until Arina had left home and was forging a life of her own. After that Ellie and Nikolai could go their separate ways…

As his chauffeur steered the car into a waiting space in front of the elegant Park Lane residence, Nikolai turned to the woman at his side. She was not quick enough to hide the anxiety in her eyes, but he swiftly banished any treacherous urge to be sympathetic. 'She is just like any other normal healthy six-year-old girl,' he heard himself explain tersely. 'But obviously we will all have to take things one step at a time.'

A delicate frown creased Ellie's smooth brow. 'I'm not expecting her to accept me on sight! Relationships take time to build.'

'Good.'

'I just want to do what's right for her.'

'Then in that case…our aims are in perfect concord.'

It was impossible for Nikolai to keep the brusque tone from his voice. There were simply too many charged and chaotic emotions coursing through his blood for calmness to be a remotely viable option…

Inside the marble-floored hallway, Ellie met the privileged and wealthy air of her surroundings with a bittersweet upsurge of both happy and painful recollection. For long moments she was battered by emotion. Aware that Nikolai's steely-eyed gaze barely left her, she took a deep breath and grimaced. 'Everything is just the same as I remember it.'

'It was only six months ago that I had the place completely refurbished.'

'The décor may have changed, but the house itself feels just the same to me.'

'Then you must have a good memory after all, Ellie. I was quite certain it was a case of out of sight and out of mind as far as we were concerned!'

His imperious gaze mocked her mercilessly, and Ellie experienced a strong urge to get this daunting and emotional reunion over with as soon as possible. Not because she didn't want to see Arina—she was *desper-*

*ate* to do so, and had been quite overwhelmed when Nikolai had turned up at the studios and told her where he was taking her. But his unforgiving and punishing attitude towards her was seriously beginning to get to her. Did he imagine that Ellie had no feelings at all about entering this house again? Did it never even cross his mind for one moment to realise that it was as difficult for her to confront the past as it was for him?

'I haven't forgotten anything about my time here.' She lifted her chin. 'Up until the accident I was very happy here, and contrary to what you might believe I haven't concocted some convenient story about losing my memory to escape whatever retribution you think I deserve! I genuinely have no recall of what happened that day.'

'That is a topic of discussion for another more appropriate time, I think. Right now it is Arina who should be our first concern. Follow me. It is almost her bedtime, and at this time of the day she will probably be playing with her toys or listening to a story read by Elsa...the au pair,' he explained.

Walking behind Nikolai's tall, straight-backed figure up the grand sweeping staircase, with its sumptuous carpeted tread and Georgian elegance, Ellie didn't have a hope of calming the nerves that seized her. Everything was simply too raw...too achingly familiar and affecting for the skills in psychology she had painstakingly acquired over the years to be of any use to her whatsoever.

Moving in silence down a corridor lined with beau-

tiful and expensive art, they stopped outside a once
familiar door. Ellie's insides clenched hard, but without
saying a word to her—as if any thoughts or feelings she
might have were totally irrelevant to him—Nikolai
rapped smartly on the cream painted oak and opened the
door. Inside a large bedroom that was a little girl's dream,
a small, pretty dark-haired girl sat on an exquisite handmade bed, beautifully decorated with fairy princess
imagery and a lilac and white quilted bedspread. Next
to her sat a kind faced, big-boned young woman, with
smiling brown eyes and sandy-coloured hair.

She immediately got up when Nikolai and Ellie
entered, her smile open and generous. She seemed genuinely pleased to see them both. 'Welcome, welcome!
And how are you today?' Her accent was definitely
from one of the Scandinavian countries. 'We have just
been reading one of Arina's favourite stories...*The
Princess and the Pea*!'

She beamed, and Ellie sensed herself immediately
warming to Arina's au pair. Nikolai's attention had immediately been captured by the child who was busy
launching herself off the low-sided bed into his waiting
arms.

'Papa!'

Ellie sensed tears prick the backs of her eyelids.
Seeing the child was a double-edged sword for her.
First of all she was poignantly reminded of the beautiful baby she had loved as if she were her own, and
whose growing-up years she had sadly missed because
of her flight to Scotland. And second the shocking re-

alisation hit her that the six-year old Arina was a perfect miniature of Sasha, with her big china-blue eyes and rich dark hair. There was very little resemblance to her beloved sister Jackie at all.

The younger Golitsyn brother had looked like a hero from some ancient folk tale, with his lustrous dark locks and ethereal light blue eyes. The pity was that his addictions had started to take their toll on his remarkable good-looks, and taint the charm that had always drawn others so effortlessly into his sphere. *Something that Ellie knew to her cost.*

Now, watching Nikolai swing the little girl up into his arms and kiss her soundly on both cheeks, she was struck by what a breathtaking picture of unity and happiness they made together, and an inexplicable pang of loneliness and envy went through her. Addressing his daughter in Russian, Ellie heard him mention her name—it seemed that he had decided to stick with Ellie and not Elizabeth after all. Returning the child to her feet, he scraped his fingers through the regimented short thick strands of his dark blond hair and smiled—simply because he couldn't seem to help himself.

The sculpted features that already had the power to command instant attention wherever he went, because they were so striking, lit up even more when backed by the inner glow of pure pleasure behind them, Ellie discovered—and she couldn't help but stare.

'Ellie used to look after you when you were very small, Arina…just a baby. Say hello.'

'Hello.'

The big blue eyes moved up and down and all over her as if noting every facet and detail of Ellie's appearance and storing it to memory. Finally, she grinned, and hopped from one foot to the other—clearly pleased with what she'd discovered.

'You look just like a fairy princess!'

'That's just what I was going to say about you!' Ellie replied, stooping low so that she would be on the same level as the little girl. Gently she touched the tips of her fingers to the child's silky-soft pink-bloomed cheek and felt something inside her—some psychic bond of love that had never been broken—leap for joy. 'In fact, I think you must be the prettiest fairy princess I've ever seen—especially as you have the loveliest black hair…just like Snow White!'

'I like that story,' Arina solemnly replied, then leaned towards Ellie and confided, 'But I like the story about Cinderella better! I don't like the way her ugly sisters were so horrible to her. Papa says they were jealous because Cinderella was kind and beautiful and they were ugly and mean and wanted to marry the prince— but in the end he married Cinderella and they lived happily ever after!'

'What a sensible prince! I think he made the right choice, don't you? And I do so like happy endings!' Ellie smiled.

'Then maybe one day *you'll* meet a handsome prince and live happily ever after too!' came the child's ingenuous reply.

Feeling Nikolai's azure-blue gaze burn with a deep

blue flame as he silently observed her, Ellie went hot and cold all over. There would be no happy ending for her in this mockery of a marriage she was being forced to contemplate...she knew that. And suddenly along with that painful realisation came the knowledge that her work helping others have better relationships—with themselves, with others—would be all she could ever really hope for in that area. Even in her own opinion she was simply too messed-up ever to sustain a long-term relationship with any man.

She had been abandoned by her father and had her faith in men compromised by her sister's widowed husband, and now there was this intimidating proposal of marriage from Nikolai. How was she supposed to feel confident in *any* potentially intimate relationship with a man? Her faith and trust had been shattered and her self-esteem demoralised.

Slowly she rose to her feet, unable to resist ruffling the top of Arina's silky dark head as she did so. The child was gorgeous, and already Ellie knew she had the kind of naturally sweet temperament that would melt even the hardest heart. *She was a daughter any mother would be proud of...*

'That is another thing about Arina.' Bending his head, Nikolai captured his daughter's hand and kissed it extravagantly. 'She is one of life's optimists! She always looks on the bright side. Don't you, my angel?'

'Did you really look after me when I was a baby?' The child turned a curious long-lashed gaze back to Ellie.

'I did, sweetheart.' Pursing her lips, Ellie wanted to smile back—but emotion locked her throat painfully tight, and she didn't want to display what she was sure Nikolai would only see as another undesirable flaw in her character if she should suddenly give way to tears.

'Why didn't you stay with me? Did you get fed up with me?'

The question stunned Ellie. Looking to Nikolai for help was futile when all he was intent on doing was watching *her* constantly—as if waiting for her to somehow trip up and further prove his negative opinions about her.

Ignoring him, she dropped back down to the child's level and folded her hand carefully in her own. 'Of course I didn't, darling! You were the most adorable, wonderful baby that ever was, and I was so sad when I had to leave you. But I was in an accident, and…' She glanced up at Nikolai and silently he shook his head, indicating that his daughter knew nothing about the car accident and that Ellie was not to elaborate. 'I got hurt, and I was in hospital for a while. Afterwards my father took me away so that I could properly get better. But I missed you so much when I left, and I thought about you all the time!'

'And now you have come back!' The child's smile was huge…as if to say *that's sorted, let's get onto something else!* Pulling her hand free, she danced across the room back to Elsa. 'Can we finish my story, please?' she begged, her father and Ellie more or less forgotten.

'Why, of course! But then you have to brush your

teeth and get ready for bed, because you have to get up for school in the morning!'

'We will leave.' Moving across the room to kiss his daughter an affectionate goodnight, Nikolai turned back to Ellie. 'I think it is time for us to go and have dinner.'

'I didn't realise you expected me to stay and eat with you.'

'You need to eat, I need to eat...of course you will stay to eat dinner! We also have some important business to complete...yes?'

Dinner was a fairly tense affair, with Nikolai at one end of the grand highly polished dining table, in the dining room with its stately windows overlooking the well-tended and manicured garden, and Ellie at the other. After his initial enquiries as to what she thought of Arina after not seeing her all this time it seemed her host was not disposed to make conversation.

It was obvious that some deep contemplation about the situation was preoccupying him, and Ellie could not really attest to minding the silence that descended between them. She was thinking hard too. Mostly wrapped up in the memories she did recall of her time in the Golitsyn household—she was quite relieved to let the time drift by with no mention of the marriage of convenience Nikolai was proposing. She knew it was only a temporary reprieve from what was looking more and more inevitable, but strangely, after a sleepless night contemplating it, and now after seeing Arina, some of her apprehension was calming down.

When Miriam brought them their coffee at the end of the meal, Nikolai suggested they take it into the drawing room. Finding herself alone with him after the attentive presence of his housekeeper and the young maid who had been helping to serve the meal, Ellie glanced round her and saw the exquisitely appointed drawing room had indeed been refurbished since she had seen it last. With its original Georgian box sash windows and sumptuous velvet drapes, it took the words 'elegance' and 'good taste' to a whole new level. Visually, it was absolutely stunning. It was a room in which to have tea in the very best fine bone china, amidst a backdrop of ever so polite conversation, Ellie decided privately. It definitely wasn't the kind of space where you could just throw down some comfy cushions on the floor and chill out, watching your favourite programme on TV!

*Not that she could ever imagine a man like Nikolai indulging in such a commonplace pastime*! He was a man made for more high-class pleasures...like fine wines, the best restaurants, and yachts in the South of France. He would most likely scorn the simple pursuits that interested Ellie.

Sighing, she let her gaze move round the room some more. With its innovative mix of contemporary and vintage furniture, and desirable art decorating the walls, it made Ellie's little flat in Hackney resemble some kind of hermit's retreat! However, the notion of envy didn't enter her mind for even a second. At this point in her life she was merely grateful to be alive and doing a job she truly loved—a job where she had a real opportunity to make a difference to young people's lives. Compared to that, Nikolai's beautiful house and staggering wealth hardly even signified.

'I'm going to have a cognac with my coffee,' he announced, interrupting her thoughts with the smoky gravel-edged tones of his compelling voice. 'What about you?' Pulling his silk tie free of his pristine shirt collar, he moved across to the burr walnut cocktail cabinet and opened it.

'Nothing for me, thank you.'

'Why not?' He raised a quizzical eyebrow.

'Because I need to try and get a good night's sleep, and alcohol doesn't really help me do that. I'm working with two new clients for the TV programme and I need to keep a clear head.'

'One small cognac will not hurt. You look like you could use a drink to put some colour back into those pale cheeks of yours!'

Knowing the colour always seemed to drain out of her whenever she was tired, but surprised that he had noticed, Ellie shrugged. 'Okay... Just a small one, then.'

'So...did seeing Arina again fulfil your expectations?' After handing her a crystal goblet-shaped glass, the amber liquid inside it glistening in the subdued lighting of the various elegant lamps dotted round the room, Nikolai went and stood by the white marble mantelpiece that was above the stunning fireplace—every inch the Lord and Master of all he surveyed.

From her position on the supremely comfortable

sofa, Ellie breathed a small sigh of relief that he hadn't joined her. 'It was the strangest experience… All this time apart and yet everything about her felt so familiar…as though I'd never left at all.' She shook her head in wonder. 'I thought she was adorable and beautiful! She's grown into the loveliest child, Nikolai!'

'I agree. Nobody would guess that her early beginnings were less than they should have been. My only wish now is that she will grow up into a happy and well-adjusted young woman. To achieve this, I have long realised, a girl should have a mother as well as a father. That is where you come in, Ellie.'

Hardly knowing what to say, Ellie fell silent. What he was proposing set her heart racing, and she tried to imagine what her life would be like living on such intimate terms with a man like Nikolai Golitsyn. The word 'intimate' conjured up particular dread for her, and she prayed that this 'convenient' marriage he was set on would not include what were her very worst fears. Surely he would find some other 'means' of satisfying that aspect of things without involving her? she thought, panicked. *But her heart was torn with a longing that contradicted that hope.*

Lifting her gaze, she found herself yet again under the ever-watchful surveillance of those azure-blue eyes. Had he guessed what was going through her mind just then? Her cheeks burned like a brand at the idea that he had. Self-consciously adjusting her position on the sumptuous sofa, Ellie took a tentative sip of her cognac. Its searing warmth had an immediate effect, and she sensed her cheeks tingle with even more heated colour. She made a mental note not to drink any more.

'From what I gleaned after the way you looked at me upstairs, when I mentioned being hurt in an accident, I gather that you haven't spoken to Arina about what happened?'

'No, and I do not intend to until she is much older! Thankfully she remembers nothing of that day, because she was too young. She only knows that her father died, and so far she has not asked me why.'

'What about her mother? Has she asked about her?'

'She knows that Jackie died giving birth to her, and that that was when you came to the house to live with us and help take care of her.'

'And what about the fact that I'm her aunt, Nikolai? Did you tell her that? Or am I supposed to keep quiet about that and act as if I am just a stranger who came to look after her when her mother died?'

'I will tell her soon who you really are. Like I said before…we need to take things one step at a time.'

The fierce look in his eyes reminded Ellie of a proud male lion defending its offspring against predatory hunters, and she flinched at the evidence of reluctance in his voice. It was further proof of his lack of trust in her, and Ellie couldn't deny that hurt. Yet beneath her pain was the steadily growing vow that she would show him that she *could* be trusted—would strive daily to prove it.

'Nikolai? I loved seeing Arina again, and the idea of becoming her mother… Well…it's an overwhelming privilege, as well as the greatest responsibility! And perhaps the very *least* I could do, considering her mother was my sister. But when it comes down to the reality of the situation, I really think this idea of yours about us getting married and me living with you couldn't possibly work!'

'One can make anything work if one is committed and dedicated to the task, Ellie.'

Nikolai moved across the room to stand in front of her, and his sudden close proximity and the disturbing clean sharp scent of his expensive cologne made Ellie's muscles go rigid with tension. Glancing up at him, she saw he really was quite formidable right then.

'And seeing the way that Arina responded to you even after all these years has convinced me that what I am proposing is absolutely right! If you do not make up your mind to do as I ask then you leave me no choice but to start legal proceedings against you! Do not make the foolish mistake of imagining I will not follow through with what I say, Ellie. I am completely serious about this!'

# CHAPTER SIX

'IF I DO agree to the marriage…what are the terms?' Quietly and with dignity, Ellie fearlessly met Nikolai's frosty gaze.

Inwardly he sensed something settle, and realised he had all but been holding his breath, waiting for her answer. Moving back across the room, he resumed his position in front of the fireplace.

'The main one would be that you agree to remain my wife until Arina is grown—shall we say twenty-one? After that we can divorce. You may leave my household, but you will remain her mother…agreed?'

'I would hardly want to bring *that* relationship to an end!' Ellie frowned and took what looked to be a reluctant sip of her cognac. 'What about my work and my commitments to people?'

'You may still pursue your career, with all that that entails—including your commitments to those people who have come to rely on you. I suppose you are mainly referring to your father? But Arina's needs must always come first. For instance, if she is ill I would expect you to stay and look after her, *not* the au pair or my house-keeper. The nature of my own work will also entail you accompanying me and Arina on essential trips abroad from time to time. I have become accustomed over the years to taking her with me whenever I go away—especially if it is a long trip—and she too has come to expect that. As she gets older I will hire a private tutor to school her whenever we are out of the country, so she will not miss out on her education.'

'Your expectations as far as me being a mother to Arina are not unreasonable, Nikolai, but I would expect some degree of flexibility from you as regards my work. For instance, when someone is having ongoing counselling it could be extremely disruptive for me to go away indefinitely…not to mention distressing to my client.'

'Then when the situation arises we will negotiate for the best interests of all concerned. I am not an ogre, Ellie…even though you may think me hard-hearted and unforgiving. I can be reasonable too.'

He allowed himself the smallest of conciliatory smiles, but Ellie did not look particularly convinced by it. *Would she resent him for good, given that he was more or less forcing her into this marriage*? This time Nikolai *did* harden his heart. He was only demanding what was owed to him *and* Arina, he reminded himself. Once he saw that Ellie was as good as her word in being the kind of mother to their daughter he expected then bit by bit she would come to see that there were definitely certain benefits to being married to a man of his considerable wealth and position. Benefits that would surely more than make up for what she might regard as her perceived lack of freedom?

'There is one more thing I have to ask.' Placing her glass on the nearby walnut side table, Ellie rose to her feet.

Where her cheeks had appeared pale before, there was now evidence of a definite rose coloured tint in them. But beneath her lovely eyes were also visible signs of strain and tiredness. Remembering she had said that she'd struggled beneath the hot studio lights all day, Nikolai frowned.

'Go on,' he said, folding his arms across his chest.

'There's no delicate way to put this, so I'll just have to come right out and say it.'

The rose-pink in her cheeks deepened almost to scarlet, and Nikolai felt a tug of intrigue and…yes…a quiet excitement deep in his belly. He had already easily guessed the nature of her tentatively voiced question, because the subject had inevitably been on his mind too.

'Are you expecting us to be intimate once we are married?'

'I have the same needs as any other red-blooded male, Ellie,' he heard himself answer nonchalantly. 'And as a woman no doubt you must share similar needs. So my reply to your question is yes…I think being intimate will be a natural consequence of us living together, and may even make the marriage better than we could have hoped for!'

Her emerald-eyed glance should have spoken

volumes as to her feelings, but right then Nikolai was so captivated by their beauty and luminosity he lost the capacity to think about what else was going on. But inside he did sense a thrill of anticipation at the idea of making love to her. *Something he had long craved since that explosive kiss they had shared all those years ago…*

'I would also like you to move in *before* we are married,' he announced, still gazing directly into her eyes. 'It will give us both a chance to adjust to the new situation, as well as getting Arina used to the idea that we will soon be wed.'

'What about my flat? I can't just leave it and not go back!' Ellie focused determinedly on the less sensitive of his proposals.

'Do you own it?'

Ellie flushed. 'I have a mortgage—like most people.'

'Then I would suggest you either make arrangements for someone to rent it or else put it on the market to sell. Let me know what you decide and I will take care of it for you if you like.'

He saw her swallow and look away.

'It seems like you've thought of everything!'

'I am accustomed to sorting things out. It is not a problem. Do you agree to my terms regarding the marriage?'

'I want to see Arina regularly and be a part of her life again, and after all this time apart from her I don't want to jeopardise that… So, yes…I agree to the terms, Nikolai.' She agreed even as the thought of their proposed intimacy danced around in her head. 'It all feels a bit unreal to me at the moment, but I expect I will eventually get used to what's happening. Now that we've discussed things…I'd really like to just go home and be by myself for a while. It's been quite a day, one way and another.'

Relieved beyond measure by her reply, Nikolai sighed and briefly moved his head in agreement to her request.

Shortly afterwards, having assured Ellie that he would be in contact again the following day, he allowed her to leave and his chauffeur took her home.

Nursing what remained of his cognac, Nikolai went to sit on the sofa in the same spot that she had occupied only minutes before. Shutting his eyes, he knew every sense he possessed was alert to not just the summery perfume that lingered there, but also to the disturbingly feminine essence Ellie had left behind her. Ellie… Mrs Elizabeth Golitsyn.

Smiling with possessive satisfaction, Nikolai opened his eyes again. He had taken the first vital step in achieving what he now knew he desired above all else—a convenient union between them, with his daughter's happiness and security paramount. He told himself he should be more than pleased. However, he had not been immune to the doubt and reluctance in the beautiful emerald eyes that had pierced him after Ellie had agreed to the marriage and his terms, and it had been a harsh pill to swallow. She had cared for his brother, *not* him! he savagely reminded himself—plus, he was blackmailing her into a marriage she did not want. Why *should* she be remotely pleased?

Both thoughts cut into him like Damascus steel, and he swallowed down the rest of his drink with little pleasure, grimacing at the fire that erupted inside his stomach. As long as Ellie kept her word and made Arina her priority then Nikolai told himself he could bear her disturbing presence. Indeed, this marriage of theirs would have compensations as well as convenience. Ellie was now perfectly aware that he expected her to share his bed, and had not even put up an argument.

Telling himself that she was at least being honest about that aspect of her nature, and would not want to contemplate a union with a man *without* sex, Nikolai pushed to his feet and depressed the switch that put out all the lamps as he left the drawing room. Turning his mind to the practicalities of the situation, he vowed to speak to Miriam first thing in the morning about preparing for the newest member of their household.

The Saturday at the end of the month was the date they had agreed that Ellie would move into the Park Lane house, and if by then she had not found someone to rent or buy her own property then Nikolai would step in and find a suitable agency to do so for her. And just as soon as a civil marriage could be arranged between them at the local register office their union would be sanctioned officially. Life would continue on more or less as normal…the only difference being that now he would have a wife and Arina a mother…

* * *

Ellie put her arm round the thin, hunched figure seated on the threadbare couch beside her. 'Jay?' she said gently, aware that the boy was crying and didn't want her to see. 'Tell me what happened.'

Scrubbing at his tears with his tobacco-stained nail-bitten fingers, he turned his resentful and hurt gaze towards her. 'I saw her… I saw me mum with her new bloke in the high street. She acted like she didn't even know who I was! I was staring at her and she looked right through me!'

'What did you say to her?'

'Nothin'!' His expression was savage. 'What was the point? She'd probably just ignore me anyway! You could see she was more interested in the loser by her side! All loved up, she was, and happy…happy that she wasn't with *me*!'

'Do you know where she's staying?'

'No—and I don't want to either!'

'It must have been hard for you…'

Absently stroking the boy's straight dark hair, Ellie soothed him as though he were a child. It didn't matter what the textbooks or the rules said—in her opinion when someone was hurting they needed the warmth and reassurance of human contact and Jay had been fending for himself since he was a small boy. His alcohol-addicted mother had inflicted a series of woefully in-adequate and violent men on her son in her desperate search for a relationship.

'Seeing her again must have opened up old wounds.

But you're getting your life together without her, Jay,'
she reminded him. 'Next Saturday you're moving out
of the shelter into a room of your own, and on Monday
you're starting your apprenticeship at the timber mer-
chants. Things are moving on for you too. Soon you'll
be earning your first real wage packet, and life is just
going to get better and better!'

The teenager sniffed and looked her straight in the
eyes. 'It'll be great moving out of here! Not that it ain't
any good, but it ain't exactly a palace is it?'

His dark gaze wryly swept the uncurtained barely
furnished room, with its tatty cushions on the floor, the
single couch, and the fireplace with its inadequate
electric bar heater. It tenderly moved Ellie that a lad
who had never had much more than this scruffy room
in the whole of his life should nurture aspirations for
something better.

'It'll be so cool, having me own place! You've been
a real friend to me, miss… I couldn't have got through
the last six months without you. The things you
said…always so positive and upbeat…well, it gave me
something to hang onto.'

Slowly moving her hand from his hair onto her lap,
Ellie smiled. It touched her more than she could say to
have someone like Jay affirm that she'd been a help to
him, and she was reminded yet again why she kept on
doing her work at the shelter even when she had a counselling practice of her own to run.

'It was my pleasure. I know it's been tough for you,
but just try and take one day at a time, hmm? Use some

of the relaxation skills I taught you when life gets over-whelming, and remember that you can always stay in touch if you need someone to talk to. Everyone here is rooting for you too…don't forget that.'

'I won't, miss…and thanks again.'

It wasn't only Jay who was moving to a new abode on Saturday. The two weeks had flown by since she and Nikolai had made their agreement. One of her colleagues at the centre had agreed to rent her flat indefinitely, and the realisation that it was now payback time swept dis-turbingly through Ellie again and again—at work, and mercilessly in the evenings, when she was back home.

Carrying her mug of instant coffee from the kitchen into the living room that particular night, it hit her even more forcefully just what she had agreed to with Nikolai. *She was doing it for Arina*, she told herself, blanking out the flickering images on the muted tele-vision screen in front of her in order to think. *And for her father…* There was no way she would run the risk of him going to prison again, should she decline the marriage and Nikolai bring a private case against them—even if his suspicions that she had stolen from him were completely unfounded.

On the phone to her earlier from Edinburgh, her dad had told her how bad things were getting with his health and Ellie's stomach had churned with anxiety and sorrow. Nikolai Golitsyn might do anything and every-thing he could to ensure his daughter's happiness, but he was also possessed of a mercenary streak that she would no doubt become all too aware of should Ellie disappoint him in his ambition to make her his wife. There was simply no talking him out of this idea of his.

Every day on the phone when he rang her at work, he reminded her of that. His mind was made up. And never far from Ellie's thoughts about the new life she had in store was the heart-racing notion of sleeping with Nikolai. She hadn't put up a fight about that because part of her hoped that if there was intimacy between them there might eventually be trust, and…and something more perhaps. Ellie wouldn't even say the word in private to herself, it seemed so impossible. The fact was—blackmailer or not—he was the man she had *always* secretly desired. But from Hackney to Park Lane! It was a surreal prospect.

Leaving her coffee on a small side table, she dropped down onto the comfy striped couch and shook her head in apprehension and wonder. Ellie wondered what her colleagues and the volunteers at the shelter would make of the dramatic improvement in the location where she lived. And there would be the stress and inconvenience of her longer journey to work everyday. It was hard to feel excitement or pleasure in the upcoming move—apart from the joy of being with Arina at last. How *could* she anticipate it with any sense of contentment or satisfaction when underlying it all was the genuinely gut-wrenching prospect of living in the one place from her past that had caused her more sorrow and regret than any part of her emotionally impoverished upbringing as a child?

\* \* \*

'Is that all of your bags, Dr Lyons?' Nikolai's house-keeper met Ellie at the front door and invited her into the hall.

'My other stuff is arriving later… Nikolai—I mean Mr Golitsyn has arranged it for me.'

'Well, then, I will take you upstairs and show you to your room!'

'By the way…where *is* Mr Golitsyn? Isn't he here?'

'No, Dr Lyons. He has taken the little one to her ballet lesson. He said to tell you that he will join you later and to please make yourself at home.'

'I see.'

*An unexpected reprieve then…*

Ellie breathed an inward sigh of relief when the housekeeper led her away from the room she had occupied five years ago. That had been beautifully appointed and decorated, but being there she knew she would have been catapulted all too swiftly into the past again, and would have felt herself at a disadvantage somehow, when she needed to garner all the positives she could muster. Determination was strengthening inside her that, for however long this strange arrangement with Nikolai lasted, she would make a decent go of it…for Arina's sake if nothing else. And, yes, she would let him see that she was a very different woman today from the inexperienced and perhaps naïve girl she'd been when she had worked for him before. He might have blackmailed her into this unwanted partnership by using Arina as a bargaining tool, but he wouldn't have everything his own way! Not by a long chalk!

Following the plump housekeeper down a corridor on the topmost floor, Ellie felt her heartbeat accelerate as another troubling thought speared her. What if she was being led to Nikolai's bedroom? She'd agreed that they would be intimate once they were married, but she'd hoped he wouldn't take that to mean as soon as she moved in. She needed time to adjust.

But, no... This exquisitely light and airy, room with its scented air, elegant armoire, and a double bed with a rich Venetian purple silk bedspread was, Miriam announced with a smile, 'one of my favourite guest rooms.' It even had a lovely balcony that looked out onto the garden.

Alone again, with Miriam's cheerful promise of a cup of tea and a slice of home-made fruitcake when she returned downstairs ringing enticingly in her ears, Ellie left her bags where they were and went and sat down on the bed. Smoothing her hand over the sumptuous silk counterpane with a softly weary sigh, she felt as though extreme fatigue—both emotional and physical—had finally caught up with her. She'd worked at the shelter nearly every night this week, after working all day at the practice, and it was no wonder her body was practically screaming at her to rest!

If Nikolai and Arina were going to be a while, would it matter if she stole ten minutes or so and had a nap? Unable to resist doing just that, Ellie kicked off the narrow-heeled pumps that had been pinching her toes all morning, and scooted up the bed to rest her head against the luxurious pillows. With another grateful sigh that seemed to arise from the very depths of her soul, she shut her eyes—and in less than a minute had drifted off into a deep, deep slumber...

'Ellie?' Nikolai knocked on the door for a second time. Miriam had assured him that Dr Lyons had not come down from her room since she had shown her there, and that had been over an hour ago. Leaving a hungry and happy Arina eating fruitcake in the kitchen with the older woman, Nikolai had come upstairs to see for himself what was keeping Ellie.

He had not set eyes on her for over two weeks now, and he could not deny that a quiet but fierce excitement was building inside him to redress that. When he received no response from her yet again, he turned the doorknob and stepped inside. A shaft of buttery golden sunlight streamed through the old-fashioned window, casting a dappled effect on the carpet that showed the shadow of trembling leaves from the oak tree in the garden. But it wasn't that captivating sight that drew Nikolai's attention.

Ellie was lying on the bed, fast asleep. The quietly hypnotic rhythm of her breathing was the only sound in the room. He moved nearer to the bed, all his muscles helplessly contracting at the vision of her lovely face, golden hair, and her sweetly curvaceous body clothed in black jeans and a lilac coloured sweater. He found himself smiling at the sight of her small slender feet with their rose-pink-painted toenails curled into the silk counterpane, and suddenly he was in no great hurry to return to the kitchen.

If Nikolai didn't confess at least to himself that he had feared Ellie might find some way of not keeping the bargain they had made he would be a liar. And now that he had the very real and captivating evidence of her presence before him something inside him knew a great longing to keep her to himself for as long as possible before resuming the rest of his day.

Stirring a little in her sleep, Ellie had a sudden furrow between her smooth arched brows. 'Sasha— no!'

The heartfelt whimper left her lips and Nikolai's muscles clenched again, this time in shock and dismay and…yes…slow-burning rage too. There he stood, admiring her beauty like the most gullible fool on the planet, relieved that she had not reneged on their agreement and grasping at the slimmest hope that things might turn out for the best after all—and Ellie betrayed him yet again… Betrayed him with a dream of his brother Sasha!

Disturbed by the images that flitted across the inner landscape of her mind, Ellie opened her stunning emerald eyes and stared at Nikolai in shock, instantly alert. 'What's wrong? What are you doing here?' She pushed herself up into a sitting position, her not quite steady hand smoothing back the lock of bright hair that had flopped onto her forehead.

'Nothing is wrong. I merely came up to see where

you were. Miriam said she brought you up here over an hour ago.'

'I fell asleep.'

'Obviously…'

Crossing his arms over his chest, Nikolai speared her with an accusing and blaming glance. 'You were dreaming about Sasha.'

'Was I?'

'You called out his name.'

'Did I? I don't remember.' Swinging her legs over the side of the bed, Ellie let her bare feet touch the floor. Swaying slightly, she stood, momentarily losing her balance.

Nikolai automatically moved forward to help steady her, his hands settling on either side of her rounded hips. He let them stay there as his furious gaze duelled with hers. He was entrapped by the enticing warmth that flowed into his palms and suddenly—shockingly—he craved a far more *intimate* contact…

'You seem to have an ongoing problem with your memory, Ellie. Can you blame me if I am beginning to believe it is a selective loss?'

'Believe what you like!' Resentfully, she freed herself and moved as far away from him as she could. 'The only reason I'm here is because of Arina and my father. I guess I'll just have to learn to live with your less than flattering opinions of me!'

Nikolai shrugged, suddenly lazily amused by her show of spirit and—despite his anger over her dream—

still aroused too. 'So be it. How do you like your room, by the way?'

He saw her indignation deflate. The slender shoulders in the lilac sweater lifted in a shrug. 'It's very nice. Pretty. I like the view over the garden.'

'Good. Once we are married you will move into my room. It too has a nice view over the garden.'

Smiling enigmatically, Nikolai had the satisfaction of seeing Ellie's expressive eyes widen. If Sasha had enjoyed the comfort and pleasure of her seductive body then why shouldn't he? There was no reason for Nikolai to feel any guilt whatsoever. After all, in a very short time she would legitimately be his wife.

'You still look a little tired. What have you been doing, Ellie? Burning the candle at both ends? Partying, perhaps, with the new celebrity friends you have made at the television studios?'

'You're determined only to think the very worst of me, aren't you?' She shook her head a little forlornly.

'I see what appears to be right in front of my eyes!'

'Then that's your first mistake! Do you make all your judgements with so little hard evidence to back them up?'

Feeling strangely chastised, Nikolai impatiently brushed off Ellie's unsettling remark and moved towards the door. 'It's time we went downstairs. Miriam has made some tea for us, and Arina is waiting to see you also.'

'Talking of Arina—what have you told her about me? I mean…why I'm staying here?'

'I explained to her a little while ago that you were her mother's sister—her aunt. I told her that when we recently met up again I was thinking about how you used to take care of her as a baby and how close you were to her. Nearly every other day she asks me… "When will I have a mother?" So I told her that I had decided you were the perfect person for the job, and that when I asked you, you said you would happily accept.'

'Children always sense a lie.'

Refusing to let her comment rattle him, Nikolai lifted his broad shoulders in their trademark shrug—a gesture he often employed to disguise his true feelings. In business particularly it didn't pay to let the opposition know what you were thinking. 'I will do whatever I have to do to make her happy! I already told you that. If you try and tell her anything different about why you are here, then I will see to it that you regret it to the end of your days!'

'Any more threats?' Ellie raised her chin defiantly.

Unable to stop the smile that tugged at the edges of his mouth, Nikolai shook his head. 'For now, Ellie… I am all out of threats. What I would like to happen is for you to come downstairs and drink tea with my daughter and me! Not too difficult a task even for you…do you agree?'

'And what about your friends? What will you tell *them* about me?' she persisted.

'I will tell them the truth. That you are Arina's aunt and my fiancée…and that we are soon to be married.' Without giving her a chance to comment, Nikolai abruptly left the room—not even glancing over his shoulder to see if she would join him…

* * *

The items Ellie had left behind her in the flat—the things she couldn't do without, like her wardrobe of clothes, her compact music system, CD collection and two bookcases of books—arrived soon after she'd finished drinking tea with Nikolai, sampling Miriam's knockout fruitcake and playing for a while with an excited Arina.

The little girl had kept giving Ellie long, assessing happy glances when she'd thought she wasn't looking, and that had made her heart squeeze. The child was very easy to love. That much was starkly and worryingly evident. And Ellie knew that the more she allowed herself to build up a relationship with Nikolai's enchanting daughter—*her niece*—the harder it would be when this pretend union of theirs failed—as fail inevitably would. And yet again Arina would be the sad casualty of that failure in a tragic story that seemed impossible to resolve.

Now, in the lovely room she had been allocated to sleep in, Ellie tried to put aside all thoughts of the future and concentrate on the present instead. The removal men who had transported her things had positioned her two pine bookcases side by side against one of the professionally painted lavender walls, and now she got down on her knees and started to excavate the six packed cardboard boxes of books they had brought too. Briefly she wondered how Jay was getting on with *his* move today.

Glancing round the genteel bedroom, with its expensive handcrafted furniture and the open balcony doors that let in the sound of birdsong and the scent of late-blooming roses from the garden, she felt her stomach momentarily turn over. The contrast in their new abodes was poignantly painful. Yet for all the room's beauty Ellie wasn't totally happy to be there at all. If it weren't for Arina—and the threat that hung over her that she might not ever see her again if Ellie reneged on the agreement she'd made with Nikolai—she would be more than content to be back in her flat in Hackney, with the constant flow of noisy traffic streaming past her door and the smell of curry wafting through the opened windows from the Bangladeshi restaurant at the end of the street.

Sighing, she turned her attention back to the task in hand. She was turning the page of a favourite hardback she'd revisited time and time again, unable to resist casting her eager gaze over the opening chapter, when her mind was seized by the memory of the dream that had earlier disturbed her nap. She'd *lied* when she'd insisted to Nikolai that she hadn't remembered dreaming about Sasha, and now the painfully real scene frighteningly replayed itself.

They were standing downstairs at the front door, and Sasha had the baby in his arms. Arina was crying loudly in distress, obviously sensing something wasn't right, and Ellie was begging him to give the baby back to her. For answer, Sasha gave her a disturbing and confused smile. He was high on drugs again, Ellie realised, as well as drunk, and he was demanding that

Ellie drive him to see a friend of his—a 'friend' that she somehow knew supplied him with drugs. His habit had worsened since her sister had died, and Ellie had often pleaded with him to give it up—if not for his own sake than at least for his child's. He always promised he would, but Ellie had long known he was finding it impossible to keep that promise.

Many times she'd threatened to tell Nikolai just what was happening, but more often than not Sasha would start pleading with her to give him 'one more chance'—and she would again keep quiet about the problem. But as he'd stood swaying at the front door in the dream—beyond reason and maybe beyond hope—Ellie fervently wished she had confided in Nikolai about what was going on with his brother. 'Please, Ellie—take me to my friend's. Or I swear I will disappear for good, and Arina and Nikolai will never see me again!' Sasha begged, glassy-eyed.

'You know I can't drive you, Sasha! I've only just passed my test, and I don't even have my own car yet!' Ellie replied, her heart thumping with foreboding and dread.

'You can drive my brother's car.'

'You're joking!'

'Then I'll phone for a cab.'

That was not a good idea… What if the cab driver went to the newspapers and exposed Sasha's drug problem to the world? His brother was both well known and respected, and had surely been through enough trauma without being dragged into the seedy orbit of a voracious and unkind media! It felt as if Ellie was in the worst dilemma of her life.

A second later there was a sound in her mind like a heavy door slamming shut, and it echoed for long seconds even as the rest of the dream frustratingly evaded her. *Was it dream or memory*? Hardly realising she was holding her breath, Ellie let out the trapped air in her lungs with a sound like a woman in labour. Into the stillness that followed came a knock at the door.

'Yes?'

She prayed it wouldn't be Nikolai. The memory of the dream clung to her like the cold slimy reeds found growing in marshes, and she didn't think she'd be able to keep her distress or her guilt hidden. But her visitor was Miriam.

'I am very sorry to trouble you, Dr Lyons—but Mr Golitsyn, he is going out very shortly and would like you to accompany him.'

'Where to?'

A fond, doting look crept over the housekeeper's face. 'To take the little one shopping for clothes! He said to tell you he would value your opinion.'

Her disturbing dream put firmly aside, Ellie rose slowly to her feet and dusted down her jeans. An undeniable sense of surprise and pleasure had inexplicably swept through her at the idea that Nikolai had thought to ask her to go with them.

'Tell him I'll be down in about ten minutes.' She smiled, inwardly assuring herself the pleasure she had experienced had been at the prospect of spending time with Arina.

'I will tell him, Dr Lyons.'

'Oh—and Miriam? Why don't you just call me Ellie?'

# CHAPTER SEVEN

THEY'D VISITED ALL the major department stores in the west end to source suitable clothing for a six-year-old, and afterwards—as if he hadn't already spent a small fortune—Nikolai had told his driver to take them to the King's Road in Chelsea.

It was clear that Arina was absolutely *loving* her shopping spree! She was a real 'girly girl', scorning jeans and more unisex clothing in favour of extremely feminine and pretty dresses, with shoes and accessories to match! And the child wasn't the only one who appeared to be in her element. Nikolai was more relaxed and at ease than Ellie had ever seen him, and definitely in an indulgent mood. Dressed in a sky-blue polo shirt and dark jeans, with a casual tan-coloured suede jacket, he looked like any other well-dressed professional enjoying an outing with his family.

Family… The word was like a pool full of sharks as far as Ellie was concerned. Part of her was torn, wanting to be the mother that Arina clearly craved and needed, and yet she was completely daunted by the very idea.

She hadn't even known her own mother, as she had died shortly after giving birth to Ellie, so what examples of motherhood could she draw upon when she had more or less brought herself up? And she was even more troubled by the idea of letting her guard slip even an inch around Arina's father. Would he or *could* he ever see past his need to make her pay for what had happened in the past and discover the real woman behind the imagined misdeeds? It was hard to believe such a thing could happen.

Whatever way Ellie viewed it, he had coerced her into making this deal with him, he didn't trust her, thought her a liar and a thief, and—worst of all— believed her to have been having an affair with his brother! The thought slammed into her like a freight train, stealing her joy at admiring yet another pretty outfit that she had helped Arina try on in the small exclusive boutique.

'Ellie?' Nikolai's hypnotic voice invaded her consciousness, and she glanced up at him in surprise across the too-warm room with its select display of colourful clothing, immediately magnetised by it.

'You were miles away.'

'Sorry,' she mumbled, fixing a smile on her face and crouching down to buckle the red patent leather shoes that went with Arina's outfit.

Outside again in the sunshine, Nikolai firmly clasped his daughter's hand, and touched Ellie's arm when she would have walked on.

'You now have a choice,' he announced seriously.

'We can either go clothes-shopping for you, or pay a visit to the Russian tearooms that have recently opened up nearby.'

'I really don't need new clothes!' she answered sharply, almost faint with embarrassment at the idea he would buy *anything* for her...let alone something as personal as clothing! But in the Russian's unsettling and riveting glance was distinct evidence of humour.

His gaze swept over Ellie's fitted black jeans, and the scooped-neck white T-shirt that hugged her breasts a little too snugly, as if he was thinking her dress sense certainly needed improving upon even if she didn't think it did! There was something else in that not so innocent glance that made Ellie break out in an almost excruciatingly hot sweat beneath her clothes as she devastatingly remembered the way Nikolai had clasped her hips when he had stopped her from stumbling in the bedroom earlier. *As if all he had needed was her consent and he would have brought them right up against his own...*

'It is an unusual woman, in my experience, who denies she needs anything when the opportunity to be taken shopping is offered to her!' he remarked in that measured, sensual way he had of speaking some-times—a way that was almost too mesmerising for words.

'Well, I've never exactly been a huge fan of shopping.' Glancing wryly down at the shiny designer carrier bags that were packed full of Arina's new clothes, Ellie hoped Nikolai wouldn't think she was simply pretending not to be interested. *It was a miserable feeling to be with someone who didn't believe you were capable of being honest.* A deep, underlying impulse arose inside her for him to see that she was both truthful and had integrity. 'I'd rather spend my free time reading a good book or going for a walk! Not that I haven't enjoyed helping Arina choose her new clothes…that's something entirely different. It's been the most fun I've had in ages!'

'I love my new shiny red shoes!' The child beamed up at her. 'Did you have shiny red shoes when you were a little girl like me, Ellie?'

The innocent question made Ellie's throat tighten briefly with anguish. When she was small all her clothing and shoes had been one hundred per cent charity donations. Except for a blue and white checked dress one of her kinder foster-carers had bought her for her seventh birthday. To this day Ellie recalled the freshly starched shop-bought smell of it with a mixture of happiness and childish hurt that it had not been her father who had bought it for her.

'No darling… I didn't.'

'So that is settled, then. We will go to the Russian tearooms!' As if sensing she had had a difficult moment replying to his daughter's question, Nikolai assumed his usual authoritative stance and stepped in to deflect any more painful enquiries. 'But first let us take these very heavy bags back to the car, before my arms either get stretched beyond repair or drop off!'

'Silly Papa!' Arina grinned up at him in delight.

The interior of the new tearooms was almost as ornate as any Russian orthodox church, with its lavish gold and black décor, and row upon row of seats upholstered in deep crimson velvet—just like pews. Between them were stout, sturdy-legged mahogany tables, and on top of them candles enclosed in intricately patterned gold lanterns.

It reminded Nikolai of many of the grandly imposing interiors of buildings he recalled from his time as a child in Moscow—clearly no expense had been spared in creating something close to authenticity. It looked as if business was going well too. Nearly every table was full.

It so happened that Nikolai was acquainted with the proprietor. In the business community in London people from the same country often tended to meet and socialise as a matter of course. And the short, stout man behind the counter, with wiry grey hair and half-moon glasses practically leapt out of his seat when he saw Nikolai and the two girls come in. No mean feat when one took into account his generous girth.

'Nikolai!'

There followed a welcome in Russian that would have pleased the old Tsar himself, Nikolai thought in secret amusement.

'Let me show you and your guests to my very best table—I reserve it for VIPs!' Beaming at Ellie and Arina, the man's face was almost florid with excitement at having the opportunity to welcome a man of Nikolai's standing into his establishment.

Nikolai knew that word would very quickly go round with all the details of his visit.

'Is this your family?' the older man enquired as they seated themselves at a table that had the best vantage point in the place—up a small flight of wide steps, with a clear view of everyone who came in the door, yet with its sensuous scarlet drapes almost enclosing them, providing a sense of privacy as well.

'Yes,' Nikolai answered in English, sensing the slight discomfort on Ellie's revealing face at the barrier of language that excluded her from the conversation. 'This is my daughter Arina and my fiancée Elizabeth.'

He uttered the words confidently, without hesitation, and immediately observed the soft rose-pink colour that invaded Ellie's cheeks. For a briefly electric moment Nikolai's gaze met hers and held it. She had the most magnetically beautiful eyes he had ever seen in a woman, and he fell into a kind of trance. It was no wonder Sasha had not been able to resist her. The thought was hardly a welcome one, and rubbed salt into wounds that were still smarting. Bitterness flowed into the pit of his stomach. If Sasha had lived, would she still be with him now? Living on the proceeds of his mother's diamond necklace?

'I am honoured to meet your lovely fiancée and your beautiful daughter!' the tearooms' proprietor declared, including them all in the effusive beam of his smile. 'Now, shall I leave you with the menu, or do you already know what you would like?'

'We have only come in for dessert and some tea,'

Nikolai replied, delving deep inside himself to restore his threatened equilibrium. 'Some blinis, perhaps? With honey or—'

'Chocolate sauce!' Arina interrupted excitedly, her dark eyes shining. 'Ellie, you must have blinis with chocolate sauce! They're my favourite!'

'Blinis?' She glanced quizzically at the child, and then at her father, her heart racing a little because of that look he had exchanged with her just a moment ago. A look that had made her insides soften and melt like marshmallows being held over a flame...

'Pancakes,' he explained.

'Oh...'

'So... We will have a selection of cream, chocolate sauce and fruit with some blinis and some tea, I think. Ellie...are you happy with tea, or would you prefer coffee?'

'Tea is fine, thanks.'

'Arina? Would you like a banana milkshake? I know that is your favourite too.'

'Yes, please, Papa!'

Briefly inclining his head in thanks, Nikolai waited until the owner had left the table before speaking again. Resting his elbows on the table and linking his hands, he told himself he was firmly back in control again, and would try not to let unpleasant and corrosive thoughts of Ellie and his brother together spoil this outing he had wanted them to enjoy together as a family.

'I never asked you before...' Ellie began, touching

the tips of her fingers to a stray wheat-blonde curl. 'Did you grow up in Russia?'

'In Moscow—yes.'

'What was it like?'

The genuine interest in her voice took him aback. 'For me and my family?' Nikolai reflected for a moment on the past, and the culture that had helped shape him. 'We were fortunate in having a very good life compared to many. My father was a scientist—a member of the intelligentsia… He became an entrepreneur when oil was discovered on our land. He provided for my brother and me all the things that anyone could wish for their children, and we were able to experience many enjoyable things…including travel. Something that was not available to everyone, I am afraid…'

'I hear it's a very beautiful city.'

'It is. Although in recent years it has undergone many, many changes. And there are over two hundred nationalities in the country that have the challenge of getting along!'

'Relationships are definitely the biggest challenge for all of us.' Looking thoughtful, then embarrassed, as though realising she'd inadvertently introduced a topic that she would prefer to steer clear of in light of the circumstances, Ellie turned to her niece, sitting beside her. 'So, how did you enjoy your ballet class this morning?' she asked.

'It was good!'

'Perhaps next time I can come and watch you?'

'Yes, I would like that. You can come and watch with Papa!'

'And when we get home today I'll help you put all your lovely new things away, but perhaps you can try them all on again first, and we can have a little fashion parade?'

'Oh, yes, please!'

Witnessing the sheer joy on his little girl's face at Ellie's suggestions, and the way her dark gaze watched the lovely woman by her side with a possessiveness and pride that made his heart turn over, Nikolai was gratefully reminded of all the qualities that he admired in Ellie. She was a natural with children. He had seen that from the start and had never forgotten it. She also had a great tenderness in her that she did not hesitate to display when she was around them. Blackmail or no, he had definitely done the right thing in choosing her as Arina's new mother. Whatever happened between them she would not disappoint his child, he was certain...

'And what about you, Ellie?' he asked, his pulse helplessly speeding up as she turned her arresting emerald gaze back to him. 'What about your own childhood? Did you always live in London?'

'Yes.' There was definite hesitation in both her eyes and her voice, and Nikolai frowned as annoyance replaced his previous magnanimity towards her. *Why did she always seem to be hiding something from him*?

'What part of London?' he probed.

'All over.' She lifted her slender shoulders in a defensive shrug. 'I moved around a lot.'

'Why did your parents not settle somewhere?'

'My mother died before I was a year old, and my father—my father wasn't around a lot of the time.'

'Why not?' *Because he was spending time in prison?* Nikolai speculated. If so, what had happened to Ellie and Jackie when he was away?

'He didn't live with me and my sister for a long time. We spent most of our childhood and early teenage years in either foster-homes or children's homes. Not always together, either.' Her pretty mouth tightened, and even Arina became still with attention.

'Your father did not want to raise you both?' Now Nikolai was feeling something very different from annoyance and suspicion.

Lifting the water jug a passing waitress had brought to their table, Ellie poured herself a glass and sipped at it carefully before replying. 'I don't think this is something we should discuss in front of Arina. Can we leave it for another time, do you think?'

# CHAPTER EIGHT

ELLIE was drawing a bath when there was a knock at the door. Cursing softly, she turned off the taps. Raising her arms to stretch out the kinks in her back, she realised the day had taken far more out of her than she'd estimated it would. Her first day as a member of the Golitsyn family—moving in, going shopping, eating blinis with chocolate sauce at the Russian tearooms, followed later by a family dinner prepared and cooked by the housekeeper. It would not normally make a body so tired, she was certain. But trying to control her emotions, always too close to the surface, and retain her composure when she seemed to be constantly under Nikolai's intimidating scrutiny had drained her right down to the marrow.

It simply wasn't possible to have any kind of conversation or contact with her formidable husband-to-be without fearing she was digging herself into an even bigger hole than she was in already. Regularly Ellie found herself wondering what other skeletons he would convince himself he'd found in her closet to trap her with.

'You are getting ready for bed?'

Her eyes nearly popped out of her head when she found the subject of her nervous musing on the other side of the door. It was an innocent enough question, seeing as she was standing there dressed only in a light cotton wrap, but the way Nikolai's eyes tracked slowly and deliberately down her body made it seem much more provocative.

'I was just running a bath before I turned in…yes,' she answered, wishing her voice didn't sound so strained and anxious.

'There is something I wanted to ask you, and with Arina present at dinner I did not get the chance. Can I come in?'

Not seeing how she could possibly refuse him, Ellie reluctantly stepped to the side. The boxes full of books she'd planned to sort earlier remained mostly unopened on the carpet, and various pieces of clothing she had attempted to arrange into some kind of order before hanging them in the wardrobe or folding them onto the scented shelves in the armoire were scattered in a riot of colour over the sumptuous silk bedspread. Seeing Nikolai glance towards the various piles, and noticing that the one in the foremost position in his eyeline was a little stack of lacy underwear she had folded, Ellie felt her limbs suddenly become as fluid as water.

'What is it that you wanted to ask me?' Her fingers fumbled with the loosely tied knot in the belt of her robe, and she prayed it was more secure than it felt.

'The same question that I asked you in the tearooms.'

He took a couple of steps towards her, then came to a standstill, dropping his hands casually either side of the straight lean hips encased in softly napped denim. A frown appeared between his dark blond brows. 'Why was it that your father did not raise you and Jackie, Ellie? I would like to know.'

Not knowing why it could possibly matter to him, Ellie sighed heavily. Psychologist or not, she was always fairly reluctant to revisit her own past—preferring to concentrate on the present as much as she possibly could. She frequently schooled her clients that they were much more than their personal histories or stories— that life could be created afresh at any chosen moment...

'When my mother died, for a long time my father blamed me for her death. She was weak after my birth, and a chest infection turned into pneumonia. He loved her so much, and couldn't get over it when he lost her. He struggled with being a single parent and then he decided he couldn't look after me and Jackie any longer. So he contacted Social Services to look for a foster-home for us both. They found me somewhere straight away, but Jackie—who was a couple of years older— was installed in a children's home. I was about three when I went to a new set of foster-carers—a young couple who had been trying for a baby for a couple of years without success. A year later they did have a baby of their own, and decided an active four-year-old was too difficult to manage as well, so I too was installed in the children's home. I spent the next few years until I was sixteen going from foster-carer to foster-carer, and sometimes back to the home. A large chunk of that time Jackie and I spent apart. Does that answer your question?'

'So when did your father come back on the scene?'

'Just before my sixteenth birthday. He'd kept in touch with Social Services, and from time to time sent money for me and Jackie. Over the years I think he really regretted giving us up. He had a change of heart, you see. He'd had a couple of failed relationships, and no doubt saw a lonely old age staring him in the face if he didn't make contact with his family again.'

Ellie's smile was thin, she knew…perhaps not quite as convincing as she wanted it to be to show Nikolai that it was all ancient history, and she was shocked by the hurt she heard in her own tone—a hurt she really thought she'd dealt with and long buried. *Especially since her father had become ill.* Ellie could only conclude that the anxieties of the day had undermined her.

'And you forgave him? Just like that?'

'Yes.' It hadn't been easy. There had been times when Ellie had wanted to punish her father for his desertion—as he had punished her and her sister—and cut him off for ever. But she just hadn't been able to bring herself to do it. Not when he had literally *begged* her to give him another chance. Besides…hadn't they both endured enough heartache and pain?

'I can't believe I did not know this. Jackie and you never really spoke of your past, but that was a tough beginning you had…by anyone's standards.'

'Maybe so.' She shrugged. 'I certainly learned some

valuable lessons about how to survive. Jackie didn't like to look back, but it's helped me in many ways. It's helped me realise that I want to help others who've had similar experiences to me. Anyway…nobody escapes life's challenges—no matter what their upbringing or circumstances.'

For a moment or two Nikolai seemed to be considering that, then he folded his arms over his chest and sighed.

'In the light of what you have just explained I think I can understand why you were tempted to have an affair with Sasha. The promise of an easier time instead of perpetual struggle must have seemed very appealing. Not that I am about to condone the affair…or the stealing of the necklace!'

After being inadvertently led to reveal some of the pain behind her upbringing, Ellie felt Nikolai's cynical assumption of her having an affair with his brother as well as being complicit in the theft of a valuable necklace like a kick in the teeth. Once again she was sick with misery. Silently she cursed the memory that eluded her, which she was certain would attest to her innocence.

'Well, I've told you what you wanted to know. I'd like to take my bath now and then go to bed. It's been a long day.'

Weary of conflict, all Ellie wanted now was for Nikolai to leave her alone and let her be for a while. But he didn't do that. Instead he moved even closer to her, and shockingly placed his hands on her upper arms.

'You would not have had an easier time with my

brother. That is the truth. He would only have added to your heartache.'

His words took Ellie aback even more than the touch that burned like flame through the flimsy cotton of her wrap. She had never heard Nikolai speak ill of Sasha before, even when it had become obvious to all the members of the Golitsyn household that the younger man had driven him to distraction with his constant demands for money, his irresponsible, lackadaisical attitude and his complete lack of concern for his baby daughter.

'What makes you so sure I wanted to be with him in the first place?'

Ellie was trembling as she asked the question, because Nikolai's hands seemed to firm against her arms rather than withdraw. Up close, he had a clean fresh smell that reminded her of newly laundered clothing spritzed with lemon. But underlying that evocative scent were darker more earthier tones, suggestive of elements much more disturbing to the senses.

Why couldn't she seem to move all of a sudden? It was almost as if she didn't *want* to be free of his touch, or the sizzling cerulean gaze that seared her soul and shook her violently awake. More awake than she had been in years...

'Perhaps you were lonely, Ellie?' His tone was husky, and suddenly the pad of his thumb was following the soft vulnerable curve of her tender lower lip, pressing her flesh with provocative intent, and wisps of his not quite steady breath were skimming over her skin like the lightest strokes from a feather.

'Loneliness would never have driven me into his arms...or made me steal for him!' Her eyes swam with tears. She had been beyond lonely for so long—but nothing, she was sure, would have made her want to try and soothe that forlorn ache with a man as unstable as Sasha. However charming he had sometimes been.

'And what about *my* arms, Ellie?'

'What?'

'Have you forgotten the evening before the accident as well?'

In shock, Ellie met Nikolai's brooding steady gaze. The scene that for the past five years she had striven hard to keep at bay played out again in her mind. What good would it have done her to recall such things when all had ended in pain and disaster? But what had transpired between them returned to her now, in a rich, full-blooded tapestry of spine-tingling memory. *Nikolai had kissed her.* Yes, kissed her as though his life depended on it. His erotically velvet mouth had plundered hers with passionately hungry demand, and Ellie had been swept away by the urgent sexual hunger that had deluged her too. His heat and hardness had burned through her clothing wherever he had touched her, and she had responded like a woman starving for breath as shock-waves of lust and rapture never before imagined or experienced had assailed her.

The only thing that had prevented the inevitable heart-pounding, pulse-racing outcome of that hot wild embrace had been the disturbing sudden peal of the telephone on Nikolai's desk. Like a scythe cutting through their stunned senses, it had brought them violently back down to earth and Ellie had fled to her room—stunned to the core by the realisation that she had been about to surrender herself to the powerful, charismatic *married* man she worked for without so much as a thought to the consequences.

With satisfaction Nikolai saw that Ellie did indeed remember what had happened between them that night. The longing and desire that had been inexorably building in his blood ever since she had opened the door and allowed him into her room increased with stunning force. Exhaling softly, he moved the pad of his thumb from her bewitchingly full lower lip to trace her fine-boned jawline, until finally he cupped it in his hand. Pleasure and need drowned him. The extremely erotic scent she exuded, and the warmth from her soft, sweetly curvaceous body had him all but hypnotised. And it only added to the agony of pleasure inside him when he hazarded a guess that underneath her insubstantial robe she was naked.

For a long moment Nikolai's will was locked in a battle for supremacy over his desire. Primal instinct vied with a logic he really did not want to entertain, and logic was losing fast. The living, breathing reality of this woman was simply too much temptation for one mortal man.

'I'm not looking for a cure for loneliness!' Her mouth working to contain her distress, Ellie stepped abruptly away from Nikolai and put herself firmly out of his reach. Suddenly the decision to take things further was no longer his. Her lush green eyes glowed like malachite in the lamplit room. 'And if I was, it certainly wouldn't be with you!'

'But you *will* share my bed when we are married, Ellie! We have an agreement, remember? Do not imagine for one moment that I have changed my mind about that part of it, because I fully intend to hold you to your word!'

'You don't have to worry that I won't keep my promise, but it won't happen until we are married…and then only under duress!'

A throaty chuckle escaped Nikolai's lips. Maybe it was arrogant of him, but he already knew that the heat between them that had erupted in that never-to-be-forgotten evening before the accident was easily going to flare up again, and would undoubtedly conclude with Ellie being in his arms and in his bed before much more time elapsed. To try and deny the kind of combustible chemistry they had would be as impossible as trying to stop a raging river from flowing downstream. No matter how much will-power or determination you applied to the task, in the end the outcome was inevitable.

'You may fool yourself that it will be under duress when you finally share my bed, Ellie… But I know you are not immune to my touch, and clearly you have needs just as I have needs. Do not trouble to try and deny it!'

'So that gives you the right to just *demand* that I sleep with you? Listen… I may have had no choice but to make this arrangement with you, but that doesn't mean that you *own* me! Why don't you just forget about the idea of sleeping with me and find some other more willing woman to accommodate you in that area?'

'Like a mistress, you mean?' Both irked and amused, Nikolai slowly shook his head. 'Why should I bother with a mistress when I will have a beautiful wife to keep me warm at night? Besides, I want to set a good example for my daughter. I want nothing to make her doubt that her father and mother are absolutely dedicated to her care and well-being, and that means that we have to present a *united* front. Intimacy between us will go a long way to helping us achieve that, I am certain. Now, go and have your bath and I will see you in the morning.'

It was only as he shut the door behind him, wincing in frustration at the desire that still held him in its taunting grip, that Nikolai recalled what Ellie had said to him at one of their earlier recent meetings. *'I was hurt and traumatised from the accident and for the first time in my life I let my father take charge and look after me.'* For a girl who had been raised the way she had— shunted from children's home to foster-home and back again—her father finally waking up to his responsibility and taking care of her when she had been hurt definitely struck a reluctantly sympathetic chord within Nikolai.

Arina could have suffered a similar fate if he had not been around to take her in when his brother had to all intents and purposes abandoned her after her mother's death. Nikolai knew Sasha had been traumatised by what had happened to Jackie, but why could he not have pulled himself together sufficiently to see that his daughter needed him? The thought that Arina could have suffered like Ellie must have suffered was like a knife score across his heart.

Returning to his room in a contemplative mood, he recalled how Ellie had flinched when Arina had asked if she had ever had shiny red shoes when she was small. The question must have speared deep into the heart of the child inside her who had been so cruelly and thoughtlessly abandoned by the very person who was supposed to love and protect her. But, no matter how much Nikolai might sympathetically regret Ellie's difficult upbringing, it didn't help to tamp down the wave of desire that flooded him every time he thought about her being naked under that thin little robe she'd been wearing…

The next morning, Ellie overslept. She didn't mean to, but as soon as her head had touched the pillow the night before, sheer emotional exhaustion had claimed her and she had yielded to it without so much as a whimper. *That almost never happened.*

Usually her mind was full of thoughts about her day—her clients' problems, and the kids at the shelter whose every day was a fight for survival and rarely anything anticipated with joy or pleasure—and Ellie would lie awake for at least an hour or two, sometimes even longer, mulling over them all, praying for ways in which she could do the most good and help them even more. To enjoy a deep, dreamless sleep was a gift she hadn't expected. And to anticipate a Sunday where she wouldn't have to work because she had moved house was another blessing.

Her thoughts turned to Arina and what the two of them could do that day. Maybe she could ask Miriam to make them up a picnic and they could spend the afternoon in Regents Park? It would be lovely to have some time to bond with the child on her own. The park was so close by, and they could walk there rather than get Nikolai's driver to transport them. The idea of a walk and a picnic galvanised Ellie into action.

Outside her window the day looked blustery and autumnal, and already the leaves on the giant oak were turning from a rich forest-green to a much lighter, burnished brown hue. Just perfect for the outing she had in mind! She dressed in jeans and a crisp white cotton shirt with a navy-blue sweater draped over her shoulders, and was almost at the door when her thoughts were suddenly ensnared by something else. Something she'd been trying so desperately hard not to dwell on. *Nikolai*…

As the tape of her memory anxiously played back what had happened between them last night, every muscle in her body locked almost excruciatingly tight. *'You will share my bed,'* he'd promised her and her mind and body had gone into meltdown at the mere idea. Frankly, it terrified Ellie that she was so acutely receptive to his touch. It seemed he only had to look at her a little longer than was necessary and she knew a frightening yearning for his hands to be on her body, her skin bare to his devastating attentions and her mouth plundered by his hot velvet kisses…

The needs he had accused her of having were obviously real—but apart from the fear in Ellie's mind that Nikolai would probably respect her even less, not more, if she easily succumbed to fulfilling them with him, there was something else that made her afraid to finally let down her guard. Something that filled her with the most tremendous anxiety and fear every time she thought about it…

She was *innocent…untouched…*had never experienced the ultimate intimacy with a man before…

# CHAPTER NINE

IN THE spacious high-ceilinged kitchen, Arina and her father were already enjoying their breakfast at the scrubbed pine table when Ellie joined them. Miriam was busy arranging fresh toast in a silver rack, and as she brought it to the table she glanced up approvingly, her homely face wreathed in a smile. 'Good morning, Dr Lyons! Please sit down and I will get you your breakfast. Would you like a full English? Or perhaps you would prefer continental-style?'

It was hard to think about food when Ellie sensed Nikolai's arresting blue gaze immediately turn her way. He was dressed casually in jeans and a white T-shirt that stretched lovingly over smooth bronzed biceps that wouldn't put a trained athlete to shame, and the mouth-watering sight of so much blatant masculinity on show so early in the morning affected Ellie much more acutely than frankly was comfortable!

'Could I possibly just have some toast and marma-lade and a cup of tea? I'm not really one for eating a lot in the morning. Thanks.'

'Good morning, Ellie,' Nikolai drawled. 'I trust you slept well?'

Ellie didn't think she'd imagined the slightly mocking overtone. 'I did, as a matter of fact…and you?'

'I am not generally a good sleeper, but as long as I have three or four hours I am fine.'

*Three or four hours? And he could look as drop-dead gorgeous and vital as that?* Ellie couldn't help but stare at him in awe.

'Sit down next to me, Ellie!' Arina patted the seat of the pine ladder-backed chair beside her, her pretty blue eyes shining with excitement and anticipation. 'Papa said we're going to the park today, and Miriam is going to make us a picnic!'

Great minds thinking alike, or some kind of weird telepathy? Ellie's stomach cartwheeled at the idea of Nikolai joining them on the trip she'd already been mentally planning as an opportunity for her to get to know her niece on her own. The fact was, like him or not, the man was just too distracting for words. How on earth was she supposed to be relaxed and at ease with him watching her every move and likely finding fault as well?

'Well… you'll never believe it, sweetheart, but I—' Just about to put her leather knapsack down on the floor beside her, Ellie heard the distinct sound of her mobile phone. The ringtone was Santana's 'Black Magic Woman,' and she sensed her cheeks flush hot pink as she caught Nikolai's eye and disconcertingly saw him smile. She bit her lip. 'I wouldn't normally answer it while we're eating but it might be work…do you mind?'

'Be my guest.'

Seeing immediately that it was Paul—the young colleague who helped run the shelter—Ellie felt her heart skip a beat.

'Hi. Did you forget today's my day off? Is anything the matter?'

'Sorry, Ellie, but I've got some bad news, I'm afraid.'

'Tell me!' Her stomach plummeting, Ellie tightly gripped the phone.

'Last night we were broken into. Nobody was hurt, thank God—most of the kids were all upstairs asleep when it happened. But the TV was stolen, along with most of the stuff that was any good in the kitchen—the toaster, the kettle and the microwave. They're all gone.'

'Oh, no!'

Furious and saddened at the same time—they'd only had a fundraiser very recently to replace all the items Paul had mentioned, because the previous ones had been so decrepit—Ellie assumed her usual 'take charge' mode. 'Did you ring the police?'

Nikolai glanced at her sharply.

'They've been here since the early hours, taking prints and so on. They are just about to leave.'

'Was there much mess?'

'Whoever it was trashed the place. It wasn't exactly Buckingham Palace before, but it's going to take a major miracle to make it anywhere near habitable again. They chucked a can of red paint up all the walls. Looks like a scene from a gangster movie!'

'Oh, Paul!'

'Don't upset yourself… We'll soon get it fixed up and shipshape again!'

The concern in Paul's kind voice almost undid her. The volunteers who worked alongside her were equally as committed to and caring of the inmates at the shelter as she was. This was a bitter blow for them too, and made a mockery of all their hard work.

Ellie rallied. 'Of course we will! Listen…I'm going to come in and take a look. Give me about an hour and I'll be with you. I'll have to get the tube. I'm not local any more.'

'Just get here when you can. I'll ring round a couple of volunteers and get them to come in and help start cleaning up.'

'Thanks, Paul. See you.'

'Who is Paul?'

Ellie blinked at the distinct coolness in Nikolai's tone. 'He's a colleague of mine at the shelter.'

'The shelter?'

'It's a refuge we set up a few months ago for kids sleeping rough on the streets. Last night it got broken into and trashed. I'm sorry, but I'm going to have to go in for a little while and see for myself what's happened. Perhaps I can come and find you and Arina in the park afterwards? I'll ring you.'

'Is your commitment at the shelter not a voluntary one? How much time does it usually demand of you?'

Not having mentioned her work at the shelter to him personally, Ellie quickly realised that in spite of his question Nikolai must have found out about it when he had had her investigated. A wave of anger swept through her. *Was he going to tell her she had to end her association with the shelter?* Prepared to do battle on that score, Ellie felt her heart beat a little faster at what she judged to be disapproval in Nikolai's hard-jawed glance.

'I usually put in at least one or two hours each night after work,' she told him. 'Now that my situation has changed, I realise I may not be able to do that *every* night.'

'Is not enough of your time already given over to work, Ellie? You have a family to think of now, and that must take precedence!'

Glancing at Arina's bewildered little face, Ellie felt a huge stab of guilt shoot through her at the realisation that she *did* give an awful lot of her time to work—both paid *and* voluntary. Now that she was effectively going to become this child's mother she would have to cut back on certain commitments. It was only fair. Thinking of the planned picnic, and knowing only too well how acutely a child could feel disappointment if let down, she vowed to make it up to the little girl just as soon as she could.

Biting back a defensive retort to Nikolai, Ellie pushed her fingers through her thick blonde hair and sighed. 'The shelter helps a lot of young people who have nowhere else to go at night. It also helps keep them away from the thugs and the drug pushers that they often encounter during the day. I *will* cut back on my commitment there, but as for this morning—I'm sorry, but I'm just going to have to go over there and make an assessment of the damage. I'll try not to be too long, and I promise I'll come and join you both just as soon as I can.'

Saying nothing in reply, Nikolai got up and moved across the room towards the cream-coloured telephone on the wall, punching in a number. Whoever he was calling answered straight away. 'Ivan—' Ellie heard him say, and then the rest of his speech was lost to her as he continued the conversation in Russian. Replacing the receiver, he glanced at the gold watch that glinted on his tanned wrist before meeting her gaze again. 'I will drive you myself to this shelter, and Ivan will accompany us.'

Shocked to her boots, Ellie stared. 'You don't have to do that! I can easily get the tube.'

'I do not think you realise the position you are now in. You are soon to become my wife! Not only does that give you the right to expect my help when you need it, but it also means that you do not take unnecessary risks and possibly jeopardise yourself or this family in any way! Ivan will be here in no time at all, and then we will go. Miriam? The little one will have to stay with you until our return. I will ring you to let you know when we are on our way back.'

'Yes, Mr Golitsyn.'

'Arina?'

'Yes, Papa?'

'Stay with Miriam and help her make the picnic.

Ellie and I will not be away for very long, and then we will all go to the park just as we planned my angel.'

'Yes, Papa.'

Not taking Ellie's advice to park the car a couple of streets away, in case it was vulnerable outside the shelter, Nikolai grimly pulled in across the road from the dilapidated building that was their destination. The expression in his eyes was steely as his gaze swept round the litter-strewn pavements and the nearby houses with their worn and neglected appearance.

His heart raced a little at the idea that Ellie should willingly expose herself to the volatile atmosphere of working in such a place. But inside him too was a reluctant admiration that she would make such a choice. It seemed to mock the fixed opinions he'd formed about her that he had convinced himself were right.

A small knot of disgruntled looking teenagers puffing away at rolled-up cigarettes—some with beer cans in their hands, and looking as if it had been months since they had had the use of soap and clean water—gathered round the shelter's entrance. A couple of them nodded their heads towards Ellie as she approached, Nikolai and Ivan close on her heels.

'Hear what happened, miss?' asked one of them—a thin youth with flattened brown hair and bloodshot eyes, his gaze warily straying behind her to the two men.

'That's why I'm here, Josh. Do you know anything about who could have done this?'

'No idea. Could've been anyone! Made a right bloody mess, though, whoever it was!' Visibly straightening his thin shoulders, Josh suddenly glared at Nikolai and his black-suited bodyguard. 'Who d'you think you are?' he mocked, clearly aiming for some kind of admiring recognition from his peers 'MI5? FBI?'

In the most seriously intimidating voice he could muster, Nikolai threw him an icy look. 'No. KGB,' he replied, and then, turning towards Ivan, said a few words in Russian.

The shock on the boy's face would have been quite comical if Nikolai hadn't been so impatient for Ellie to assess the damage inside and return home with him again. The boy swore, and a second later moved aside to let them all pass.

'You shouldn't have scared him like that!' Ellie admonished Nikolai, but there was the smallest, disconcerting glimpse of humour at the corners of her mouth. 'Besides, weren't the KGB disbanded?'

Nikolai shrugged. 'He deserved it.'

As soon as they entered what seemed to be the main living area, at the end of a scruffy hallway, they saw that it did indeed resemble the film set of a bloody gangster movie. The vivid red paint that covered the walls was a shocking assault on the senses, and glancing round at the smashed up furniture and crude messages on the patches of wall that weren't submerged in scarlet Nikolai sensed a wave of burning fury engulf him. This was no fit place for Ellie to be! He wanted to take her by the shoulders and march her out of there as swiftly as her shapely legs would carry her!

But, seeing the desolation and sadness in her beautiful green eyes as she surveyed the stark evidence of the break-in, he suddenly felt as protective of her as the precious child he had adopted as his daughter. The feeling genuinely took him aback…

'Oh, God!' She rubbed her hand over her cheek, moving her head from side to side in anguish. 'Where do we start to put this right?'

'Ellie… Hi…'

A young man with tousled fair hair, dressed in worn denims and a black T-shirt, joined them. He barely spared the two men with Ellie a glance before putting his arm around her shoulders. Nikolai was instantly gripped by anger of a different kind.

'This is even worse than I imagined it would be, Paul!'

'I wanted to try and spare you too many details.'

'What did the police say?'

As though suddenly aware that Nikolai's intimidating gaze was taking unflattering measure of her young colleague, Ellie stepped slightly away from him and the man's arm dropped—reluctantly, it seemed to Nikolai—to his side.

'What could they say? You know how regularly this kind of thing happens round here! Just that they'll make the usual enquiries and get back to us when they have anything. In the meantime, I don't know how anyone can stay here with the place in this condition.'

'You're right. But where will they go?'

'On the streets…where they usually go. They'll

manage. Give us a week or two and we might be able to get the place reasonably habitable again. But as for replacing the items that were nicked—I don't know how we're going to get those. By the way…who are your friends?'

'Oh… This is Nikolai and—'

'I am Ellie's fiancé.' Thinking he might as well put the man straight as soon as possible as to his relationship with Ellie, Nikolai moved protectively to her side.

'Fiancé?' Paul looked dumbfounded. 'You never said you were engaged!'

'It happened rather suddenly.' Giving him a weak smile, Ellie turned her gaze imploringly to Nikolai, as if to say *please don't say anything more*!

Did she have feelings for this man? he wondered jealously. Could his investigators have been wrong about her not having anyone she was interested in?

'What are these items that need replacing?' Forcing himself to change the subject, he immediately assumed authority.

'Most of our kitchen equipment and…' Ellie shrugged forlornly and Nikolai got the distinct impression that she was close to tears. 'What you see broken here. Most of the stuff was second-hand, but still… Anyway, I can replace most of the kitchen stuff. I can bring them from my flat, seeing as I'm not living there now.'

'You don't have to do that, Ellie.' Sounding irked, Paul narrowed his gaze almost accusingly as he surveyed the Russian. 'She's always giving us her own stuff or ploughing her own money into the shelter. It's not right!'

'Indeed, she should not have to do that,' Nikolai agreed, the faintest grim smile at the edges of his mouth. 'If you would make me a list of everything that needs replacing, I will see to it that it is taken care of. I will also arrange for a complete clean-up to be done of the property. Excuse me.'

Turning away from them all, Nikolai reached for the mobile phone in his jeans pocket and made a call. When he'd finished, he turned back to find Ellie staring at him in wide-eyed surprise. Right then he could not tell if she was pleased by his gesture or merely suspicious of it. But he just wanted to get her out of these stark and grim surroundings and back to somewhere more conducive to putting a smile on her lovely face again. *And if anyone could make her smile it would be Arina*, he thought proudly...

'A crew will arrive in about half an hour's time. They will see to everything.'

Shaking his head almost in disbelief, Paul replaced his scowl with a reluctant smile. 'This is very good of you, Mr...er...?'

'Golitsyn.'

'Right.' Still perplexed, Paul glanced at Ellie. 'Congratulations, by the way.'

She frowned. 'For what?'

'On your engagement!'

'Oh.' Her arresting emerald gaze moved warily back to Nikolai. 'Thanks.'

\* \* \*

'Now it's Papa's turn to try and catch you, Ellie!' Clapping her small hands together with glee, Arina was clearly enjoying the game of tag she'd been playing with Ellie and her father. Relieved to put the problems of the shelter behind her for a while, Ellie was too.

It was the perfect day for spending time in the park, just as she had concluded earlier. The sun was shining, but there was a welcome cooling breeze, and the majestic trees surrounding them still shimmered with their raiment of leaves. However, the mere idea of a supremely fit and athletic Nikolai chasing her with the sole aim of catching her induced a heat in Ellie that was nothing to do with the exertion of the game.

A disconcerting awareness of the man's more physical attributes had been building in her all morning, and when he had accompanied her to the shelter and insisted on replacing all the items that had been stolen or broken, as well as arranging for the place to be professionally cleaned up, Ellie had helplessly found her unsettling attraction for him growing. *Despite* her automatic suspicions of his motives.

'Run, Ellie—run!' shouted Arina from beneath the large oak tree they'd been picnicking under. 'Papa's started counting!'

'Coming—ready or not!' her father proclaimed, with a definite lascivious glint in his eye, and Ellie pounded across the grass for all she was worth, despite being slightly disadvantaged by her limp.

To her immense frustration, she didn't get very far before an electric stirring of the air made all the hairs at the back of her neck stand up, warning her that Nikolai was right behind her. Arms with all the strength of iron bars pinioned her to his strong hard body, and Ellie's breath left her lungs in a disconcerting whoosh. Before she could get her bearings, Nikolai had pushed her to the ground. Just before she hit the earth he somehow arranged it so that he hit it first, and her fall was cushioned by his long, prone body.

Finding herself staring down into his teasing smiling face, into twinkling eyes as blue as the great dome that was the sky above them, Ellie was hardly aware that she breathed at all in those few electrifying seconds.

'Now I have you right where I want you, *laskovaya moya*!' he triumphantly declared—and kissed her.

As soon as Nikolai's lips touched hers, and his velvet tongue smoothly infiltrated Ellie's mouth, she melted and froze all at the same time. Suddenly he manoeuvred her body so that her denim-clad thighs were spread either side of his tight lean hips. Trying hard not to succumb to the prowess and danger of his slow, seductive kiss and failing dismally, Ellie became not only aware of the overwhelming effect he was having on her own aroused libido but also of how Nikolai's arrestingly fit body was so acutely responding to hers. His hardness pushed against her centre, and she gave a little yelp of shock mingled with a pleasure so fierce that her womb contracted and her nipples stung as though bitten.

Reluctantly, she stopped Nikolai kissing her. It seemed that the taste of him had not just infiltrated

Ellie's mouth but the rest of her senses too, and she felt drugged, dizzy with a sensuality she hardly remembered was possible.

'Arina will see!' Ellie stared back at Nikolai in genuine alarm. If she had ever forgotten what his touch could do to her she had just been well and truly reminded and had good cause to be apprehensive of a repetition. Seducing her would be so easy for him she told herself. After all, it was a normal and even necessary function for a vital and healthy male specimen like him. But for Ellie it would be much, much more complicated…

'We are not doing anything to be ashamed of!' Easing himself up into a sitting position as she rolled away from him, Nikolai considered her with mocking amusement as he brushed some loose blades of grass from his jeans. 'I want her to see that we like each other and to feel secure in the fact.'

'*Like* each other? When did you decide that?'

'Would you prefer that I hated you?'

'Why change the habit of a lifetime?'

'I do not hate you, Ellie. What you did was unforgivable but I have since been reminded that you *do* have some admirable qualities… And I would be a liar if I said I was not attracted to you.'

'By "attracted" you mean you want to have sex with me?'

His shoulders went rigid for a moment, and his sensual lips compressed a little, as though he was offended. 'A crude way of putting it, perhaps—but, yes…I will not deny it!'

'And will that be in return for doing what you did today at the shelter?'

Now Nikolai was even more offended. 'What I did was a spontaneous gesture, not something planned to extract sexual favours from my wife-to-be!'

'Why did you help me?'

'I—'

'Papa—you caught her!'

Out of breath from running, Arina suddenly appeared beside them, her plump cheeks pink from exertion, clearly delighted at seeing them sitting so close together on the grass.

'Yes, angel.' Her father laughed, that devastating twinkle in his eye again as he turned his gaze back to Ellie. 'Unfortunately poor Ellie did not run fast enough!'

# CHAPTER TEN

ELLIE sat in frozen animation on the floor, the boxes of books she'd started to open surrounding her. A searing knife-like pain had just throbbed through her skull, and in the midst of her unpacking she'd stopped still, willing it not to repeat itself. Assuring herself it was probably just a stress headache after what had happened at the shelter, she felt her breath catch at the disturbing scene that was starting to unfold in her mind—like a scroll she was slowly rolling opened to read the writing right to the end…

It was a repeat of the disturbing dream she had had about Sasha. But this time it went beyond the point where he was begging her to drive him to his friend's. His dark handsome face was contorted with frustration and irritation, and the baby was crying in his arms. He swore savagely beneath his breath, and then, realising he wasn't helping his case, regrouped himself and flashed Ellie one of his most disarming boyish smiles.

'What if I promise you that after this…after you drive me to my friend's…it will be the last time, the very *last* time, I ever take anything—drink or drugs—and I ask Nikolai to get me some help? What if I do that, Ellie? It's what you've always begged me to do, isn't it? Give me this one last chance and I'll show you that I *can* get clean. Please, Ellie! Don't condemn me when I'm ill! Addiction is an illness, you must know that! My friend's place is only about a mile away. I want to see him because he's let me down, Ellie. He sold me some bad gear and I've got to speak to him!'

'Maybe you need to go to the hospital rather than your friend's, Sasha? What have you taken? What did he give you?' Alarmed, Ellie honestly feared for him if she left him to his own devices. He had a disturbingly frantic look in his eyes and clearly wasn't capable of making rational decisions right now. *If only he would ask Nikolai for help then everything could change*, Ellie thought fervently. Given time, he might even come round to seeing how precious and important his baby girl was, and at last forge a real loving bond with her just as Jackie would have longed for him to do.

Arina's cries turned to a snuffly whimper and Ellie longed to hold the child and comfort her.

'I don't need the hospital! I just need to see my friend and sort things out!' Sasha slurred, his balance wavering a little as he held the baby.

Ellie stared at him in horror. 'Give me Arina, Sasha… Let me take her and then we can get in the car and go. I promise I'll drive you, but let me take the baby first!'

'I am sorry, Ellie… But I need you to do this for me,

and the baby is my insurance! Here are the car keys.' Sasha dragged them out of his jeans pocket and pressed them into Ellie's hand. 'Let's go.'

He marched towards Nikolai's smart gold coloured Mercedes parked kerbside, and she realised that he had taken his brother's keys. She had no choice but to hurry after him. Arina was her first and most urgent concern. She had to get her away from Sasha soon, before the worst happened and he dropped her!

The quiet street seemed to be free of passersby that afternoon, but even if she stopped someone for help there was no telling what Sasha might do in his current state of mind. *He was right.* He *was* ill. She didn't think she had ever seen him quite this bad before. So, with the car keys he had shoved into her trembling hand enclosed in her palm, Ellie climbed into the driver's seat, her gaze nervously on the wriggling baby in his arms, sick to her stomach at the volatile and potentially dangerous situation she found herself in.

'If I'm going to drive anywhere you need to put Arina in her baby seat. We can't travel with her on your lap. It's too dangerous. You absolutely *have* to do this!' she said firmly.

'Don't fret,' Sasha said impatiently. 'I'll put her in the car seat—don't worry. But then we've got to go.'

Swallowing hard, Ellie felt her hands clammy with fear as Sasha fumbled to get the baby in her car seat, then returned to the passenger seat and told Ellie to start driving.

'Have you strapped her in properly?' she demanded, twisting round to see for herself.

'Yes, yes!' Sasha replied. 'Now let's go!'

The scene started to fade, and—still kneeling on the carpet in her bedroom—Ellie pressed her palms to the sides of her face and briefly shut her eyes tight. She breathed out heavily. This time she knew what had just been revealed to her was no dream. It was pure shocking memory, and it had left her reeling, occurring out of the blue like that.

Knowing for certain that she had not willingly got into the car with Sasha that day, had only done so because he'd been high and she'd feared he might do himself or the baby harm if she didn't—Ellie felt immense relief roll through her. But how she would relate this unpalatable record of events to the man she had now agreed to marry she had no idea.

There was no doubt in her mind that Nikolai had loved his brother, despite all his faults—that was surely why he sought to avenge his death by blackmailing her, she realised. But the truth would surely test that love, and possibly make Nikolai feel more strongly than ever that he had somehow failed Sasha. Knowing the level of responsibility for his brother that he had always taken upon his shoulders, Ellie didn't doubt that. But being able to reveal the truth to him at last might not exactly endear Ellie to him either—for all that she'd longed for her memory to return.

From inside her bag, which lay on the bed, her mobile phone rang. Still in a bit of a daze, she jumped up to answer it. Having not rung her father yet, to tell him about the situation with Nikolai and that she had moved back into his house, Ellie thought for a worried moment that it might be him. But the caller was Paul from the shelter.

'Ellie? Just wanted to let you know that the cleaning crew your fiancé arranged turned up and did the most amazing job on the place you've ever seen! It looks even better than before. I know that's not saying much, but everyone here is over the moon! Say thanks from us all, will you?'

Dropping down onto the edge of the bed, Ellie clutched the phone to her ear with relief. Now at least the kids who'd been staying there would not have to sleep on the streets tonight. Nikolai had indeed done a wonderful thing.

She frowned at the wave of longing that suddenly swept through her at the thought of him, and her cheeks burned as she remembered that disturbing game of catch in the park, when he had caught her and kissed her…

'Of course I will,' she told Paul. 'I'm just so pleased the place is habitable again! It means we can think about our plans for improvement—as we'd hoped we could before this happened.'

'It's just a thought…but I wondered if you fancied meeting me for a quick drink? I'm in Leicester Square with a couple of friends of mine, and thought you might like the opportunity to celebrate everything turning out so well?'

Grateful for a chance to distract herself from thoughts of Nikolai, and the disturbing revelations about Sasha her returning memory had revealed, Ellie didn't hesitate to accept Paul's invitation. 'Sounds good. Give me about an hour and I'll join you. Where will you be?'

In the kitchen, having cleaned up after dinner, Miriam was having a final tidy round before she retired to her own rooms for the night.

'Miriam? Do you know where Mr Golitsyn is?' Ellie asked, her heart thudding at the very real chance Nikolai might suddenly appear from wherever he'd gone after putting Arina to bed and take her by surprise. She had kissed the little girl goodnight earlier, after he had suggested Ellie might like to finish her unpacking.

'He has gone into his study to do some work, Dr Lyons…I mean Ellie.' The older woman smilingly grimaced, remembering that Ellie had told her to use her first name. 'He asked me to tell you that he would be busy for a couple of hours and to help yourself to anything you need in the meantime.'

Breathing a soft sigh of relief, Ellie released the blonde curl she had been absently twirling round her finger and did up the buttons on the three quarter-length jacket she wore over her jeans. 'Well, I've just had a phone call from a friend of mine, inviting me for a drink. If Nikolai wants to know where I've gone, would you tell him? I'd rather not disturb him if he's working.'

'Of course! I hope you have a nice evening.'

'Thanks very much… Goodnight, Miriam.'

'Good night, Ellie.'

\* \* \*

It was useless trying to work when his concentration was shot to pieces! Why was he even bothering to attempt to read his letters when his secretary could look them over for him in the morning at his office?

Throwing down his fountain pen on the desk, Nikolai rose to his feet and circled his shoulders forwards and then backwards, moving his head from side to side to try and erase some of the strain in his ridiculously tense muscles. All his thoughts had been preoccupied with Ellie...that was why he could not work. Deliberately removing himself from her company shortly after dinner, to read a bedtime story to Arina, he had told himself that some time spent without her lovely face and sultry perfume distracting him was just what he needed to help straighten out his mind about her.

Seeing the shelter today, and learning that it was Ellie who had set it up in the first place, had made Nikolai seriously reflect on why a girl he had accused of stealing a valuable necklace and aiming to run off with his charming but reckless brother would spend her time helping disadvantaged teenagers sleeping rough on the streets. It did not make sense. If she was only interested in acquiring money and living a more wealthy existence herself. The two behaviours just did not tally.

Doubt started to creep into his mind about Sasha's behaviour in the past. Had Nikolai overlooked too many of his less than charming character traits and perhaps extended him too much benefit of the doubt because he had felt so responsible for him and loved him? *With both their parents gone, what else could he have done*? Yet who knew what might have really occurred that fatal day of the accident? Thinking too about Ellie's obvious affection for Arina, Nikolai felt something deep down inside him telling him that what she had said was true...*She would never have knowingly or willingly put the child at risk*...Not even for Sasha, if she'd cared for him!

Shaking his head, he uttered her name out loud in sheer frustration. His body throbbed with the need to hold her, and that kiss they had shared earlier in the park had only poured petrol on the fire that already simmered hotly inside him. If he did not get her into his bed soon he might have to seriously consider ringing up one of his previous lovers after all! He knew that he wouldn't. Since seeing Ellie again it was impossible for him to even *think* of being intimate with someone else.

There was a knock at the door. Scraping his fingers through his hair, Nikolai found himself tensing even more at the idea it might be Ellie. When he saw his small rotund housekeeper in her wrap-around floral apron standing there instead, in the softly lamplit hall, disappointment crashed in on him like a wave.

'Yes, Miriam?'

'I have a message for you from Ellie, Mr Golitsyn.'

'Well?' he snapped impatiently. 'What is it?'

'She has gone out for a while with a friend. She did not want to disturb you. As I was just on my way up to bed, I thought I had better come and tell you.'

'Who is this friend? Did you see him or her?'

'No, Mr Golitsyn.'

'When did she leave?' Nikolai demanded, his mind and heart racing at the idea that Ellie might be running out on him and Arina again, and berating himself for starting to see the good in her instead of the bad.

'About half an hour ago, Mr Golitsyn.'

'And you are sure she did not mention who this friend was?'

'No. I am sorry.'

Wishing that Miriam had come and told him all this earlier, still Nikolai realised he could not blame his good-hearted housekeeper for Ellie going out. And in spite of the agreement they had made he could hardly keep her prisoner in what was now her home…*could he*? Yet the steel-like muscles in his stomach cramped painfully at the idea that she had gone out with some unknown male admirer.

'Go to bed, Miriam. I will wait up for Ellie. Sleep well.'

'Yes, Mr Golitsyn.' Unable to banish the concern that she had somehow done something wrong, the housekeeper sighed and lifted her shoulders in a resigned shrug.

'Did you have a nice evening?'

Rising from the armchair he had been sitting in whilst waiting for her return, Nikolai did not know how he managed to keep his tone so calm and civilised. It was after midnight, and he had endured wave upon wave of fear and doubt that Ellie had left him for good.

Perhaps she had concluded that it was worth the risk

of her and her father going to prison after all to get away from Nikolai? Now, his worsening mood poised on a precarious knife-edge, he let his gaze flick in reluctant and helpless admiration over her appearance. With the lamp light from the hallway outside the sitting room wreathing her hair in a halo of gold, in contrast her pale skin appeared almost luminous—whilst her emerald eyes glinted like dark fire as they registered her surprise at seeing him.

'Nikolai! You didn't need to wait up for me. It's late, and I have the key you gave me to let myself in.'

'Where have you been?'

'Didn't Miriam tell you?' Ellie frowned, 'A friend of mine rang and invited me out for a drink. I would have told you myself, but you were working and I didn't want to disturb you.'

'And this friend of yours…Was it male or female?'

'What?'

'You heard me perfectly well, I am sure.'

'I don't believe this! Are you going to cross-examine me every time I set foot outside the door? Maybe next time you'll make me take Ivan as well! Then you can spy on who I'm with and keep me prisoner all at the same time!'

His temper finally spilling over, Nikolai swore savagely beneath his breath, his hands clenched into fists of tension and fury down by his side. 'You go too far!'

'No!' She took several strides towards him and jabbed her finger in the air. 'It is *you* who go too far!'

Reacting instinctively, Nikolai caught her slender-boned wrist and gripped it tight.

She gasped. 'Let go of me!'

Seeing fear in her eyes, he stared at her in stark cold horror as he realised she thought he was going to strike her. Before he could let her go, her face crumpled, and she moved her hand across her eyes to hide her distress. Again, acting purely on instinct, adrenaline pumping through his veins like white water, Nikolai impelled Ellie urgently into his arms.

'I wasn't going to hurt you. I swear to you I would cut off my hand before I laid it on you in anger, *devochka moya*!' *My little girl...* It was the same endearment he used sometimes when speaking to Arina, and it had slipped out quite naturally.

Nikolai's hand was smoothing over the silken fall of Ellie's alluring shampoo-scented hair—faint notes of sandalwood and orange—and, unable to resist, he kissed the top of her head... Once, twice, three times. The contact only deepened his frustration and desire. It was nowhere near enough to satisfy the building need in him for complete fulfilment...not when his lips ached to kiss and taste and explore every exquisite inch of her and his body longed to be one with hers. If previously Nikolai had been angry, then what he was experiencing right now was light years away from that emotion and silently, devastatingly, it shook him to his very foundations.

Trembling, Ellie pressed herself closer into his chest with a sigh. 'One of my foster fathers hit me across the face once when he was angry…I've never forgotten it.'

'I am sorry that you experienced such brutality from a man who should have protected you…Let me assure you that I would never, *never* do such a thing to you!'

'I know…'

Softly pliant and warm, and no longer defensive, Ellie let her hands come to rest either side of Nikolai's hips. Even though her touch was feather-light, it burned through the tough material of his jeans. Volcanic heat pulsed through his bloodstream and made him hard. Cupping her face, he let his hungry gaze briefly scorch her before he lowered his mouth and claimed her softly opened rose-pink lips in a kiss that transported him far from this world… 'Come with me…' his voice beseeched her, when he could finally bear to tear his lips away from the sweet wild honey taste of hers. 'Come with me, and for a few hours we will shut out the world and think only of each other.'

## CHAPTER ELEVEN

FINDING herself in a situation she had both feared and yet secretly longed for, Ellie let her nervous gaze move slowly round Nikolai's sumptuously designed bedroom, with its silk wallpaper and antique furniture. She heard the ominous click of the door shut behind her. Sensing his eyes burning into her back in the way that she'd often found him studying her—with the most disturbing and yet heart-stopping intensity—she felt her mouth go dry and a quiver of excitement ripple through her.

It was hard to take her own eyes off the stately and astonishing four-poster bed that loomed up in front of her. Complete with mirrors in the headboard, and enough brocade and silk cushions on top of the luxurious purple counterpane to please Cleopatra herself, surely it was a bed made for seduction? *What was she thinking of?*

Ellie grimaced at her own question. The problem was that she *wasn't* thinking. Her brain was not the part of her anatomy she was engaging at all! All she knew was that this man made her feel something deep and powerful…something she hardly *dared* to feel… And she wanted—no, *needed* to sample more of that spellbinding sensation. It might not make any sense to an outsider, given their past traumatic history together, and yet there it was.

All through the evening spent with Paul and his two cheerful companions she had hardly been able to think about anything but Nikolai, immersed in his work again. Didn't he ever long to make a real connection with someone? she'd thought, almost desperately. With Arina and work his two main priorities, had he relegated any hopes he might have had for a deeper relationship with a woman to a completely lost cause? After all, he had strongly asserted that he was only interested in a marriage of convenience now, after his first marriage had failed so miserably.

All evening the strongest impulse to return to the house and be with him had been building inside Ellie. Despite his anger towards her over the past—despite all of that—she knew something inside him was trying to reach out to her, and from the moment she had seen him again, she had been slowly and inevitably moving towards that call.

She turned round to face him. 'This is a lovely room.'

Nikolai smiled at the comment. And this time the only danger reflected in that riveting gesture was the seductive promise that glinted in his eyes and lingered round the edges of his compelling mouth. 'Made all the lovelier by your presence, my angel.'

Struck dumb as he approached her, it seemed to Ellie that every inch of her skin was alive with the sensation of his touch—even though he hadn't physically made contact with her yet.

Also silent, Nikolai reached out for her, to slide his arm round her waist and lift her up high against his chest as easily as if her weight amounted to nothing. His glance boring into hers like simmering blue flame, he laid her down on the sumptuous bed, and with another enigmatic smile drew his hand lightly down the centre of her chest.

Ellie gasped as one by one he flicked open the three half-moon-shaped mother-of-pearl buttons on her blouse, discovering that she had a penchant for very feminine underwear. She saw the pleasure in his sexy blue eyes deepen as they skimmed the semi-sheer floral bra she was wearing, with its pink satin bow in the centre and prettily decorated straps.

Murmuring, 'Beautiful…' Nikolai reached behind Ellie's slim back and undid the fastening.

When his hands palmed her exposed breasts she bit her lip and briefly closed her eyes, hardly prepared for the storm of need that rippled hotly through her. When he pinched her aching, tingling nipples and sublime languorous heat invaded her—the aroused velvet tips surged hotly into his hands and made her gasp again.

Leaning back to shrug off his shirt, Nikolai smiled lazily. Getting the distinct message that he planned to take his time making love to her, and would relish every moment, Ellie sighed, surprisingly content and quite prepared to wait. After all, what did she have to complain about? Just the sight of him was a feast for the senses.

Bare-chested now, he was long bodied and lean-waisted, with heavenly broad shoulders that she longed to rest her head against. The sight of his golden-tanned torso, silky smooth and perfect, with its mouthwatering display of toned lean muscle and smattering of dark blond hair over flat male nipples, made another surge of heat flow into Ellie's already melting centre, and her thighs quivered to contain it.

'Now we have to get rid of some of these clothes, don't you think?' Smiling like the cat that got the cream, Nikolai peeled off his own jeans and then Ellie's.

While she still reeled with the new sense of urgency and demand in his touch, he covered her near naked body with his and kissed her. It was the most deeply erotic and exploratory kiss she had ever encountered. Her senses were already saturated with the clean, yet musky warm scent of the man as his hard body pressed her down into the bed—and the taste of him was like hot summer nights under the stars. Ellie could have wept with pleasure.

What Nikolai did not know was that no man had ever held her this intimately before—but very soon he would find out. A small stab of unease stole away her joy for the briefest moment, but then her lover moved his sensuous velvet mouth from hers onto her breasts, and she forgot everything but the sheer ecstasy that she was drowning in.

Her hands were moving over his body too, in an instinctive need to give him back some of the pleasure he was giving her. As her palms cupped the tight smooth buttocks beneath his black silk shorts, she felt them clench and his sex—already like steel against her belly—seemed to grow even harder. Emitting a sound that was very like a satisfied growl, he lifted his head, gave her a wicked smile, then kissed her passionately on the mouth, his tongue thrusting hotly inside her.

Disengaging himself only temporarily, Nikolai started to inch Ellie's delicate floral panties down over her hips and then with the minimum of fuss deftly removed his shorts. Kissing her again, as though he could scarcely bear being apart from her for even a second, he slid his hand down between their bodies over the soft tiny curls between her quivering thighs. While Ellie was absorbing this new, fiercely erotic delight he stroked his fingers across her hot moist centre. She sighed out her pleasure and shock on a husky breath.

The feelings that this most intimate of touches elicited were so intense that shuddering emotion brought tears to her eyes. It was frightening to sense all her defences being as expertly and vividly demolished as they were being now. Vulnerability was always scary, but she was so tired of being numb with grief and pain and regret. To feel *anything* was surely better than that?

Now Nikolai was murmuring to her in Russian, and it was the sexiest sound Ellie had ever heard, even though she didn't know what his words meant. Her hands moved tenderly over his short fair hair and round the rough coating of stubble that studded his hard jaw.

'What are you saying?' she asked softly, with a helpless catch in her voice as he inserted a finger deep inside her. Her muscles tightened in shock around him.

'I am saying,' he began, 'that you look and feel and taste like heaven to me, my bewitching, lovely Ellie... And that...' he spread her a little more with his fingers and she gasped '...I want to be inside you...right now.'

As he positioned himself at the apex of her thighs and started to slowly inch himself inside her Ellie knew great relief that Nikolai didn't just thrust into her without care, thinking only of his own urgent need for satisfaction. It made her heart swell with tenderness towards him even more. But she couldn't help but freeze for a moment as he started to fill and stretch her, and he glanced down at her with the faintest suggestion of a frown on his handsome face.

'I am not hurting you?' he asked with concern.

'No.' Her smile was quick to reassure him.

'Then it has been a long time, perhaps?' He frowned again.

Unable to bear the idea that he clearly thought she had shared her body with other men before him... namely his *brother*...Ellie reached out to touch his cheek. 'I'm fine, Nikolai...really. It's just that—'

'What?' Now his whole body stiffened, and he stopped moving inside her, the honed muscles in his biceps taut as iron as he held himself above her.

'I've never been with a man like this before,' she breathed, anxiety making her bite her lip.

'You have *never*? You are telling me you are innocent?'

'Yes.'

*Would he stop making love to her now that he knew the truth? Perhaps even believe she was using her virginity as some kind of manipulative tool?*

But Nikolai wasn't regarding her with disapproval at all. Instead there was the most beguiling smile hovering about his delectable lips.

'You are so beautiful,' he murmured, before claiming her mouth in another all-consuming and avid kiss.

Slowly he started to move inside her again, encouraging her to wrap her firm, shapely legs around that perfect lean waist of his, so that he could go deeper. Surprised, and secretly delighted at how her body responded so meltingly to his possession, realising that pain had hardly featured at all, Ellie finally allowed her tense body to relax. *It would be all right.* This was a totally natural and beautiful experience between a man and a woman. It was only her past anxieties around men in general that had made her resist sampling it before. *But then no man she had ever met apart from Nikolai had made her want to surrender her virginity before*.

Giving herself up to the sensations of joy and ecstasy that were building like a storm about to break inside her as Nikolai's thrusts became more rhythmic and urgent, it was Ellie who confidently and eagerly sought his mouth and claimed it. Soon after that her huskily voiced gasps littered the air as wild sensation dissolved into never-before-imagined bliss.

As she fought to gain purchase on the torrent of emotions that engulfed her, her lover held himself still above her, groaned out loud, then slowly lowered himself against Ellie's chest as she registered a sensation of scalding heat and dampness drench her insides. As he cupped her face, his blue eyes had never regarded her with such searing scrutiny before.

'Why did you wait so long to be with a man?' he asked.

'I've never met a man I wanted to be with like this before…that's why.' For Ellie there was no conflict involved whatsoever.

'Not even my brother?' Nikolai's gaze was fierce again, and she saw doubt and deep inner turmoil flit across the brilliant azure irises.

'I was never with Sasha in an intimate situation— and I was certainly never attracted to him either!'

'I have been tormented these past five years, thinking of you and him together in just such a situation as this!'

'But now you *know* that can't be true!' Ellie's chest was tight with fear that Nikolai would somehow not believe she'd been a virgin after all. She was also stunned to learn of his torment about her and his brother, and to hear such jealousy in his voice.

Sighing heavily, he moved his hands into her silken blonde hair. 'Yes… I know that you were innocent until you gave yourself to me just now. It is a gift no man should take for granted, *angel moy*, and it was wonderful! It makes me more certain than ever that it is right you should become my wife.'

Why? Because he wanted to possess her? *Own* her instead of *love* her? Her heart hurt at the very idea. Surrendering her innocence to Nikolai had been no small thing for Ellie. And now she had to face the most unexamined but possibly terrifying idea of all… She loved him—and on some deeply shocking level she knew that she *always* had.

'Why did you break up with your first wife?' she asked, aware that she was potentially ruining something precious by stirring up the past again.

But she wanted to know about Nikolai and Veronika—the woman who had seemed to have made him so cynical and hard about marrying for love again.

Rolling away from her to lie on his back, Nikolai stared up at the ceiling. Feeling chilled without the warmth of his heavenly body, Ellie pulled an edge of the silk counterpane across her breasts.

'She was unfaithful to me…maybe more than once. I was away working a lot of the time, and she did not always want to come with me. You must have been aware when you came to live here after your sister died that my marriage was a sham. It had been over for a long time, really. When I look back now, I wonder how I could ever have chosen such a woman to be my wife! Apart from our Russian heritage we never did have very much in common. But I was young when I met her, and she acted like I hung the moon!' He lifted a shoulder. 'I suppose I fooled myself she was genuinely in love with me, and with all the responsibility of the family business thrust upon me I needed an ally. I was looking for a companion and friend as well as a lover Ellie…'

Turning his head, Nikolai studied her closely. Ellie wanted to say to him *You're so far away, lying over there… come back to me…* But because she had no certainty of anything right then as far as their relationship was concerned she held back the words.

'I'm sorry for the pain she must have put you through,' she said softly instead, genuinely meaning it.

His eyes widened. 'You never cease to astonish me—do you know that? You always seem to be thinking about somebody else's suffering and not your own! Why is that?'

'I don't particularly want to dwell on my own pain. I've sought to come to terms with it as best as I can, but I decided long ago that the past wasn't a good place to live and it was better to concentrate on trying to build a healthier future instead.'

'I feared that you would die when you were in the hospital.'

As he leaned up on an elbow, Nikolai's glance was grave and concerned. Her heart turning over in surprise and sorrow, Ellie sat up too. 'No!' she exclaimed. 'I was hurt badly, yes… But I knew I would recover. I'm a survivor, Nikolai. I *do* know that about myself.'

As soon as the words were out of her mouth she flinched—because Sasha had *not* survived. *Would Nikolai resent her for that for ever?* How would they make this planned marriage between them work if he could never let go of blaming her?

Thinking about the memory that had partially come back—no doubt stimulated by her return to this house—Ellie felt her stomach knot painfully at the idea of telling him just *why* she had been in the car with Sasha that day. *He'd loved his brother so much, and he'd already suffered such great torment and grief over his death.* Even if it meant exonerating herself at last, she was still torn about telling Nikolai what she now knew to be the truth about the events of that day.

'I saw you limping the other day, when I picked you up from the studios,' he remarked thoughtfully. 'Did the surgery leave any scars?'

Tucking some hair behind her ear, feeling suddenly shy, Ellie held the edge of the sheet over her breasts as though it were a life-raft. 'It did…but they're actually not too bad.' Smiling, she moved some of the fabric away from her legs to reveal the two long scars that were about half an inch in width, running up the front of each bare, shapely thigh.

There was also one at the side of the ankle she had broken too. That was the cause of her limp. The surgeon concerned had done a fantastically neat job of sewing her up again after the operation, and Ellie had never wasted time fretting over the appearance of her scars. That had partly been because up until now—until she'd known for certain she had not voluntarily got into the car with Sasha and taken Arina with her—she had been racked with such terrible guilt and thought she'd deserved them.

Now Nikolai was touching each pale pink slightly raised blemish in turn, gently stroking his fingers across the tight repaired skin, his fascinating cheekbones appearing even more hollow and defined as his gaze became almost hypnotised by what he was viewing.

'Now it is my turn to tell you that I am sorry you endured so much pain…I truly regret that. But the truth is, Ellie, there is nothing that could spoil such incandescent beauty as yours…nothing!'

The hands that were touching her were suddenly coaxing her trembling thighs apart, running up the insides of them with renewed mesmerising purpose. Shivering, Ellie barely had time to register her surprise when Nikolai ripped away the silk that she was modestly covering her nakedness with and covered her trembling form with his body instead.

'Now that I have you right where I want you I find that I cannot get enough of you! Something that I secretly always knew would be the case!'

And his velvet tongue slid in between the moist seams of Ellie's quivering mouth and made her forget both the past *and* the future, to concentrate vividly and unequivocally on the present…

*The hands that covered the soft leather of the steering wheel were damp and slightly shaking.* All through the nightmare car journey through London's busy traffic Ellie drew on every resource she had—mental, physical and emotional—to get her through the dreadful ordeal. Once they reached Sasha's friend's house she told

herself that she would seize the chance…*any* chance…
to get Arina safely away and back home to Nikolai—
to the man she knew loved her more than he loved his
own life.

But the alcohol and drugs he had taken were seriously messing with Sasha's head, and all through the
drive he had been alternately muttering and then falling
into a trance. Ellie seriously feared for him if she left
him with this so-called friend, but she would cross that
bridge when she came to it. Right now, for Arina's sake
if no-one else's, she simply *had* to focus all her concentration on the road ahead.

She was momentarily and shockingly distracted
when Sasha suddenly grabbed the wheel, babbling
something about someone trying to get him, and
shouting in terror. Frantically trying to get back control
of the careening vehicle, Ellie inadvertently veered to
the right of the queue of traffic in front of her. Before
she could straighten the wheel she had to deliberately
yank it even further right as an oncoming Land-Rover
headed straight for them. Suddenly they were motoring
towards a nearby lamppost instead.

*From that moment on, time had taken on a slowed-
down almost dream-like quality…and Ellie had
watched events unfold as though she was an observer
looking down on the scene instead of being part of it
herself.* The last thing she remembered was Sasha
yelling and Arina crying, and then…and then *nothing*.

Merciful blackness had descended like a stormy
raincloud blocking out the sun, and the next thing she

recalled was waking up in hospital with the too-harsh lighting on the ceiling almost blinding her with its vulgar and painful intrusion…

'Sasha!' she cried out loud—a final picture flashing through her mind of his head slumped forward onto the dashboard covered in blood.

With her heart beating as if it would beat right out of her chest, Ellie opened her eyes to discover she had been dreaming, and was still in the opulent bed she had been sharing with Nikolai for most of the night.

*But it was not just a distressing dream,* she realised… It was the full and complete return of her memory of what had happened that day—and why the accident had occurred.

Pressing her hands either side of her head, Ellie couldn't help murmuring beneath her breath… 'Dear God!' Now a little more conscious, she glanced round. Disturbingly, there was no sign of her attentive and ardent lover. All that remained of his presence was the sexy aroma of the aftershave that he wore and—as she discovered, touching the sheet—the warm imprint where his body had so recently been…

# CHAPTER TWELVE

*SHE HAD been calling out for Sasha again.* Finding himself disturbed beyond belief as he had watched Ellie tossing her head from side to side and whimpering like a child in a way that rent his heart in two, Nikolai had finally got out of bed, pulled on his discarded jeans and silently left the room.

She had sworn to him that there had been nothing intimate between her and his brother, but even having found to his shocked surprise that she was indeed innocent, still Nikolai found himself wondering if she had secretly nurtured feelings for him. Why else would she dream about him so often? he asked himself. *And why else would she have willingly got into the car with him that day and taken Arina with her?*

Gripped by frustration at having no answers to any of these questions, and feeling an increasing sense of despondency that he never would, Nikolai made his way to the drawing room. He went to the drinks cabinet and poured out a generous measure of cognac. Tipping it down his throat in one hit, he grimaced at the burn that seared his stomach, but welcomed the temporary relief of pain it brought with it. It seemed he was destined to fall for women who found it impossible to love him just for himself and not feel they yearned to be with somebody else.

Shocked by the thought, and disparaging of the uncharacteristic wave of self-pity that washed over him, Nikolai moved barefooted across the elegant moonlit room and placed his empty glass on the white marble sill of the mantelpiece. Ellie's evocative scent still clung to him, and the realisation made him grow hot all over and instantly hard. She had been the most responsive and exciting lover, and Nikolai had revelled in teaching her the many ways of loving… What he had told her was true. He *had* always known that when he eventually made love to her it would never be enough. He had known it very soon after she had come to the house to be Arina's nanny, he remembered. There'd been something about her smile and her innocence that had bewitched him from the start. So much so that he had found himself seeking out her company whenever he was home, finding excuse after excuse to be in the same room as her and Arina, and fantasising about them becoming a 'real' family. *It had been his secret wish, and he had revealed it to nobody.*

Not until that evening in his office, when Ellie had brought him tea and somehow they had found themselves in each other's arms—not until then had he believed he might be able to turn his secret wish into a reality. But the next day all his hopes had been devastatingly smashed by the car crash that had stolen his brother's life, endangered his baby daughter and not only wounded Ellie but revealed her—so he had believed at the time—to be a liar and a thief.

Now, remembering his visit to the shelter for street kids she had set up, and witnessing the level of devotion she had to both the people who used it as well as the volunteers who worked there, he could not see how she could possibly be *either* of the uncomplimentary things he had accused her of being… Yet how could he trust her unless he knew for sure? He had been betrayed by a woman before, and it had left him feeling both bitter and wary of entering into another similar relationship. More to the point…could he trust revealing his heart to Ellie if she really had loved Sasha and preferred him to Nikolai?

'I've been looking for you.'

Caught up in his thoughts, Nikolai had not registered the soft creak of the door opening. Now he saw Ellie, barefoot and robed in that thin pink wrap he had seen her in before, regarding him with an expression on her lovely face that seemed uncertain and maybe even a little shy…

'I could not sleep,' he said gruffly, spearing his hand through his hair.

'Did I disturb you?' Closing the door behind her, Ellie hugged her arms over her chest and slowly walked towards him.

Outside, a full moon was shining. There was no need for lamplight or other light of any kind with the brightness it bestowed on the room. With her long blonde hair curling over her shoulders, her radiant skin and soft green eyes, she resembled a vision of loveliness and purity that took Nikolai's breath away.

'Yes, you disturbed me.' He smiled ruefully. 'But then you always do.'

'That's not what I meant.' Was that a blush he glimpsed seeping into her pretty cheeks? 'I was talking in my sleep…I might even have cried out,' she continued, looking torn.

Slowly Nikolai inclined his head. 'You called out for Sasha,' he told her, his heartbeat suddenly picking up to an uncomfortable speed.

'Most of my memory has come back.'

'*What*?'

'It must have been returning to this house that prompted it… I've been having dreams about what happened that day. Not just dreams, sudden memory recall too. I was going to tell you…'

'What do you remember?' The question had almost got lodged in Nikolai's throat he was so tense about the answer.

'What I'm about to tell you…you might not want to hear.'

Rubbing the flat of his hand across his bare ribcage, Nikolai sighed. 'What you consider I may or may not want to hear should not prevent you from telling me the truth, Ellie. Just come right out and say it.'

She stared at him for some time before uttering a word…as if she was considering how best to reveal what had to be said. When she finally started speaking there was a new look in her eyes, he noticed. A look that seemed more determined and resolved.

'You remember that Sasha had been drinking that day, before you left to go to your office?'

He moved his head in a brief nod.

'Well…what you may not have known was that he was high on drugs too. He had been taking them for some time…maybe at first to help him get over Jackie…who knows? Anyway, he begged me not to tell you about it. That afternoon, after you'd gone, he was agitated about getting to his friend's house—I think he was a dealer, Sasha said that he'd given him something bad…' Ellie flinched.

'He said he had to speak to him, and he pleaded with me to take him there. He said he would get a cab if I didn't, but I saw he was in no fit state to go anywhere alone, and I was worried that someone might find out who he was—that he was related to *you*, Nikolai—and the press would be on you like a ton of bricks! He was holding Arina and she was crying. He told me that she was his "insurance" to make sure I drove him where he wanted. He was really off balance, and I feared he might drop her. I had no choice but to agree to drive him. I made sure Arina was strapped into the car seat and we left. All the way Sasha was muttering, sounding more and more distressed. I realised then that I couldn't leave him alone with this supposed friend of his, and that I would have to do something—get help in some way. But I had to concentrate on driving safely—particularly because Arina was with us.' She bit her lip and glanced momentarily down at the floor. 'I think he might have been having hallucinations of some kind.'

Nikolai's stomach sickeningly turned over. 'What happened then?'

Ellie's hand touched her throat, and she seemed to turn even paler in the moonlight streaming in through the opened window. 'All of a sudden he cried out and grabbed the wheel. He was muttering something about someone trying to get him. The car was swerving badly all over the road. I tried to get back control but he wouldn't let go of the wheel. All of a sudden I saw that a large four-by-four was heading towards us. With all my strength I managed to yank the wheel to the right, but that left us heading towards a lamppost by the side of the kerb. I don't remember much else after that, except waking up in hospital.'

Biting back the strong curse that hovered on his lips, Nikolai sucked in a breath and held it for a couple of seconds before audibly releasing it. *How blind could one man be*? he thought, anguished. Why had he not seen that Sasha was more addicted than he'd realised? And not just to alcohol but to drugs too?

Ellie was regarding him with an anguished look in her eyes. 'I'm sorry, Nikolai… Sorry that you had to find out such a shocking thing only now.'

For a long while Nikolai said nothing. Somehow words seemed woefully inadequate to begin to describe what he was feeling. He had received the most appalling shock—but part of him was already blaming himself for not seeing the truth long before. Had his sense of responsibility and his love for his brother prevented him from acknowledging that he might be numbing his pain with something other than drink? Why hadn't he moved heaven and earth to get him the help that he needed? Instead Nikolai had sought refuge from his own pain in work and in taking care of Arina, and in the meantime Sasha's addiction had got out of control and become potentially dangerous. In not seeing what was going on Nikolai had endangered both his daughter *and* Ellie. The shame and regret that pulsed through him in that instant knew no bounds.

'Nikolai, are you all right?' Stepping closer to him, Ellie reached for his hand. He could see by her expression that its icy temperature shocked her. He smiled grimly. 'Right now? No... I fear it may take quite some time before I am all right again after what I have just heard.'

'I've told you the truth. I swear it!'

'Do not distress yourself, my beautiful Ellie. You can rest assured that I believe everything you have said. It has come as a great shock, yes... But what has shocked me more is that I *knew* my brother was a potential danger to himself and those around him when he drank and lost control, and I did not persuade him hard enough to get some help. If I had known he was hooked on drugs too then I would have tried even harder! I took Arina under my wing because I loved her, but I did not protect *you* as I should have done, Ellie. I cannot begin to tell you how much I regret that.'

'You loved him,' she said softly, her emerald eyes shining as she glanced up at him. 'And you acted out of the best of intentions.'

Reaching out, Nikolai tipped up her chin. 'Is there no end to your capacity to forgive?' he asked huskily.

'Most people are only doing the best that they know how to do,' she answered. 'Blaming and holding grudges only brings more pain. Why are you smiling?'

'I am smiling, Ellie, because I am in awe of your virtue, and I find myself wondering how a mere mortal man can ever deserve or live up to such a woman as you?'

'I'm no saint! I have plenty of flaws and faults, just like anyone else!' She frowned. 'There is something else I wanted to say.'

'Go on.'

'I don't know how that necklace got into the car, but I absolutely *know* that I did not steal it, Nikolai—and neither was my father involved in any way!'

Lifting a shoulder, he dropped his hand to his side. 'I believe you. It is clear as day to me that Sasha must have taken it—*and* all those other things that went missing from time to time. A drug habit is expensive…no matter how much money you have! Our argument was mainly over money, and he knew that I kept the necklace in my room. He must have taken it before he came downstairs to find you and demand that you take him to see this friend of his.' Moving away from Ellie, Nikolai released a resigned and weary sigh. 'You are absolved of all blame in everything I have ever accused you of. As of this moment you are free to leave, whenever you desire.'

'Leave?' Ellie echoed in shock, her beautiful eyes wide.

'Yes.' Nikolai held her gaze for a long and anguished moment. 'And you will of course be compensated for all the distress I have unwittingly caused you…*substantially*. I will not prevent you from seeing Arina whenever you want. Now I think we should both go back to our respective beds and get some sleep. We can talk about this again in the morning, if there is time before you leave to go to work. Good night, Ellie.'

Unable to look at her for a second longer without acting on his overwhelming desire to sweep her up into his arms and carry her straight back to his own bed, Nikolai walked to the door with a heavy tread and went out, leaving her standing there…

'Ellie, I did a beautiful picture of you and I made you into a princess!'

'Did you, darling? Let me see!'

Sipping the fragrant Italian coffee Miriam had kindly given her when she'd arrived in the kitchen earlier, Ellie felt her heart leap with pleasure at the sight of the little girl dressed in her green and grey school uniform. Having tried to prepare herself for Nikolai walking through the door at any moment, anticipating his arrival with a mixture of longing and trepidation after their abrupt parting in the early hours, she bit back her disappointment when it was Elsa she discovered close on the child's heels instead.

The blonde au pair greeted her with a cheerful smile. 'Good morning!'

'Good morning. Now, Arina…you must come and sit on my lap and show me this wondrous picture you have done of me!' Giving the child's drawing her full attention once she had climbed up onto her lap at the breakfast table, Ellie felt a wave of overwhelming emotion grip her when she saw with what care and loving detail the portrait had been composed.

Ellie had been drawn wearing a long sparkling yellow dress, with her wrists adorned in bright jewelled bracelets. On her head resided a crown decorated at regular intervals with what she guessed were meant to be emeralds. Her hair was long and rippling—the same butter-yellow as her dress—whilst her lips were candy-pink and her eyes the most startlingly bright green Ellie had ever seen!

'Oh, sweetheart!' she exclaimed, giving the little body on her lap a warm, heartfelt hug, 'This is amazing! Nobody told me we had such an incredible artist in our midst!'

'I'm glad you like it, Ellie.' Jamming her thumb into her mouth in a sudden fit of shyness, Arina looked flushed with pride at the praise.

'She loves to draw!' Elsa confirmed, helping herself to some coffee from the percolator and bringing it to the table to join them.

'Yes,' Miriam agreed, in the midst of opening a

cupboard and selecting some cereal boxes. 'But even the greatest artists have to eat before they start their day! Which cereal will you have this morning, my sweet?'

'Good morning, everyone.'

Into all the activity, Nikolai arrived, dressed smartly in a charcoal-grey tailored suit to die for, clean-shaven and showered. His arresting cologne lightly permeated the air.

Gazing at him as an archaeologist might gaze at the find of her life—in wonder, awe and gratitude—Ellie knew her longing for him had no bounds. There had been no conflict in her mind at all last night, when he had told her she could leave. He thought he'd given her a viable option. Ellie knew there *was* no option! She loved him, and she loved Arina, and there was no question of her leaving. All she had to do now was convince Nikolai that she meant it, and pray he wanted her to stay too.

'Ellie? Will you step into my study for a moment?' His glance was fleeting, almost as if he dared not risk looking at her for long, in case he exposed his true feelings.

'Of course…Arina, darling, do you mind if I catch up with you later? If you're gone when I come back, have a great day at school, won't you? I'm looking forward to hearing all about what you've done!'

'Shall I draw you another picture?' Arina asked with excitement in her eyes as Ellie helped her down from the table.

'That would be lovely!'

'You should not tell Arina you will be here when she

gets home if you are planning on leaving today!' Nikolai scolded Ellie once they'd reached his study and he had shut the door firmly behind them.

'I never told you I was leaving!'

The tension rolling off his broad shoulders was palpable, and Ellie's heart welled with love and sorrow at the pain he was obviously going through, believing that she was going to walk out on him.

Walking right up to him, and ignoring the look of puzzlement on his handsome sculpted face, she began to straighten the blue silk tie he wore. It didn't need straightening at all, but Ellie could no longer put off being near him or touching him for another second!

'*This* is my home now…here with you and Arina. The only reason I would even contemplate leaving is if you tell me right to my face you don't want me here.'

'Why would you want to stay? I have not made any of this easy for you. I have blamed you and punished you, even *forced* you into agreeing to marry me because of my inability to believe in your innate goodness…to trust you. No one could blame you for hating me under the circumstances!'

'Hate you?' Hot tears swam into Ellie's eyes. 'Oh, Nikolai—I don't hate you! I *love* you! Don't you know that by now? Why do you think I didn't go with any man all these years? It was you and only you I yearned to be with!'

'It was?' He appeared genuinely stunned.

Smiling now, as well as crying, Ellie kissed him gently on the mouth and touched her palm to his smoothly shaved cheek. 'I think I had a crush on you from the very first day I saw you! I told myself it was just a silly fantasy, and that a man like you would never look at a girl like me in that way. But then I saw how tender and loving you were with Arina and it melted my heart, Nikolai! It made me wonder how it would be to have a man who was capable of giving so much love to a motherless child—give some of that love to *me*.'

'I will show you, my darling…I will show you how it will be—because I too have loved you from the first! From the moment I saw how wonderful and natural you were with Arina I yearned to make you my wife…for us to be a real family! But of course I was still married at the time, and then the accident happened. My plans for the future all turned to dust. I *never* would have prosecuted you or your father for the theft of the necklace. I only said that to manipulate you into agreeing to marry me. Do you believe me?'

'I do. You're a good man, Nikolai. The very best! Not many men would take their brother's child, raise her as his own and be so utterly devoted to her! And it must have been devastating for you to lose your only brother in such a tragic way… I've thought about that many times over the years, even though I couldn't recall how it had happened. I could understand you being angry as well as hurt, and wanting to blame someone for what happened.'

'I should have trusted you…seen more clearly the treasure I had in front of me instead of thinking you had betrayed me! It was only because of my lack of faith in love and relationships that I did so, Ellie.'

'But you trust me now?'

'With my life!'

With her heart singing at the idea that Nikolai really and truly loved her, Ellie boldly moved her hands away from his tie, to slide them down the front of his shirt and undo the button on his jacket.

'What are you doing?' Capturing her hand, he deliberately stilled it.

Her heart started to race in case he had changed his mind and did not want her after all. 'I was wondering…'

'Yes?' He was trying to look stern but failing miserably.

Seeing the smile that kept tugging at his delicious mouth, Ellie immediately relaxed.

'I was wondering if you had to dash off to work early today?'

'Why? Is there something you need?'

'Oh, yes!' Ellie started to push his jacket off his shoulders, and this time Nikolai made no move to stop her. 'I need *you*, my love… What I mean to say is,' she started, unknotting his tie, 'I need you right now!'

There was no preamble to their urgent lovemaking. Too impatient to divest Ellie of her skirt and blouse before achieving the erotic union with her body that he craved, Nikolai pulled her to the floor with him. Down to the deep, tightly woven pile of the exquisite handmade rug he had bartered for with a stallholder in Istanbul many years ago, because it was the custom. He slid her white cotton panties over her bare legs and thrust deep inside her. At the low moan she released he bent to kiss her, and it was as though a fire in him that had been simmering hotly inside his blood for years suddenly burst into an inferno of need and passion. He loved this woman so much! And finally learning that she loved him too had fostered in Nikolai a deep and abiding belief in miracles.

Ellie would be his light and his joy in the years to come—of that he had no doubt. And when Arina had grown and left home—along with any other the children he prayed they might have together—she would continue to be the lover, friend, ally and companion he had always hoped for.

Her heat and delicious melting softness drawing him closer and closer to the edge, Nikolai gazed down into her bewitchingly lovely face, seeing that she too was about to slide deeply into bliss.

'Ti viy-desh za me-nya?' he murmured, before ejecting his seed deep inside her.

'What does that mean?' She clung to him, her body trembling in the aftermath of their urgent loving, arms tight round his shoulders.

Breathing hard, and shaking his head in wonder at the unbelievable pleasure that was making every cell in his body vibrate with joy, Nikolai gave a smile that was infinitely tender. 'I just asked you to marry me,' he explained.

'Didn't I already agree to?' she teased.

'I want you to marry me of your own free will, Ellie... Not because I have coerced you!'

'I know that, my love.' She sighed, drawing his face down to hers. 'And I am…I will! It's what I want more than anything in the world… You, me and Arina… A real family at last!'

# EPILOGUE

IN THE garden of his childhood home six weeks later, outside the window of the study that had once been his father's, whoops of joy and laughter rang out, drawing Nikolai away from the article he had been rereading for a second time—an article in a newspaper his secretary had sent to him from London. The headline read:

## PONY-TAILED PSYCHOLOGIST MARRIES RUSSIAN OIL BARON IN FAIRYTALE WEDDING IN MOSCOW

Beneath this was a large black and white photograph of Ellie and Nikolai at their wedding in the cathedral— with Arina as bridesmaid, standing in front of them, carefully holding onto her posy of fresh flowers.

He had heard it said that a man's wedding day was meant to be one of the happiest, most joyous days of his life, and Nikolai could more than attest to the truth of that. The experience had surpassed even his most longed-for dreams. And if they had enjoyed a fairytale wedding, then Ellie had more than resembled a fairy-tale princess, in the most ravishing of white dresses, designed by one of Italy's top fashion designers. With her flowing blonde hair, sparkling green eyes and the sheer joy that she so naturally emanated, she had been the loveliest bride in the world.

Every day since they had married Nikolai had woken in their bed beside her and counted his blessings. Every day she made him smile, and every day he learned anew just how generous and selfless her heart was. When he had asked her what she would like for a wedding present, after barely a minute's thought she had looked him squarely in the eyes and said, 'A donation for the shelter would be wonderful! Would you mind?'

So the shelter had its donation, and Nikolai's pledged continued support, and he had added even more meaning to this new, happier life he was leading with his interaction and association with the teenagers who for one tragic reason or another no longer had homes of their own.

'Papa! Are you going to come out and play with us? We're playing tag, and we want you to be it and try and catch us!'

Laying down the newspaper on the desk in front of him, Nikolai smiled, got up from the large leather armchair he'd been sitting in, and leaned out of the opened casement window.

'I'm counting to one hundred, and then I'm coming—ready or not!' he exclaimed, chuckling beneath his breath as he left the room and went out to join his lovely wife and pretty daughter…

# A NIGHT WITH CONSEQUENCES

BY
MARGARET MAYO

**Margaret Mayo** was reading Mills & Boon® romances long before she began to write them. In fact she never had any plans to become a writer. After an idea for a short story popped into her head she was thrilled when it turned into a full-scale novel. Now, over twenty-five years later, she is still happily writing and says she has no intention of stopping.

She lives with her husband Ken in a rural part of Staffordshire. Margaret's hobbies are reading, photography, and more recently watercolour painting, which she says has honed her observational skills and is a definite advantage when it comes to writing.

# CHAPTER ONE

THIS was an unbelievable opportunity, thought Kara. Flying to Italy with her boss for the firm's annual conference was any woman's dream. She would have liked it to be hers, but unfortunately—sadly—it wasn't. It never could be.

Not that Blake Benedict was a man who could be so easily dismissed. He was aggressively handsome, with strong dark features that guaranteed a second look. And she had stolen many of those. According to gossip he was divorced—acrimoniously—and had sworn never to get married again. But he was not short of girlfriends. Far from it! They vied for his attention like bees around a honeypot.

Not so Kara. She did not want him to notice her, and had always tried to make herself invisible by wearing dark classical suits and little make-up, dragging her hair back unbecomingly. Her hair was actually her crowning glory, a deep, rich auburn, but there was no way she could wear it loose for the office.

The fact that he never gave her a second look told her that her efforts to hide her sexuality really did work. She made a point of being extremely efficient, and even though he rarely heaped praise on her shoulders she knew that he was more than satisfied.

But the very thought of joining him in Italy sent unease curling down her spine. It was impossible. And yet how to tell him? What if he insisted? What if he said that it was part of her job?

She had felt very fortunate when she'd got the position as PA to Blake Benedict, head of the Benedict Corporation—a worldwide organisation whose head office was in London. The agency had lined up another girl, but she had fallen ill at the last minute and Kara had been sent in her place. The first time she had set eyes on him she had felt a whoosh of something dangerous slide through her body. Never, ever in her life had she felt anything like it.

Blake was head and shoulders taller than most men, with a square dimpled jaw and dark, closely cut hair that held a hint of silver at the temples. His grey eyes were deep-set and his nose looked as though it had been chiselled out of fine stone—as did his lips. They were so beautifully moulded that Kara occasionally found herself holding her breath as she envisaged being kissed by them. This feeling was something entirely alien to Kara and unnerved her greatly. She had never kissed a man, never even been out with a man—her father had seen to that! And even though her domineering father was no longer alive his presence still hung over her.

Not that Blake would ever be interested in Kara. She was not beautiful; she was not blonde or gorgeous. She was an ordinary woman with ordinary features and no man ever looked at her twice. But she was the luckiest woman in the world to have landed this job. It had come at just the right time.

'It's not a problem for you, is it?' Blake was surprised that Kara did not look excited. She had not said that she did not want to go, but the look in her eyes reminded him of a doe in a car's headlights and he could not understand why. Their yearly convention was an opportunity every one of his other personal assistants had jumped at.

He had to admit that Kara was different, and if he hadn't been desperate after Olivia had left he would perhaps not have hired her. He liked beautiful women around him and Kara was—well, she made no effort to make herself look glamorous. But she had come with good references and she was damned good at her job. In fact she had made herself indispensable.

And he needed her in Milan. She had dealt with every aspect of the conference; she had practically organised it herself. She knew exactly what the agenda was. So he was going to make very sure that she went with him no matter what excuse she came up with.

She looked extremely nervous, perched on the edge of the chair, and for the first time he noticed what delicate ankles she had—it was all he could see of her legs in the ridiculous long skirts she insisted on wearing. And her flat shoes were the most unflattering things he had ever seen. But her ankles? Why had he never noticed them before? 'Are you going out tonight, Miss Redman?' He had no idea what had prompted the question, but it suddenly seemed important for him to know.

'Is the question relevant, Mr Benedict?'

It was not the answer he'd expected and it amused

him. He even thought that he heard fire in her voice, and there was certainly a spark in her blue eyes. An almost violet-blue. Something else he had never noticed. They were totally amazing when she widened them, when her long silky lashes fluttered as she waited for his reply. This was a new and interesting side to his PA. A side that he felt himself wanting to explore.

Despite that, though, it didn't please him that she was not readily agreeing to his wishes. 'If I am holding you up then perhaps we can have our little talk another time?'

'You're not holding me up.' Kara did her best to ignore the sarcasm he had injected into his voice. 'But there really is nothing to talk about. I can't join you in Italy—it's as simple as that. I'm sorry.'

She held her breath as she waited for his response. She imagined that no one had ever said no to him before. Blake Benedict was law. Everyone jumped at his bidding. And why not, when he was the successful owner of one of the largest IT solutions companies?

Blake's was a success story beyond most people's wildest dreams. It was a story that every member of staff knew. From a little boy of five who'd been able to use a computer better than most adults, he had started his first business venture at the age of sixteen, writing troubleshooting computer programs, and now he had thousands working for him. He was revered by all and no one ever thought of saying no to him. This was why Kara had taken him by surprise. But she simply could not leave her mother even for a few nights. It would be far too dangerous.

Her daring clearly astonished him, though. A deep

frown grooved his brow and narrowed his grey eyes.
And when he spoke his voice had developed a hard
edge that she was not accustomed to hearing when he
spoke to her. 'There is no such word as *can't* in my
vocabulary, Miss Redman. I'm sure you've worked for
me long enough to know that.'

Of course she had, but her priorities were equally
important. 'I—I appreciate what you are saying, but I
do have a life outside work and—'

'And that life is so important that you cannot dedicate
yourself to your job?'

Kara quivered at the caustic harshness, at the bullet
hardness of his eyes, which had turned almost silver,
but nevertheless she stuck to her guns. 'Mr Benedict,
I do not think you can ever say that I do not do my job
properly.' She had worked late so many times that she
sometimes felt she spent more time at work than she did
at home.

'Maybe not. In fact you're very good,' he admitted.

Grudgingly, she thought. Praise did not come easily
from this man. He was a fair employer, though. His
staff were treated fairly and paid high wages and they
rewarded him by doing their jobs well. Few people left
his employ.

Why couldn't he see things from her point of view?
Did he not think that his staff had lives of their own?

'So who is it that has priority on your time? A boyfriend, perhaps?' The lift to his brows told her that he
clearly thought this was not a good enough excuse.

Kara knew he would not rest until she had told him
the truth, or as much of it as she cared to reveal. 'If you
must know, I look after my mother. She cannot manage

without me.' And she prayed that he would not try to delve any deeper into their circumstances.

For a fraction of a second he hesitated—this was evidently something he had not expected or even thought about. Kara wondered whether he had a mother who equally relied on him. Or maybe not. Blake's work was his life. During the eleven months she had worked for him he had not taken one single day's holiday.

'And there is no one else who can look after her? No other family member?'

Kara was tempted to say, *Would I be talking like this if there was? Don't you think I'd jump at the opportunity of going to Italy?* But she didn't. She lifted her chin instead and met the glare in his eyes with one of her own. 'I'm an only child and my father's dead.' And felt her heart pound as she waited for his response.

His brows lifted fractionally. She would not have noticed if she had not been staring him in the face.

'I see. That is unfortunate. I am sorry.' And he actually looked it. 'What is wrong with your mother?'

'It's her health,' she answered. 'It is not good. She depends on me.'

'And you are sure that there is no one who could possibly keep an eye out for her?'

Kara hesitated. There was her mother's sister, who had always said that she would love to have her stay any time Kara wanted a break, but she had never taken her up on it. It hadn't seemed fair. She wasn't sure that her aunt realised how fragile Lynne had become.

But she'd hesitated too long, and Blake Benedict seized the opportunity, his eyes narrowing on her face. 'I can see from your expression that there is someone.'

Kara compressed her lips and nodded. 'Actually, there is my aunt. Possibly! I would have to ask her.'

'Then do that tonight, Miss Redman. And if the answer is no then I will personally hire a nurse.'

Meaning that he intended her to go to Milan with him whether she wanted to or not! Kara wasn't sure whether to feel annoyed or flattered—it was impossible to decide between the two. She hadn't told Blake the whole truth when she'd said that she could not leave her mother because of her health; it was something far more serious than that. But it was none of his business and she had no intention of talking about it. 'I'll see what my aunt says. Is that all, Mr Benedict?' She kept her eyes level on his in an endeavour to look more confident than she felt. She did not want him to know exactly how fearful she was about leaving her parent.

'That is all.' And already his head was bent over paperwork.

Kara's mother was all for her going. 'Of course I'll stay with Susan. She'll love to have me. She'll let me stay for as long as I like.'

'It will only be for a few days,' Kara hastened to assure her. 'I would get out of it if I could, but Mr Benedict is adamant that he needs me.'

'You worry too much about me, my darling.' Her mother's blue eyes, so much like Kara's, smiled tiredly. 'The change will do me good.'

'Of course I worry,' insisted Kara. 'I have every reason to. You don't think he'll find out where you are?'

Her parent's lips thinned and a deep shadow crossed

her lined face. "You mean the rat who's hounding us for money? Your father certainly didn't do us any favours, did he? But it's unfair that you should have to shoulder the burden. Why all your hard-earned cash should—'

'I don't care about that as long as *you* are all right,' Kara insisted.

'I'll be safe at Susan's,' her mother assured her. 'It's you I'm thinking about. It will do you good to go away.'

Kara tossed her head, her eyes flashing dismissal. 'You're making it sound like a holiday. It won't be, I assure you. Mr Benedict will probably work my fingers to the bone.' The mere thought of going, of being at his beck and call all day, every day, of spending even more time with him than she already did, was not her idea of fun.

'He's realised your true potential, that's what. I bet you're the best PA he's ever had.'

Kara shrugged and smiled, but she didn't tell her mother that Blake Benedict had implied that as well.

'Where are the others?'

Blake had sent a car for Kara and met her at a small private airfield, and as she stepped up into his executive jet she expected the other managers to be already on board. Instead it was empty. The engines were running, they were ready for take-off—and there was only the two of them!

'They've gone on ahead. I thought we could use the time to talk. You have worked for me for almost twelve months and yet you are still a mystery to me.'

His smile told her that he had planned this all along: a

smile designed to put her at her ease, but instead setting alarm bells off in her head. A one-to-one with Blake Benedict was the last thing she wanted. And she could not understand why he was taking this sudden interest. Unless there was something else he was after!

Rumour had it that the last two PAs who had gone with him on these trips had been given their marching orders as soon as they had got back. The rumour machine also said that he'd had affairs with them while they'd been away. Was that what he had in mind? An affair? Did he think it was about time he broke through her personal barrier?

Sheer, cold horror shot down her spine. She had not thought of this before, and it was too late now to back out of the trip. She would need to be careful—erect a shield and not let it slip for even one second.

She felt uneasy at the thought of being at his mercy for the duration of the flight, and when they were cleared for take-off and rose into the air she felt as though she had left her stomach behind. And it wasn't because of the altitude!

It was a luxurious plane, with deep comfortable seats—not that she would have expected anything less—but being on it alone with her employer made everything fade into insignificance. Blake Benedict filled the whole space. It felt as if they were the only two people in the universe.

Which was ridiculous! But how could she help it? She had never found herself in a situation like this before.

Thankfully they had a stewardess, who was prepared to attend to their every need. Except that when Blake insisted Kara sit at his side on a couch so that they could go over the programme of events the woman made herself invisible.

Not surprisingly the laptop lay unattended at his side, and when he half turned in his seat towards her the air in the plane thickened until it became unbearable. Kara had only to inhale to smell the very essence of him. Even if she closed her eyes she could feel him, feel his strength, his omnipotence. Breathing him in was like taking a drug; it settled in every part of her body, making her feel more alive than she ever had in her life.

More aware!

More afraid!

What was happening to her? In all the time she had worked for him she had never felt like this. On the other hand she had never been completely alone with him. Not this alone. It was different in his office—the whole atmosphere was different. She felt awkward now, unsure of herself. Men were a mystery as far as she was concerned.

'You have nothing to fear, Miss Redman. Or may I call you Kara? It's such a pretty name it's a shame not to use it.'

A pretty name! No one had ever said that to her before. A further shiver of awareness ran through her.

'We cannot live together and not be on first name terms.'

'What do you mean, live together?' she asked quickly and sharply, feeling her heart give a giant leap.

'A figure of speech,' he answered, with a lazy shrug and a smile.

A dangerous smile!

'I'm talking about the hotel.'

'Of course,' she answered faintly, hoping that her room was as far away from his as possible. She had booked the whole top two floors but had not been able to stipulate who stayed in which room. They would be allocated on arrival. Except Blake's! He always, but always, stayed in the executive suite.

'I'm glad that you're not wearing one of those terrible suits today.'

Kara felt swift colour rise in her cheeks. She had packed two of her work suits, but she had relaxed her own rules this morning and put on jeans and a spicy pink sweater, completely unaware that the colour complemented her skin colouring and made her look alive and vibrant and very, very pretty—even though she wore no make-up and her hair was tied back in its usual functional style.

Blake too had foregone the dark suits he wore for the office and was wearing an impeccable ivory linen suit which contrasted against the tanned darkness of his skin, making her feel deathly pale by comparison. His jacket had by now been discarded, and although his dark hair was brushed back in its usual style a few strands had been loosened by the wind, making him look younger and less fearsome—and more frighteningly human!

'Why don't you tell me a little more about yourself?' he suggested softly.

A frisson of something Kara failed to recognise shivered through her. It felt dangerous. 'What is there to tell that you don't already know?'

'I know nothing,' he said, 'except that you apparently spend most of your time looking after your mother instead of getting out and enjoying yourself. It's very creditable, of course, but I'm sure she would be the first to agree that you need a life of your own.'

'I am not unhappy doing what I do. Since my father died she has no one—why shouldn't I spend my time with her?' Her voice rose defensively without her even realising it.

'I'm not suggesting that you shouldn't, but you should try and maintain a balance too. You're like me, an only child, so at least we have something in common. What was your childhood like? Did you have lots of friends when you were younger or have you always been a stay-at-home girl?'

'Pretty much,' she admitted.

'Did you have a happy childhood? What was your father like?'

'Why all the questions?' she asked, her voice unconsciously sharp. He had touched a raw spot. There was no way in this world that she was going to tell him what a rotten father she had had, and that even now he was dead he had left them with a whole host of new problems. 'I thought we were supposed to be going over the conference notes?' She inched away from him, curling herself into the corner, unconsciously using the defensive posture she had always adopted when her father threatened her.

Blake's eyes narrowed thoughtfully. 'You're right. It should be business.' But he could not help wondering why Kara was so averse to talking about herself—or her father. Perhaps she had loved him so much that she found the loss still painful? The way she had turned in on herself when he mentioned him suggested that.

He had no idea how long it had been since her father's death, but could not remember her asking for time off to attend his funeral so it must have been before she'd started working for him.

A pity she did not want to talk. He would have enjoyed finding out more about her. She intrigued him. Overnight she had practically turned from an ugly duckling into a swan, knocking him for six in her tight-fitting jeans and hot pink sweater. He had not wanted to take his eyes off her. Unless the dark suits were her office uniform and outside of work she always dressed like this! It would be interesting to see what she had brought with her for the conference.

He opened his laptop, staring at the screen without truly seeing it. All he could see was Kara. The intriguingly, surprisingly beautiful Kara. He could not understand why she kept her raw beauty hidden. She had truly fine features—her nose with a delightful little curve at the tip, amazing blue eyes, and a cupid's bow of infinitely kissable lips. They all begged to be explored.

Kara was glad that Blake had stopped asking questions. She had begun to feel suffocated—or was the rapid beat of her heart caused by a surprising and unwarranted attraction towards him? Her father had banned her from having boyfriends, and even after his death she had never found the time or the inclination. So this was the first occasion she had ever been close to a man who had shown an interest in her, and she found it a scary experience.

When finally Blake began concentrating on the screen in front of him Kara allowed her head to drop back and closed her eyes. But it was not easy ignoring him—not when his cologne teased her nostrils, not when she knew his leg was mere inches away from hers, not when she sensed that sometimes his eyes were on her instead of his computer.

Quite how she managed it Kara did not know, but somehow she fell asleep. She was woken by Blake's light touch on her shoulder as he told her that they were about to land and she needed to put on her seat belt.

Embarrassed now, she moved to her original seat and sat rigidly upright. Blake on the other hand was totally relaxed, a smile turning up the corners of his lips. Had he watched her while she slept? Kara went hot at the thought. Had her mouth fallen open? Had she looked stupid? 'I'm sorry I fell asleep on you,' she said quietly.

'And very beautifully too. It was quite something, having you resting your head on my shoulder. My usually prim and proper PA behaving like a real woman for once.'

Alarm raced through Kara. Her head on his shoulder! Was that what she had done? Her heart went wild, leaping within chest as though it was trying to escape. 'I really am sorry.'

'No need to apologise,' he said, shaking his head. 'It was my pleasure.'

His pleasure! Another source of heat seared the surface of her skin. This was too embarrassing by far. 'It was very rude of me.' She sat up even straighter. 'I didn't sleep very well last night. That must be why.'

'Was it the thought of joining me today that kept you awake?' His grey eyes met and held hers and Kara shivered. There was something in the tone of his voice that alarmed her.

It was wrong to judge all men by her father—but her mother had told her to be careful, that men were not always what they seemed. And all she knew about Blake was that his affairs were legend. There was no way on this earth that she wanted to become another statistic.

But how to answer his question? 'It was the thought of what lay ahead,' she said, which in itself was not an outright lie. 'I've never been to Italy.'

'Then I will enjoy improving your education, showing you places that you have only read about or perhaps seen on the television.'

'Mr Benedict.' Kara put on her most professional demeanour. 'I am sure we will not have time for sightseeing. You have a very full schedule.'

His slow smile said it all. 'There is always time for enjoyment, Kara.'

# CHAPTER TWO

IT SEEMED like no time at all before they were being driven to their hotel, and because Kara had booked the rooms and seen photographs of it she knew what to expect. Except that the grandeur of the building actually took her breath away. The architecture was stunning. But what stopped her breathing altogether was the discovery that her room was right next door to Blake's.

And it was clearly actually part of his suite, because it had an adjoining door. Fortunately locked, but that did not make her any happier, nor ease her alarm. Had he asked for her to be put here?

There was only one way to find out. She walked the few yards along the corridor and tapped on his door, entering at the sound of his voice. 'Why have I been roomed next to you?' she asked bluntly, without even waiting for him to ask what she wanted.

'Does it bother you?' Blake did not look in the least concerned. He did not even look surprised—which told her that he must have been expecting a reaction.

'Actually, yes, it does,' she retorted.

'For what reason?' Grey eyes captured blue.

'Because—well—' She lifted her chin a fraction higher, realising that she actually didn't have a particularly good reason. 'Because it doesn't feel right. I should be with the others. It's as though you're giving me some exalted presence.'

Dark brows rose and he folded his arms across his magnificent chest. He had taken off his jacket and undone the top buttons of his shirt, revealing a scattering of springy dark hairs against darkly tanned skin.

Kara had only ever seen him in a collar and tie. She had never seen the flesh and blood man beneath. Although it shouldn't have affected her, it did. He suddenly looked less daunting and more human. And—she hated to admit it—sexy.

'For your information, I was thinking of practicalities.'

Kara hardly heard what he was saying. She was still staring at his chest, which was quite magnificently muscled. Did he work out somewhere? A private gym, perhaps? Or did he have his own gym? She realised she actually knew nothing about Blake; she had never been interested. But now all sorts of questions sprang into her mind. She was seeing the man now, and not her employer, and could not ignore the way her pulse raced that little bit faster.

'It makes perfect sense,' he said now. 'You are my right-hand woman. You are the trigger to this whole conference running smoothly. There are sure to be things we need to talk about. I need you close to me.'

He needed her close to him! They were the only words that penetrated through the haze that fogged her brain. Close to him!

Then she blinked and everything snapped back into

place. 'I do not agree, Mr Benedict. There is no need for us to—'

Her words were abruptly cut off. 'Miss Redman—Kara—it is too late to change now. The hotel is full.' His expression suggested that she was making a mountain out of a molehill. 'But if it will make you feel any better I promise not to intrude on your privacy.'

Kara felt hot colour flood her cheeks. Was that really what he thought she had been thinking? She somehow managed a glare before turning around and marching back to her room. After her initial concerns she had been excited at the thought of coming here, of hopefully seeing something of Milan, but now new fears began to build. What had happened to the barrier she had supposedly erected? One look at a V of exposed chest and she had gone to pieces. How stupid was that? She was behaving like a teenager instead of a twenty-six-year-old woman.

Unfortunately she would now see Blake Benedict in a completely different light, and it could spoil the whole conference—unless she took herself in hand. Even with his shirt buttoned up and a tie in place, his jacket over his magnificent chest, she would still remember what she had seen. It would still haunt her thoughts and she would hunger to see it again, perhaps to even touch! Oh, God, this was crazy. She was turning into someone she did not recognise.

She needed to be careful. Blake's attitude towards her had changed as well. She knew that. He had never really taken the time to get to know her before. She had been a faceless woman who quietly and efficiently kept his office running. But something had happened on the flight over. He had taken a second look, and a third, and seen a changed person. And if her instincts were anything to go by he was taking a very real interest in her now.

On the other hand maybe she *was* making a mountain out of a molehill. Maybe she was seeing things that were not there. Embarrassment coloured her cheeks again, made her wish that she had not gone to his room. The time to confront him would have been if he had stepped over the mark. It was going to be sheer hell facing him now. It would take all of her courage to keep her chin high and pretend that nothing was wrong.

After unpacking she stepped under the shower. They would soon be attending a pre-conference dinner, where everyone could get to know each other. A supposedly relaxing evening before the work really started. The trouble was that she could not get over her unease that Blake Benedict was on the other side of that door.

Was he showering too? Was he standing there naked? Was all that fabulous flesh exposed? All hell let loose inside her body. Despite the fact that she kept telling herself everything was in her imagination she could not shut him out of her mind.

Which was ridiculous when she thought about it. She had worked with this guy for nearly twelve months and not felt even a second's interest in him—so why was it happening now? Was it because, for the first time, she was seeing him as a human being instead of a man driven by work? Or was it the reverse? Was it because he appeared to be taking an interest in her?

Was that it? Was she falling under his influence? Was it because he was the first man ever to take an interest in her? Please, God, don't let me be so weak as to fall for him, she prayed. Please don't let me be like all the rest.

When it was time to get dressed she was undecided whether to wear one of her work suits or a black dress that she had once bought for a New Year's Eve party she had never actually gone to. It had been only a few months after her father had died and she had felt uncomfortable about leaving her mother. But was the dress too dressy for tonight? Should she save it for the last evening?

As she wasn't used to going out like this she was still debating when a sharp rap came on her door. 'Kara, are you ready?'

Kara groaned inwardly. 'Almost! I'll be down shortly.'

'I'll wait for you.'

Mild panic skittered; goosebumps rose on her skin. 'There's really no need. I can find my own way down.'

'I want you with me.'

It was a command, and Kara knew he would not go away. But she was not going to let him in—not when she was standing in her bra and panties. Embarrassing heat attacked her at the mere thought.

Hastily now, because it was the quickest and easiest, she pulled on the dress. She had already fixed her makeup, but there was no time to do anything with her hair other than a swift flick of the brush.

She opened the door just as his hand was raised to bang on it again. It stayed where it was. He simply stood there looking at her. God, she must look awful. 'Is there something wrong?' She ought to have taken another look in the mirror. 'Am I overdressed? Should I change? I didn't really know what to wear.'

'You look—stunning. Absolutely stunning.'

Blake could not take his eyes off her. The dress fitted her body like a glove—as though she had been poured into it. And what a figure she had! A perfect hourglass! Never before had he seen her dressed like this. Nor had he realised how thick and luxuriant her hair was, or that it was reddish-brown with copper highlights. Wearing it loose made her look sensational. It brushed her shoulders and swung like a silken curtain when she moved.

Why she usually hid herself beneath shapeless clothes he had no idea. Unless it was simply that she thought tailored suits were the correct uniform for work. Which, he suddenly decided, was OK by him.

Otherwise, if she flaunted her fabulous figure as some of the girls in the office did, she would have all the male members of staff drooling over her. And he did not want that. He surprised himself by suddenly feeling very protective towards his PA.

After his welcoming speech to the other delegates he introduced her. 'Gentlemen, may I present to you Kara Redman, my PA? The most competent assistant any man could wish for. She will be at your disposal during the next few days—for work-related reasons only. Anything personal you keep to yourself.'

His last words created the expected laughter but Kara felt embarrassed. She had not dreamed for one moment that he would introduce her so publicly, and for him to say that... Her cheeks burned and she felt on fire.

When the food was served and everyone's attention

was taken she looked at him and said quietly, 'Did you have to make a joke of me?'

Blake's brows rose questioningly. 'It wasn't a joke. It was for your own protection. I've already seen one or two of the men here eyeing you up.'

'And you think I cannot look after myself?' She was totally embarrassed. Admittedly she'd never had to fight men off, but he didn't know that.

'My apologies,' he said drily.

Despite her initial concerns Kara enjoyed the evening far more than she had expected. She enjoyed meeting the people she had been in touch with, putting faces to names, and all seemed to be going well—until after their meal, when everyone mingled and one of the guys from New York suggested to her that she was more to Blake Benedict than his PA.

'What makes you say that?' How could he even think it, yet alone put it into words? Was everyone else thinking the same? Was that why they thought he had made that hands-off statement about her earlier?

'I've seen the way he looks at you. He's like a guard dog on patrol. I just wanted to see if I stood a chance. You are a stunning woman. Any man would give his right arm to go out with you. Blake's a lucky a so-and-so if he's already got you.'

'No one has *got* me,' she retorted, flashing her blue eyes. 'Blake Benedict is my boss and that's all there is to it.'

'Is that so?' he asked with a slow smile, and he moved closer—so close that Kara could feel his breath on her cheek.

She took a step back and felt herself cannon into a rock-hard chest.

'Is everything all right here?'

Blake's voice sounded in her ear and she felt his hand on her waist. The next moment both arms came around her and she was held prisoner against him. Her first instinct was to pull away—but, knowing it would make a fool of him when he was trying to save her from this man's advances, she made herself relax.

Amazingly, her world shifted. She was aware of nothing except the hard strength of his body, the soft thud of his heart against her back—and the pounding of her pulse. These were new and unexpected feelings, and except for the time on the plane she had never been this close to a man. She had certainly never felt her heart flutter because of a man's touch! This was not her employer any more. This was Blake, the man.

For a few mind-blowing seconds they were the only two people in the room. Her heart began its own roller-coaster and her mouth grew dry. She could not speak even if she wanted to, so it was a relief when the other man backed away.

Once he had gone Kara struggled to free herself, feeling mortified now by her reaction to Blake, unable to understand what had come over her. Thank goodness he had no idea that she had been turned on by him. It would be so embarrassing if he knew—if he even suspected it. She put on her most indignant face. 'I am capable of looking after myself.'

'I've no doubt,' he answered calmly, a tiny smile turning up the corners of his mouth, 'but Miles can be very persuasive. He also has a wife at home. I should have warned you that on occasions like this a lot of the guys seem to forget they have other commitments, like wives and families.'

Kara began to realise how little she really knew about men and life. All thanks to her father! But she would learn, and she would learn quickly.

'I've seen the way some of them are already looking at you,' he continued. 'And why should they not? You are incredibly beautiful.'

Kara could not stop a flush of hot blood. No one had ever called her beautiful before. And for it to be her boss! 'It's kind of you to say so,' she said primly, at the same time wishing that she had gone with her first instincts and worn a boring suit. None of this would have happened then. No one would have looked at her twice. 'But, like I said, I don't need a bodyguard.'

'That may be the case,' he admitted, 'but surely you're not going to take away my credit for doing the gallant knight thing?'

Kara laughed. The first time she had really felt comfortable with him. 'For which I thank you. But shouldn't you be mingling with your colleagues, not worrying about me?' She did her best to sound prim again, though was aware that she failed dismally.

'But I do worry, since this is your first conference. I feel obliged to look after you. And I will only *mingle*, as you so delightfully put it, if you accompany me.'

He looked at her with such determination that Kara did not dare refuse. She was conscious, though, as they stopped and talked to each individual in turn, that he was reinforcing the impression that she belonged to him. His hand was on her elbow often as he guided her around the room, and her worst fear was that they would leave together at the end of the evening. And that maybe he would insist on her joining him in his room for a nightcap.

Her heart beat unreasonably fast at the mere thought of it, and the tales she'd heard about his other PAs would not go away. Not that he'd given her any reason for alarm, but even so...

When he was called away for a moment, Kara saw her opportunity and almost ran up the stairs in her haste to escape, closing the door to her room and leaning back against it as though at any moment it would burst open and Blake Benedict would walk in.

It was not until her breathing returned to normal that she realised how stupidly she was behaving. Blake had not said or done anything to make her believe she was in danger, so why was she panicking? Her problem was that she did not know how to handle men. She had never had a boyfriend. She had never even dated. Not one single date. How pathetic was that, at her age?

She got ready for bed and crawled into it but was unable to sleep. Her mind was far too active. Too much was going on in it for her to relax. That Miles man, for instance, and Blake's intervention! She was grateful, but she also felt extremely foolish. He must think her a real *ingénue*.

Finally she heard Blake's door open and close, followed by the murmur of his voice. At first she thought he had someone with him, but then realised he was on the telephone. Even when there was silence she still did not settle down.

Her fertile imagination saw him undressing, and

she couldn't stop herself visualising the hard, strong lines of his body. She even imagined threading her fingers through those dark chest hairs. How would it feel? Would they be soft and springy? Or quite firm? Would the heat of his body transfer itself to her fingers? Would he capture her hand and hold it against his beating heart?

She had absolutely no idea. But she did know that something was happening to her own body just by thinking about it. And if she carried on like this she would get no sleep tonight.

But how to stop her thoughts? These were new feelings. Her body felt vibrantly alive and she could not help wishing that he would unlock the door and tiptoe into her room and slide into bed beside her.

What she would do if he actually did she had no idea. Probably scream at him to go away. Ask him what the hell he thought he was doing. But her body warred with her mind. For the first time ever in her life it burned with excitement.

How she managed to sleep Kara was not sure, but somehow she did. She slept well, and was woken only by her alarm. Feeling self-conscious now about the attention that had been paid to her yesterday, she slipped on a white blouse that fastened right up to the neck and one of her dark suits. Then, as there was still plenty of time before breakfast, she went down to the conference room and put out the notes that would be needed during the day.

She did not hear Blake enter, and gave a tiny cry of alarm when she turned to leave and cannoned right into him.

'Steady, Kara.' And although it wasn't necessary his arms came around her.

Immediately the tantalising smell of his cologne stung her nostrils and the crazy sensations from last night came rushing back, threading their way from her throat right down to her stomach. 'I'm sorry,' she said huskily, at the same time pulling away from him. 'I didn't know you were here.'

'Are you afraid of me?' he asked, a frown pulling his brows together.

'Of course not.' Her reply was instant and fierce, and she looked him straight in the eye. But whether he believed her was another thing. If the truth were known she would not have believed herself.

'Good, because we're going to be spending an awful lot of time together. Have you eaten breakfast yet?' And when she shook her head, 'Then perhaps you will join me and we can go over today's agenda?'

They had already gone over it many times, thought Kara, but refusing did not appear to be an option. The dining room was full, and all eyes were turned on them as they made their way to Blake's table.

Blake had never come across any woman who intrigued him as much as Kara Redman did. He could not make up his mind whether she truly was the innocent she appeared or whether she was putting on an act.

'We're two of a kind, do you know that?'

Kara stopped picking at a croissant and frowned at him. 'What makes you say that?'

'It's simple. We've both lost our fathers, we have no siblings, and we're both career-minded. Maybe my career has taken me on a different path from yours, but you're very good at what you do, very conscientious, which in my eyes makes you the perfect PA. I wish never to lose you.' And that had to be the truth.

'It's very kind of you to say so.'

'Do you mind if I ask how long it's been since your father died? I gained the impression the other day that his death had hit you hard. My father died when I was just eleven, so I've had some time now to get used to it.'

Instantly Kara's face changed. A mask came over it, and when she spoke her voice had become much cooler. Blake instantly felt her withdrawing from him. 'I'd really rather not talk about him, if you don't mind. My father was—well, he wasn't a very nice man. And that's more than I should have told you. I'm sorry.'

'And I'm sorry that I asked.' Her confession had stunned Blake and he wished now that he had said nothing. Kara's hurt still sounded raw. Maybe one day he would discover exactly what sort of man her father had been, but for the time being he needed to bring the conversation round to something pleasant.

'I lived here for a while,' he told her. 'It's a beautiful country. My mother is half Italian.'

To his relief a spark of interest brightened her eyes. 'Does she still live here?'

'Actually, no. She prefers England. Says she likes to be closer to me. But I do have cousins in Seville.'

'And will you be visiting them after the conference? I've never known you take a holiday.'

'I doubt it,' he answered. 'My work means far more to me than spending time looking up relatives. How about you? Where do you go when you take your annual leave?'

Kara shrugged and looked as though she wished he had not asked her *that* question either. 'I stay at home. My mother isn't well enough to travel.'

Of course. He was forgetting her parent's illness. 'In that case you have no right criticising me,' he said, accompanying his words with a smile. Sometimes Kara looked as though she was terrified of him and he had no idea why. She intrigued him, and he felt a very real need to get to know her better while they were here.

Kara found the first day of the conference an eye opener. She was spellbound. Watching Blake take command, the respectful interest everyone had in him, the energy that buzzed around the room, somehow invigorated her as well. She felt more alive than she had in a long time.

She had expected to sit quietly by Blake's side, making notes, feeding him any information he did not have readily to hand, but somehow she found herself being drawn in.

Maybe the fact that she was fully conversant with everything helped. She had made it her business to be the most efficient PA Blake had ever had so that he would never feel the need to get rid of her. And she felt very proud of herself when she was able to answer any question that he threw her way.

'A very successful first day,' he announced when the meeting broke up. 'Thanks to your excellent organisational skills. You've done me proud, Kara, thank you.'

Kara felt swift colour flood her cheeks. 'I only did what I'm getting paid for.'

'And more,' he said, his eyes locking into hers so that she felt a swift river of heat tumble its way through her body. 'Remind me to give you a rise when we get back. For now, I think we should get some air before dinner. We need to stretch our legs.'

Kara was not sure whether this was a command or a suggestion. 'I actually thought of relaxing in my room.' The whole day had proved more exhausting than she had expected.

'Nonsense!' he said briskly. 'You need fresh air and exercise. It's either a walk—I could show you some of the sights Milan has to offer, La Scala for instance—or—' his eyes lit up as he spoke '—we could take advantage of the swimming pool. You do swim, Kara?'

Every nerve in her body shuddered. The mere thought of seeing all that exposed, bronzed, muscle-packed flesh, scared her to death. It was not that she did not want to see him, she did—her heart raced at the thought—but she was afraid that she might give herself away in the process.

'I do,' she answered, unaware that her voice had gone suddenly husky. 'But I think I'd prefer to walk. In any case I haven't packed a swimsuit. I had no idea that swimming was part of the agenda.'

Blake smiled his appreciation at her attempted humour, his eyes crinkling at the corners and making him look—different. Softer, kinder, poles apart from the tough-guy businessman she had got to know so well. This new man frightened her. He sent prickles of heat across her skin and an ache low down in her belly.

'They do have a shop here in the hotel that sells that sort of thing.'

'I'd still rather walk,' answered Kara quietly, since she wasn't being given the option of going back to her room. He was overpowering her, and wasn't giving her any time to herself. And, although she did feel a need to drag some fresh air into her lungs, she could do that just as easily in the hotel gardens—alone!

Amazingly, though, once they set off she began to relax. She even found herself chatting to him as though he was an old friend. Not divulging anything personal, but commenting on the shops that lined the streets, selling jewellery and handbags and all sorts of interesting things. But it was definitely La Scala itself that entranced her.

'I've always wondered about this place,' she exclaimed as they stood looking at the elegant building.

Blake smiled indulgently. 'Do you like opera?'

'Sometimes,' she admitted. 'It depends if I'm in the right mood.'

'And what mood would that be?' he asked, half-turning to face her.

As she met those stunning dark eyes her body flooded with new and different sensations, different emotions that spun her into a whole new world. A world of hunger and desire. A world where there was just Blake and herself. Blake making love to her, teaching her, encouraging her. She felt embarrassed by it. This should not be happening.

But how to help herself? She had the feeling that Blake could read the thoughts in her mind. The countless thoughts that raced round and round, confusing her and worrying her, bringing swift colour to her cheeks, and she wished now that she had gone to her room and shut herself in.

In London Blake was her boss, her employer, and she had never let herself think of him in any other way. She had not even wanted to. But now that she was far away from home, away from the safe and familiar, she was changing, relaxing—and almost welcoming the attention he was paying her.

'When I'm feeling sad,' she admitted in answer to his question, surprised to hear that her voice sounded normal. 'I don't really understand opera, but it somehow helps me. Not that I've ever been to a live performance.'

'Is that so?' Blake's brows lifted. 'Then we will have to see whether we can remedy that while we're here. Watching an opera being performed at La Scala is a serious sensation in itself.'

Swift alarm stabbed at Kara's chest. Attending a concert with Blake went far beyond anything that was reasonable and sane. 'I doubt whether we'll have time.' And even if they had would she really want to go with him? Sit with him for two or three hours, or however long it lasted? This new-found awareness would fill her to such an extent that she would be unable to concentrate on what was going on on the stage. She put on her very best office voice. 'You have a very full schedule, Mr Benedict. And even if you didn't, I doubt you'd get tickets at this late stage. They must be sold out months in advance.'

'Are you trying to get out of it?'

'I am.' There was no point in lying.

Blake laughed at her honesty. 'Tut-tut, Kara. Have

you not realised yet that I always get my own way? And perhaps you could learn to call me Blake?'

There was a whole world of difference between calling him Blake in her mind and saying it to his face. Maybe she was old-fashioned, but using his surname was what she needed more than anything right now. It held up the barrier. It prevented intimacy. It reminded her of who he was.

Not that her body took heed of any barriers. The longer they were together the more aware of him she became. And the more uncomfortable she felt. It was such a foreign feeling that she wanted to turn and run in case he sensed it.

Blake was a man of the world. He knew all about women. If he looked too deeply into her eyes he would be able to see how much he affected her. He would guess at the riot of emotions he had stirred. And he might play on it. Take advantage. Hammer away at her senses until she weakened.

The thought of weakening, of allowing him to flirt and tease, maybe even go further, caused a fast, heart-thumping eruption of excitement, of actual physical need. She turned and began to walk away. Finally she was beginning to appreciate what all the other girls in the office talked about.

'You do understand, Kara—' his voice came closely over her shoulder '—that running away tells me more about you than if you had stayed and argued.'

Blake knew that it was not going to be easy getting Kara Redman to relax in his company. For a few minutes earlier, when they had been window shopping, she had become animated, but as soon as he had suggested doing something that would throw them into close contact she had frozen.

The question was, why? And how long was it going to take him to find out? Kara was the most private person he knew. Other women were always eager to talk about themselves, to show off, to preen like a peacock in front of him. Not so Kara. And the less she opened up the more intrigued he became, the more determined to prise open the shell of security she had wrapped around herself. There had to be a reason and he wanted to know what it was. Whether it really was because of her father or whether it was something else.

'I am not running away.'

He smiled at the hint of defiance in her voice. 'Good, because I want you to relax. I want you to enjoy your time spent here. It's not all about the conference, and since you've never been to Milan before I think you should see something more of the city than the inside of a hotel. In my humble opinion La Scala is the *pièce de résistance*. You cannot possibly leave without embracing a performance here. And I would be honoured to be the one to introduce you to the delights of live opera.'

'It's very kind of you Mr—er—Blake, but your diary is full.'

'As you constantly remind me.' He smiled as he spoke, sensing how difficult it had been for her to use his first name. 'Nevertheless we will make time.' He saw the apprehension in her blue eyes, and the way her teeth bit nervously on her lusciously plump bottom lip— something else he had never noticed before.

He was tempted to kiss away her nervousness, to taste those delicious lips for himself. But he knew that to do so would be fatal. Kara Redman was without a doubt the most intriguing female he had ever come across, and if it was the last thing he did he was going to remove the barriers she had built around herself. And he would take great pleasure in doing so.

'I actually think we should be getting back,' said Kara, looking pointedly at her watch. 'Dinner will be in an hour, and I need to shower and—'

'You are right, of course,' said Blake, but she need not think that he had given up on the opera. The idea of them sitting together watching a performance, her slender body close to his, touching him perhaps, of letting her delicate perfume entrance him, maybe even finding himself far more aware of his surprisingly beautiful assistant than of what was going on onstage, was something that would not go away.

Kara Redman had begun to get beneath his skin like no other woman ever had. He'd been out with lots of beautiful women since his divorce, but their beauty had been skin-deep. His assistant was very different. Once he had really looked at her he had seen a strikingly good-looking woman—and he would never be able to understand why she hid her amazing figure beneath sensible clothes. She was also superbly intelligent. In fact she was one hell of a woman—and he could not believe that he had not realised this months ago.

# CHAPTER THREE

RELIEF flooded Kara when she finally got back to her room, and she gulped in great breaths of air. Spending time with Blake left her feeling breathless and exhausted. Crazy feelings swirled in her stomach—desire mixing with unease. Hunger with fear.

What she could not understand was why she was experiencing these feelings now when she never had before. What was the difference between working for him in London and working with him here? The fact was that he'd never taken her walking in London. They had never met outside the office. In fact everything was different.

Even Blake was different. He was no longer the man who barked orders. Who expected them carried out to the letter in the shortest possible time. He had become human. And in so doing he had triggered something inside her that was scary. Because of her father she had always kept her feelings tightly controlled, everything hidden behind a mask.

And when Blake had shown not the least interest in her, when *no* man had shown interest, it had been easy to remain behind her mask of self-preservation. Now it was in danger of slipping. In fact it had already begun its downward slide. A few kind words, a desire to get to know her, and something inside had sprung into life. An amazing new life that both scared and excited her.

As she showered Kara wished with all her heart that she had been able to get out of this conference. Blake could quite easily have managed without her. All the arrangements had been made, the paperwork was done—there was nothing he needed that he hadn't got. She had seen to everything.

She found herself scrubbing at her skin more energetically than was necessary, and asked herself whether she was trying to rid her body as well as her mind of him. Which was laughable! Blake Benedict was not a man anyone could forget easily, and she'd had more than her fill of him over the last eleven months.

It was a wonder she didn't dream about him. Actually, now she remembered she *had*—the very first day of her job. After a gruelling eight hours she had convinced herself that she would never be able to do the job to his satisfaction, and had gone home to bed to experience a dream that had disturbed her deeply. Not because it was erotic—thoughts like that hadn't entered her mind—but because he had assumed the mantle of the devil.

After that she used to tell her mother that she was working for the devil. She had never learned a job so quickly in her life. She had taught herself always to be prepared—and she had been. Always ready with an answer to his quick-fire questions. Until he'd changed from Blake Benedict, business tycoon, to Blake Benedict, human being. A human who was interested in her!

Dressing for dinner, Kara chose the skirt from her black suit, teaming it with a red blouse with a deep

V-neck. Her mother had bought it for her last Christmas, but she had only worn it once, feeling that it was too pretty and too feminine to wear for work.

When she walked into the dining room, taller and more elegant than ever in her black high-heeled sandals, every eye turned in her direction. But the only person she saw was Blake, watching each step that she took.

'You look stunning,' he said softly as he stood to hold out her chair. 'Red suits you. You should wear it more often.'

Kara smiled her thanks, not trusting her voice. He looked particularly handsome too, in a handmade navy suit and a pale blue silk shirt. His red and navy tie, also silk, was as immaculate as always, and as he bent over her, ensuring she was seated comfortably, his cologne— the one he always wore and which was an integral part of him—drifted beneath her nostrils like an aphrodisiac.

And when his hand touched her shoulder, when it lingered longer than was necessary, she felt a shiver of sheer pleasure run all the way down to the tips of her toes. 'You smell divine, Kara,' he whispered in her ear.

*So do you*, she wanted to say, but could not—dared not. It would be far too intimate. She was not sure that she liked him complimenting her either—not here, not with so many eyes on them.

She was relieved when a waiter placed a napkin on her lap and handed her the menu. Now she could breathe! Except that every breath she drew seemed to bring her nearer to Blake, and when she stole a glance at him from beneath her lashes she saw that instead of studying his own menu he was watching her.

'What's wrong?' she asked, trying to make light of it, which was practically impossible when her heart had just leapt. 'Do I have a spot on my nose?'

'Your nose is delightful. It's a very kissable nose.'

Kara's eyes widened in shock.

'You do not like compliments, Kara?'

The truth was that she was not used to compliments. What made her nose kissable, anyway? It was just a nose. She didn't answer his question.

'As are your lips.'

Kara refused to listen. She did not even look at him any more. She concentrated on the menu instead, ignoring the fact that her stupid pulse had begun to race again and heat was prickling her skin. One of her downfalls was the way that she blushed so easily, and she prayed that her cheeks did not colour now.

Even when their order was placed there was no escape. There was just the two of them. For no reason at all everyone else had faded into the background. Wine was poured and Blake proposed a toast. 'To my most efficient PA—long may you continue to work for me.'

Kara could not drag her eyes away from his. She had never really noticed before how thick his lashes were, or how the grey of his eyes seemed to change colour according to his mood. She had seen them turn a light silver at the office, when someone was being less than efficient, but at this moment, when his attention was concentrated solely on her, when his thoughts were deep and unreadable, they were much, much darker. And they held an expression that she could not read but one that both scared and excited her at the same time.

Here in this beautiful hotel, in this beautiful country,

something was happening to her. It was as though her old life in England was being slowly erased. Memories were fading and something far more exciting was taking over. It was a transitory thing, she knew, but it would surely be foolish not to make the most of it.

He made her feel as though they were the only two people in the room, commanding her attention in such a way that everything except him was blotted out. And for the moment this was all right with her. It was a new experience—one she would treasure when they got back home and everything returned to normal.

She took a sip of her wine and smiled shyly at him. 'You're very kind.'

'It is no more than the truth.'

'I enjoy the job.'

'And are you also enjoying the conference?'

Kara nodded. 'I've never attended anything like this before, and I have to confess I was a little nervous, but, yes, I am enjoying myself.' Except when he paid her too much attention!

'Every man here envies me. And why not, when you are a very beautiful woman?'

This time colour really did flood her cheeks. 'It's very kind of you to say so.'

In response he simply gave her a smile that caused a further skittering of her senses.

The waiter returned with their food and Kara was glad of the respite. It gave her time to take a few deep breaths and tell herself she was in control. That having a man flatter her like this should be a joyful experience, not scary.

And somehow it worked. Gradually she began to

relax and enjoy the evening. She drank more wine than usual, unaware that her eyes were brighter and her cheeks flushed with happiness. They talked incessantly, and Kara laughed out loud at some of his anecdotes.

It was not until the end of the meal, when he passed her an envelope and then watched her face closely as she opened it, that she was suddenly stuck for words. Inside were tickets for *Faust* the following night. Kara blinked twice and swallowed a sudden lump in her throat.

'Think of it as a thank-you from me to you for all the hard work you've put in,' he said, watching the changing expressions on her face.

'I—I don't know what to say. I didn't expect it. I didn't think that you would be able to—'

'But you are pleased?' He looked suddenly anxious, not something he usually did. 'And hopefully a little excited?'

'Yes, but—'

'But nothing, Kara,' he said, his voice firm now. 'All I want is for you to enjoy it.'

Privately Kara doubted whether she would remember anything of the opera. Sitting here talking to him when the room was filled with other people was one thing, but going to the theatre, seated so close that their bodies would touch, when there would be no escape, was another.

She would be far too aware of Blake, of the emotions he was amazingly managing to arouse in her. Alien feelings that sometimes made her feel happy and at others scared her witless.

Admittedly she was beginning to feel more at ease with him. He had never done or said anything to alarm her; he was in fact always the perfect gentleman. So perhaps she was worrying for nothing. It was just that she was not used to being treated so kindly. To have Blake make this generous gesture brought a lump to her throat and tears to her eyes.

Immediately he frowned. 'Now what is wrong? You are still not happy?'

'Of course I'm happy. It's just that no one's ever done anything like this for me before.'

Blake reached across the table and took her hand, enclosing it gently with his other one. 'That is such a pity. You are a gracious woman, Kara, and you should be treated accordingly.'

His sympathy, the look of compassion in his eyes, completely overwhelmed her, and it was a big struggle to control her tears. She swallowed hard and smiled. 'I'm being silly. I'm sorry.'

Blake lifted her hand to his lips. 'I am the one who is sorry. Sorry that you have not enjoyed the pleasures in life that a beautiful woman like you should. But now I think it is time we retired to our rooms.'

Before she made a complete fool of herself in front of everyone—that was what he was saying. Kara smiled weakly and allowed him to take her elbow and lead her upstairs.

# CHAPTER FOUR

JOINING Blake for a nightcap went against every one of Kara's self-imposed rules. The trouble was he had a way of making her break them. He had made her laugh tonight; he had been fun company—something she had never imagined her employer being. He had made her almost cry as well, with his generosity.

'What would you like? More wine, perhaps, or coffee? A brandy, even?'

'Coffee, please,' she answered. 'I've already drunk more than I'm used to.' Not that she was drunk or anything like that. She'd only had two glasses, but that was one more than normal. In fact she rarely drank alcohol. Christmas and birthdays were about the sum of it.

Expecting him to lift the phone and order their drinks, Kara was pleasantly surprised when he crossed to the open-plan mini-kitchen at the other end of the immensely spacious sitting area and proceeded to make the coffee himself.

It gave her time to look around the sumptuous suite. Soft cream leather sofas, deep-piled cream rugs gracing American walnut floors, original paintings on the walls, crystal chandeliers. No expense had been spared. The room she was in was furnished well, but this was something else. And she knew what it had cost just to book it for a few days! Almost more than she earned in a year.

Floor-to-ceiling glass doors opened onto a wide balcony, allowing views across the spacious gardens. Well-manicured lawns were softly sculpted by trees and shrubs, and she could see a water fountain in the distance. The swimming pool was not visible, but she knew from the brochure that it was as stunningly attractive as everywhere else.

'Here we are.' Already Blake was joining her, setting out a coffee pot and two china cups on the low table that sat between two of the sofas. Cream and sugar followed.

'I'll pour,' Kara said quickly. It would give her something to do and would stop her from looking at him—at those large capable hands with their perfectly manicured nails. She did not know what had got into her but she could imagine those hands on her skin, holding her, touching her. Arousing her!

Alarm bells rang in her head. Perhaps she ought to leave right now; perhaps it had been a mistake allowing herself to enter his room. When her hand shook as she lifted the pot Blake immediately leaned forward and took it from her. 'Careful, it's very heavy. I should hate you to scald yourself.'

Their coffee safely poured, they both settled back on their seats—opposite each other. Another mistake! He never took his eyes off her. 'I think it's about time that you told me something about yourself, Kara. You've been evasive for far too long.'

A swirl of unease circled her stomach. 'There's not really much to tell that you don't already know.'

'I know you're very wary of men. Who did that to you?'

It was such a direct question that there was no escaping it. But she was silent for so long that he spoke again.

'Was it a boyfriend? Someone who let you down badly? Is that why you—?'

Kara drew in a deep breath, held it for a few seconds, and then let it go quickly. 'My father didn't allow me to have boyfriends. I told you he wasn't very nice, didn't I? The truth is that—that he used to beat me.' There—the words were out, the confession made. The hardest thing she had ever had to do. She looked down at her hands twisting on her lap and did not see Blake's frown, the shock in his eyes. 'I'd really rather not talk about it.'

Her heart began to race and she started shivering, and the next second he was on the sofa beside her, his arms around her, saying nothing but making the sort of shushing noises one would make to a crying baby. It was not until her heart settled, until her body stilled, that he began to murmur words of comfort.

'It's all right, Kara, you're safe with me. No harm will come to you. I will never hurt you, I promise. You can relax. Just close your eyes and relax.'

She heard the words through the thick blanket of her mind. And gradually, as he kept repeating them like a mantra, her father was, for once, amazingly forgotten. She was aware only of Blake's warmth, of the strong arms holding her, of his heartbeat against her body.

And when he touched his fingers to her chin and

turned her face up to his she saw not her employer, not Blake Benedict tough businessman, but warm, human Blake. A Blake whose grey eyes were soft with concern. Without even realising what she was doing she snuggled up closer.

Never in her life had she felt as safe as she did now. No man had ever held her like this, made her feel secure, as though her whole world had turned around and no one would ever mistreat her again. She had not believed it possible. And for it to be her employer, of all people! Her father had always drummed it into her that she was a worthless creature whom no man would ever look at twice. He had said it so often that she had believed it.

Kara knew that she ought to move now that she had recovered, but pulling away from Blake was the last thing she wanted. And Blake seemed in no hurry to let her go either.

'Are you sure you don't want to talk about it?' he enquired softly. 'It might help.'

'No, I'm sorry. I couldn't.' It was too humiliating by far. Even though her father was dead she still did not want to talk about him. 'I never will. And I'm sorry I—'

'Do not keep apologising, Kara. I'm glad that you've told me. It helps me to understand you.' He trailed a gentle finger down the side of her face, pausing a moment before tracing the outline of her lips. Then he touched her fingers to his mouth and kissed them before placing them against her lips again. 'You're a beautiful lady, both inside and out, and you do not deserve to have gone through what you have. I reiterate my promise that I will never do anything to hurt you.'

Kara let out her breath slowly, feeling her body relax. She liked him holding her, she liked him touching her, she liked what he was saying to her. It was almost as though she had been transported into a different world— a world where everything was beautiful and sensual and no one ever hurt anyone. A world she had never known before.

'Maybe you should drink your coffee,' he said, 'before it gets cold.'

'I'd rather you held me a little longer.' The words slipped out before she could stop them and she was horrified. 'I'm sorry. I'm being silly. I shouldn't have said that.'

'My beautiful Kara, I'm glad that you did. It proves that you trust me.' His eyes had darkened but they still held the softness, the tenderness, and Kara guessed that he had never held a woman like this before and not kissed her.

She was grateful to him. And she actually experienced a sense of relief that she had told him about her father. It felt cathartic—as though a whole weight had been lifted from her shoulders, finally giving her permission to move on.

He continued to stroke the side of her face, gently sweeping back tendrils of hair that got in his way, and Kara enjoyed the touch of his fingers so much that when he again traced the outline of her lips they parted of their own volition, the tip of her tongue coming out to touch and taste him.

She heard the faint groan in the back of his throat and had no idea what it meant. Was he saying *please don't do that*? Or, *if you do I won't be responsible for my actions*? It was embarrassing to be totally innocent in the ways of men.

And the trouble was that the longer she remained in his arms the more intense her emotions became. She reached out and touched his cheek, feeling the faint rasp where his strong black hair was already growing again. He put his hand over hers, holding it there for a few seconds before moving it slowly so that he could press his lips to her palm.

Then he folded her fingers over the kiss and gave her her hand back. 'Especially for you, my troubled one.'

Kara did not want her hand back; she wanted to continue to touch him. She wanted to trace the outline of his face, his beautifully sculpted lips. She wanted— When she suddenly realised exactly what it was that she wanted it took her breath away. She wanted him to kiss her—really kiss her. Something she had shied away from all her life. She had shied away from any sort of contact with a man.

But Blake was more than just a man! She closed her eyes and thought about what it would be like for him to kiss her. Would it be light and sweet, or deep and tempestuous? Would it fill her with pleasure or dread? She felt him move and guessed that he was going to put her away from him, move back to the other sofa—with the coffee pot between them. And her heart suddenly ached.

But then she discovered that he was simply positioning himself more comfortably in order *to* kiss her. It was a gentle kiss, an experimental kiss, but the touch of his lips on hers was like lighting the touchpaper on a firework. It fizzed quietly at first, but then exploded into a galaxy of sparks and showers, of crackling noises and body-tingling sensations.

Sensations such as she had never experienced before. Stimulation such as she had never experienced before. *Whoa!* she thought. What was happening here? How could a simple kiss create such strong feelings? Except that it was not simple. It was a complex kiss, one that spun into every corner of her body, creating tingles and hunger and all sorts of crazy emotions. It was like pins and needles everywhere.

She was afraid to open her eyes and look at him. This was a man of the world who had made love to endless women. Experienced women. Women who would readily respond. Whereas all she was doing was submitting. It would hardly be enough for him.

But letting him know what he was doing to her, what was happening to her, felt frighteningly like revealing her soul. Shame suddenly crept over her, shame that she was allowing the kiss, and she struggled to free herself.

Immediately Blake let her go. 'I'm sorry, Kara, I thought you were ready for this. I want to help you—if I may be permitted to do so? Not all men are the same. You need to know that. There are some good guys around.'

Finally she looked at him. And what she saw in his face was nothing but compassion. He was not judging her or comparing her. 'I'm sorry,' she said, her voice no more than a husky whisper now. 'It's just that I'm not used to—'

'I know and I understand. I'm sorry I misjudged the

timing,' he said gruffly. 'Go to your room if you want to.' And he did indeed look truly sorry. Sad, even.

Kara did not want to leave; she did not want to be alone—not yet. She wanted to feel Blake's strong arms around her again. They had held comfort and—and something else she could not put a name to. 'Will you— will you just hold me?' she asked, feeling tears gathering in her eyes.

His answer was to pull her gently against him, his arms folding round her. How long they sat there like that Kara did not know, but it felt like a very long time. She could feel the regular beat of his heart and peace stole over her until gradually she felt completely at ease with him.

The threatened tears never materialized, and when she eventually went back to her room she felt like a new woman. She even—and this thought really scared her— wondered what it would feel like to have Blake in bed beside her. Except that she knew it would be hard for him, if not impossible, to sleep with her and not want to make love. But she was not ready for that yet.

Her mind was slowly adjusting to the idea that such a relationship could work without her feeling that she was doing something wrong, something her father would not approve of. But he had been such a big influence in her life that it was too soon yet to let go of the old and welcome the new.

At least she was getting there.

Blake's eyes caught Kara's as she joined the conference the next day. Her confession last night had knocked him for six. Any man who hurt a woman, whether it was physically or verbally, was the lowest of the low as far as he was concerned. And her father's abuse had certainly left Kara with some problems.

She had trembled so much when he had held her that he had feared she might break down. It was a miracle that she had grown into the competent woman she was. Clearly work had been her saviour. Only when she was working was she in control of herself.

Certainly she had been on edge in his suite. He had felt her fear. But then, surprisingly, she had let him kiss her. It had taken every ounce of his not inconsiderable self-control to contain the kiss. How he had managed it he was not sure, and as delicate as it had been it had still sent a raging heat through his body.

Kara had no idea how lovely she was—how sexy, how alluring. He could understand now why she always dressed down, why she never made anything of herself. If she dressed as most of the other women in the office did then she would have every man in the company after her. And that, he realised now, was the last thing he wanted.

She did not know it, but after he had kissed her her eyes had assumed a sparkle he had never seen before, and her skin had glowed. It had been the hardest thing in the world not to kiss her again. And even harder to let her return to her room!

'Are you all right?' he asked her now. 'Did you sleep well?'

'Yes, thank you,' she answered, her eyes meeting his shyly. 'And I'm sorry about last night.'

He shook his head. 'Think nothing of it. You have nothing to be sorry for.' He was the one who was sorry—sorry that she had been caused such suffering at the hands of a monster like her father. His blood still boiled every time he thought about it.

'It actually helped, telling someone,' she admitted with a wry twist to her lips. 'I didn't think it would. I've kept it bottled up all these years. But when I went back to my room I felt a sense of relief. I slept better than I've done in a long time.'

'Then I'm glad that I could be of service.' How any man could treat his daughter like that he had no idea. It was perhaps fortunate that he was no longer alive or he would have felt like confronting him, giving him a taste of his own medicine. He wasn't usually a violent man, but anyone who could harm his own flesh and blood did not deserve to be treated humanely.

'And the opera tonight? Are you looking forward to that too?'

Kara nodded. 'Actually, yes, I am.' After last night she felt much more at ease with Blake. Whether it was because he now knew something about her past, or because she had spent so much time with him and got to know him better she wasn't sure. But she was beginning to see him as a man instead of her boss. A good-looking, sexy man who had lit a fire inside her. The idea that confession was good for the soul had certainly been true in her case. She felt as though a great big weight had been lifted from her shoulders and now there was a whole bright new future ahead.

'I thought we might have dinner somewhere first. Unless you'd prefer to eat after the theatre?'

'I think before.' She could imagine that a late dinner would lead to a late evening, and that could lead to…

Kara allowed her thoughts to go no further. The way she had relaxed in Blake's company last night, responded to him, still scared her slightly. It was hard to get it out of her mind.

'What do I wear?' she asked him now. 'I'm not sure I have anything suitable.'

Blake smiled. 'The black dress you wore the other night will be perfect, Kara.'

Dinner was everything Kara had expected it to be. The restaurant was not far from the theatre, and served exquisite food in stunning surroundings. She chose sole fillet with asparagus for her main course, and it was truly the most delicious fish she had ever eaten.

But her attention was not on the food. It was on Blake instead. Ever since that kiss he had filled her body and her mind, and she was beginning to wonder whether it was wise spending so much time with him. Her heart seemed to have developed a mind of its own, fluttering like a captured bird whenever he spoke to her, whenever he was near.

'What are you thinking?'

His voice was low and gruff and it created an unimaginable stream of sensations that sped through her body like a fast-flowing waterfall. Sitting opposite him like this, feeling his oh-so-attractive grey eyes constantly on her, was not a situation she felt comfortable with. 'I was actually wondering what I'm doing here.'

An instant frown caused his dark brows to scurry together. 'You are not looking forward to the opera?'

'Of course I am. But—' How could she explain how

she felt? 'I'm actually nervous about spending time with you.'

Blake reached across the table and rested his hand on her arm. 'Kara, all I want is for you to enjoy some free time, which I fear has been lacking in your life.'

He dared not say that besides wanting to spend time getting to know her he wanted to make love with her. It would send her scuttling for shelter more quickly than if she was fleeing a thunderstorm. But the truth was the more time he spent with her, the more excited his body became, the more hungry he grew. Kara was without a doubt one very intriguing female—sexier, he guessed, than she had ever dreamt she could be. She lit fires within him that would never be assuaged until he had made her his. But he would never, ever force himself on her. If and when they did make love it would be because she wanted it too.

'I do trust you, Blake,' she said now, her eyes wide and beautiful and more violet than blue.

He wished that she had not used those words because it made him feel ashamed of his thoughts. He squeezed her hand and then let it go.

*Faust* was everything Kara had expected—and more. She sat entranced throughout the whole performance, hardly even aware of Blake at her side, or the fact that his eyes were often on her, or that his hand held hers. Tears ran down her cheeks at the end, when Marguerite mounted the scaffold where she was to be hanged for killing her child—Faust's child.

Blake produced a handkerchief and dabbed at her

tears. At the same time his arm came around her, holding her firmly against him.

'That was lovely,' she managed to say. 'I truly enjoyed it.'

'And that is why you are crying?'

'It was sad, but beautiful too. Thank you for tonight. It is an evening I will always remember.'

In the car on their way back to the hotel Kara did not mind when he put his arm around her again. She nestled her head on his shoulder and closed her eyes. She felt as though she was in another world—a world where bad things never happened, where there was light and laughter...and Blake!

If anyone had asked her a few weeks ago whether she fancied her boss she would have laughed at them, would have declared herself a man-free zone. But all that was changing, and Blake was the reason. He was giving her confidence in herself, assuring her that she was a very beautiful woman—and at the same time revealing that he was enchanted by her. Blake Benedict enchanted by her! It was the stuff of dreams.

'Shall we indulge in a nightcap?' he asked as they stepped out of the private lift that had swiftly taken them up to his suite.

Kara surprised herself by agreeing. She had enjoyed his company so much this evening that she did not want to be on her own again yet. There was something about Blake here in Italy that was different. He was charming and considerate and she truly felt relaxed with a man for the very first time in her life.

'What would you like?' he asked. 'Brandy, perhaps? Or maybe wine?'

'Actually, coffee would be good—if that doesn't sound too boring?'

'Coffee it is, then, and it doesn't sound in the least boring. In fact it's probably wise.'

He lifted the phone as he spoke, and Kara loved hearing him speak in Italian. It made him seem excitingly different. It added to the glamour of the evening. It was hard to believe that she was here again with her boss at this time of night and they were going to settle down for a quiet drink together. She needed to be fresh and alert tomorrow. Perhaps it had been a mistake coming here. Maybe she ought to have gone straight to her room and to bed.

And in the end it was the coffee that proved to be her undoing. As she sat opposite Blake in a deep comfortable chair, nervously aware that his eyes never left her, Kara's hand trembled as she took a sip of her drink and some of the hot liquid spilled down the front of her dress.

Instantly Blake jumped up, took the cup from her, and began dabbing his handkerchief on the stain. It was a much too intimate gesture, and Kara's heart began to thud painfully against her ribcage—especially when he draped his arm around her shoulders to hold her steady. 'It's all right, Blake, it's nothing. I—'

Her words were cut off when his eyes met hers, when she saw the dark hunger in them, when all the breath seemed to leave her body.

'Forgive me—I have to do this,' he said, his voice rougher than she had ever heard it. And she swiftly realised that he wasn't talking about the damp mark on her dress, but something far more intimate.

And, amazingly, this time her lips were ready for his. The rhythm of her heart altered and she closed her eyes. Why fight the inevitable? All evening she had been far too aware of Blake to not want to experience his kiss again.

Blake quickly realised that what he had intended as a gentle kiss, not wanting to frighten her, or rush her into anything that she was still not ready for, was swiftly turning into something else. Kara's lips had parted on a sigh that suggested secret desire, and when he cautiously deepened the kiss, when he felt her response, when she kissed him back with a hunger that took him by surprise, he was unable to stop himself.

Fire built between them as their tongues entwined and danced and tasted and explored, as he nibbled her lower lip and she did the same to him. Every pulse in his body threatened to explode. And he knew that it would take every ounce of self-control to put her away from him afterwards.

Kara found it difficult to breathe; she could not understand what was happening to her. How could she allow Blake to kiss her like this? How could she want his kiss when she had always hated men with a vengeance? The lure had been building from day one, and the taster she'd had yesterday had woken something inside her, but even so...

Cautiously she risked looking at him, and her breath caught in her throat when she saw the raw desire in his eyes—gone in an instant, shielded from her gaze. If any man had looked at her like that in the past she would have run a mile, but she knew without a shadow of doubt that Blake would never pressure her into anything that she was not ready for.

And the fact was—and this was as much of a surprise to her as it would be to Blake—she actually wanted him to make love to her.

She closed her eyes again, allowing the moment to seep into her mind, into her bones, into her heart, feeling an unaccustomed ache in the lower regions of her stomach. If Blake ended the kiss now she would feel bereft. She would have had a taste of heaven snatched away from her as quickly as it had arisen.

Of their own volition her arms snaked around him, trapping him, her body urging itself against his raw masculine hardness. It shocked and excited her at the same time. Never in her wildest dreams had she ever envisaged that she would be in a situation like this.

The wild throb of his heart beating against her own told her without words that excitement ran through his veins too, and that he was also deeply affected by what was happening.

Why, she asked herself, when for nearly a year she had worked for this man without ever feeling anything, was this happening now? No, that was wrong. She *had* been aware of him; how could any woman not be? But her fears were such that she had allowed her thoughts no purchase.

Now they were in danger of escaping the tight confines she had kept on them—in fact they had already escaped. They were not at the galloping stage yet, but they were sufficiently free of their reins to taste freedom. And, oh, how she liked it.

Based on pure instinct now, she ground her hips

against him, shocked by his hardness, but actually glorying in the fact that she was able to do this to a man. To Blake. Not *any* man—never any man. Would he allow her to set the pace? Already she was in danger of running rather than walking, and she could hear the drumbeats of her heart echoing in her ears.

Words seemed irrelevant. Words would shatter the atmosphere that cocooned them. And when Blake trailed his fingers down the exposed arch of her throat, pausing on the fluttering pulse he found there before moving lower to feel the soft swell of her breast, Kara's breath caught in her throat. Her eyes fluttered open.

Blake was watching her, gauging her reaction, but she saw behind the reassurance he sought a hunger that matched her own. The grey of his eyes had deepened to charcoal, almost blending with the blackness of his pupils, though when he saw her looking at him he instantly lowered his lashes.

Kiss followed kiss followed kiss—deep, heart-stopping kisses that sent her spinning into a world she did not recognise, a world where senses were paramount. In these last few minutes she had become a woman—a woman filled with emotions she had often wondered about but never expected to experience. She felt as though she had been born again. And she wanted this moment to go on for ever.

It was disappointing, therefore, when Blake lifted his head, when his hands fell to his sides. Her first thought was that she had let him down, and she felt tears welling—until he tentatively suggested that they make themselves more comfortable.

Which must be why they ended up in bed!

Kara could only vaguely remember Blake lifting her into his arms and carrying her to his bedroom. For some reason her mind had gone numb. She had been aware of nothing except the feelings churning round and round inside her—feelings that needed both feeding and assuaging.

What had begun as a tingle had developed into a stampede of pulses, of hot pounding blood, of her heart beating so hard and so fast that she was afraid it would burst.

And all because he had kissed her!

Except that a kiss from Blake was more than just a kiss. It was a full-scale attack on her defences. It stripped away barriers, leaving her open and vulnerable. And bursting with excitement! If this was what making love was all about then she was glad that she had not gone through her whole life without ever knowing what she was missing.

Their kisses became more intense, more hungry, more *everything*, in fact. Not only did he kiss her mouth, make it his, sucking and nibbling, creating deep wells of passion that both shocked and thrilled her, he trailed kisses down the arch of her throat, causing her head to fall back in utter abandonment, and somehow he managed to remove her clothes at the same time.

When she heard his swift intake of breath Kara did not know what was the matter—until she felt his fingers touch a certain place on her back. Then she knew!

'How did you get this scar?' he asked, his voice unusually quiet.

Kara struggled with the truth, but decided that she needed to be honest. 'It's from the buckle on my father's belt. He didn't mean to hurt me that badly.' Not that he had ever said that, or even apologised. He'd been blind drunk at the time.

'Whether he meant it or not, it should never have happened,' growled Blake. 'Did he beat your mother as well?'

Kara nodded.

Blake swore.

'It's a good job he is no longer alive or I would have great difficulty in keeping my hands off him. Only cowards hit women. Did you never report him, Kara?'

'I was too afraid,' she confessed. 'He was a very big man. He'd probably have killed me.'

Blake swore again under his breath and cradled Kara in his arms. He held her for a long time, until he felt them both relax again, until he was able to push to the back of his mind everything that was bad and evil.

'You are so brave,' he told her, over and over again. 'Brave and beautiful.' He kept stroking her skin, and when she lifted her lips up to his he groaned and kissed her, and his heart leapt when she took his hand and put it on her breast.

Kara closed her eyes and gave herself up to the moment. Blake's touch caused her breasts to engorge and become incredibly sensitive, and the moment when her nipples tightened into excruciatingly responsive buds was an experience she would remember for the rest of her life, even if it never happened again.

But even that feeling increased when he kissed her breasts, sucking her tingling nipples into his mouth, nipping them with his fine white teeth, until every one of her bones melted.

'You are all right with this?'

Blake's voice was gruff and hoarse, and his eyes, raised to hers, held an expression that shook her rigid. They were filled with an emotion that suggested he was in the grip of something much stronger than himself, something he was struggling to control.

And it was all because of her!

How could that be? How could kissing her do this to him? She was inexperienced, she didn't know what was expected of her, and she wasn't even very pretty. She was—

'Kara?'

She looked at him, unaware that her eyes were huge and shiny, that her cheeks were flushed and she already looked as though she had been well and truly made love to.

'Do you want me to stop?'

She rocked her head from side to side, not trusting herself to speak. How could she when both her body and mind felt as though they no longer belonged to her? Somehow he had cast his spell over her and she was now his to do with as he liked. She had gone from being a woman who was afraid of men to someone whose body was filled with a desperate need to be touched.

Needing no further encouragement, Blake trailed kisses across the divide from her breasts to her navel. All she had to do was lie there and enjoy! *All she had to do!* It was impossible. She could not keep a limb still. She wriggled and squirmed and was completely unaware of the sounds she made—sighs and cries, even tiny screams of pain. Yet it wasn't pain at all.

And Blake was enjoying making her aware of her

body, of its erogenous zones, of the sensations just the lightest touch of his fingers or tongue could create. It was almost an act of cruelty. Delicious, mind-blowing cruelty.

But none of it—nothing—prepared her for the moment when he explored the most intimate part of her. She was shocked and stunned when she discovered how swollen and sensitive she had become, how moist, how responsive she was to his touch, how her body seemed to arch so that he could explore her more fully. She had never in her life known that such sensations existed, that simply by touch she could feel ready to explode.

Her fingernails dug into his shoulders, her body lifting from the bed almost of its own volition. 'Make love to me, Blake,' she said hoarsely, almost without knowing that she spoke. 'I want you to make love to me.'

'If you're sure?' His voice was as hoarse as her own.

'I'm sure.'

And when he finally lowered himself over her, when he began to enter her, protecting himself first, she could hardly breathe. She was shocked, therefore, when he stopped, when she heard him swear softly.

Was she doing something wrong? She wasn't experienced like his other girlfriends—was that it? Should she be doing something? Helping him? Sadly, she had no idea.

'Blake?'

'You're a virgin.' The words choked from his throat.

'I thought you knew that.'

'What I mean is that I cannot do this to you. I've never made love to a virgin before. It would be wrong to—'

Kara touched a finger to his lips. 'You're not doing anything I do not want. Please, Blake—please don't leave me like this. I want it as much as you do.' And she wrapped her legs even more tightly around his hips, grinding herself against him.

Blake groaned again, and after only a moment's further hesitation plunged himself into her.

She felt a brief moment of pain, and then came the pleasure. Intense, mind-blowing pleasure.

'Blake!' Kara heard herself call his name over and over again, felt her hands clawing his back, heard him telling her that it was all right to let go.

And seconds later her world exploded.

# CHAPTER FIVE

IT WAS the last day of the conference. As Kara walked into the room she felt sure that every person present must know that she had let Blake make love to her last night. Her reflection as she brushed her hair had shown a different woman. A woman with stars in her eyes and a bloom to her skin. A woman who had well and truly been made love to.

She had spent the whole night in Blake's bed, only returning to her room this morning to shower and dress. She had not gone down to breakfast—food was the last thing on her mind. And now she was afraid to look at Blake, because she knew that if she did her hormones would jump all over the place again.

'You were amazing last night,' he whispered when she reached his side. 'I trust you have no regrets?'

'We shouldn't be talking like this,' she whispered fiercely. 'Let's get on with things.' Even so, she was unable to really concentrate, too conscious of what had gone on between them, and she was relieved when at lunchtime the conference finally drew to an end.

Blake's closing speech included his thanks to her for all the hard work she had put in both prior to and during the last three days. 'I do not know what I would have done without my wonderful PA,' he said. 'The fact that everything has gone without a hitch is all down to Kara. Her organisational skills are second to none. I think a round of applause is in order.'

Hot colour flushed her cheeks as every pair of eyes turned on her. 'I only did my job,' she muttered, smiling awkwardly. And when he presented her with a bouquet of pink roses she was even more self-conscious.

'You deserve some recognition,' he said firmly. 'None of my other assistants has ever reached your high standards. I can fault you on nothing.'

It was not until they had said their goodbyes to everyone and finally gone up to his suite that he shocked her still further. 'I have another surprise for you.'

His voice was no more than a low growl in his throat now, and it sent a shiver of expectation across Kara's skin. She braved a glance at him and saw the way that his lips were trying to contain a grin. He looked, she thought, like a little boy who was doing his best not to give away a secret.

'A reward for a job well done.'

She waited.

'We're going on a few days' holiday.'

Kara's mouth fell open. She could not help it. This was the last thing she had expected. 'What do you mean, a holiday? I can't. I have my mother to think of. I couldn't possibly leave her any longer.' Even though the thought of spending more time with Blake was exciting, her mother was her top priority. Besides, Blake *never* took holidays. What was he talking about?

'She doesn't like staying with her sister?' he asked, a

sudden frown replacing his smile. 'Or—are you perhaps afraid of what is happening between us?'

Kara was glad that they had left the others behind. This was not a conversation she wanted anyone else to hear. 'I'm not afraid.' The denial was instant, but she could see that he did not believe her. 'My mother relies on me. She needs me. And it will be too much for Aunt Susan if she has to look after her for any longer.'

Dark brows lifted. 'I think maybe we should let your aunt be the judge of that. Why don't you call her?'

It sounded as though he was giving her no choice. And, although she would have dearly loved to spend more time with him, making magical love—and it had truly been magical—she knew that it would be impossible. 'You do not fully realise my situation. I'm sorry, Blake, but—'

'I'm not forcing you to stay,' Blake said, trying to make his voice sound as gentle and persuasive as possible. 'But I do think you deserve some relaxation. You've worked very hard and I'd like to show you my appreciation.' She enchanted him, and one night of passion was not enough. He wanted to spend more time with her. Taking her virginity and then coldly dismissing her to resume normal office life was not what he wanted. She deserved better. He wanted her to know that it had not been a one-off. He did not want her to think ill of him.

Not that he was looking for anything long-term. He had no intention of settling with any woman ever again. To hell with all that. One go at marriage was enough. But at least he could show Kara that not all men were bad.

'OK, I'll ring my mother,' she said, still sounding reluctant, 'and see what she says. Maybe a couple of days. I don't want to lumber Aunt Susan with her for too much longer.'

Blake would have liked to spend more than two days with her, but he knew that to push the issue would end up with her refusing to go with him at all. 'I'm sure you won't regret it,' he said, touching his hands lightly to her shoulders and dropping a kiss on her cheek.

The sweet, dewy softness of her skin and the intoxicating smell of her was almost his undoing. What he really wanted to do was kiss her and pleasure her again. But he did not want her to think that he was using sex as a way of persuasion, so he reluctantly backed away, leaving Kara to go to her room.

Her mother, surprisingly, was happy for her to stay longer. 'You deserve a break,' she said. 'And your aunt is glad of my company'

'Everything is all right?'

'Of course. I'm safe here, Kara.'

Kara knew what she meant. Her biggest fear was that the loan shark her father had lumbered them with might catch up with her.

Her father, as well as being a bully and a tyrant, had taken out a loan in her mother's name, telling her that it made good business sense for tax purposes. Her mother had been too frightened of him to argue. His building company had begun to go downhill because he had spent most of his money on gambling and drinking, but it had not been until after his death that they'd discovered the loan had never been repaid and that exorbitant interest rates made it look as though it never would be.

The man after their money was a sharp-faced, cold-hearted individual, without an ounce of compassion. She could not leave her mother to deal with him. Even thinking about him caused her to shudder. But she could not tell Blake about him either. Her mother did not want anyone to know. She found the shame of the whole situation too embarrassing, even though it was most of Kara's salary that went towards paying off the debt.

Kara quickly packed and drew in several deep, steadying breaths before taking the few steps along the corridor back to Blake's room. His door was open, as though he was waiting for her. And his suitcase was also ready to go. His brows rose as he waited for her to speak.

'I'll come with you,' she said quietly.

'Your mother and aunt are all right with it?'

'Yes.'

'But you are not?'

'I've never been on holiday with a man.' In fact she had never been on holiday. Even saying those words caused her heart to flutter alarmingly. Would she be throwing herself in at the deep end without being able to swim? Would she regret it? Would she lose her job because of it? A multitude of questions swam through her mind.

'You are afraid of me?'

Not Blake. It was her feelings that she was afraid of. She was afraid that at the other end of the spectrum it would all be too much for her, that she would never want it to end. That she would have a taste of heaven before going back to her own private hell.

Although she did not disclose her thoughts, the conflict in her eyes was clear for Blake to see. With a groan he pulled her against him. 'You have nothing to fear, Kara, not while you're with me. I want you to be happy, that is all. You've looked tired this last couple of days. I guess I've put too much pressure on you. Let this be my way of saying thank you.'

Kara buried her head in his shoulder, feeling stupid tears again. God, why did this man always make her want to cry? The plain fact was that no one had ever been this kind to her before, and she was totally overwhelmed.

'Are you packed?' he asked, gently putting her away from him.

Kara nodded.

'Then let's go.'

'Where are you taking me?'

He smiled—the sort of smile that flipped her heart and made her want to lift up her face for his kiss.

'I'll let that be a surprise.'

A car and driver were waiting, and on the journey Kara spent her time looking at the stunning landscape, trying to ignore the fact that she was with her boss and that she had spent last night in his bed. Even sitting beside him, not even touching, she was overwhelmed by the feelings he managed to arouse.

Finally they arrived at a beautiful white villa overlooking the shores of a huge lake.

'Welcome to Lake Como,' he said. 'And to what used to be my grandmother's house.'

Kara's eyes were as big as saucers. 'Who lives here now?'

'No one permanently,' he admitted. 'Since her death it's been kept for any family member to use. I suppose you'd call it a holiday villa.'

A holiday villa! That had to be the understatement of the year. Who could afford to keep a villa like this and not use it? She truly was moving in exalted circles.

'Is anyone else staying here at the moment?'

Blake shook his head. 'There is staff, of course, so we won't be completely alone.'

Keeping it staffed when no one was using it sounded like an alarming waste of money. And Kara could not help wondering whether he had brought his other PAs here—the ones he'd sacked on their return to England. Did he use it as a love nest? Had she been sucked in by his kindness? Was she right to be nervous?

She could not deny that the villa was enchanting, though. It looked like a fairy-tale castle, nestling into the hillside above the lake. But even so it did not make her feel any better about spending two whole days entirely alone with Blake—despite his assurance that whatever they did was up to her.

And it did not help when they were greeted by his army of employees, who looked at her as though she was someone very special. Too polite to do anything other than smile, she was relieved when they melted away after Blake had introduced her.

'They think that you and I are an item,' she whispered. 'I could see it in their eyes.' Blake had spoken in fluent Italian, while hers was non-existent, but they wouldn't have looked at her with such interest if they had known that she was really just his PA on a few days' holiday with her boss. No, they thought she was his girlfriend. She was sure of it.

Dark brows rose, hands waved airily. 'You are right. They probably are imagining that you are special since I have brought no one else here. But it is of no consequence. Do not let it worry you.'

At least he had assured her of one thing, and he sounded and looked more Italian than English at that moment, thought Kara. But it did little to alleviate her fears.

'Would you like me to show you around? Or perhaps you are tired and would prefer to rest?'

Resting sounded good—except that she would have felt safer in a hotel. If *safer* was the right word. Safer from what? From whom? Herself or Blake? She was afraid that she had been thrown in at the deep end. That this was not going to be the recreational break she had expected. For one reason because they were going to be totally alone, and for another because she was seeing Blake in an entirely different light!

Her feelings were running dangerously high. She felt an awareness that scared her rigid. She wanted to feel his arms around her, to feel the hard pulsing strength of him. Despite her misgivings, she wanted him to make love to her again. How could that be?

'I am a little tired,' she agreed. 'This is all so new and so—' She struggled to find the right words to say what was in her mind.

'Exciting?' he suggested, an eyebrow lifting, his body very still as he waited for her reply.

He was right—but perhaps not in the way he thought. What would he say if he knew how intense her emotions were? That she actually would welcome him holding her, maybe even kissing her, maybe even making love to her again? It was beyond sanity. She had never wanted a man even to touch her, and now she was craving it. One taste and she was hooked.

She drew in a deep breath. 'Different.' It hardly described her feelings—or maybe it did. Maybe it was the exact word. Every cell in her body was different. No longer calm and in control. They were dancing all over the place, hot and hungry for this handsome man.

It was strange that she was thinking of him now as more Italian. Had he truly changed or was it all in her mind? Was it this place?

'You never expected to find yourself here?' he questioned, his soft smile suggesting that he knew exactly how she was feeling. 'It is a shame that you do not want to stay longer. But perhaps after a couple of days spent in this very beautiful part of Italy you will change your mind? You will allow me to—'

Kara did not let him finish. 'No! I *must* go home, Blake.' Even saying the word *home* brought back the fears that awaited her there. She could not afford to let herself be distracted by him.

Something had happened to her here in Italy—something she dared not think about…something that needed to be crushed. There was no room in her life for romance—or whatever name she cared to put on what was happening to her now. No room at all.

'Kara—'

Quite how it happened she was not sure, but the next second she was being held against the rock-hardness of his chest, her head pressed into his shoulder, one strong, warm hand stroking her hair.

Blake could not bear to see Kara so agitated. He wanted to soothe away the fear he had seen in her eyes. Was it really because she was worried about leaving her mother, or did it go much deeper? Something to do with her father? Perhaps she had nightmares about him? Perhaps she was fearful that if she stayed too long she would give herself away in the middle of the night? Or was it being alone with him that she was afraid of?

He continued to murmur her name and smooth her hair against her nape until he felt her tension easing. 'No one is going to force you to stay against your will. Whenever you want to leave I will take you.'

She lifted her face to his, and when he saw tears in her lovely blue eyes he could not help himself. All his good intentions failed. This was a wounded woman and he wanted to make her better. His hand slid round to cup her chin and at the same time his mouth came down on hers.

What started as a gentle, reassuring kiss soon turned into something else. Into something fast and furious. Her lips parted on a sigh that suggested secret desire, and when he deepened the kiss, when he felt her response, when she kissed him back, he knew he could not resist.

Together they went upstairs, their mouths still clinging, and in his room he began to slowly undress her. In actual fact he would have liked to rip her clothes off and make love to her straight away, but he knew that to do so might make her fearful of him. And he did not want that. She had been fearful of her father. Once in a lifetime was enough to fear a person. He needed to be gentle.

As each inch of flesh was exposed he feathered it with kisses—and listened to her quiet moans of ecstasy. She tasted good, and her perfume made him even headier with desire. He would never have dreamed that his once prim PA could be so sensual, so sexy, so alluring.

Kara was aware of nothing except the fact that Blake's kisses, his touch, his energy, totally consumed her. They made love slowly and beautifully, over and over again. They did not surface, did not even stop to eat; food was the last thing on their minds. She had entered a world where nothing else mattered except the senses.

The touch of Blake's hands on her body. The excitement when he found that some parts of her were more responsive than others. The taste of his skin when she kissed him, when her lips dared to explore places that she had never let herself even think about before. The clean male smell when his body was so close to hers that they became one. The sight of him when he had just made love to her—his face both soft and raw at the same time, so different from the normally controlled man who had always scared her to death. And the sounds they both made when they were no longer in command of their bodies—grunts and groans, cries and shouts.

She knew that she would re-enter the real world soon, but she did not want to think about that. She was enjoying this new-found sexual liberation too much. She did not want it ever to end.

Even when Kara awoke the next morning she was still locked in her time bomb of happiness. She had learned so much from Blake. She had even instigated their lovemaking on one occasion. Her blood ran hot at the memory. What must he have thought?

'Kara?'

She suddenly realised that his eyes were open and he was watching her.

'Are you all right?'

'I—I feel—' *Embarrassed* was what she wanted to say, but the words would not come. How could she have behaved so wantonly? What had happened to her?

Blake finished the sentence for her, as he had on a previous occasion when she'd been stuck for words. 'Like a real woman? As though you've been on a voyage of discovery and found what you've been missing all these years?'

'I feel—different,' she confessed, her voice nothing more that a whisper.

He smiled. 'In a good way, I hope. You were magnificent.'

Magnificent! Oh, wow! Kara Redman, magnificent! They were words she had never expected to hear.

'And I don't know about you, Kara, but I'm hungry.'

Hungry? How could he think of food at a time like this?

'I'm going to jump in the shower. Care to join me?' And, before she could respond, 'Perhaps not. Or we'll never get any breakfast.'

He left the room without waiting for her answer and Kara pulled the sheets over her head. She had only to think of Blake's hands on her, stroking and teasing, his mouth nibbling and tasting, to feel swift arousal between her thighs and an almost insatiable urge to run after him.

It was crazy, it was totally insane, but she could not help herself, and she was still lying in the same position when Blake returned. He pulled the sheet aside and stood looking down at her. 'What are you doing, curled up under there?'

He looked magnificent, and completely unperturbed that he was as naked as the day he was born. Her eyes refused to move away from the muscled hardness of his chest, the damp curls of dark hair that arrowed down to narrow hips and— When she realised where her eyes were going Kara sat up with a stifled curse.

'I was waiting to use the bathroom.' And before she could give herself away she fled.

By the time she returned Blake was dressed in a white polo shirt and dark chinos, but his eyes were hungry as he looked at her wearing one of his cotton robes, tightly belted around her waist. She half expected him to make love to her again. But he didn't.

'I took the liberty of ordering a few clothes for you,' he said instead. 'I hope you don't mind, but I guessed you hadn't brought enough with you for a few extra days. Take a look in the wardrobe.'

Kara's mouth fell open when she saw dresses and skirts, tops and shorts—everything she could possibly need. 'You've bought these for me?'

'Yes.'

'I don't know what to say.' She was totally overwhelmed.

'You don't have to say anything, Kara.' All he wanted was to keep her here for as long as possible. She had turned into the most amazing lover. Ever since he had seen her transformation she had tortured his soul, but he had feared after last night that she might accuse him of simply bringing her here with the sole intention of seducing her.

But, no, she had been willing. At every opportunity he had given her the option to call a halt but she hadn't. Considering that she had never been with a man before, she responded to him with a passion that was both amazing and surprising. And definitely exciting. She had even pleasured him in a way that could only come from instincts as old as the age of man.

Two days with Kara would never be enough. He did not want full commitment; that was not what he was after. Not after what his ex-wife had done to him. As far as he was concerned there was no way of telling whether all women were the same, so it was far better not to let his heart get involved.

Besides, Kara would never bind herself to any man; she too had been badly hurt. But there was no reason why they could not indulge in an affair—maybe even a long-term one. She had shown that she was capable of enjoying intimate pleasures. Oh, yes, she had shown him in a very big way. A surprisingly big way! He had unleashed a tigress.

'I'll see you downstairs,' he said quietly. 'Otherwise I might be tempted to make love to you again.'

Kara felt colour flood her cheeks—especially when she saw the raw need in his eyes, which at one time would have scared her to death. Now it simply incited.

Once he had gone she dressed swiftly in a lilac cotton top and a lilac and white floral skirt—both of which fitted her perfectly. She marvelled that Blake had known her size. She brushed her hair and left it loose, and then hurried downstairs.

'You look beautiful,' were his first words. 'That colour matches your eyes. Did you know they are sometimes more violet than blue? Especially when we're making love,' he added with a knowing smile.

A swift tremor ran through Kara. She'd had no idea that her eyes were so expressive.

'And you should always wear your hair like that.' He threaded his fingers through it and pulled her face close. 'It suits you. You are a beautiful woman.'

With her heart racing she fearlessly met his eyes. It was amazing how much braver she felt now, so much more sure of herself. And even though her mind told her that she needed to be careful, her body took not the least bit of notice.

She had become a real woman, with all the needs and desires that went with it. No longer repressed, no longer hating all men. At least not this man! Not Blake. Blake had shown her that he was nothing like her father. He treated her with respect, with care, with gentleness.

Her eyes grew moist. Because she had never allowed any other man into her life she had never had the opportunity to judge for herself whether they were different. She had not even wanted to find out. She had judged herself of little value. Wasn't that what her father had told her, time and time again?

But now she knew differently. Blake would never have crossed the dividing line between business and pleasure if he had not found her attractive. And he would never have forced himself on her. After her initial paranoia she felt perfectly safe in his presence. She was not plain and worthless after all. She was beautiful and desirable. He had told her so.

'Kara, you are crying. Why?'

'I'm not,' she protested quickly. 'My eyes are watering, that's all.'

He smoothed a gentle thumb over her eyelids and then dropped a kiss on each one in turn. But he did not let her go. He kissed her on the lips instead, and all the fire and emotion that had burned so brightly last night came rushing back.

She was about to return his kiss, her arms already beginning to slide around him, when a woman's soft voice behind made her pull guiltily away.

'Breakfast is awaiting us,' he said.

The living area spread across the whole of the back of the villa, with floor-to-ceiling windows and sliding glass doors opening out onto a terrace dotted with plants in pretty coloured pots. It was there that their table was laid. Below was an arched entrance to landscaped gardens.

But it was the view that entranced Kara. The view over the lake. She could have stood there for hours, simply looking at it. The soaring mountains, boats, people, birds. Constantly something to look at, to take in, to capture in the memory of her mind. 'I wish I had my camera.'

'Maybe it's not the last time you'll come here.' Blake had been watching her, smiling at her pleasure, but now from behind he slid his arm around her waist and held her against him.

Kara chose to ignore his suggestion. 'It's certainly a beautiful location. Do you have a boat?'

'Naturally,' he said. 'And if it is your wish we will go out on it after breakfast.'

'Yes, please,' she said eagerly. 'I'd like that.' It was comforting being in his arms. Comforting and safe. Thanks to Blake, she was learning to trust. Considering that she had not wanted to join the conference in the first place she was now enjoying herself in a way that had been unimaginable a few days ago.

Blake was not the man she had imagined. She had always thought him to be a bit of a Lothario. And maybe he was. But at the moment he was treating her with delicacy and a genuine concern for her state of mind. He was allaying her fears, teaching her that everyone was not the same.

And it was working. *She* was not the same! She had become a different woman. She had felt a change in her in Milan, and even more so here, in this delightful part of Italy. How had he known that it would appeal to her? That it would bring out yet another side of her that she had not known existed?

He was changing her life, changing her views on life. And just for a few seconds she knew that she never wanted this period to end.

Breakfast was made up of an assortment of pastries washed down with cappuccino. Kara could not help thinking that if she lived here for any length of time she would become as round and plump as his housekeeper. Not that the cakes weren't delicious, but she was surprised that Blake had not asked for bacon and eggs.

Afterwards they explored the terraced gardens, and finally they reached the shores of the lake and a small cruiser moored there. Blake helped her into it, and she watched him as he started the engine, then untied the boat and guided it away from the shore. In everything he did he was confident and assured. She could not help but admire him.

Kara was silent to begin with, completely over-awed as they passed more magnificent shore-side villas. Dotting the tree-clad hillsides higher up were more modest houses, whole villages of them. And above them, above everything, the sky was the deepest blue she had ever seen, reflecting in the waters, which looked tempting enough to swim in.

'Everything's so beautiful,' she said on a sigh, her hands clasped in front of her as her eyes darted all over the place.

'Including you,' he said quietly.

For a brief second Kara remembered that Blake was her boss. But he was also her lover! Wasn't he? Her body grew suddenly hot at the thought, and she was unaware that her eyes were shining, that her cheeks had delicately flushed.

'Why have you always hidden yourself away behind plain clothes?'

The question was unexpected, and it surprised her. 'I think you know the answer to that.'

'Because of your father.' It was a statement, not a question. 'Why didn't you both leave him?' His head turned, his eyes locking into hers. 'Wouldn't it have been the wisest thing to do?'

'It sounds so easy, doesn't it? Just leave the monster

behind. But we couldn't. He— He—' Kara swallowed hard. 'He threatened us. I don't know what he would have done if we'd tried, but we felt that it was more than our life was worth. Not that our life was very good...'

Blake swore. 'It is a good job your father is dead, because I would personally—'

'Blake, please.' Kara put her hand on his arm. 'I should not have told you any of this. It's too private and too painful. Please, I don't want to talk about it any more.' Because if she did she would end up telling him about their money problems, and she knew she could not do that.

He closed his lips, but Kara could see that he was not comfortable keeping silent.

'That is why you tried to make yourself look like a nobody? To keep out of his way? You did not want him to know what a beautiful daughter he had. And it made you fearful of all men.'

Kara shrugged. 'Why don't you tell me about yourself instead?' she suggested, trying to inject lightness into her voice.

Dark brows rose. 'You mean you want *my* sad story? This was not intended to be a soul-baring mission. Today was supposed to be all about making you happy.'

'I am not unhappy,' she said immediately.

'But my insensitive questioning has brought back unhappy memories. I am sorry.'

He took her hand and pulled her against him, then draped his arm about her shoulders while he steered with his other hand. And when she looked up into his face he smiled and kissed her.

Instantly her problems were forgotten. Kissing Blake

was like turning on an electric lightbulb; it made her glow with energy. She knew that when they flew back to England all this would be over. Her life would return to normal. But she did not want to think about that now. She wanted to make the most of every moment.

They spent their whole morning exploring various inlets and promontories, stopping for lunch at a very beautiful hotel. Sometimes they were talking, sometimes sitting quietly watching other boaters, or the antics of water skiers in the distance, although Kara frequently found that Blake was watching her instead of the scenery.

The lake was much bigger than she had thought, and she could not help dreaming that one day she might be lucky enough to come back here and explore it all. 'You are very fortunate, having a villa in a place like this,' she said. 'And yet I have never known you take a holiday from work in all the time I've been working for you. Why is that? Why don't you use it?'

A shadow crossed Blake's face. 'I have secrets too, Kara. My memories of the villa are not entirely happy.'

He closed his eyes, and Kara could see that whatever the memory was it still haunted him. And if this was so why had he brought her here? She felt a cold shiver run down her spine.

'Perhaps we should not have come,' she said, unaware that her voice had changed, that she was emotionally pulling away from him.

'I wanted you to see it. I wanted to take pleasure from your enjoyment.'

'At the cost of yours?'

'I decided that it was time to let go of the past. I saw

someone who had been hurt as much as I had, but in an entirely different way, and I wanted to help. I hope I have done that?' Blake knew he was taking a big risk, talking like this, but it had felt right bringing Kara here, and now that he had seen the change in her he was glad that he had. But how did Kara feel? He held his breath as he waited for her answer. He was not usually so cautious when it came to his female acquaintances, and he absolutely never told them anything about his personal life. For some reason Kara had got beneath his skin. She was beginning to unleash her own demons too, and in the process revealing a side to her that he would never have guessed existed. She excited him in so many different ways.

She nodded slowly. 'I do feel a changed person here.'

'Then I have done what I set out to do, and helped myself in the process. You and I, Kara, although you may not believe it, are two of a kind.'

Kara shook her head. 'How can we be alike? Our lives are so very different, Blake! I can't imagine that there is anything similar about our lives at all.'

'Perhaps I do owe you an explanation,' Blake agreed after a few moments' thoughtful silence. But it was not going to be easy. Kara was the complete antithesis of his ex-wife. The two women could not be more different. Kara so innocent and honest; his wife two-timing and scheming.

He drew in a deep breath and let it out slowly, unaware that his unhappy memories were showing on his face. 'I was married once, a long time ago, to a woman called Melanie. When I married her I thought myself the luckiest guy in the world. She was blonde and beautiful and full of life. She enjoyed going out, socialising, parties—but I was busy building up my business. Nevertheless, I believed that I had got the balance right between work and pleasure.'

Kara waited, almost holding her breath. This was a side to Blake that she had never seen. A sad and sensitive side that she had not known existed.

Then his lips twisted wryly and a dark shadow crossed his face. 'Melanie, however, thought otherwise.'

He drew in a harsh breath and closed his eyes as memories flooded back.

'On holiday right here—a holiday she had insisted on taking, and one that started so happily, where she could not have been a more attentive and loving wife—she told me that she was pregnant. And, although I had not wanted to start a family so soon, I could not deny that the thought of being a father gave me great pleasure.'

He was silent for a moment and Kara could see the turmoil in his eyes, the wretchedness and the hurt, and she almost wished that they had not started this conversation.

Another sigh shifted through him, causing his eyes to grow hard and his jaw to tighten. Finally he spoke again. 'It was not until we got back to England that I discovered through a well-meaning friend that Melanie had been seeing another man. At first I was totally disbelieving, declaring that my wife would never do anything like that, but once the thought had been introduced into my mind I began to see that there could very well be some truth behind the accusation. Her behaviour was often erratic, and she would stay out much later than I had ever really noticed before. She would end phone calls as soon as I walked into a room, and she had started to spend a lot more money on seemingly quite trivial things. I knew I had to confront her and give her the opportunity to explain.'

Kara knew how hard it was for Blake to talk to her like this, and she was afraid to say anything for fear that he would close up and not finish his story. So she simply sat there looking at him, waiting, wondering.

'Initially she denied that she had been having an affair, and was angry with me for accusing her. I felt torn, but my suspicions would not go away, I knew by now that there was definitely *something* going on. Eventually, after another of her late-night parties, the truth came out. I think she had argued with her lover and was scared he might reveal her secret to me. Finally she broke down and told me that the baby was not mine but this other man's. Apparently he had told her he did not want to be a father, and once he had found out that she was pregnant had told her that their relationship was over.'

By the time Blake had finished his lips were grim and his eyes stone-hard. Kara almost wished that he hadn't told her. It was scary, seeing Blake like this. 'So she thought she would pass it off as yours?'

She felt for Blake. She felt his fury, his anger, his disappointment that his wife had cheated on him. And she wanted to throw herself into his arms and comfort him.

'I was so furiously angry. I could not believe that I had actually been sucked in by her lies. Her apologies afterwards meant nothing. I cast her out of my life and began divorce proceedings immediately. But it made me wary. I've trusted no woman since, and I'm definitely never going to get married again.'

'I'm sorry.' Kara did not know what else to say. What was there to say in the face of such duplicity? She did not know how Melanie had had the nerve to try and deceive him. She must have known that the truth would come out sometime.

'So you see,' he said finally, after a long silence when they were each deep in their own thoughts, 'we really are two of a kind.'

Never in a million years would she be like him, thought Kara. She did not have that hard edge that he hid behind. Her emotions came too easily to the surface. 'Have you seen her since?' She could not help asking the question.

'No. Nor do I want to,' he answered curtly. 'I'm sorry I've told you, I did not want anything to spoil our day.'

'I'm actually glad that you have,' she said softly.

'And I think it's about time we set off again.' He visibly shrugged off his mantle of discontent. Nevertheless he was silent for a while—until he found a secluded spot where he switched off the engine and tied up the cruiser. And Kara found out exactly what he had in mind when his dark gaze met hers, when she saw the searing hunger in his eyes.

'I need this, Kara. I've been wanting to do it all day.' His voice was no more than a low growl now, a growl deep in his throat, vibrating through her nerves, making her shiver with anticipation. At one time she would have felt fear if any man had approached her like this, but not so with Blake.

Although her body quivered her mind was open to him, and when his hands slid around her and she felt herself urged against his lean hardness, when she felt the full force of his arousal, hunger raced through her like quicksilver and there was no way on this earth that she could have resisted.

He had turned her into someone she did not recognise—and yet she did not hate herself for being weak. She could not. The pleasure was too intense. Simply being here and feeling the heated emotions spinning from one to the other was sufficient to capture her mind as well as her body.

Her eyes were on his mouth as it drew closer to hers, on his intensely sensual lips that could cause such devastating excitement. Unconsciously she touched her tongue to her own lips, moistening them in readiness, and she saw Blake's eyes narrow, the way he drew in his breath and became motionless.

What began as a gentle kiss grew swiftly into something hard and demanding. They each fed from the other, their bodies melding together as though this was where they rightly belonged.

Kara felt as if she was drowning in the waters of the lake, as if she was being swallowed up by the silky warmth that swam through her limbs and caused her head to spin. The mere taste of his lips was like an aphrodisiac, inciting her to return his kiss with a passion that both shocked and thrilled her.

Somewhere—somewhere in the back of her mind—rang a warning bell. Don't get into this too deeply, it said, or you might be sorry. But she did not listen. She liked what was happening. She wanted more of it. She was like a child who had been let loose in a sweet shop. She wanted to taste everything.

Heat gathered and swirled between her legs, her heart thundered, and when Blake took her hand and led her down to the cabin she made no demur. Urgently now, he stripped off his clothes, and Kara did the same. She felt no inhibition, though had anyone asked her a few days ago if she would strip off in front of a man she would have told them they had to be joking.

He feathered her skin with tiny kisses, causing her to buck and wriggle. Kara had never realised before how many sensitive areas she had. He was opening up a whole new world, and her enjoyment went beyond anything she had ever experienced.

It would be time to take a step backwards when they returned to London, when he would once again become her boss and she would be his perfect PA. There was no reason for her to believe that this would carry on. His affairs never did. But at least he had said that she would not be thrown out of her job. Not in so many words, but he had said that he never wanted to lose her—which amounted to the same thing, didn't it?

'I love the paleness of your skin,' he muttered, as his mouth moved from her breasts to trace a path over her stomach and towards his ultimate goal. 'Too many women think a tan makes them look healthier and more beautiful, but you are simply perfection.'

Kara loved the compliment he had paid her. And when his hungry mouth finally reached the soft whorls of hair at the apex of her thighs neither of them wanted to speak. The only sounds they made were of pleasure. The only movements they made were purely instinctive.

Kara could not believe how easily or how swiftly Blake brought her to her climax. It seemed that he had only just touched her and her world exploded. Again! As it had last night! What must he be thinking? It couldn't be very much fun for him.

'I'm sorry,' she said, her voice low and hoarse.

'Sorry?' he growled. 'Don't be. It's a compliment. Would you like to return the favour?'

What? Kiss him? There? Kara felt the blood rush to her face. He was asking too much. How could she? But within minutes she found herself teasing Blake in the same way as he had teased her. And whatever she was doing she must have been doing it right, because with the deepest groan she had ever heard he suddenly swung her onto her back and within seconds of protecting himself had entered her.

Kara lifted her hips to accommodate him and they both rode the storm together. She thought that she was going to black out, so intense was her pleasure, so many waves washing over her time and time again, and afterwards they both lay sated, unable to move, no strength left in their bodies.

Blake watched Kara, lying perfectly still with her eyes closed, and she lay there for so long that he wondered whether she was hating him now, whether he had overstepped the mark. There was a stillness about her that was scary. He felt sick to the bottom of his heart—until her eyelids fluttered open and she smiled. 'I think I have gone to heaven.'

Relief flooded through him. 'I was beginning to think that you thought badly of me.'

'How could I?' she asked, sitting up. 'I never knew that making love could be so beautiful. My mother always said—' She stopped abruptly and shook her head. 'Please forget I said that. I love my mother dearly. I would never say anything against her.'

Blake guessed that her mother's opinion on sex would have been based on the man she had married. The man who sounded like a complete monster. He forced himself to smile. 'We're not all the same. Myself and many other men besides me see women as objects of beauty, to be treated with respect and fairness. We would never demand anything they do not want to give. One day, Kara, you will find a man to love, and you will see that I am right.'

Kara felt as though he had just thrown her into the lake and left her to drown. He had just confirmed her suspicions that this was nothing more than a fling as far as he was concerned. A holiday romance! Something she would remember for the rest of her life but he would not.

How she managed to give the impression that there was nothing wrong she did not know. She glanced at her watch and pretended to be surprised at the time. 'We should be getting back.'

Despite what he had said, however, Kara still managed to feel total awareness, and she knew that if he wanted to make love to her again she would let him. He was in her bloodstream now; she could not get rid of him. He was a part of her and she was a part of him.

# CHAPTER SIX

Kara and Blake had finished their dinner, and were seated outside on the terrace watching the sun slide slowly down behind one of the mountains. This surely had to be the most perfect place in the world, she thought, and felt sad that they had only one more day left.

She wondered whether she dared ask Blake if they could stay a little longer, but then remembered the fuss she had kicked up in the first place. And of course her mother would be expecting her! She suddenly sat up straight. How could she have forgotten her mother? How could she have spent a whole day without even thinking about her?

'Is something wrong?'

'I was thinking about my mother, wondering whether she's all right. I feel guilty now for—for enjoying myself.' *Enjoying* was too feeble a word to describe the emotions that had set her body on fire. It should have been something like seventh heaven or paradise, and she was glad that the darkening sky hid the hot colour that now flooded her cheeks.

'Then why don't you ring her?' And he tossed her his phone.

Even as he spoke her own phone rang, and as soon

as she heard the panic in her mother's voice Kara knew that something was wrong—very, very wrong—and she moved away so that Blake would not overhear.

'You need to come home,' said Lynne urgently. 'He's found out where I am. He was here just now, demanding money. I'm scared, Kara. He was really nasty. I've never seen him quite like that before.'

Kara felt her blood run cold. She had never heard her mother sound so worried. She was usually resigned to their lot in life. But she knew that she must not panic—even though she wanted to! She drew in a long breath and spoke as steadily as she could. 'Of course I'll come. Try not to worry. I'll speak to Blake. I'll be there as soon as I can.'

She spent a further few minutes trying to pacify her mother, who had a weak heart. Kara knew how dangerous it was for her to get worked up like this. And she needed to draw in a few more deep breaths herself before returning to Blake's side. Her heart was racing all over the place.

His dark eyes were questioning as he looked at her. 'Is something wrong? You've gone very pale.'

'My mother's not well. I need to go home.' She couldn't tell Blake the truth because it would to be embarrassing to admit to this man that her father had tricked them in such a blatant way. And, knowing Blake as she now did, he might want to do something about it. They would then be in his debt. And did she really want that?

The answer was a resounding no. Besides, once they got back to England their intimate relationship would be over. She was sure of it—convinced of it. He hadn't made her any promises. Far from it! Kara was certain that Blake wouldn't want to carry on their affair under the noses of his staff. No, a line would be drawn under the whole affair. It would be back to business as usual. Telling him about their debt would be a huge mistake!

She would need to treat these last few days as nothing more than a pleasant interlude. An overwhelming interlude! More than overwhelming, actually, but she could think of no other superlatives to describe what had happened to her. At least she would have memories. Totally amazing memories that she would hold for the rest of her life.

'I am sorry. Of course you must go.' Even as he spoke he was on the phone, and in what seemed like no time at all they were on their way to the airport.

The good thing about being with Blake was that he got things done, thought Kara. Money talked.

'What's happened to your mother?' he asked her now, genuine concern on his face. 'Is she in hospital?'

Kara shook her head, unaware that her eyes were shadowed and her face so drained of blood that she looked ill. 'She has a weak heart and amongst other things she suffers panic attacks—really bad ones. A legacy from my father, I'm afraid.' None of this was a lie; she was not making excuses to avoid the truth. 'She needs me. I should never have come away. I blame myself for this. I—'

'Kara!' Blake took her icy cold hands into his. 'You mustn't blame yourself. Everyone needs a break at some time. Perhaps you should get someone in to help with your mother? I'd be willing to—'

'No!' Kara almost shouted in her need to stop what

he was saying. Involving Blake in their family affairs was the last thing she wanted. Both she and her mother were too embarrassed by what they saw as their failings to want anyone to witness it—let alone the man who paid her wages!

If they had stood up to her father all those years ago, been brave enough to walk out on him, then none of this would have happened. But they hadn't, and now they were forced to face the consequences.

And the man they owed money to was becoming more and more demanding, more frightening with every visit. Kara was giving him practically every penny of her salary and it still wasn't enough. It was hard to believe that he had found out where her mother had gone.

If she hadn't thought her parent would be safe with Aunt Susan she would never have agreed to go to Italy in the first place. Even if it had cost her her job! The man had no conscience. He didn't care who he frightened so long as he had enough cash to fund his extravagant lifestyle.

During the flight Blake respected Kara's wish to remain silent, even though he didn't understand it. His attempts to talk to her had led to nothing, and he hated to see her so deeply troubled. He would be worried, too, if it was his mother, and he could understand her distress—but he did wish that she would let him in so that he could talk her fears through with her.

Instead she sat bolt upright, her eyes staring into space, her mind on whatever lay ahead. He would be there for her, he determined. He would give her any help she needed. If her mother needed hospital treatment then he would arrange it—pay for it, even.

Although he hadn't wanted it to happen, Kara had got through to him like no other woman ever had. He hadn't planned, didn't even want a permanent relationship, but something had happened. She had opened a tiny crack in his heart. And her pain was now his pain.

'Are you sure there is nothing I can do, Kara? I could phone ahead and arrange for—'

'*No!*' The word was immediate and loud, and then she said, 'I'm sorry. I didn't mean to snap. But I'm used to my mother's—attacks. She'll be all right once I'm there.'

'If you're sure? Because—'

'I'm sure,' she reiterated, her eyes flashing a vivid blue.

Blake felt sad at the loss of the beautiful woman he had found, the woman who had given herself so willingly. Who had transformed herself from someone plain and introverted into someone beautiful and outgoing. She had retreated back into her shell and he had no way of knowing what was going through her mind. 'If there is anything I can do,' he said again, 'you know you have only to ask.'

'I know.' Her voice was quiet once more. 'And, thank you, but we'll be all right.'

It was as though she didn't trust him, as though she wanted to compartmentalise the two sides of her life, and he could not understand why. He would have expected her to welcome his help after the time they had spent together, the closeness they had shared and enjoyed.

When the plane touched down he heard her on her phone, calling a taxi. 'Kara, please—let me take you. It will be so much easier. I have a car waiting.'

But she vehemently shook her head. 'I need to cope with this on my own, Blake.'

Kara saw the shock on his face but she had to do this. She did not want him knowing anything else about her private life. She refused even to think about the word *help*, as it brought with it feelings of both shame and hope.

When she got to her aunt's house and saw the state her mother was in she was glad that she had not let Blake bring her.

Her aunt Susan was all for them going to the police, but her mother was adamant. 'I'll be all right now Kara's home,' she kept saying. And when later that same day they returned to their own house she did indeed begin to look well again.

Kara knew that her mother was frightened, but she wondered whether part of her reaction was simply because Kara had not been around to rely on. An ache filled Kara's heart. For the first time ever she felt that she was being held back from a life that could be a whole lot better. She had experienced that life, had tasted a little bit of heaven—and unfortunately that was all it was ever going to be. One taste! A taste that would have to last her a lifetime.

Not that she'd truly expected anything more from Blake, but her brief experience of life on the other side meant that it would be hard going back.

Her mother, once she was settled and comfortable, naturally wanted to know all about her time spent away. And although Kara had no intention of telling her what had taken place between her and Blake, she could not hide the light in her eyes or the bloom to her skin as she spoke about her time in Italy.

'Tell me to mind my own business, but it looks to me as though something happened while you were there. You look as though you've fallen in love, Kara!'

In love! Bright colour flooded her cheeks even as she shook her head. 'I'm not in love, Mother. I'm never going to fall in love.'

'But something happened in Italy, didn't it?'

There was no hiding it. Kara shrugged, trying to give the impression that it was nothing. When actually it had meant everything to her. 'I did have a little romantic—liaison.'

Her parent smiled, suddenly looking happier than Kara had seen her in a long time. 'I knew it. Who is he? Are you going to see him again?'

Aware that her mother would not rest until she knew the truth, Kara drew in a deep sigh and let it go slowly. 'Actually, it was my boss.'

'Blake Benedict?' Shock registered on her mother's face. 'Was that wise, my darling? Doesn't he have a terrible reputation?'

'I guess.'

'And are you going to continue this affair?'

'Of course not,' Kara answered. 'I don't want the whole office knowing. It was just a—a holiday romance. A fling.'

Her mother looked at her wisely. 'You're not into flings, Kara. I hope he doesn't hurt you.'

'Blake won't do that,' she declared blithely. 'We've reached an understanding.'

At least she was assuming they had. They had not

actually talked about it, but she could not see Blake wanting to continue their affair now they were back in England. It had been exciting while it lasted—more than exciting. It had been an intense sexual experience. But she had resigned herself to the fact that that was all it was.

It was with trepidation, after spending the weekend at home, that she turned up for work on Monday morning. Blake looked both surprised and pleased to see her when she walked into his office.

'How is your mother?' were his first words. 'I wasn't sure that you'd be in today.'

'She's much better, thank you.' And *she* was all right too, now that she had seen him! One look into his face and she felt like a real woman again. What she would have liked was his arms around her, the strong, reassuring beat of his heart against hers.

'Are you sure?'

'Perfectly sure. Once we got home she was fine.'

'I didn't realise you were back in your own house or I would have come to see you. I had no idea where you were. I've been worried, Kara.'

'That's very kind of you, Mr Benedict.'

'*Mr Benedict?*' Dark brows shot up. 'What is this?' And then his face cleared. 'It's because we're at work, isn't it? You want to keep up appearances? Don't you think it might be a little difficult?'

'I wasn't even sure whether I still had a job. I know you said that you never wanted to lose me, but—'

'Kara!' Blake's eyes widened in astonishment. 'Whatever gave you that idea? I would be lost without you.'

For some reason she hadn't been able to help thinking

about the gossip that had flown around the office before her and Blake's trip to Italy. It had been common knowledge that his relationships with women were fleeting! Her thoughts must have shown on her face.

'Ah! Let me guess. You've heard that two of my previous PAs left after their respective conferences? And you, my innocent Kara, like everyone else, put two and two together and decided I'd bedded them and then dismissed them. The rumour amused me, but for your information it was the strain of working for me that they could not handle. Whereas you, my beautiful one, cope with *everything* admirably.'

Kara felt her usual blush coming on.

'And even in those dreadful clothes you are still sexy. I think I might struggle to keep my hands off you. You are both prim and desirable at the same time.'

'You flatter me, Mr Benedict.' She had gone back to her regulation dark suit, with flat-heeled shoes, her hair dragged back and her face bare of make-up. 'But what happened between us in Italy should be forgotten. I work for you, Mr Benedict. Let's leave it at that.' They were the hardest words Kara had ever had to say, but she truly believed that it would be for the best. 'Shall we start work?'

Continuing to see Blake would mean involving him in her family life, and that was something she did not want. She felt a very real need to keep her private and business lives totally separate.

Both his disbelief at what he was hearing and his displeasure that she was actually saying these words were very clear in his eyes. 'Can you really tell me, Kara, that you can stand there and look at me and feel nothing? Are you saying that even at this moment you do not feel a resurgence of the hunger we both felt?'

Kara sucked in a deep breath. 'Of course I feel it. But I choose to ignore it. And by so doing it will go away.'

'And if it doesn't?'

'Mr Benedict, you must realise that an office affair is not what I want. I should never have led you to believe that I would be OK with this kind of thing.' She felt extreme heat even saying those words. It curled around her stomach and made her feel ill. She had been fool-ish—very foolish. If word got out every person in every department in the building would know. She would be talked about. Speculation would be rife. There would be no getting away from it. She would be a laughing stock. Another gullible woman sucked in by the enigmatic Blake Benedict.

The idea made her stomach clench, and Kara knew already that she wouldn't be able to take being the centre of office gossip. She might even have to leave because of this foolish encounter with Blake! And if she left there would be no money to pay off… She let her thoughts go no further, they were far too disturbing.

His dark eyes met and held hers, and although she wanted to she could not look away. There was something mesmerising in them and she could actually feel herself being pulled back into that space she had inhabited for a few days. A few days of sheer unadulterated pleasure. A few days to last her the rest of her life!

'Will you do me the honour of dining with me to-night?'

Her heart quickened its beat and she took a step back, though still her eyes were locked into his. 'Have you not heard a word I've said? I cannot carry on an affair with you. Not right here under the noses of your staff.'

'So, our affair—it was all right while we were where no one knew you?'

'I lost my head,' she admitted. She had actually done more than that. She had lost her virginity. 'I let the magic of Italy carry me away. But I've come to my senses and—'

Her words were cut off when he swiftly closed the space between them and slid his arms around her. The next second his mouth was on hers and every sane thought fled. How could she fight when instant desire flared? When her body ignited? It was both crazy and beautiful at the same time.

It was not until he had thoroughly kissed her and was satisfied that she would no longer deny him what he wanted that Blake let her go. 'You lost your head in the most delightful way. You cannot deny that you want me—as much as I want you. I'll do my level best to keep my hands off while we're at work, though I cannot entirely promise. You're an incredible woman—do you know that? You're refreshingly different. Again I ask myself why I never noticed you before.'

'Because you go for glamour,' retorted Kara swiftly.

'Which I have now discovered can come in all sorts of guises,' he said on a groan. 'You may be dressed in the most conservative suit I've ever seen, you may not be wearing a scrap of make-up, but in my eyes, Kara, you are extremely beautiful. And I want you.' Even as he spoke, even as his voice turned low and throaty, his arms were tightening around her again, and his mouth claimed hers in a kiss that shot her into space.

Blake asked himself why he was doing this. Why he was persisting with Kara when she had told him quite clearly that their brief affair was over. Was it his wounded pride? Was he not used to women turning him down? Or had she really got beneath his skin in a way that no woman had since his marriage broke down?

He *had* actually intended ending their affair when they got back, feeling that he wasn't being fair to Kara, but found that he couldn't do it. More especially after her scare with her mother. She needed someone in her life—someone to care for *her*. Her mother was not the only one who had been traumatised by a beast of a man.

He had hardly slept the whole weekend for thinking about Kara, wondering how she was coping, wishing there was something that he could do. And when she'd turned up in one of her straitjacket business suits he had felt immensely disappointed. He had not expected her to come into the office, but he was glad that she had. Very glad!

The way that she dressed was in fact to his advantage. He did not want anyone else seeing what a stunning woman she really was. He would never get enough of her. Not that he wanted permanency, but contrarily he did not want to let her go. At least not for a long time yet!

'Am I being persuasive enough?' He deliberately kept his voice low and sexy as he posed the question. 'Isn't this what you want, Kara?' Because it was as sure as hell what *he* wanted. The merest touch of her lips against his fired a wild need through his body. Simply looking into her amazing blue eyes created a surge of adrenalin. There was no way he could work with her all day and not be allowed to release the energy she created. Kara had become a part of his life and he did not want to let her go.

'Mmm.'

It was the only sound he heard from her. Already he could feel her beginning to respond to him, the defences she had built so determinedly starting to crumble, and in little more than a few seconds her body arched involuntarily into his, her hips tight against him, her lips parting hungrily.

He should have felt guilty, but he didn't. Kara had turned into the most amazing woman—truly amazing— and he did not want to think that her strong virtues could hold him to ransom. He would not let them! He would do everything in his power to ensure she changed her mind.

Kara felt that she had let herself down. If she had not given herself to Blake in the first place then this would not be happening. She had become like every other one of his PAs—enchanted by Blake's seductive power.

He'd flattered her when he had probably seen very little that was beautiful about her. And she had responded to that flattery and given in to him. And why? Because she'd been available to him at the conference and he was too virile a man to go without sex for long. Colour flamed her cheeks and she tried to pull free.

To no avail. Blake's arms tightened resolutely. 'Do not think I'm unaware that your need is as great as mine.'

It was—but didn't he know that people would talk?

That her life would be hell if anyone found out she was being bedded by her boss? This was insanity of the highest order, and she ought to have known that from the beginning. What a crazy fool she had been to even *think* that Blake Benedict would settle for anything less than a full-blown affair.

'Kara…' His voice murmured softly against her mouth. 'It is all right. Everything is all right.'

No, it wasn't. It was all wrong. Everything she was doing was wrong. Except that another part of her mind, the insane part, was urging her to accept everything that Blake had to offer. He made her feel more feminine than she ever had in her life. He had given her a good feeling about her body. He had given her confidence. She had become a different woman, and if she was honest with herself then she truly liked that person.

But that was then and this was now. Circumstances were different. She could not go through with it. Except that there was still a part of her, a part of her head that was not connected to her brain, that was telling her it was all right to let go. That she deserved some pleasure in her life. That she could not remain a prim spinster because of the insecurity her father had beat into her, or because she needed to stay at home to help and protect her mother from the man who was ruling both their lives.

In the end she gave in to the primal urges that were taking over. She could no longer deny herself the excitement of being in Blake's arms, of his kisses, of his touch. Already an army of pleasure-seeking gremlins were marching through her body, tracking along nerves and veins, infiltrating her blood stream, resulting in her melting against him, accepting his kisses, returning them with a fervour that should have scared her but instead only increased her hunger.

When finally they both paused for breath, with Kara clinging on to Blake because she knew her legs would buckle if she let go, he said softly, 'My driver will pick you up at seven-thirty.'

'My mother—'

'I'm sure your mother will not mind you dining with me. Would you like me to talk to her?'

'No!' Kara's response was instant. 'I'll tell her myself.' Which meant that she had agreed to his suggestion—as he had known all along that she would.

She was not sure what her mother would say, though. Lynne had not been slow in voicing her opinion that the Blake Benedicts of this world did not take women seriously. Especially their personal assistants. And Kara really had no wish to heap any more trouble on their shoulders.

It was too late now to back out. She had given her answer by letting him kiss her. But when she got home at the end of the day, when she told her mother that she was dining with Blake, her parent's reaction was not what she expected.

'It sounds as though he is a good man after all,' she said. And when Kara came downstairs in one of the beautiful new dresses that Blake had bought for her, tears filled her mother's eyes.

Kara knew that she was thinking her father had been the reason why she had never worn fine clothes before. Her heart ached—both for herself and for her mother.

As she slipped into the waiting saloon Kara did not

see the other car parked on the opposite side of the road, or the driver watching her intently; nor was she aware that it pulled away and began to follow them.

Her head was in the clouds. Despite her own initial concerns she was excited to be dining out with Blake. Although she had been resolute in her decision today to let none of her time spent in Italy intrude, once Blake had kissed her every good intention had fled. And now she was filled with unbelievable anticipation.

As the city was left behind Kara began to wonder where they would be eating. The glass partition between her and the driver prevented her from asking, and it was not until he halted in front of a set of iron gates, passing through them as they opened to follow a long drive, that she finally realised she was being taken to Blake's home.

Pinpricks of excitement—or was it fear?—heated her skin, and she sat forward on the edge of her seat. But even though she was expecting something impressive nothing prepared her for the grandeur that confronted her eyes. It was a stunningly beautiful mock-Tudor-style house overlooking its own lake—not as large as Lake Como, but imposing all the same. And the house was quite simply huge, making Kara wonder how one man could live there alone.

He came out to greet her, casually elegant in pale grey linen trousers and a matching short-sleeved shirt. 'Welcome to my home.' He kissed her gently on the lips, and even that one light touch created a sizzle of excitement, and with his arm about her shoulders he led her inside.

Kara was totally speechless—even more so when

she saw the huge oak-panelled entrance hall. A staircase with barley-twist balustrades ran right up the centre, and she caught a glimpse of a galleried landing either side.

'I wasn't expecting this,' she said.

'Where did you think I lived? In some smart London apartment?'

'It would make more sense.' Surely this place was too big for him?

'I like space. I like the countryside. Quite simply I like it here. Besides, I do a lot of entertaining—corporate sometimes. It suits me perfectly. Would you like a tour, or are you hungry? I believe dinner is almost ready to be served.'

'Then we will eat first,' declared Kara, still breathless from both her impression of the house and Blake's nearness.

'Once again you look stunning,' he said, with something deep and throaty in his voice—something that sent a further quiver of hunger though Kara's veins. 'But no less sexy than you did today, in that terrible suit of yours.'

'How dare you call my suit terrible?' she said with pretended indignation, tossing her head, her thick glossy hair brushing the side of her face as she looked him straight in the eye.

His lips quirked. 'Of course—I was forgetting. It is your suit of armour. But unfortunately for you it doesn't work against me any more. You're ravishing, Miss Redman, whatever you wear.'

'Should you really be saying that to your personal

assistant?' she threw back, enjoying this teasing side to her employer.

'There are lots of things I'd like to say to you,' he growled, 'but none that would be appropriate for the moment. Perhaps later...'

The innuendo in his voice created a further chaotic river of excitement, and she could not help wondering whether he would suggest that she stay the night.

The dining room was as impressive as the entrance hall, with a polished oak floor and a beamed ceiling, and a long oak table in the centre that seated at least a dozen people. Laid for the two of them, it looked slightly incongruous. A bowl of sweetly scented pink roses freshly picked from the garden stood in the centre, with matching candles either side in silver candelabrum.

'You have gone to all this trouble for *me*?' she asked in an awed whisper.

'You do not think you are worth it? Come, let me prove that you are.' His kiss turned her hunger for food into hunger of a very different kind. And when his hands cupped the cheeks of her bottom, urging her against him, she was left in no doubt about his need of her too.

'Blake!'

'Mmm? Blake what?'

'We should not be doing this. We should be taking our seats. What if—?'

'Ahem!'

The sound of someone clearing their throat caused Kara to spring away. She felt one of her embarrassing guilty blushes coming on, but Blake was as calm and relaxed as if all they had been doing was talking.

'Ah, Mrs Beauman. This is Kara, and we are both absolutely starving. Kara—my housekeeper.'

'Pleased to meet you, Kara,' said the short, cheerful woman. 'Blake surprised me when he said he had invited a guest for dinner. I usually get more warning.'

'I hope I'm not inconveniencing you,' said Kara at once.

'Not at all.'

Kara waited until Mrs Beauman had left before she turned to face Blake. 'Well, that was embarrassing. I hope she knows I'm just your PA!'

'You are not my PA tonight, Kara. You are my— friend. My lady-friend. My—whatever you would like to call yourself. My lover, perhaps?'

Again that telltale blush, but more furiously this time. 'Please don't call me that, Blake. I know it's what I was in Italy, but things have changed.'

'Have they?'

'Of course they have. I keep you telling you that.'

'Except that your body tells me differently,' he said, his voice a deep growl in his throat. 'Don't try to hide or deny it. But let's not think about that now. Let's take our seats. Mrs Beauman does not like to be kept waiting.'

The meal was scrumptious. That was the only word Kara could use to describe it. Everything was home-made and tasty and tempting. They started with a very flavoursome carrot and coriander soup, followed by lamb chops with garden peas and new potatoes. Then fresh raspberries and cream for dessert.

There was nothing fancy about it, but everything was delicious. She ate too much, and drank too much, and by the time they had finished she was so relaxed that she was laughing and chattering as though Blake was a lifelong friend instead of the man she worked for.

Afterwards, instead of touring the house, they took a walk in the grounds. 'We need to walk our dinner off first,' said Blake, and Kara agreed. She was excited by the swimming pool, with its own changing rooms and sauna, but even more enthralled by the log cabin that stood in a lightly wooded area. It had a living room-cum-kitchen, a bedroom and a shower room, with decking at the front.

The house was lovely, but so big. This was cosy—this was something else. Intimate. Sexy. And clearly Blake thought so too. He caught her in his arms as they were viewing the bedroom and pulled her down on the bed. 'I've been wanting to do this all day,' he growled. 'You've been driving me insane, do you realise that?'

Kara had been determined not to let Blake make love to her tonight. If she let him get away with it now she would be for ever at his mercy. But what was a girl to do when her heart ruled her head? When her body craved fulfilment? When the most amazing man in the world, a man who could have any woman he liked, desired *her*? How could she refuse him?

# CHAPTER SEVEN

'YOUR house is incredible.' Blake had just given Kara a guided indoor tour, and she had lost count of the number of rooms—each one furnished to an incredibly high standard. By comparison it made the house she and her mother lived in look like a doll's house.

'I will take that as a compliment.'

They were sitting in the conservatory, which looked out over the lake and the gardens beyond. The inky dark sky was laced with a myriad stars and a sliver of silver moon. The lake and surrounding area was lit by hidden lights. It reminded Kara of Lake Como.

'I still don't see why you want something so huge,' she said. 'Was it once your family home?'

Blake gave her one of his body-tingling smiles and shook his head. 'We didn't live anywhere this grand. My mother actually still lives in the house where I was born.'

Kara had seen a photograph of his mother standing proudly beside Blake at his graduation. She looked a very strong and very fine woman. 'And was that a photo of your father I saw in the drawing room?' She had meant to ask him at the time, but somehow their mouths had been otherwise engaged. She found it strange that he never talked about his father, though she supposed it was because he had lost him when he was so young.

Blake nodded. 'It was taken some years before he fell ill.'

'You look like him.'

'So I've been told.'

'What was he like?'

'He was very strict. He'd help me with my homework, make sure it was done, but he was of the old-fashioned school, believing that children should be seen and not heard. He was an academic, actually, his head always stuck in a book. He was kind and fair, though, and it was a sad day when he died. He'd been ill a long time and it was expected, but even so I wasn't too young to feel it.'

He went quiet for a moment, and Kara felt sorry that she had asked the question. She had not meant to bring back sad memories. If only her own father had been of such good character her life would have been so different. 'I expect your mother still misses him?'

He nodded. 'She does. She talks about him often. She has never found anyone else to love. I'll take you to meet her one day.'

Faint alarm filled Kara. Should she be flattered or worried? 'Won't she get the wrong impression? Won't she think there's something serious going on between us?'

'My mother knows I will never get married again.'

It was a clear statement of fact which put her firmly in her place, thought Kara. He had unmistakably confirmed what she had known all along. And even though her heart sank like a lead weight in a pond she tried to keep her tone light. It was all very well her surmising things, but to have them so clearly defined was not a happy feeling.

'She might think you've changed your mind,' she said, surprising herself with the lightness of her tone. 'Or do you take all your girlfriends to see her?'

'Certainly not! I've taken no one,' he declared—more forcefully, Kara thought, than was needed. 'There's no one I've wanted my mother to meet. However, you, my lovely Kara, are different. You may not believe this, but you might even be changing my mind about women! I'm beginning to believe that there are perhaps still one or two who are trustworthy.'

'I'm glad if I've restored your faith,' she said demurely. 'At least I've been of some service.'

'Some?'

The gleam of light in his eyes should have warned her. Despite his affirmation that he wished to remain single to the end of his days, she was still living on a high from their earlier lovemaking. It had taken on a whole new dimension. Felt different in the log cabin. She had given herself freely to him before, but there, in the woods, it had been as though they had taken a step back in time. As though they were the only man and woman on earth, and in their safe little place they could let go of everything. She would never have believed herself capable of being a temptress, of the things she had invited Blake to do, what *she* had done. Even thinking about it sent a fierce heat through every corner of her body.

'My beautiful Kara, *some* does not even begin to describe what you have done to me. Not only are you a sensational lover, but you do not have a bad bone in your body.'

'I do my best,' she said demurely, fluttering her eye-lashes, fully aware that it would send his temperature soaring again. She was becoming a *femme fatale*, and actually quite liked the feeling of power it gave her.

His voice got slower and deeper and his eyes grew darker. 'I don't want this night to end—stay with me.'

'You know that's impossible.' She glanced at her watch and was horrified to see how late it was. 'I'm sorry, Blake. I must go,' she said, jumping to her feet. 'I didn't intend to stay this long.' She hated to admit it even to herself, but once again she had forgotten all about her poor mother.

'Of course. I'll drive you.' Blake had only drunk a small amount with their meal. Kara had wanted to keep a clear head too—especially as she was not used to drinking. Not that it had stopped her losing her head when Blake made love to her. His lovemaking was far more intoxicating than any amount of alcohol.

She knew that when she went to bed later she would relive every single action in minute detail. It was doubt-ful she would get any sleep. And yet he would expect her bright-eyed at the office first thing in the morning. Where she would have to act like she had never acted before. It was going to be hard hiding her emotions from the rest of the staff.

When they reached her house she turned to give Blake a quick peck on the cheek, but he was out of the car before her. 'I think it's about time I met this mother of yours, don't you?'

Swift alarm shot through her. 'She's probably in bed,'

she lied, knowing full well that her mother would be waiting up and wanting a full report on the evening.

'In which case I shall kiss you goodnight and leave. But it would be ungentlemanly not to see you safely indoors.' Even as he spoke his hand was on her elbow and he was walking her up the garden path.

Luck was not on her side. As soon as Kara opened the door her mother called out to her. 'Kara? Come and tell me all about your evening! I hope you didn't let that man—'

'Would "that man" be me, by any chance?' asked Blake, popping his head round the door that led straight off the tiny hall.

Kara wished the floor would open and swallow her up, but Blake simply looked amused and walked further into the room.

'Mrs Redman, I can assure you that I have taken very good care of your daughter. Let me introduce myself. I'm Blake Benedict, your extremely beautiful and extremely capable daughter's employer. She is worth her weight in gold to me. I would never jeopardise her future.'

Kara felt hot colour stealing over her neck and cheeks. He was going way over the top. But already Lynne was in his thrall, smiling up at him, completely oblivious to the fact that she was in her nightie. 'That is very reassuring to hear, Mr Benedict. I confess I was a little worried, but—'

'But now that you have met me your fears are allayed? It is good to hear. And, please—call me Blake. You are as charming as your daughter. I hope I shall see more of you in the future. But for now let me bid you goodnight.'

He took her hand and pressed a kiss to the back of it, and when Kara walked with him to the front door she said, 'Thank you for being so kind to my mother.'

'I imagine she has had little attention paid to her over the years, so the pleasure is all mine.' He tilted her chin with his fingers and kissed her gently. 'Thank you for this evening. And if you're late in the morning I shall understand why.'

'I shall not be late,' she told him quietly. Whatever was happening between them, she still intended to do her job properly.

As Blake drove home he found himself humming an old love song, and alarm bells rang in his head. Surely he wasn't falling in love with Kara? Surely not? She was beautiful and exciting, and he enjoyed being with her, making love to her. She was refreshingly different. But that was all it was—wasn't it? Enjoyment? He was not looking for a long-term relationship. Commitment. Hell, no! Once was enough. He was done with that sort of thing. Love and marriage was definitely off his agenda. He intended remaining single to the end of his days.

He had meant what he said when he'd told her that she was helping him to change his mind about women, but it still did not mean that he wanted to get serious.

Happy now that he had convinced himself he was in no danger, Blake did not even notice that he had begun humming the love song again—and in the weeks that followed he did not question his actions. As far as he was concerned they were indulging in an affair which would one day end with no regrets on either side.

It stunned him, therefore, when he turned the corner to her road one day, ready to pick her up because he had planned a lavish dinner with a show to follow, to see her in the arms of another man.

At first he could not believe his eyes. Something harsh and sharp ripped through him and his first instinct was to confront them. But even as he watched the man let her go and turned and disappeared, while Kara hurried into the house.

Blake sat there for a few minutes, trying to reconcile himself to what he had seen.

When he finally picked her up she said nothing. She did not even look guilty. He began to wonder whether he had read the scene correctly.

He needed to ask. He knew that if he didn't it would fester in his mind. 'Who was that man I saw you with?'

Kara frowned. 'What man?'

'Outside just now, when I turned the corner.'

'Oh, you saw him?' The words popped out before she could stop herself, and she felt the blood drain from her face. 'He was no one.' But her heart did a painful drumbeat. How she wished that he was no one. How she wished that he wasn't their worst nightmare.

'No one? When he had his arms about you?'

Kara shivered. Blake looked so cold and condemning that she was suddenly afraid. 'He came to see my mother. He was saying goodbye, that's all.'

She wished that she could tell him about the loan shark, but it was such a deep stigma—so horribly embarrassing and shameful. It was something she and her mother had to deal with themselves. And now the unpleasant man had unfortunately seen her with Blake, realised she had a wealthy boyfriend, and was upping the interest on the loan again.

Blake's brows lifted. 'It was a funny goodbye. It looked as though he was kissing you.'

Spitting fury into her face was more like it. He had shoved his nose right up to hers and she had been scared to death. He had never been quite this aggressive before. 'It was just a peck on the cheek,' she said, mentally crossing her fingers that he would believe her.

Finally he relaxed. 'You had me worried, Kara. I thought I had competition.'

'There is no one else I'd rather be with,' she said, smiling gently and touching the tips of her fingers to his face. She actually felt as guilty, as if she *had* been two-timing him, and it was hard to control a tremor.

He took her hand and pressed a kiss into its palm before giving it back to her. 'Let's enjoy our evening out.'

Kara did enjoy her evening, but she could not forget the close shave she'd had and wondered whether she ought to stop Blake coming to pick her up. She had no idea how it had started, because he had always used to send his driver. But lately he had come for her himself, and he always made it his business to have a few words with her mother.

Lynne thought he was amazing. She thought him a good man, and good for her daughter, and had expressed the opinion that they might have a future together.

'You're being silly, Mum. Blake's not the settling down type. One marriage was enough for him.'

'Then why are you wasting your time with him if there is no future in it?'

'It's not a waste,' answered Kara. 'I'm experiencing life.' She wasn't going to tell her mother—not yet, at least—that she thought the signs were hopeful. Blake had only the other day begun to talk about something they might do in the future. And if that didn't mean he was serious then she did not know what did.

But life had a way of kicking her in the face when she was least expecting it, and of making niggling fear become reality.

# CHAPTER EIGHT

KARA stared at the tiny window, refusing to believe her eyes. This was not right. It could not be a true reading. But it was. She was deluding herself. It did not lie. She had known without the test. It had merely confirmed her fears. She slumped down on the edge of the bed, suddenly feeling icy cold. She was pregnant.

How it had happened she had no idea; Blake had always been so careful. Her out-of-control heartbeat echoed so loud in her ears that it was deafening. A baby! A baby who would take time and money. How could she clothe and feed a baby when already almost every penny of what she earned went towards paying off their debts?

Please, God, don't let this be real, she prayed. Don't let this be happening. But the truth was there in front of her. Nothing could be more real.

Blake would not want to be lumbered with a child—hadn't he told her he had no intention of playing happy families? She could imagine his disbelief when she did confess. He might even blame her. Wasn't that what men did? Some men anyway, at least.

He might even suggest paying for a termination, although she really had no idea what his thoughts on the matter were. Even thinking about it was enough to fill her with horror. Then she shook her head. No, he wouldn't want that—and neither would she, no matter how hard things got.

What she really ought to be thinking about was how she was going to cope. Once she had to leave work she could see no way out of their financial difficulties except to move away—somewhere the loan shark wouldn't find them. Otherwise how could she provide for a baby when he was sucking all their money from them?

Tears raced down her cheeks as she sat there looking at the evidence, willing it to change. But no power on earth could do that. She had to face the fact that she was to become a mother, with all the complications that involved.

How could she tell her own mother, even? How could she admit that she had got them into deeper trouble? The future looked bleak. Even if they moved and escaped the claws of the money-lender they had no savings to fall back on. It didn't look well for the future.

She waited until that Friday to tell Blake the news. It had become a habit for her to go to his house for dinner. He invariably tried to persuade her to stay the weekend but she never did, insisting that she could not leave her parent. Always, but always, they ended up in bed, and it would be very late when she got home.

This evening Kara felt nervous, and began toying with her food. Blake was not going to be happy; that was a certain fact. She felt sure that he did not see her as a permanent fixture in his life. Ought she to get out of here now and say nothing? Except that a few months down the line he would notice anyway. There would be no hiding the fact that she was pregnant.

'Is something wrong?' A faint frown grooved Blake's brow and his eyes were full of concern. 'You've been chasing that piece of chicken around your plate for the last five minutes. Are you not feeling well?' He reached his hand across the table to touch hers. 'You've looked a little pale all week. Do you think you're coming down with something?'

Finally Kara looked at him and made herself smile, ignoring the butterflies that were creating havoc in her stomach, trying to look as natural and joyful as possible. Perhaps if she looked happy he would be happy. 'I have some news for you.'

His brows rose. 'Go ahead.' He smiled expectantly.

It was now or never. 'I'm—pregnant, Blake.' There was no other way she could say it. No way to cushion the blow. 'I'm having your baby.'

But he didn't look happy. She had been hoping for too much. His expression was one of total disbelief and his eyes fixed firmly on her face, making her shiver inside. 'You cannot be.'

'I think I should know whether I'm pregnant or not,' she said, trying her hardest to ignore his reaction. It was a shock for him, the same as it had been for her. He needed a few minutes to let it sink in. She prayed this was the case. 'I'm definitely having your child, Blake.'

Her heart stopped beating as she waited for his response, and she did not like what she saw. A frown drew his brows together in a hard, straight line, narrowing his eyes, turning them into silver slits, and he looked at her as though she was a complete stranger telling him something he did not want to hear. There was none of the compassion and warmth that had been there a few seconds ago. Nothing but stone-cold disbelief.

'Tell me this isn't true.' His whole body was taut, every muscle clenched, his eyes silver and dangerous.

Her stomach began to churn uncomfortably. It was almost as though he was saying that he did not want their child. Which would be the cruellest thing in the world. Too cruel even to contemplate. She knew that he'd been hurt in the past, cheated on by his wife, but even so…

'I've done a test,' she said, quietly but firmly, keeping her eyes level on his despite the churning of her stomach. 'I'm definitely pregnant.'

Kara heard the breath hiss out of Blake's body as he turned away to look out of the window. She saw the tenseness in his shoulders and knew that she had to say something to defuse the situation. It was going to take him time to get his head round it. But the fact remained that she was carrying his child, and there was nothing either of them could do to change it.

'Are you certain that it's mine?'

Before she could answer he turned around, and Kara was shocked by the light blazing from his eyes. 'Of course I am.' Her jaw dropped and she stared at him in disbelief. 'How can you even suggest that I might have been with someone else? You have taught me everything I know about relationships, about trust, about making love.'

'Love?' He tossed the word into the air as though it did not exist. 'I don't believe in love—not any more. We had sex—very good sex.'

Although Kara knew where he was coming from, his harsh words still hurt. 'I'm not like Melanie, Blake.' She kept her voice soft and calm—just about. It was difficult in the face of such opposition. 'I can promise you I've been with no other man.'

'I saw you in the arms of someone else.'

His eyes had taken on a scary sheen and she shivered inside. 'And I told you who he was. Why would I want any other man when I have you?' It was hard to believe that he thought she was capable of going behind his back. She was not like his ex-wife; she would never, ever do anything underhand. Surely he knew that? Surely he knew her well enough by now?

She felt as though her whole world—her new and beautiful world—was crumbling at her feet stone by stone. Everything they had built up together being destroyed because he couldn't accept that she was pregnant with his child. Did he think she was happy about it?

It was a struggle even to breathe. Had it been his intention all along to have fun at her expense and then drop her as he had all the other women in his life? And now that she had announced she was pregnant it had put a whole different complexion on things.

Blake had taught her more about herself than she would ever have discovered if she had not been with him. He had made her believe in herself. She had finally become a confident woman. And now he was throwing it all back in her face. Her father had been right. She was a worthless creature. She had sold her body—and for what? The only way now was downhill.

Her tears finally came, and she swung away so that he would not see. She did not want him accusing her of turning them on so that he would take pity on her. Pity was the last thing she needed. What she wanted was for him to accept that they were having a baby. She wanted him to comfort her and assure her that he would look after her. She needed him. She did not want to go through this alone.

Blake's mind was in turmoil. He did not want children. Love and marriage and the whole happy family thing was not for him. He'd tried marriage once and it hadn't worked. He did not want to do it again. He had sworn he would never do it again.

He closed his eyes. Something had gone terribly wrong and he needed time to think about it. His whole world was spinning out of control and he was clinging on for dear life. It was hard to get his head round what Kara had just told him. He wanted to be alone.

'We will talk about this again later,' he said, trying to remain calm while inside a wild storm was raging. 'It would be best if you left now.' He spoke into his mobile, and seconds later Kara was being driven away.

The hurt in her eyes remained with him.

Drawing in a deep breath, trying to wipe the picture from his mind, Blake poured himself a large glass of whisky and sat down. He would be a very pathetic individual if he did not accept that Kara was telling the truth. She was so very different from any other woman he had gone out with. And nothing at all like Melanie. And yet he had questioned whether the baby was his.

It had been a gut reaction. The very thought of being a father scared him rigid. His mother had told him, some years after his father's death, that she would have liked more children, but her husband had been dead set against it. He'd actually not wanted Blake in the first place, although he had loved him once he was born.

And, since Blake was never happier than when he was working, he often felt that he was following in his father's footsteps. But if it was true and Kara *was* expecting his baby then everything would change. This did not make him feel happy. He needed time to think.

He had been thrown by the dramatic change in Kara in Milan; she had gone to his head. She had turned into a beautiful woman almost overnight—a beautiful, sexy woman who had welcomed her own femininity, who had been startled by it but had grown with it. He had watched her develop and mature and take pride in her sensuality, and he had felt something grow within himself too.

And now, in an instant, whatever it was that had been developing inside him—whether it was love or infatuation of some kind—had dealt him a body-blow. He hated himself for doubting Kara, for questioning her relationship with the man he had seen her with. And he blamed Melanie for making him wary.

Or was it his own take on the whole baby thing that was refusing to let him accept that he was about to become a father?

A few whiskies later, he was still thinking about his problem.

Kara wished that she had stuck to her guns and not gone to Milan—then none of this would have happened. And if she had not weakened it would not have happened either.

Life was cruel. It had been hard when her father

was alive, and even afterwards with the debts he had left them, but this was worse! Having Blake believe, if only briefly, that she would trick him into thinking that another man's baby was his had created the deepest, darkest fear she had ever experienced.

Even when her father had hit her she had not felt like this. She had cowered away and run to hide, but she had not felt as though her world was coming to an end. There had been a sort of inevitability about it—as though somehow it was all her fault and she deserved it.

But she did not deserve *this*!

The moment Kara walked into the house her mother asked her what was wrong. She thought of saying nothing, but her parent was not stupid and she would have to know the truth sooner or later. There were most likely still traces of tears on her face even though she had done her best to dab them dry.

'I think my relationship with Blake is over.'

Lynne said nothing, wisely waiting for her daughter to explain.

But seeing the sympathy on her mother's face caused her to lose what frail hold she had on her composure. Tears filled her eyes and rolled down her cheeks. 'He sent me home.'

Her mother still remained silent, holding out her arms instead. Kara walked into them, feeling like a child once again, when her mother's kisses had always made things better. Not that they would this time. Nothing could make her feel better.

'I'm pregnant, Mum, with his baby, and he's not happy about it.'

This did have her mother snapping to attention. 'You're pregnant?' And her eyes, so very much like Kara's, though their intense blue had faded over the years, widened in dismayed surprise.

Kara nodded, her misery mirrored in her expression. 'Whatever you do, don't censure me. I did not mean it to happen. We've always been careful. I don't know how it happened, but it has.'

Lynne stroked her daughter's hair and looked sadly into her face. 'I won't confess I'm not shocked, but it's not the end of the world, my darling. Blake must be in an equal state of shock. He'll need time to get over it. But he'll come round, you'll see. He's a good man.'

'I wish I could be as sure as you.'

'Men are strange creatures—you should know that,' said her mother. 'Look at your father.'

Kara did not even want to think about her father. 'I thought Blake was different.' She moved away, walking to the other side of the room. 'He's the only man I've ever felt comfortable with, the only one I've ever trusted. He brought me to life. He made me feel good about myself. But he's no different to the rest, Mum, when it comes down to it.'

Her mother's eyes widened again. 'I'm sure that's not true. It's my guess that in a few days' time he'll accept the inevitable. He cannot turn his back on you—not when he's the father.'

'He even questioned whether he was the father.' She might as well tell her the whole truth.

Lynne's brows drew together in a deeply disbelieving frown. 'But if you're not out with him you're always home. Why would he think that?'

'He did see me with someone,' she admitted, with a wry twist to her lips.

Confusion clouded her eyes. 'Who? A work colleague?'

Kara shook her head and remained silent, but her mother would not let it go. 'Then who?'

'The loan shark.'

'The loan shark?'

'Yes. Outside the house one evening. He was threatening me. I didn't tell you because I didn't want to alarm you. Blake saw him from a distance and thought we were kissing. I—*Mum!*' She lurched forward as she saw her parent slump in her chair.

What followed afterwards was like a nightmare. The ambulance. The hospital. The waiting. Kara blamed herself. She should never have mentioned that horrible man. He was her mother's worst enemy. Pure evil. The bane of their lives.

She spent all night at the hospital, worrying herself sick, feeling better only when her mother was declared out of danger. A suspected heart attack was ruled out, but Kara was told that her mother needed to rest and be kept calm. Because of her weak heart an attack in the future was not an impossibility.

A day later Lynne was allowed home. She looked pale and needed to rest, but insisted that Kara did not take any time off work. 'I'll be all right. If you don't go Blake will think you're staying away because of him—because you're scared.'

'Of Blake? Never!' she declared fiercely. She was more fearful for her mother's state of health. Nevertheless her parent was right. She did need to go. Neither of them mentioned the crook who was after their money, but Kara watched her parent sometimes sinking deep into her own thoughts, while her own were all over the place. She wished over and over that she had not brought him into the conversation. It made her more aware than ever of the effect the whole thing was having on her mother. How were they ever going to manage when the baby came along? Kara's hopes for the future were very bleak.

She arranged for a neighbour to sit with her mother while she went to work on Monday, and it was a relief to discover that Blake was absent—although she knew that he had been in earlier because he had left her a whole list of instructions. Her heart—which had been dancing all over the place at the thought of coming face to face with him again—quickly settled into its usual rhythm.

It was almost the end of the day before he returned, and when he did he called her in to his office. Kara kept her chin high and her eyes brave, even though her pulses were racing.

'Sit down,' he said roughly, when she remained standing in front of his desk.

Kara sat. Glad to do so because her legs were in danger of collapsing beneath her. There was something about Blake's expression that sent ice slithering down her spine. A few short weeks ago, even a week ago, she would never have imagined that their relationship would be put in jeopardy. She was the happiest she had ever been. And now she had no idea what her future held.

# CHAPTER NINE

'I CANNOT say in all truthfulness that I am happy about this situation, Kara,' said Blake, his eyes a light, telling silver.

'And you think I am?' she asked, hearing the sharpness in her voice but unable to do anything about it.

'We were both in shock the other day. I perhaps said things I should not have done.'

He could say that again! She did not like her honesty being questioned.

'We need to talk. Will you come home with me tonight so that we can discuss this matter over dinner?'

*This matter!* He made it sound like a business deal. And the way she was feeling at this moment she did not want to join him for dinner, tonight or any night. It was spending so much time with him that had got her into this mess. 'I don't see why we can't talk here and now.'

A frown dragged his brows together. 'It's hardly conducive.'

'To what? Intimacy?' Oh, God—why had she said that? Why had she even thought it? Except that intimacy was what they experienced every time she went to his house. Nevertheless she went on bravely. 'Have you any idea how much this is going to change my life, Blake?'

'I've thought of nothing else.'

'Is that so?' Still Kara couldn't keep the irony out of her voice. 'Or were you perhaps thinking more of yourself? The way it will change *your* life? Your single life. Your free and easy life. Because, believe me, I'm not going to bring this child up on my own. You're the father and you're going to play a part too.' How brave her words sounded—not that she was feeling brave. Anything but.

'I would not want it any other way' he said. 'I may not have planned on this child, Kara, I freely admit that. It has stunned and shocked me, but I *will* be involved in its upbringing.'

What exactly did that mean? Be involved? On what basis? A part-time father? Or would he do the honourable thing and suggest marriage? Her heart raced at the thought of being married to Blake. Suddenly she could think of nothing she would like better than to be married to Blake, to go to bed in his arms every night and to share her deepest fears over the future. Being Blake's wife would be the perfect solution to this problem, but Blake had said he would never marry again. And she had no idea what was in his mind now.

She already knew his views on marriage, but now there was a child involved—*his* child. Did he believe in a child having two parents who were tied together by marriage? Or was he a modern man who believed that marriage was not necessary to raise a baby? She did not doubt that he would provide for her and the baby, but how about personal support? Would she get that?

Would he want her to live with him? Or would his support come in the form of financial security? There was so much they had to talk about.

'I'm not trying to get out of anything, Kara, but I need to know your plans.'

'I've not had time yet to make any,' she threw back crisply.

'It has come as a great shock to both of us,' he agreed. 'I will obviously get you the best medical attention possible. I will personally—'

Kara held up her hand and shook her head at the same time. 'Don't think that throwing your money at this is the answer, Blake. What would have been nice was your belief in me. Have you any idea how much it hurt when you questioned whether the baby was yours? I guess I was stupid, naive. You didn't want anything long-term from me. You're simply after yet another affair. I'm just one in a long line.'

How she managed to speak without breaking down Kara had no idea, but she was not going to give Blake the pleasure of knowing how much he had upset her. Anger was her best form of defence.

'That is not the case.'

'What? I'm *not* one in a long line?' His affairs were common knowledge in the office. Everyone knew what he was like.

Blake shrugged. 'I admit I have had girlfriends. You already know that. But you are different.'

'And isn't that what you say to them all?' Her words came hot and fast, and she didn't care. Her whole world was crumbling about her feet. It had been bad enough when her father was alive, but now it was a thousand times worse. What she needed, what she really wanted, she suddenly realised, was his instant reassurance that this baby would bring them even closer together. She could do without the whole marriage thing, but she could not do without Blake. She knew now that she had fallen in love with him. He had made her feel wanted and special and free for the first time in her life, but his attitude now was causing her nothing but heartache.

'Such a question does not deserve an answer, Kara.' His jaw tensed, muscles working in his cheeks as he strove to keep a hold on his temper.

Perhaps it had been below the belt. But she was angry. Damned angry. She felt that it was only grudgingly that he was offering her the support she needed, for duty's sake. She and the baby were a mistake that Blake wanted cleared up. She would have to take his help, of course—she would be a fool not to—but, oh, how she longed for him to have offered it straight from his heart.

'The first thing we need to do is make a doctor's appointment to get your condition confirmed.'

'I don't need it to be confirmed, Blake.' She kept her eyes steady on his, challenging him.

'But you still need to see a doctor. I wish to take care of you.'

He wished! Kara wished that she had never gone to Italy with him. It was turning out to be the biggest mistake she had ever made! What a fool to fall in love with her boss—a man who clearly had a heart of stone. It was the worst thing she had ever done. But he was throwing her a lifeline, and she would be an even bigger fool to turn it down. 'Very well,' she answered reluctantly.

'Do you want to take some time off work?'

He was being so damned practical! All she wanted was his love! But that was an empty dream now. It would never happen. He was doing what he was doing because it was the right thing. 'I would appreciate a few days. My mother's not well. She's been in hospital.' She would love to tell him the reason why, but their relationship was clearly over. She would never share those secrets with Blake now.

'Why didn't you say?' he asked at once, his eyes sharp with surprise. 'You should not have come in under those circumstances.'

'And have you thinking that I was being a coward? Not a chance, Blake.' She saw the way his nostrils dilated, the flare in his eyes quickly disguised, and felt a grim sort of pleasure.

'I'll drive you home,' he said. 'You should be with her.'

Kara's chin tilted. 'There's no need. I have my car.'

It was not until she'd left his office that Kara realised how badly she needed to breathe. She drew in deep lungfuls of air, closing her eyes and holding on to the edge of her desk as she felt her world swing on its axis. She did not see Blake follow her. Knew nothing until she felt an arm about her waist, her head pulled down on his shoulder.

'I'm taking you home,' he said firmly. 'No arguments. You're in no fit state to get behind the wheel.'

Thanks to you, she thought, wanting to pull free but unable to stop herself responding to his touch. Crazily, in spite of everything, she wanted to relax and let him take care of her. She wanted his strength to be her strength. It would be so easy. And yet so dangerous!

She sat silently beside him in the back of the car, hardly conscious of him issuing instructions to his driver. It was not until they reached her house, when Blake jumped out and made to walk up the path, that she spoke. 'There's no need for you to see me in. I'm—'

'I believe there is,' he said sharply. 'Besides, I'd like to see your mother. To a degree I feel at fault. If there is anything I can do to help, then—'

'We don't need your help, Blake,' she said with fierce determination, wanting to tell him the whole truth, confess the desperate situation they were in, but knowing it would do her no good. 'All we want—all I want is to get on with my life.'

Blake's eyes sparked determination. 'You're forgetting that I am a part of your life now.'

And trying to stop Blake when he had set his mind on something was like trying to hold a London double-decker bus up in the air single-handedly.

Lynne's face was a picture when Blake followed Kara into the house. 'Mrs Redman,' he said immediately. 'Kara tells me you've been in hospital. I trust you're feeling better?'

Kara saw the surprise on her mother's face and spoke quickly. 'Blake says that I can take a few days off to look after you. Isn't that good of him?'

Her parent looked from her to Blake and then back again. 'Yes, it is. Thank you, Blake.' But her words were stilted, and Kara knew that she did not mean them.

'It is my pleasure,' he answered.

'I will take the rest of this week off, if that's all right,' said Kara quickly, anxious to get rid of him, out of her house and her life, so she could start the difficult task of moving on and getting over him—as if that would ever be possible! 'But I will be at my desk first thing on Monday morning.'

Kara did not realise quite how tense she was until he had left, then she sank down on a chair and closed her eyes. But she soon snapped them open again when her mother spoke.

'What have you told him?'

'Nothing. Just that you've been in hospital. He didn't ask why and I didn't volunteer anything. You don't really think I'd tell him about our money troubles?'

Lynne closed her eyes, and she was silent for so long that Kara began to feel worried. 'Mum?'

'Blake's a good man, you know,' Lynne said, looking at her daughter now.

Kara sighed. 'I know. He's promised to help, but I have a feeling that deep down inside he hates me now. I just know it. Me and this baby are going to be a complication in his life and he doesn't like it. Oh, Mum, everything was going so well between us. I really thought my whole life was going to change. I've been such a fool.'

'You have been no such thing, Kara,' said Lynne, pulling her daughter into her arms. 'Blake just needs time to get used to the idea of the baby.'

During the week that followed Kara tried to push Blake out of her mind—except that it was virtually impossible. The practical half of her hated him. The other half, the sentimental half, grieved that she might never see him again, might never be held in his arms or share his bed again. He had taught her what love was all about and she had embraced it with both arms—and now they were empty, and destined to remain that way.

The only person she would have to love would be her baby. Blake's baby! The baby he didn't want! He was going to take care of her welfare during her pregnancy, and hopefully later he would want to play a part in the baby's life. But as far as she could see it would only be duty that kept him close. Commitment and marriage were anathema to him.

She'd half expected him to pay them a visit, or at least telephone to say that he had made her an appointment with a doctor, but she heard nothing. A whole week of nothing. And although her mother's health improved, her own temper did not.

It was not until she arrived for work on Monday morning that Kara found out why he had not been in touch—and her heartbeat accelerated to such a degree that she felt sure it was not good for her.

Blake had been involved in a car accident a week earlier. He hadn't been in the office since, and was now convalescing at home.

*A week ago!* The day he had left her house!

Kara's heart went cold. Why hadn't he told her? Wasn't he well enough? Or did he think she had worries enough? Maybe she ought to go and see him? Or telephone him at least?

She was kept busy all day, but as soon as she got home she rang him. 'Blake, it's Kara. I've heard about your accident. Why didn't you let me know?'

A few seconds went by before he spoke. A few worrying seconds. Was she doing the wrong thing, phoning him? Did Blake want nothing more to do with her now? Was that why he hadn't told her about his accident?

'I thought you had enough to contend with.'

Had he perhaps thought she wouldn't care? Even hearing the sound of his voice sent a tingle through her body. 'How are you?'

'Recovering.'

'Can I come and see you? No one seems to know exactly what your injuries are.'

There was a long pause before he answered. And when he did speak his voice was oddly quiet. 'I'd like that.'

'I'll be there straight away—if that's OK?' It seemed important to her that she should not wait. Though if she had stopped to ask herself why she would not have been able to give an answer. She ought not to care. But she did. She loved Blake despite everything, and she was concerned for him—she wanted to see for herself what his injuries were.

'Only if you let me send my driver for you. I'm not sure your car will make the journey here and back.'

Kara smiled into the phone. Her car was so old that it was a wonder it hadn't given up the ghost a long time ago.

When she arrived at Blake's house she was let in by his housekeeper. 'I'm warning you, Kara, he is not a good patient—he's very grouchy. You'll find him in his study. His injuries haven't stopped him playing with his computer.'

Playing! What Kara saw on the screen as she entered the room was columns of figures. He was working.

Naturally. She might have known it would take a lot to keep Blake away from his work.

The moment she looked at him, the moment her eyes met his, Kara knew that it had been a mistake to come. No matter how she tried, she could not hate him. The love inside her flowed through her limbs like warm honey. All she wanted to do was go to him and feel his arms around her. She wanted back the man she had fallen in love with in Italy.

'What happened, Blake?' she asked quietly, walking towards him. Apart from some marks on his face she could see no other sign of injury.

'I'm sure you don't really want to know.'

'Of course I do,' she said at once. 'I wouldn't be here otherwise.'

Blake shook his head and closed his eyes, as if reliving the scene. 'It was the night I last saw you. I couldn't sleep. So I decided to take the car out—anywhere. I didn't care. I drove too fast. But it was the drunken idiots in the other car who caused the accident. A head-on collision. I was lucky. I have five broken ribs as well as some pretty bad bruises.'

'Five?' she asked in horror. 'Oh, Blake!' Instinct made her go to him and rest her hand across his shoulder. She bowed her face to his and touched her lips to his cheek. 'I'm sorry—so sorry.'

'It was not your fault,' he growled.

Kara felt that it was. 'If you hadn't been angry at me then you wouldn't have driven so fast.'

'Come here.' He urged her down on his lap, his mouth seeking hers, and Kara did not have the strength to refuse him. Her blood burned hot and strong as his kiss deepened, and every thought that it was wrong to be allowing this after the way he had reacted to her pregnancy disappeared.

All she wanted was his kisses—his hot, hungry kisses. They did more than breathe life into her. They consumed her, made her totally his. Everything else was forgotten. This was the Blake she had known in Italy—the Blake who had taught her the pleasures of the flesh and the intimacy of loving someone.

She heard the soft noises emanating from the back of her throat, felt her body melt against him, and felt too the way he was losing hold. It seemed that his pain was forgotten as he devoured her mouth; all he wanted was to kiss her. And this was what she wanted too. She had missed the passion between them, the sensations that warmed and thrilled her, the knowledge that Blake found her desirable.

Without even realising what she was doing Kara twisted around so that she was straddling his legs, careful not to press against his chest. The look in his eyes was one she remembered well: the glazed look of a man filled with raw need over which he had no control.

She too felt as though she was drowning…swimming against a current too strong to fight. *I love you, Blake.* The words filled her head but she did not speak them—knew that she dared not. Instead she touched her hands to the sides of his face and this time she kissed him, allowing her tongue to explore the shape of his lips, the moist heat inside his mouth, finally touching her tongue to his.

Blake groaned, and his hands came behind her head so that he could take control. His kisses were fierce and deadly, filling her with an emotion that was almost too painful to bear. She needed to remember that this was pure sex. Nothing more. It did not mean that their relationship was back on.

'Kara!' He breathed her name. 'Tell me I have been a fool to ever suspect you.'

Hope filled her. 'You are a fool!' she replied immediately.

'I want to make love to you, Kara, but my ribs—they hurt too much.'

'Then *I* will make love to *you*,' she said.

Her heart beat fast as she slid to her knees and slowly unzipped him, releasing the fastening on his waistband and tugging his trousers down over his hips. His boxers followed, and she almost got up and ran when she saw how hard and ready he was for her.

But she couldn't change her mind now. She had gone too far. And when she began to drop tiny kisses along his thighs, heading towards her target, his hands came down to touch her head, his fingers threading through her hair, holding her so tightly that she could not move even if she wanted to.

She chanced a glance at him and saw that his head had fallen back and his eyes were closed. He looked as though he was already in heaven. Sensing her looking at him, he lifted his lids and met her gaze head-on. 'Don't stop,' he groaned, his eyes glazed with pure emotion.

He had taught her how to pleasure him like this and Kara took her time, exulting in the noises he made, in his involuntary movements. She felt herself growing closer to her own orgasm, and was afraid it might happen before Blake reached his. But it didn't, and when he finally let go it was as though the earth had shifted beneath her feet too.

She stayed where she was, silent and fulfilled, while Blake's hands held her head. It was a deep moment of togetherness.

Blake was not used to admitting that he was ever wrong. But he had been wrong even suspecting for one second that Kara would look at another man. If there was someone else she would not have been able to do what she had just done. She would not even have come here. She cared. It had been a gesture of love.

Love! The forbidden word.

Even before today, before she had arrived and self-lessly put his needs before her own, he had berated himself. He had been judge and jury without all the facts, without any real evidence. It would be ungentlemanly of him now not to give her the benefit of the doubt.

'I am sorry I misjudged you. I should have known that—'

Kara closed his lips with her finger. 'Please, say no more. Don't spoil the moment.'

In response he took the tips of her fingers into his mouth. 'I've been a complete swine. Do you forgive me?'

'Of course.'

'Then will you stay a while and keep me company?'

Kara nodded.

'I do not deserve you, Kara,' Blake said, before capturing her head and kissing her.

In the days that followed Blake surprised himself by feeling more content than he ever had in his life. He was

even beginning to think that against his better judgement he had fallen in love again—with Kara. His initial
reservations about becoming a father were fading into
the background.

And when he went with her to the obstetrician there
was no doubt in his mind that he wanted to be a permanent part of their child's life. He wanted to watch him
grow every step of the way. He would play with him in
a way his father never had.

And he wanted Kara beside him.

He was going to ask her to marry him.

# CHAPTER TEN

KARA could not wait to get home and tell her mother how her appointment with the obstetrician had gone—how excited Blake had seemed. But the instant she walked into the house and saw her mother's pale, worried face, the way that she was shaking uncontrollably, everything else went out of her head.

She crossed the room in seconds, her heart pounding. 'What's the matter?' Her mother's skin looked almost grey, and Kara feared that she was about to suffer a heart attack. 'I'll call the doctor.'

Her hand went towards the phone but her mother stopped her. 'He's been here.'

'Again?' She knew very well who her mother meant, and her already fast heartbeat increased. 'Why? What does he want now?' His visits were becoming far too frequent for Kara's peace of mind, and she was afraid that all the worry would affect her baby.

Lynne pulled a face. 'He's seen Blake coming and going more often lately. He knows he's rich. He's upping the payments again.'

When her mother mentioned by how much Kara gasped. 'But that's more than I earn. He can't do that.

What did you tell him?' She feared that their nightmare was never going to end.

'That our circumstances haven't changed. Not that he believed me.'

'You shouldn't have opened the door to him.'

'I didn't know it was him,' said Lynne, her eyes pained. 'I thought it was you and that you'd forgotten your keys. He shouldered his way in, Kara. I was terrified!'

'We need to call the police,' said Kara at once. 'He can't do this. It's gone too far.'

'The police can't do anything, Kara,' her mother said, fear evident in her voice. 'The contract he has is legal, remember? He'll deny using threats against us and it will be our word against his. But there might be a solution,' she added, lifting her brows and looking at her hopefully. 'You could ask Blake to lend us the money so we can be rid of him once and for all.'

'Ask Blake?' Kara closed her eyes and shook her head. Getting pregnant by him was embarrassing enough. To ask for money to solve their personal problems would be a step too far.

'I feel so foolish for having let it get this far. And I hate that I have involved you. But I do not think my heart can stand much more.'

Tears filled Lynne's eyes now, and Kara held her mother close. To ask Blake would be painful and humiliating in the extreme. And yet her mother was right. He was in a position to help. And then the loan shark wouldn't be on their backs all the time, demanding payment. It would be a fair deal. They would know exactly where they stood. But it was still an awful lot to ask of him. He'd only just got over the shock of the baby.

'You could tell him that it's to buy stuff for the baby,' said her parent. 'Men have no idea how much these things cost, so I'm sure he won't ask questions.'

The amount she needed to borrow would buy an awful lot of baby things, thought Kara. But because her parent still looked pale and fragile, her breathing difficult, as though she was indeed on the verge of a heart attack, Kara finally reluctantly nodded. 'Very well. I'll ask him.'

Her mother's relief was instant and some of the colour returned to her face. 'You're a good girl, Kara, and I'm sorry to have to burden you with this.'

It was going to be the hardest thing she had ever had to do. Telling Blake that she was pregnant would be nothing compared to this.

When she went to work the next morning she went straight into Blake's office. It was no good sitting thinking about it. She had to ask him immediately.

'What's wrong?' His grey eyes scanned her face. 'You look pale. Are you not feeling well? If that's the case you shouldn't have come to work.'

He looked so concerned, so very concerned, that Kara almost backed out. How could she do this? But seeing her mother's pale and anxious face in her mind's eye was a warning that she *had* to go through with it.

'I'm all right,' she insisted. 'It's just that I need to ask you a favour—a very big one.' Her heart raced, thumping so hard that it felt as if it was trying to burst out of her chest. Perspiration gathered under her arms, and her whole body was pulsing with anxiety.

'Ask away,' he said. 'Is it something to do with your mother? I thought she didn't look very well the last time I saw her.'

'I—I need some money, Blake,' she said, not answering his question. 'I wouldn't ask if it wasn't necessary.' She swallowed the lump that had gathered in her throat and forced herself to look at him. She didn't want Blake guessing how hard this was for her. She had lain awake all night worrying. But her mother's health was at stake here. She was left with no choice. It was either asking Blake to help or ending up losing her home or her mother—possibly both.

'But of course. What was I thinking? You need to buy things for the baby.'

Relief flooded her that she did not have to actually lie. 'You've no idea how much they cost these days.' How could she sound so normal when every nerve tingled with fear? When the blood pumped hotly and uncontrollably around her body? Never in her life had she done anything like this, and she hoped she never had to do so again. Fear froze her limbs and dried her mouth, and she was sure he must see how uneasy she was.

'I will open a bank account for you at once. Shall we say five thousand pounds?'

Kara closed her eyes. How could she tell him that that was not enough? That she wanted five times that amount? It was difficult to comprehend how the sum her father had initially borrowed in her mother's name had grown to that amount. But it had. Interest had piled on top of interest, and now they were facing dire consequences if it was not repaid. There was no one else she could turn to except Blake.

When his finger lifted her chin she shuddered, opening her eyes, feeling her throat close up as she stared into the darkness of his gaze. His brow was furrowed but he spoke softly. 'What is wrong, my beautiful Kara?'

'It's not enough,' she whispered.

She felt the way his body grew tense, even though his expression did not change. 'Not enough? Pray tell me what you are going to buy for this baby of ours?'

The inflection in his voice worried her. 'There are lots of things,' she said hesitantly. 'A pram, a cot, a pushchair, clothes—all sorts. I need to turn a room into a nursery, so there'll have to be new furniture. I'll need about twenty-five thousand pounds.' Her heart was thumping so loud she feared it would jump out of her chest.

He looked long and hard into her eyes, making Kara wish herself a thousand miles away. Never in her life had she felt as embarrassed and as uncomfortable as she did at this moment. She had promised her mother, though, and she had to go through with it.

'And do you really think I believe that's how much things for a baby costs?' he asked, his voice taking on an even harder edge. 'I would suggest—' his fingers dug deeply into her forearms, bruising, hurting, but she did not flinch '—that this is for your own personal gain. Am I right?'

His eyes burned into her, and Kara felt her insides begin to shrivel, but she could not let her parent down. 'You may think what you like, Blake, but I am not in the habit of begging for money without just cause.'

Blake hated the way he was thinking, but it very much looked as though Kara had had a taste of the high life and found that she liked it—that she preferred it to the simple life she led with her mother, and was now trying to cash in on it. He did not know how much it cost to prepare for a baby, but he was damn sure it wasn't nearly as much as Kara was asking. It was not that he minded giving her money for his unborn child, but he did not like being taken for a fool.

Unbidden memories of Melanie flashed into his mind. Melanie trying to pass off another man's child as his. Melanie wanting a share of his wealth. And once the idea was implanted he could not get rid of it. He could not ignore the fact that he had seen Kara on her doorstep in the arms of another man.

He had found it difficult to accept her story that he was a friend of her mother's—the woman lived a solitary lifestyle. He had been deeply suspicious at the time, but had nevertheless given her the benefit of the doubt. Even apologising for questioning her.

It hurt to think that he had been so wrong. He truly had thought Kara was different. Damn it, he had been going to ask her to marry him. She had got beneath his skin in a way he had never expected—or even wanted.

And now this! What was it about him that made women think he was an easy target? The Melanie incident had made him wary, and he had stuck to his guns all these years. So why had he let his guard down now? Why had he let Kara creep into his life and into his heart?

She was looking at him now as though she wished that she had never asked. As well she might! Every vestige of colour had left her face. He wanted to tell her to go, to get out of his life. His disappointment was a hard and bitter pill to swallow.

'And that cause would be…?' he asked grimly, hoping against hope that he had once again jumped to the wrong conclusion.

'I can't tell you Blake.' Kara hung her head, her devastating shame complete.

'You cannot? Or you do not want to?' He let his eyes rest on her face for several long seconds, and when there was no answer, when she refused to look him in the eye, when she looked miserably down at her feet instead, he said grimly, 'Let me tell you what *I* think, Kara. I think you are trying to play me for a fool. I think you are using the baby you are carrying for financial gain. I think you are trying to trick me as Melanie once tried, and—'

'How dare you?' Fire immediately lit Kara's eyes, and she flashed them into his face. 'I would *never* do a thing like that. This *is* your baby and you'd better believe it. Forget about the money, Blake. I can see that it was a mistake asking for your help.'

He looked into her face, seeing a mixture of both anger and despair, and for some reason it created deep unease inside him. What he should be doing was kicking her out of his life. Instead he found himself making a proposition.

'I *will* give you the money—but on one condition. You move in with me permanently.' He might be crazy suggesting it, but he could not easily dismiss her. Despite his disappointment that she had tried to make money out of this situation, she had got beneath his skin in a way none of the others had. Blake was convinced there was something else going on here, and he was determined to get to the bottom of it. Why did she want so much money? There was only one way to find out, and that was to keep her as close to him as possible.

'Move in with you?' For just a moment hope bloomed in Kara's chest. Hadn't she wanted this all along? To live with Blake? To have a future with him? But as she looked at the coldness in his eyes now she saw that he was not offering her a future. He was offering her a prison. He would own her in return for the money. Would men always be in control of her life? First her father, then the loan shark and now Blake. If she accepted Blake's offer of the money she might be free of one shackle around her neck, but she would simply be replacing it with another one. She knew what her answer must be. 'I can't do that, Blake.'

Blake thought for a moment. Her answer had confused him. If she moved in with him then she would be given exactly the kind of lifestyle she wanted—one far removed from the life she had now. So why was she turning his offer down? Did she need the money for another purpose than funding her lifestyle? What was she keeping from him?

He couldn't help wondering whether her mother was in on the act too. The moment the thought entered his mind he put it into words. 'Does your mother know about this request for money? Is she a part of this *let's see what we can get out of Blake* plan?' And the way Kara flinched, the way she averted her eyes, looking anywhere but at him, the way hot colour came rushing back into her face, told him exactly what he wanted to know.

Disappointment flooded him in cruel waves. He felt

as though someone had taken a knife to his heart and sliced it in two. The once innocent Kara, his PA who had served him in a quietly efficient way, had turned into a carbon copy of every other woman he had dated.

If it wasn't for the fact that she was carrying his baby he would send her packing right here and now. He might be many things but he wasn't cruel enough to do that. He would tell her, though, that she would not get a penny more out of him than was necessary for the upbringing of his child—not until he found out exactly why she wanted so much money.

'I'm sorry I asked.' Kara had never felt so humiliated in her life. The look in Blake's eyes made her want to turn and run and never see him again. She had known all along that it would be a bad idea asking him for money, but foolishly she had never expected it to turn out like this. She had naively hoped that Blake would simply hand over the cash, no questions asked. But this was Blake Benedict, businessman extraordinaire! Once again Kara realised how badly she had misjudged his feelings towards her.

'And I am sorry you asked too,' he said, the quietness in his voice more deadly than when he had raised it. 'Shall we start work?'

Kara would have liked nothing more than to turn around and run. She had demeaned herself for nothing. She wanted to walk out of the office and never see Blake again. But that would mean losing her job, and she could ill afford that—especially now. She was not sure, though, how she was going to get through the rest of the day. At least it was Friday, so she would have the weekend to come to terms with her humiliation.

The atmosphere between them was decidedly icy, and it was a relief when Blake was called away early.

When she got home and told her mother that he had refused to lend them the money, deliberately omitting the fact that he had suggested she move in with him, Lynne broke down in tears. 'What are we going to do now?'

Fearing for her parent's health, Kara put her arms around her and held her close. 'We're going to forget about it for the time being. I'll make us a nice cup of tea, and we'll watch TV and push Blake and the loan shark and everyone else right out of our minds.'

It was easier said than done, but at least Lynne calmed down, and on Saturday Kara suggested some retail therapy. 'Even if we only window shop,' she added, 'it will do you good to get out of the house.'

They had a good day—Kara even managed to forget about Blake. She had spent the whole night tossing and turning, reliving her humiliation at his expense. Deep down inside she knew she couldn't blame him for refusing her the money, since she hadn't told him the truth about what it was for. It was ridiculous to have expected him to believe that it was all for the baby.

But her mother's sanity meant more to her than anything else. Lynne was a very private woman who kept herself very much to herself. She had always hidden from her neighbours the way her husband treated both her and her daughter, and over the years they had learned not to ask questions.

And so Kara felt that it was only right that she respect her mother's privacy, even though it had made it hard asking Blake for help. She could still feel the deep humiliation. She had wanted to turn tail and run and never see him again. What they would do when she finally had to leave work because of the baby Kara did not know—how would she ever repay the debt then? But she refused to think about it. Her main concern was her mother, and for her sake she needed to keep bright and cheerful.

Except 'bright and cheerful' flew out of the window when the loan shark decided to pay them yet another visit. They'd had a good day at the shops, even buying only the very cheapest of baby clothes had lifted their spirits and they had been in a good mood when they arrived home.

It was early evening when the doorbell rang, and unsuspectingly Kara went to open the door—only to be confronted by the man who held a tight grip over their lives. Quickly Kara stepped outside and closed the door behind her, so that her mother would not know who stood there.

'Do you have the money?' he growled.

'If you mean can I give you any more than we are already doing, then the answer is no,' said Kara bravely, even though inside she was quaking with fear. She knew that this man was not averse to using force to get what he wanted. 'And if you do not stop harassing us I shall call the police.'

Her brave words had no effect. His top lip rose scornfully, his narrow eyes ugly and condemning. 'This is a legitimate loan. There is nothing they can do.'

'But you cannot keep upping the payments or threatening us in this way.' She felt that her protest was in vain, but she had to try something. 'We can't pay you money we haven't got.'

'You're forgetting the rich boyfriend,' he jeered, his breath smelling of tobacco and something as unpleasant as the man himself. 'Don't think I haven't seen you with him. What I'm asking for would be a pittance in his eyes. Ask him for it.'

'I can't do that,' she declared, surprised to hear her voice still coming out strong and steady when all hell was still breaking out in her body. Her heart was thumping like a mad thing and every pulse stampeded. 'I refuse to involve someone else in your fraud. The only people I'm prepared to go to are the police.'

Strong hands gripped her shoulders and he thrust his face up close. 'I want my money.'

And she wanted him to leave her alone. She pushed as hard as she could against his chest and he let her go—but not before he had made a further threat. 'I'll come back every day until I get what I want. You'd better believe it.'

'And if you do that I will definitely go to the police. *You'd* better believe *that*.'

Not until the door was safely shut behind her did Kara feel safe. She leaned back against it, breathing deeply, forcing herself to calm down before she faced her mother again.

# CHAPTER ELEVEN

A SLEEPLESS night had left Blake tired and out of sorts. He could not shut Kara out of his mind. Deep down inside he did not want to believe that she was capable of feathering her own nest at his expense. He couldn't help wondering whether there was some other reason why she had asked him for such a large amount of money. But what? He paid her a good wage, she and her mother lived comfortably, so why the need for more? It was puzzling in the extreme.

When Kara had changed from a mouse into a beautiful woman she had delighted him. She had tugged at a corner of his heart. She had almost made it her own. Almost! Thank goodness he hadn't got to the point of asking her to marry him. Wouldn't that have been a grave error of judgement? He'd thought he had learned his lesson when Melanie deceived him. Now he realised that he was still vulnerable. And vulnerability meant mistakes.

Over and over he asked himself the question whether he knew Kara at all. Whether he had ever really got to know her. Discovering her avaricious side was not a pleasant thing. It had angered and dismayed him. Nevertheless he felt disquiet about the way he had handled the situation. Maybe he should go and see her, talk to her in her own surroundings, try to find out exactly why she wanted so much money.

He had been due to go out to dinner with a banker friend, but at the last minute he cancelled, deciding that a visit to Kara was more important. If he left it until tomorrow he would have another night without sleep. He needed to sort this matter out once and for all.

Even so he felt an unexpected quickening of his senses as he neared her house. Whatever he might think of Kara now, there was no getting away from the fact that she was expecting his baby. It was the hardest thing he had ever had to accept—and it still gave him night-mares. He had never seen himself as a family man—never wanted to be a family man. Which was why he found it hard to believe that it was happening to him now.

Because he did not want her to see him coming, to give her time to decide what she would say to him, he parked in an adjoining street. But as he rounded the corner he could not believe what he saw. Kara in the arms of that man again!

His blood began to boil—until he looked more closely and saw that this was no cosy clinch, as he had first imagined. The man was hostile. It looked as though he was actually threatening Kara!

Blake hastened his step, but before he got close the man let her go, sliding into his car and driving swiftly away. And while he watched the man leave, making a mental note of his number plate, Kara disappeared inside the house.

He wasn't going to let this go, though. And he wasn't

going to be satisfied until Kara told him exactly what was going on. He strode along the street and banged on the door. He wasn't surprised when no one opened it. She was probably scared that the man, whoever he was, had returned.

So he phoned her. 'Kara, it's me. I'm outside. Let me in.'

A moment's silence before she spoke. 'What are you doing here?' she asked, and he thought he heard tears in her voice.

'I need to speak to you.'

'I don't want to speak to you. Go away.'

'I'm going nowhere,' he declared firmly. 'Open the door, Kara, before I break it down.' He wouldn't have done that, of course, but it worked. He heard the key being turned in the lock, heard a bolt being withdrawn, and the thought that she needed to lock and bolt herself in turned his stomach. Who was this man, and why was he harassing her?

Kara's white and drawn face shocked him. He immediately wanted to pull her into his arms and tell her that whatever it was that was happening in her life he would take care of it. But he guessed that she wouldn't let him.

'What are you doing here?' she asked again.

'I came to talk about the money you asked me for. But it has begun to look as though there are far more important things to talk about. Who was that man?'

If Kara's face could have gone any paler then it did. Her eyelids closed for a few seconds, and when she clutched the wall for support he put an arm about her shoulders and led her into the sitting room, where her mother also looked as though she was on the verge of collapse.

Once Kara was seated he sat down himself, looking from her to her mother and back again. 'Are you going to answer my question?'

Kara closed her eyes for a moment before looking at her mother. 'Can we have a little privacy, please?'

'Kara, are you sure this is for the best?'

'Mum, we can't go on like this any longer. I have the baby to think of now, and things are only going to get harder for us. I have to tell Blake.'

Lynne actually looked relieved as she nodded and left the room.

Once they were alone Kara told Blake the whole story—about the loan her father had taken out in her mother's name, about the payments constantly rising. 'It's a never-ending nightmare,' she added, once she had finished.

'And this is why you wanted all that money?'

She nodded, her arms folded across her chest, her eyes sadder than he had ever seen them.

'Why didn't you tell me before, Kara? I could have sorted all this mess out for you!'

'Because my mother did not want anyone to know,' she answered with a wry twist to her lips. 'It's very shameful to have been duped by the man she once loved, the man she married. She would have been deeply embarrassed. She's not the sort of person to share her problems with strangers.'

Blake wanted to take her into his arms and comfort her, but he felt that was not the right thing to do considering the way he had spoken to her yesterday. She would probably push him away, and he did not want that.

His deepest concern at the moment was the degenerate who was doing this to them. Anger had risen in him as she spoke—anger that any man could prey on two helpless females the way this man did. He played on their fear, driven by greed, uncaring that he was making their lives a living hell. And they probably weren't the only people he was harassing.

Neither had he helped by parking his Bentley outside their house! In fact he was the one who had exacerbated their problem. He curled his fingers into his palms. 'Do you know where this guy lives?'

Kara shook her head, at the same time looking quite alarmed. 'You're not thinking of confronting him?'

'Someone has to,' he growled. 'He cannot be allowed to get away with this. What he is doing is unlawful.'

'It doesn't stop him.'

'Of course not. There are plenty of con men like him around. But they usually get their just desserts in the end. He'll come unstuck—you'll see. Meantime, I definitely think you should come and live with me. You *and* your mother. He'll soon give up when he realises that you no longer live here.'

'It's not the answer,' said Kara, although her heartbeats had hastened at the thought. The loan shark would find them wherever they were. The only way they would get this man off their backs was to pay him in full the amount he claimed they owed.

'I'm not giving you a choice.' His grey eyes were relentless on hers. 'You will be safe, both you and your mother, and our baby. I promise you that. I'm not sure that all this stress is good for you or the little one.'

It wasn't good for them, Kara knew that. But she knew that Blake was only offering her his home in order to keep the baby safe and keep her under his spell. The other option was staying here and living with the nightmare of the loan shark everyday.

She had her mother to think of too. All this worry was not doing her health any good. She deserved better. She had put up with so much during her life that it would not be fair to put her through any more. Not when Blake had offered them a lifeline.

'I don't seem to have much choice, do I?' she asked quietly, unaware that her eyes reflected her sorrow.

'Not if you know what's best for you. For you both.'

Kara drew in a long, ragged breath, and released it on a sigh.

'So you agree? You'll move in with me?'

She nodded. 'I'll tell my mother.' She didn't dare look him in the eye. In a way he was saving their lives, but she was not happy about it.

Her mother, though, was both delighted and overwhelmed. 'Thank you, Blake,' she kept saying. 'Thank you, Blake. You have no idea how much this means to me.'

'I think I do,' he answered gruffly. 'What I want you both to do is pack up whatever you'll need for the time being, and I'll organise transport for the rest tomorrow.'

Everything was moving so fast that Kara felt dizzy. Blake took one look at her and ordered her to sit down.

In contrast her mother seemed to have taken on a new lease of life, bustling around, collecting everything she thought they would need.

And finally they left behind the house where so much misery had occurred. Kara knew that this was only going to be an interim period in her life, but she could not help feeling relief. Not that she expected to be entirely happy living with Blake. The closeness they had once shared was gone, and there was no way she could go on living with him permanently. He wouldn't want that either, she felt certain. He was doing his Good Samaritan act but it was only a temporary solution to their problems, and he was really only doing it to ensure his baby was safe.

Her mother, though, was in seventh heaven. 'Whoever would have thought we'd end up living somewhere like this?' she asked. 'Blake's a good man, Kara.'

'It's not permanent, Mum,' said Kara, unaware that there was a sharp edge to her voice. 'I don't want to be beholden to him.'

Lynne frowned. 'How can you be beholden when you're expecting his baby?'

'You're forgetting we're only just about friends. There's nothing between us any more.' Except her heart refused to believe it. It went on the rampage every time he was near. But there was nothing she could do but ignore it—pretend it wasn't happening. The honeymoon period was over. Their relationship was held together by the baby and nothing more.

'Are you sure, Kara?'

'Of course I'm sure. And we're not going to stay here any longer than necessary.'

Lynne's voice was filled with alarm when she spoke. 'We're safe here, Kara. Can't you see that? Safe for the first time in our lives.'

'Yes, but— Well, we'll see,' she accepted reluctantly. She was thinking of herself rather than her mother, which was incredibly selfish. But living with Blake was not her idea of fun.

Later that evening when her mother had gone to bed early, Blake invited Kara to join him for a drink.

'If you make it a hot chocolate,' she said.

A single brow rose. 'I actually like hot chocolate. Mrs Beauman will be delighted. She thinks I drink too much alcohol.'

Such mundane conversation, when Kara guessed he would much prefer to talk about their circumstances. 'My mother really appreciates what you are doing for us,' she said. 'It's as though a whole weight has been lifted from her shoulders.'

Blake nodded. 'I can well imagine it. There was no way I could allow you to go on living there, a perfect target for that unscrupulous money-lender. Why didn't you tell me about him before, Kara?'

'How could I?' she asked. 'He's the biggest embarrassment of our lives. We both felt so ashamed, and we wanted no one to know.'

'As though it was your fault?' he asked with surprising understanding. 'When in fact it was that useless man of a father who got you into this mess?'

Kara closed her eyes. The only good part of her whole life had been the time she'd spent in Italy. Only then had she been able to forget her problems. She'd been the happiest she had ever been. Except that the pleasure she had experienced then had now given way to a whole new set of problems. Unconsciously she put a hand on her stomach.

Blake's eyes narrowed. 'Are you all right, Kara? All this upset cannot be very good for your—for *our* baby.'

'I'm OK,' she said. 'A touch weary, that's all.'

'And is the little man all right?'

Kara could not help but smile. 'He—or maybe *she*,' she corrected, 'is doing fine.'

When his housekeeper came in, setting a tray down on the table beside them, she was still resting her hand on her stomach.

Mrs Beauman's smile was warm and welcoming. 'It's good to see you again, Kara. I hope you and your mother will be very comfortable here. You must tell me if there is anything that you need.'

'I will,' promised Kara.

Their hot chocolate was in a Thermos jug, with two china mugs on the side. Blake leaned forward and filled their mugs.

Kara waited until he had finished before saying, 'Does Mrs Beauman know about the baby?'

Blake shook his head. 'I saw no reason to tell her.'

Because he was ashamed? Because this was an interim period in his life? Kara had no idea what the future held. Of one thing she was certain: she could not go back to their house again. They would need to find somewhere else to live—somewhere they would never be found by the obnoxious man who was harassing them. Maybe even move to a different part of the country.

She had always fancied living in Scotland. That

would be a good place. Far enough away to forget her troubles. But would her mother like it up there? And how would they manage when they had no money?

'Do you still want me to carry on working for you?' she asked. 'Because I would really like to do so.' She did not tell him that it was to try and build up her bank balance and fund their move.

Blake smiled—one of those smiles that turned her heart over and sent a zillion sensations through her body, darting along nerves and arteries, looking for escape but finding none. 'Nothing would please me more, Kara. I will miss you when you stop work to have the baby. You're the best PA any man could ever wish for. It will be hard finding your successor.'

His best PA! Was that all she meant to him? Her pleasure died. He couldn't have made it any plainer that their affair was over, that the only reason they would stay in touch was because of the baby.

She picked up her mug of chocolate and cradled it between her hands, and as silence settled between them she wondered whether she was jumping to the wrong conclusion. Blake had been talking about work, not their personal life.

It was her hormones. They were all over the place. She did not know what to think any more. So much had happened today that all she longed for now was sleep. Peaceful, refreshing sleep. It would be the first night in a long time that their money worries hadn't troubled her.

'Would you mind very much if I went to bed?' she asked as soon as she had finished her drink. She had sipped it so quickly that her mouth stung. 'It's been quite a day and I'm tired.'

'But of course,' he said at once, standing up.

He held out his hands and she had no option but to take them. And when he had pulled her to her feet he pressed a kiss to her brow. 'Sleep well, Kara.'

And that was it. No arms around her, no holding her close, no mouth-to-mouth contact. It was the sort of kiss you'd give a friend, but not a lover. She might as well get used to the idea that their situation had changed. That Blake no longer wanted her in his bed. She was ultimately going to be the mother of his child, and he would see her all right, but as for anything else...

# CHAPTER TWELVE

BLAKE had tried to appear calm and in control for Kara's sake, but inside he was seething that any man could stoop so low as to put the fear of hell into two defenceless women. Kara was even more vulnerable at the moment. He had seen how distraught she was, how terrified, and the thing that hurt most was that *he* had had a part to play in it.

He had not stood by her when she came to him for help. He had been brutally angry instead, believing the very worst of her. And although she was grateful to him for rescuing them he sensed that she had lost all faith in him in every other respect. He was almost afraid to touch her, in case she brushed him away. Rejection was not something he could handle. The fact was that whatever had been growing between them was gone. Ruined by his own stupidity.

He bowed his head in his hands, wondering how he could go on working with her, having her live in his house, without ever being able to touch or kiss her. Or bed her. It was a fate too hard to contemplate.

But first things first. He needed to sort out the villain who had been blighting their lives.

* * *

It did not take him long to discover who he was and where he lived, and on Monday evening after work, after he had taken Kara home and knew that she was safe, he drove to the man's house.

A very fine house. Bought, decided Blake, feeling renewed anger rise in his throat, on the proceeds of his underhand, heartless treatment of innocent people. A woman answered the door—an over-made-up blonde, wearing a low-cut blouse and a tight black skirt. 'Yes?'

'I've come to see Mr Draydon.'

'And who shall I say is calling?'

'Benedict. Blake Benedict. And tell him I'm in a hurry.'

When she moved to shut the door Blake put his foot in the way. It had been a telling action, suggesting that he wasn't the first caller to want to see this man.

Blake's grey eyes were hard when the loan shark finally appeared. He had taken so long that Blake was on the verge of entering the house and seeking him out.

'Yes?' Already he seemed on the defensive.

'Mr Draydon?'

'That's right. Do I know you?'

'Not until this moment. But I think you will remember me for some time to come.'

The man frowned.

'Do you get a great deal of satisfaction from frightening defenceless women? Extracting money from them that they can ill afford? I'm actually talking about one woman in particular, but it's my guess that she's not the only one you're trying to defraud.'

The man's eyes narrowed. 'I have no idea what you're talking about.'

'No? Does the name Mrs Redman ring a bell?'

Blake saw the flash of enlightenment in the man's eyes before he blanked it off. 'She is on my books, yes.'

'And for how long has she been "on your books"?'

'What are you getting at?' he asked with a sudden snarl. 'And what's it to do with you?'

'I am suggesting,' said Blake loudly and firmly, ignoring his question, 'that you are illegally demanding money from her and her daughter. I am suggesting that the loan has already been paid many times over. I have seen the original documents and I know how much you have taken from them. I'd now like to see your books.'

This was Blake on the warpath. Blake in his immaculate handmade suit and silk shirt. Blake with an expression so hard it might have been carved out of stone, causing the other man to lose some of his bravado.

'If you do not comply I shall not hesitate to go to the police,' he added, not for one second allowing his eyes to drop from the other man's.

'You'd better step in.' Mr Draydon's eyes darted this way and that, checking to see whether anyone was watching.

Perhaps, thought Blake, this was not the first time he had had some irate client turning up on his doorstep.

Inside, the house was as Blake had guessed it might be—filled with expensive furniture, clearly bought with his ill-gotten gains. But he made no comment, simply standing and waiting while the man went to find the necessary paperwork.

What Blake saw, what he read, the figures that leapt out of the pages at him, tripled his heart-rate. He wanted to lash out at the man. He wanted to make sure he never did this to anyone again. The sum of money that Kara and her mother had paid him over the years compared to the sum of the original loan—including interest—went far beyond anything he had expected.

This man was a crook—an out-and-out crook—and he deserved to be behind bars. But that was not why he was here. He was here for Kara's sake. Kara and her mother.

'I think you will agree,' he said, his tone so cold and hard that it would have flattened a lesser man, 'that their debt has been paid. Actually it has been paid many times over, but we will not go into that. Not now.' He eyed the man threateningly, suggesting that if he did not do as he asked then he would be in even deeper trouble. 'What I want you to do, Mr Draydon, is tear up those documents right here in front of me, and let's have an end to this. Otherwise, as I said, I'll get the police involved. This is nothing short of fraud.'

By the time Blake had finished speaking the man had begun to look very nervous. 'It is an unfortunate oversight on my part. I will give you the papers. You can do with them what you like.'

'How generous—considering how much you've conned out of the Redmans,' said Blake, his voice infused with such sarcasm that it was a wonder it didn't flatten the man. In front of him he tore each piece of paper into quarters, before stuffing them into his own pocket. 'Goodbye, Mr Draydon. I wish never to see you again.'

Once in his car, Blake sank back into the seat, closing his eyes for a few seconds, letting his breath out. How he had kept his hands to himself he did not know. The man should be in jail, not living the high life on his proceeds from a crooked business. But at least he had got him off Kara and her mother's back. That was the main thing. They could live safely now, without any fear of some rogue money-lender knocking on their door.

Except he did not want them to leave—at least he didn't want Kara to leave. He had done the unthinkable and fallen in love with her. Despite the vows he had made to himself, he had fallen in love!

The discovery rocked him.

Blake knew that Kara was loyal, trustworthy, kind— and she was carrying his baby! Not that that was the key factor. He would have loved her even if she wasn't pregnant. He had never met anyone like her, and he doubted he ever would again. The thing was, did he stand a chance with her? Or had he ruined everything when he had turned down her plea for help when she needed it most?

The house felt empty without Blake. Kara knew that she ought to feel relieved he had gone out, but instead she wandered from room to room, not knowing what to do with herself. Her mother was content to sit in her bedroom and watch television. She was used to smaller spaces, she said, and the size of the house overwhelmed her.

But Kara could not sit still. She paced up and down

like a caged animal, and when Blake finally returned she wanted to run to him, wrap her arms around him and feel his strength flow into her. But she did none of this. She simply looked at him and smiled weakly.

He had such gorgeous eyes, but she thought they looked tired at this moment and she wondered where he had been. Not that she dared ask. It was, after all, none of her business. It wasn't work-related, she knew that—because *she* always kept his diary up to date.

'Have you eaten?' she asked.

Blake shook his head. 'I'm not hungry, Kara. Come and sit with me. Are you happy here?'

Kara frowned, wondering why the odd question. 'I'd obviously be happier at home,' she told him quietly, 'but not under our present circumstances.'

Her answer seemed to disappoint him, but it was the truth. Living with him but not *being* with him, not making love with him, was sheer hell. She wanted to cry because what they had once had was gone. She could not understand why he had changed from an attentive lover to someone who was almost a stranger. He was polite and correct, and this wasn't the Blake she knew—the Blake she had fallen in love with.

Unhappily, the next few days followed the same pattern. At the office it was pure business, and at home he was kind and courteous—but nothing more. Her mother still stayed in her room, believing she was doing the right thing leaving them together, and Kara did not tell her what was really going on.

So she was not entirely surprised by his question one

evening over dinner. 'Would you prefer to go home, Kara?'

'Is this a trick question?' she asked with a frown. 'You know I would. But how can I?'

He drew in a long breath and said quietly, 'You have nothing to fear any more.'

Her frown deepened. 'I don't understand.'

'The whole issue of the loan has been sorted. Mr Draydon, your loan shark, won't bother you any more.'

Kara felt her mouth fall open. 'He won't?' It was a stupid question, but what was she supposed to say? 'How do you know?'

He smiled grimly. 'I went to see him. He's written off your loan.'

Kara knew the money-lender wouldn't have agreed as easily as Blake was suggesting, but hope began to rise in her heart. 'How did you find him?' In all these years she had never known where he lived.

'Ways and means,' he said dismissively. 'The point is that you and your mother are free of any debt. You have nothing more to fear.'

'Oh, Blake.' Instinctively Kara rose and rushed around the table, throwing her arms around him. 'Thank you. Thank you from the bottom of my heart. You are a wonderful man, Blake. Thank you again.' And before she could stop herself she was kissing him.

But it was a short-lived kiss. He gently put her from him. 'I think you ought to tell your mother.'

'I will—I will in a minute. She'll be as relieved as I am. I can't thank you enough, Blake. This is a dream come true. We can go home now and get out of your hair. Of course, once the baby's born I'll always let you see him.' She missed the pain that crossed his face. 'And you can come with me for the scans. I don't want to deny you any part of our child's life.'

Realising that she had been talking too quickly and not taking any notice of Blake's reaction, Kara pulled up short when she saw the hurt in his eyes. 'I'm sorry. I'm getting carried away, aren't I?'

'I don't want to just come for the scans, Kara. I want to be with you every step of the way. I have to confess that being a father scares the hell out of me, but what scares me more is the thought of losing you. I love you. I love both you and our unborn child.'

Kara could hear the words, but she wondered whether she was imagining them. Whether she was hearing what she wanted to hear and not what he was actually saying. 'You love me?' she asked, knowing that she must sound stupid—but this had come like a bolt from the blue.

'With every breath in my body.'

'But—But—'

'But nothing, Kara. It's true. You've bewitched me. You've changed me. I doubted myself for a while, but now more than anything I want you by my side for always. I want this child and I want more children with you. I know I'm jumping the gun here, but…'

Kara closed her eyes, hardly listening to him now, letting her breath out in a slow, steady stream. She found it hard to believe that this was happening. Blake loved her. He loved her unconditionally. How magical was that?

And then he kissed her. And the magic continued un- abated. And when they went upstairs to tell her mother that a wedding was in the offing Lynne said that she had known all along that it would happen.

'It was just a matter of time,' she said.

Two years later Kara and Blake were out walking in Hyde Park, pushing their twins' pushchair alongside the Serpentine, discussing what name they should give to the baby she was expecting in three months' time. It was going to be a girl—a little sister to Ben and Mark. The twins, who had come as a shock to both of them, had been named after Blake's father.

'I think,' he said now, 'that it's only fair she should be named after your mother.'

Her mother would be over the moon, thought Kara. She had moved back into her little house, finding Blake's mansion far too intimidating, and she was truly happy for the first time in her life. Even her health seemed to have improved.

'Her middle name's Rosemary,' said Kara. 'We could call her Rose. I think I'd like that.'

'Then Rose it will be,' he said. 'She'll be like a beautiful flower—the same as her mother. I love you, Kara, so very, very much. I never thought I'd be this happy.'

'I love you too, Blake Benedict. You're my hero—do you know that? You rescued me from my miserable life when I thought there was never going to be any escape. I shall love you to the end of my days.'

'And I shall love *you*, my adorable Kara—to the end of *my* days.'

# MILLS & BOON®

## Want to get more from Mills & Boon?

Here's what's available to you if you join the exclusive **Mills & Boon eBook Club** today:

- ✦ *Convenience – choose your books each month*
- ✦ *Exclusive – receive your books a month before anywhere else*
- ✦ *Flexibility – change your subscription at any time*
- ✦ *Variety – gain access to eBook-only series*
- ✦ *Value – subscriptions from just £3.99 a month*

So visit **www.millsandboon.co.uk/esubs** today to be a part of this exclusive eBook Club!

# MILLS & BOON®
# By Request

**RELIVE THE ROMANCE WITH THE BEST OF THE BEST**

## A sneak peek at next month's titles...

**In stores from 18th September 2015:**

- **His After-Hours Mistress** – Margaret Mayo, Trish Wylie & Tina Duncan

- **Rich, Rugged and Royal** – Catherine Mann

**In stores from 2nd October 2015:**

- **Scandal in Sydney** – Marion Lennox, Alison Roberts & Amy Andrews

- **His Girl Next Door** – Soraya Lane, Trish Wylie & Jessica Steele